HIS MASTERPIECE

ÉMILE ZOLA

HIS MASTERPIECE

Translated by Ernest Alfred Vizetelly

ALAN SUTTON
1986

Alan Sutton Publishing Limited
30 Brunswick Road
Gloucester GL1 1JJ

This translation first published 1902

British Library Cataloguing in Publication Data

Zola, Émile
  His masterpiece.
  I. Title
  843'.8[F]   PQ2499.C5

  ISBN 0-86299-293-1

Cover picture: detail from Le Déjeuner
sur l'Herbe *by Edouard Manet. Jeu de Paume,
Louvre, Paris. Photograph: Bridgeman Art Library.*

Printed in Great Britain
by The Guernsey Press Company Limited,
Guernsey, Channel Islands.

BIOGRAPHICAL NOTE

ÉMILE ZOLA (1840–1902) was thirty-one when he wrote *La Fortune des Rougon-Macquart*, and he had already gained considerable experience of life. He was born in Paris on 2 April 1840, but in 1843 the family moved to Aix-en-Provence where his father, an enterprising engineer from Venice, had finally gained permission to build a canal system to provide the town with regular fresh water. Unfortunately, François Zola died in 1846, before his project was complete, leaving his wife and child with very little money. Madame Zola, with her parents, was forced to live among the poor of Aix, so Émile would have early become accustomed to the rough life of the poverty-stricken. However, money was found to send him to school, where he did well at first, but soon found his own creative writing more entertaining than schoolwork, and he enjoyed playing truant with his great friend, Paul Cézanne (the painter-to-be).

In 1858, he was very distressed by his family's move to Paris. He missed Cézanne and the country life. Although he attended school, he failed his *baccalauréat*, partly through nerves and partly through ignorance. At the end of 1859 he accepted employment, found by a friend of his father, in the Excise Office. After two months of clerical drudgery he 'opted out' and lived as a destitute in the poor Latin Quarter of Paris. He tried to write, but spent much of his time daydreaming and observing life in a frenetically busy Paris, a city in the throes of an architectural rebirth, which was doing nothing to improve the lot of the poor. At this time he met and befriended the artists who were to be the leaders of the new Impressionist School, and he was in regular communication with Cézanne. He was finally rescued in 1862, when he was hungry, cold and ill, living in a filthy lodging house frequented by thieves and prostitutes: some poems were accepted for publication in a provincial newspaper, and yet another friend of his father found him a post with the publishing company Hachette.

During the next eight years Zola gained a reputation as a controversial journalist and writer. His defence of the scorned painter, Manet, particularly marked him as a rebel, while his novel *Thérèse Raquin* (1867) was described as 'putrid literature . . . a mass of blood and mud'. Such an extreme reaction, of course, was good publicity and Zola was not afraid of such criticism. In the meantime, he had left Hachette, and was working as a freelance writer for various journals and provincial papers. He met Alexandrine Aubert, a seamstress, whom he eventually married, and moved into a small house near Montmartre. All this time he had been reading widely: philosophy, history and physiology, and had become acquainted with the Goncourt brothers, who had helped him to form his own literary philosophy.

At last he was ready to plan what was to become the major work of his life: *Les Rougon-Macquart: une histoire naturelle et sociale d'une famille sous le Second Empire*, which begins with *La Fortune des Rougon-Macquart*; includes *Nana* (1880), *Germinal* (1885), *La Terre* (1887), and concludes with *Le Docteur Pascal* (1893). As Zola explains in his preface to *La Fortune*, his aim is to explore a fictional family in a scientific way, showing what he believed to be the inevitable effects of heredity and environment on this extended family and on the societies in which they lived, throughout the time of the Second Empire (1852–70). With his own concept of 'naturalism', founded on his scientific reading, Zola was developing the realist tradition of Flaubert and Turgenev, using the same infinite variety of character and circumstance as Balzac, whom he admired and sought to emulate. But, unlike Balzac, who worked from intuition and imagination, Zola did an enormous amount of research and planning for his novels, experiencing, wherever possible, the places and activities which he described. And, of course, he developed themes and variations based on personal experiences. Plassans, for example, is the Aix of Zola's childhood; many of the Rougons are based on families he knew there. Miette, the heroine of *La Fortune*, was probably inspired by Louise Soltari, for whom Zola is believed to have cherished a romantic and undeclared love, while Silvère personifies his own romantic nature. When considering the plot of *La Fortune*, it is worth noting that Louise had died in 1865, and with her many of Zola's romantic dreams. The position of *La Fortune* as the first of the *Rougon-Macquart* series explains why the development of the plot is frequently interrupted with character description and historical explanation.

Unfortunately, the original serial publication of the novel was interrupted by the Paris siege and civil strife of 1870–71. During this time Zola moved out of Paris, but in 1871 he returned, to become immersed in the Rougon-Macquart world for the next twenty years. In 1872 he changed his publisher and laid the foundation for a lasting friendly relationship with Charpentier, who was attracted by Zola and his plan for the series. But it was not until the publication of *L'Assommoir*, the seventh of the series, in 1876, that Zola's work started to sell really well and he achieved his ambition of establishing himself as a powerful controversial literary figure in France. He was also becoming wealthy, and by 1878 he was able to buy a second house in Médan, outside Paris, which grew bigger as his work progressed, and where he regularly entertained a group of young admirers, including Guy de Maupassant and Paul Alexis, his first biographer.

In Russia, on the other hand, Zola had been accepted as a popular writer for some time and his link with St Petersberg had been further strengthened by his friendship with Ivan Turgenev, then living in Paris. The kind-hearted Russian had introduced Zola to the publisher Stassyulevitch, who agreed to pay Zola for the proofs of his novels and to commission a series of essays for his magazine, *The European Herald*.

In spite of his success, the 1880s were difficult years for Zola. In 1880, first his friend, the writer Duranty, died, then Gustave Flaubert, who had been an admired and close friend for eight or nine years, and finally his mother; in 1883, Turgenev and Manet died. Zola had always been of a nervous disposition, which manifested itself in psychosomatic disorders, and these were exacerpated by the bereavements, as Zola succumbed to depression. He was also, as usual, working under considerable pressure, producing a novel almost every year, as well as other literary work for the stage and the press. In 1885, after painstaking research, *Germinal* was published, a resounding success. In it is the character of Souverine, a Russian political emigré in the unlikely situation of working in a French mining community. It is believed that this character was suggested by Turgenev, who, when he died, had been planning a novel on the Russian revolutionary movement. Zola was thus expressing some of the ideas and theories of his dead friend. A year later, *L'Oeuvre* appeared, a study reflecting Zola's disillusionment with the Impressionist movement. After supporting them in their early ventures, he had lost interest in his former friends when they became more preoccupied with light and technique than with subject matter, and he felt that Cézanne and the rest were artistic failures. This negative outlook, expressed in the novel, finally severed Zola's relationship with Cézanne and the movement generally. In 1887, just as he was concluding *La Terre*, Zola was the victim of a cruelly personal attack from a group of writers who, presumably resenting his success, accused him of obscenity in his novels and in his private life. The erotic elements of his novels and his childless marriage were probably conducive to the form of the attack. Although he maintained his usual rather bluff exterior in the face of these insults, it is difficult to believe that the dark, bearded figure with deep brooding eyes, as portrayed by Manet, did not hide a sensitive and vulnerable interior, and it is possible that the attack lead to a self-appraisal, and his subsequent positive action.

During the years of tension, Zola had put on weight, and he became aware that because of his involvement in his work, he was no longer experiencing life at first hand – he was becoming removed from reality. So, in 1888, he took himself in hand. He lost weight, and his personality brightened; he began to practise photography, for which he showed considerable talent. Then he fell in love with Jeanne, who had been employed by Madame Zola to help with the household sewing. He secretly provided for Jeanne to move into an apartment in Paris, courted her and she had two children before Madame Zola found out. After the initial shock,

Madame Zola decided to remain with her husband, and consequently he maintained both households until his death.

The *Rougon-Macquart* series was finished in 1893, but Zola went straight on to produce a trilogy concerned with religious and social problems, *Les Trois Villes*, and then started his final series, *Les Quatres Evangiles*, novels which were to be both moralistic and optimistic about the future. The fourth of this series was never written.

On the whole, Zola's work was not well received in England at the end of the nineteenth century, but he was respected in some quarters, and in 1893 he was invited to visit London by the Institute of Journalists. He stayed for five weeks, spending time with the writer George Moore, and the Vizetelly Company, who were the first translators of his books into English. His second and final visit to England, in 1898, was under very different circumstances, as a result of the notorious Dreyfus Affair.

In order to point out the immorality of the French military courts in failing to recognize the innocence of a French Jewish army officer, who had been wrongly accused of passing information to the Germans, and in order to provoke further action, Zola wrote a letter to the press, entitled *J'accuse*. This famous diatribe successfully lead to a resumption of the case, and Zola was forced to flee to England to avoid a prison sentence, as the court persisted in asserting the innocence of the likely suspect and the guilt of Dreyfus. He stayed in Surrey and Upper Norwood for nearly a year, until finally the Appeals Court agreed to grant a petition for a retrial, and Zola decided to return home, whatever the consequences. No action was taken against him, and he was eventually absolved in the general amnesty which followed Dreyfus' pardon in September, 1899.

His involvement with the Dreyfus Affair aged Zola, and slowed him down in his writing, but he completed *Verité*, the third of *Les Evangiles*, and he was planning the fourth when the accident happened which caused his death on the night of 28 September, 1902. He died of carbon monoxide poisoning, the result of a blocked chimney in his Paris apartment. There is a theory, and a distinct possibility, in the light of the emotional reaction to the Dreyfus case, that the chimney had been purposely blocked, but there is no evidence. He was buried in Montmartre, but his ashes were transferred to the Panthéon in 1908.

Between 1871 and 1902, Zola had produced twenty-six full-length novels, eight volumes of essays, three volumes of short stories and a collection of plays. The *Rougon-Macquart* series demonstrate a mammoth literary feat, an artistic construction of immense variety and vitality. Zola was, according to Professor F.W.J. Hemmings '. . . the first of those who raised sociology to the dignity of art, he was the prophet of a new age of mass psychology, mass education and mass entertainment, an age in which the part is never greater than the whole'.

SHEILA MICHELL

HIS MASTERPIECE

I

CLAUDE was passing in front of the Hôtel de Ville, and the clock was striking two o'clock in the morning when the storm burst forth. He had been roaming forgetfully about the Central Markets, during that burning July night, like a loitering artist enamoured of nocturnal Paris. Suddenly the rain-drops came down, so large and thick, that he took to his heels and rushed, wildly bewildered, along the Quai de la Grève. But on reaching the Pont Louis Philippe he pulled up, rage-fully breathless; he considered this fear of the rain to be idiotic; and so amid the pitch-like darkness, under the lashing shower which drowned the gas-jets, he crossed the bridge slowly, with his hands dangling by his side.

He had only a few more steps to go. As he was turning on to the Quai Bourbon, on the Isle of St. Louis, a sharp flash of lightning illumined the straight, monotonous line of old houses bordering the narrow road in front of the Seine. It blazed upon the panes of the high, shutterless windows, showing up the melancholy frontages of the old-fashioned dwellings in all their details; here a stone balcony, there the railing of a terrace, and there a garland sculptured on a frieze. The painter had his studio close by, under the eaves of the old Hôtel du Martoy, nearly at the corner of the Rue de la Femme-sans-Tête.[1] So he went on while the quay, after flashing forth for a moment, relapsed into darkness, and a terrible thunder-clap shook the drowsy quarter.

When Claude, blinded by the rain, got to his door—a low, rounded door, studded with iron—he fumbled for the bell knob,

---

[1] The street of the Headless Woman.—ED.

and he was exceedingly surprised—indeed, he started—on finding a living, breathing body huddled against the woodwork.
Then, by the light of a second flash, he perceived a tall young
girl, dressed in black, and drenched already, who was shivering with fear. When a second thunder-clap had shaken both
of them, Claude exclaimed:

' How you frighten one! Who are you, and what do you
want?'

He could no longer see her; he only heard her sob, and
stammer:

' Oh, monsieur, don't hurt me. It's the fault of the driver,
whom I hired at the station, and who left me at this door,
after ill-treating me. Yes, a train ran off the rails, near
Nevers. We were four hours late, and a person who was to
wait for me had gone. Oh, dear me; I have never been in
Paris before, and I don't know where I am. . . .'

Another blinding flash cut her short, and with dilated eyes
she stared, terror-stricken, at that part of the strange capital,
that violet-tinted apparition of a fantastic city. The rain had
ceased falling. On the opposite bank of the Seine was the
Quai des Ormes, with its small grey houses variegated below
by the woodwork of their shops and with their irregular roofs
boldly outlined above, while the horizon suddenly became
clear on the left as far as the blue slate eaves of the Hôtel de
Ville, and on the right as far as the leaden-hued dome of St.
Paul. What startled her most of all, however, was the
hollow of the stream, the deep gap in which the Seine flowed,
black and turgid, from the heavy piles of the Pont Marie, to
the light arches of the new Pont Louis Philippe. Strange
masses peopled the river, a sleeping flotilla of small boats and
yawls, a floating washhouse, and a dredger moored to the
quay. Then, farther down, against the other bank, were
lighters, laden with coals, and barges full of mill stone,
dominated as it were by the gigantic arm of a steam crane.
But, suddenly, everything disappeared again.

Claude had an instinctive distrust of women—that story of
an accident, of a belated train and a brutal cabman, seemed
to him a ridiculous invention. At the second thunder-clap
the girl had shrunk farther still into her corner, absolutely
terrified.

' But you cannot stop here all night,' he said.

She sobbed still more and stammered, ' I beseech you,
monsieur, take me to Passy. That's where I was going.'

He shrugged his shoulders. Did she take him for a fool?
Mechanically, however, he turned towards the Quai des Céles-
tins, where there was a cabstand. Not the faintest glimmer of
a lamp to be seen.

'To Passy, my dear? Why not to Versailles? Where
do you think one can pick up a cab at this time of night, and
in such weather?'

Her only answer was a shriek; for a fresh flash of lightning had almost blinded her, and this time the tragic city
had seemed to her to be spattered with blood. An immense
chasm had been revealed, the two arms of the river
stretching far away amidst the lurid flames of a conflagration.
The smallest details had appeared: the little closed shutters
of the Quai des Ormes, and the two openings of the Rue de
la Masure, and the Rue du Paon-Blanc, which made breaks in
the line of frontages; then near the Pont Marie one could
have counted the leaves on the lofty plane trees, which there
form a bouquet of magnificent verdure; while on the other
side, beneath the Pont Louis Philippe, at the Mail, the barges,
ranged in a quadruple line, had flared with the piles of
yellow apples with which they were heavily laden. And
there was also the ripple of the water, the high chimney of
the floating washhouse, the tightened chain of the dredger,
the heaps of sand on the banks, indeed, an extraordinary
agglomeration of things, quite a little world filling the great
gap which seemed to stretch from one horizon to the other.
But the sky became dark again, and the river flowed on, all
obscurity, amid the crashing of the thunder.

'Thank heaven it's over. Oh, heaven! what's to become of me?'

Just then the rain began to fall again, so stiffly and impelled by so strong a wind that it swept along the quay with
the violence of water escaping through an open lock.

'Come, let me get in,' said Claude; 'I can stand this no
longer.'

Both were getting drenched. By the flickering light of
the gas lamp at the corner of the Rue de la Femme-sans-
Tête the young man could see the water dripping from the
girl's dress, which was clinging to her skin, in the deluge
that swept against the door. He was seized with compassion.
Had he not once picked up a cur on such a stormy night
as this? Yet he felt angry with himself for softening. He
never had anything to do with women; he treated them all as

if ignorant of their existence, with a painful timidity which he disguised under a mask of bravado. And that girl must really think him a downright fool, to bamboozle him with that story of adventure—only fit for a farce. Nevertheless, he ended by saying, 'That's enough. You had better come in out of the wet. You can sleep in my rooms.'

But at this the girl became even more frightened, and threw up her arms.

'In your rooms? Oh! good heavens. No, no; it's impossible. I beseech you, monsieur, take me to Passy. Let me beg of you.'

But Claude became angry. Why did she make all this fuss, when he was willing to give her shelter? He had already rung the bell twice. At last the door opened and he pushed the girl before him.

'No, no, monsieur; I tell you, no——'

But another flash dazzled her, and when the thunder growled she bounded inside, scarce knowing what she was about. The heavy door had closed upon them, she was standing under a large archway in complete darkness.

'It's I, Madame Joseph,' cried Claude to the doorkeeper. Then he added, in a whisper, 'Give me your hand, we have to cross the courtyard.'

The girl did as she was told; she no longer resisted; she was overwhelmed, worn out. Once more they encountered the diluvian rain, as they ran side by side as hard as they could across the yard. It was a baronial courtyard, huge, and surrounded with stone arcades, indistinct amidst the gloom. However, they came to a narrow passage without a door, and he let go her hand. She could hear him trying to strike some matches, and swearing. They were all damp. It was necessary for them to grope their way upstairs.

'Take hold of the banisters, and be careful,' said Claude; 'the steps are very high.'

The staircase, a very narrow one, a former servants' staircase, was divided into three lofty flights, which she climbed, stumbling, with unskilful, weary limbs. Then he warned her that they had to turn down a long passage. She kept behind him, touching the walls on both sides with her outstretched hands, as she advanced along that endless passage which bent and came back to the front of the building on the quay. Then there were still other stairs right under the roof—creaking, shaky wooden stairs, which had no banister, and suggested the unplaned rungs of a miller's ladder. The landing at the top was so small that the girl knocked against the young man, as he fumbled in his pocket for his key. At last, however, he opened the door.

'Don't come in, but wait, else you'll hurt yourself again.'

She did not stir. She was panting for breath, her heart was beating fast, there was a buzzing in her ears, and she felt indeed exhausted by that ascent in the dense gloom. It seemed to her as if she had been climbing for hours, in such a maze, amidst such a turning and twisting of stairs that she would never be able to find her way down again. Inside the studio there was a shuffling of heavy feet, a rustling of hands groping in the dark, a clatter of things being tumbled about, accompanied by stifled objurgations. At last the doorway was lighted up.

'Come in, it's all right now.'

She went in and looked around her, without distinguishing anything. The solitary candle burned dim in that garret, more than fifteen feet high, and filled with a confused jumble of things whose big shadows showed fantastically on the walls, which were painted in grey distemper. No, she did not distinguish anything. She mechanically raised her eyes to the large studio-window, against which the rain was beating with a deafening roll like that of a drum, but at that moment another flash of lightning illumined the sky, followed almost immediately by a thunder-clap that seemed to split the roof. Dumb-stricken, pale as death, she dropped upon a chair.

'The devil!' muttered Claude, who also was rather pale. 'That clap wasn't far off. We were just in time. It's better here than in the streets, isn't it it?'

Then he went towards the door, closed it with a bang and turned the key, while she watched him with a dazed look.

'There, now, we are at home.'

But it was all over. There were only a few more thunder-claps in the distance, and the rain soon ceased altogether. Claude, who was now growing embarrassed, had examined the girl, askance. She seemed by no means bad looking, and assuredly she was young: twenty at the most. This scrutiny had the effect of making him more suspicious of her still, in spite of an unconscious feeling, a vague idea, that she was not altogether deceiving him. In any case, no matter how clever she might be, she was mistaken if she imagined she had caught him. To prove this he wilfully exaggerated his gruffness and curtness of manner.

Her very anguish at his words and demeanour made her rise, and in her turn she examined him, though without daring to look him straight in the face. And the aspect of that bony young man, with his angular joints and wild bearded face, increased her fears. With his black felt hat and his old brown coat, discoloured by long usage, he looked like a kind of brigand.

Directly he told her to make herself at home and go to bed, for he placed his bed at her disposal, she shrinkingly replied : ' Thank you ; I'll do very well as I am ; I'll not undress.'

' But your clothes are dripping,' he retorted. ' Come now, don't make an idiot of yourself.'

And thereupon he began to knock about the chairs, and flung aside an old screen, behind which she noticed a washstand and a tiny iron bedstead, from which he began to remove the coverlet.

' No, no, monsieur, it isn't worth while ; I assure you that I shall stay here.'

At this, however, Claude became angry, gesticulating and shaking his fists.

' How much more of this comedy are we to have ? ' said he. ' As I give you my bed, what have you to complain of ? You need not pay any attention to me. I shall sleep on that couch.'

He strode towards her with a threatening look, and thereupon, beside herself with fear, thinking that he was going to strike her, she tremblingly unfastened her hat. The water was dripping from her skirts. He kept on growling. Nevertheless, a sudden scruple seemed to come to him, for he ended by saying, condescendingly :

' Perhaps you don't like to sleep in my sheets. I'll change them.'

He at once began dragging them from the bed and flinging them on to the couch at the other end of the studio. And afterwards he took a clean pair from the wardrobe and began to make the bed with all the deftness of a bachelor accustomed to that kind of thing. He carefully tucked in the clothes on the side near the wall, shook the pillows, and turned back a corner of the coverlet.

' There, that'll do ; won't it ? ' said he.

And as she did not answer, but remained motionless, he pushed her behind the screen. ' Good heavens ! what a lot of fuss,' he thought. And after spreading his own sheets on the couch, and hanging his clothes on an easel, he quickly went to bed himself. When he was on the point of blowing out the candle, however, he reflected that if he did so she would have to undress in the dark, and so he waited. At first he had not heard her stir ; she had no doubt remained standing against the iron bedstead. But at last he detected a slight rustling, a slow, faint movement, as if amidst her preparations she also were listening, frightened perchance by the candle which was still alight. At last, after several minutes, the spring mattress creaked, and then all became still.

' Are you comfortable, mademoiselle ? ' now asked Claude, in a much more gentle voice.

' Yes, monsieur, very comfortable,' she replied, in a scarcely audible voice, which still quivered with emotion.

' Very well, then. Good-night.'

' Good-night.'

He blew out the candle, and the silence became more intense. In spite of his fatigue, his eyes soon opened again, and gazed upward at the large window of the studio. The sky had become very clear again, the stars were twinkling in the sultry July night, and, despite the storm, the heat remained oppressive. Claude was thinking about the girl— agitated for a moment by contrary feelings, though at last contempt gained the mastery. He indeed believed himself to be very strong-minded ; he imagined a romance concocted to destroy his tranquillity, and he gibed contentedly at having frustrated it. His experience of women was very slight, nevertheless he endeavoured to draw certain conclusions from the story she had told him, struck as he was at present by certain petty details, and feeling perplexed. But why, after all, should he worry his brain ? What did it matter whether she had told him the truth or a lie ? In the morning she would go off ; there would be an end to it all, and they would never see each other again. Thus Claude lay cogitating, and it was only towards daybreak, when the stars began to pale, that he fell asleep. As for the girl behind the screen, in spite of the crushing fatigue of her journey, she continued tossing about uneasily, oppressed by the heaviness of the atmosphere beneath the hot zinc-work of the roof ; and doubtless, too, she was rendered nervous by the strangeness of her surroundings.

In the morning, when Claude awoke, his eyes kept blinking. It was very late, and the sunshine streamed through the large window. One of his theories was, that young landscape painters should take studios despised by the academical figure painters—studios which the sun flooded with living beams. Nevertheless he felt dazzled, and fell back again on his couch. Why the devil had he been sleeping there? His eyes, still heavy with sleep, wandered mechanically round the studio, when, all at once, beside the screen he noticed a heap of petticoats. Then he at once remembered the girl. He began to listen, and heard a sound of long-drawn, regular breathing, like that of a child comfortably asleep. Ah! so she was still slumbering, and so calmly, that it would be a pity to disturb her. He felt dazed and somewhat annoyed at the adventure, however, for it would spoil his morning's work. He got angry at his own good nature; it would be better to shake her, so that she might go at once. Nevertheless he put on his trousers and slippers softly, and walked about on tiptoes.

The cuckoo clock struck nine, and Claude made a gesture of annoyance. Nothing had stirred; the regular breathing continued. The best thing to do, he thought, would be to set to work on his large picture; he would see to his breakfast later on, when he was able to move about. But, after all, he could not make up his mind. He who lived amid chronic disorder felt worried by that heap of petticoats lying on the floor. Some water had dripped from them, but they were damp still. And so, while grumbling in a low tone, he ended by picking them up one by one and spreading them over the chairs in the sunlight. Had one ever seen the like, clothes thrown about anyhow? They would never get dry, and she would never go off! He turned all that feminine apparel over very awkwardly, got entangled with the black dress-body, and went on all fours to pick up the stockings that had fallen behind an old canvas. They were Balbriggan stockings of a dark grey, long and fine, and he examined them, before hanging them up to dry. The water oozing from the edge of the dress had soaked them, so he wrung and stretched them with his warm hands, in order that he might be able to send her away the quicker.

Since he had been on his legs, Claude had felt sorely tempted to push aside the screen and to take a look at his guest. This self-condemned curiosity only increased his bad temper. At last, with his habitual shrug of the shoulders, he was taking up his brushes, when he heard some words stammered amidst a rustling of bed-clothes. Then, however, soft breathing was heard again, and this time he yielded to the temptation, dropping his brushes, and peeping from behind the screen. The sight that met his eyes rooted him to the spot, so fascinated that he muttered, 'Good gracious! good gracious!'

The girl, amidst the hot-house heat that came from the window, had thrown back her coverlet, and, overcome with the fatigue of a restless night, lay steeped in a flood of sunshine, unconscious of everything. In her feverish slumbers a shoulder button had become unfastened, and a sleeve slipping down allowed her bosom to be seen, with skin which looked almost gilded and soft like satin. Her right arm rested beneath her neck, her head was thrown back, and her black unwound tresses enwrapped her like a dusky cloak.

'Good gracious! But she's a beauty!' muttered Claude once more.

There, in every point, was the figure he had vainly sought for his picture, and it was almost in the right pose. She was rather spare, perhaps, but then so lithe and fresh.

With a light step, Claude ran to take his box of crayons, and a large sheet of paper. Then, squatting on a low chair, he placed a portfolio on his knees and began to sketch with an air of perfect happiness. All else vanished amidst artistic surprise and enthusiasm. No thought of sex came to him. It was all a mere question of chaste outlines, splendid flesh tints, well-set muscles. Face to face with nature, an uneasy mistrust of his powers made him feel small; so, squaring his elbows, he became very attentive and respectful. This lasted for about a quarter of an hour, during which he paused every now and then, blinking at the figure before him. As he was afraid, however, that she might change her position, he speedily set to work again, holding his breath, lest he should awaken her.

And yet, while steadily applying himself to his work, vague fancies again assailed his mind. Who could she be? Assuredly no mere hussy. But why had she told him such an unbelievable tale? Thereupon he began to imagine other stories. Perhaps she had but lately arrived in Paris with a lover, who had abandoned her; perhaps she was some young woman of the middle classes led into bad company by a female friend, and not daring to go home to her relatives;

or else there was some still more intricate drama beneath it all ; something horrible, inexplicable, the truth of which he would never fathom.   All these hypotheses increased his per-plexity.   Meanwhile, he went on sketching her face, studying it with care.   The whole of the upper part, the clear forehead, as smooth as a polished mirror, the small nose, with its delicately chiselled and nervous nostrils, denoted great kind-liness and gentleness.   One divined the sweet smile of the eyes beneath the closed lids ; a smile that would light up the whole of the features.   Unfortunately, the lower part of the face marred that expression of sweetness ; the jaw was pro-minent, and the lips, rather too full, showed almost blood-like over the strong white teeth.   There was here, like a flash of passion, something that spoke of awakening womanhood, still unconscious of itself amidst those other traits of childlike softness.

But suddenly a shiver rippled over the girl's satiny skin. Perhaps she had felt the weight of that gaze thus mentally dissecting her.   She opened her eyes very wide and uttered a cry.

'Ah ! great heavens ! '

Sudden terror paralysed her at the sight of that strange room, and that young man crouching in his shirt-sleeves in front of her and devouring her with his eyes.   Flushing hotly, she impulsively pulled up the counterpane.

'Well, what's the matter ? ' cried Claude, angrily, his crayon suspended in mid-air ; 'what wasp has stung you now ? '

He, whose knowledge of womankind was largely limited to professional models, was at a loss to understand the girl's action.

She neither spoke nor stirred, but remained with the counterpane tightly wrapped round her throat, her body almost doubled up, and scarcely showing an outline beneath her coverings.

'I won't eat you, will I ? ' urged Claude.   'Come, just lie as you were, there's a good girl.'

Again she blushed to her very ears.   At last she stammered, 'Oh, no, monsieur, no—pray ! '

But he began to lose his temper altogether.   One of the angry fits to which he was subject was coming upon him. He thought her obstinacy stupid.   And as in response to his urgent requests she only began to sob, he quite lost his head in despair before his sketch, thinking that he would never be able to finish it, and would thus lose a capital study for his picture.

'Well, you won't, eh? But it's idiotic. What do you take me for? Have I annoyed you at all? You know I haven't. Besides, listen, it is very unkind of you to refuse me this service, because, after all, I sheltered you—I gave up my bed to you.'

She only continued to cry, with her head buried in the pillow.

'I assure you that I am very much in want of this sketch, else I wouldn't worry you.'

He grew surprised at the girl's abundant tears, and ashamed at having been so rough with her, so he held his tongue at last, feeling embarrassed, and wishing too that she might have time to recover a bit. Then he began again, in a very gentle tone:

'Well, as it annoys you, let's say no more about it. But if you only knew. I've got a figure in my picture yonder which doesn't make head-way at all, and you were just in the very note. As for me, when it's a question of painting, I'd kill father and mother, you know. Well, you'll excuse me, won't you? And if you'd like me to be very nice, you'd just give me a few minutes more. No, no; keep quiet as you are; I only want the head—nothing but the head. If I could finish that, it would be all right. Really now, be kind; put your arm as it was before, and I shall be very grateful to you—grateful all my life long.'

It was he who was entreating now, pitifully waving his crayon amid the emotion of his artistic craving. Besides, he had not stirred, but remained crouching on his low chair, at a distance from the bed. At last she risked the ordeal, and uncovered her tranquillised face. What else could she do? She was at his mercy, and he looked so wretchedly unhappy.

Nevertheless, she still hesitated, she felt some last scruples. But eventually, without saying a word, she slowly brought her bare arm from beneath the coverings, and again slipped it under her head, taking care, however, to keep the counterpane tightly round her throat.

'Ah! how kind you are! I'll make haste, you will be free in a minute.'

He bent over his drawing, and only looked at her now and then with the glance of a painter who simply regards the woman before him as a model. At first she became pink again; the consciousness that she was showing her bare arm—which she would have shown in a ball-room without thinking at all about it—filled her with confusion. Nevertheless, the young man seemed so reasonable that she became reassured. The blush left her cheeks, and her lips parted in a vague confiding smile. And from between her half-opened eyelids she began to study him. How he had frightened her the previous night with his thick brown beard, his large head, and his impulsive gestures. And yet he was not ugly ; she even detected great tenderness in the depths of his brown eyes, while his nose altogether surprised her. It was a finely-cut woman's nose, almost lost amidst the bristling hair on his lips. He shook slightly with a nervous anxiety which made his crayon seem a living thing in his slender hand, and which touched her though she knew not why. She felt sure he was not bad-natured, his rough, surly ways arose from bashfulness. She did not decipher all this very clearly, but she divined it, and began to put herself at her ease, as if she were with a friend.

Nevertheless, the studio continued to frighten her a little. She cast sidelong glances around it, astonished at so much disorder and carelessness. Before the stove the cinders of the previous winter still lay in a heap. Besides the bed, the small washstand, and the couch, there was no other furniture than an old dilapidated oaken wardrobe and a large deal table, littered with brushes, colours, dirty plates, and a spirit lamp, atop of which was a saucepan, with shreds of vermicelli sticking to its sides. Some rush-bottomed chairs, their seats the worse for wear, were scattered about beside spavined easels. Near the couch the candlestick used on the previous night stood on the floor, which looked as if it had not been swept for fully a month. There was only the cuckoo clock, a huge one, with a dial illuminated with crimson flowers, that looked clean and bright, ticking sonorously all the while. But what especially frightened her were some sketches in oils that hung frameless from the walls, a serried array of sketches reaching to the floor, where they mingled with heaps of canvases thrown about anyhow. She had never seen such terrible painting, so coarse, so glaring, showing a violence of colour, that jarred upon her nerves like a carter's oath heard on the doorstep of an inn. She cast her eyes down for a moment, and then became attracted by a picture, the back of which was turned to her. It was the large canvas at which the painter was working, and which he pushed against the wall every night, the better to judge it on the morrow in the surprise of the first glance. What could it be, that one, she wondered, since he dared not even show it? And, meantime, through the vast room, a sheet of burning sunlight, falling straight from the window panes, unchecked by any blind, spread with the flow of molten gold over all the broken-down furniture, whose devil-may-care shabbiness it threw into bold relief.

Claude began to feel the silence oppressive; he wanted to say something, no matter what, first, in order to be polite, and more especially to divert her attention from her pose. But cudgel his brain as he would, he could only think of asking: 'Pray, what is your name?'

She opened her eyes, which she had closed, as if she were feeling sleepy.

'Christine,' she said.

At which he seemed surprised. Neither had he told her his name. Since the night before they had been together, side by side, without knowing one another.

'My name is Claude.'

And, having looked at her just at that moment, he saw her burst into a pretty laugh. It was the sudden, merry peal of a big girl, still scarcely more than a hoyden. She considered this tardy exchange of names rather droll. Then something else amused her.

'How funny—Claude, Christine—they begin with the same letter.'

They both became silent once more. He was blinking at his work, growing absorbed in it, and at a loss how to continue the conversation. He fancied that she was beginning to feel tired and uncomfortable, and in his fear lest she should stir, he remarked at random, merely to occupy her thoughts, 'It feels rather warm.'

This time she checked her laughter, her natural gaiety that revived and burst forth in spite of herself ever since she had felt easier in mind. Truth to tell, the heat was indeed so oppressive that it seemed to her as if she were in a bath, with skin moist and pale with the milky pallor of a camellia.

'Yes, it feels rather warm,' she said, seriously, though mirth was dancing in her eyes.

Thereupon Claude continued, with a good-natured air:

'It's the sun falling straight in; but, after all, a flood of sunshine on one's skin does one good. We could have done with some of it last night at the door, couldn't we?'

At this both burst out laughing, and he, delighted at

having hit upon a subject of conversation, questioned her
about her adventure, without, however, feeling inquisitive,
for he cared little about discovering the real truth, and was
only intent upon prolonging the sitting.

Christine simply, and in a few words, related what had
befallen her. Early on the previous morning she had left
Clermont for Paris, where she was to take up a situation as
reader and companion to the widow of a general, Madame
Vanzade, a rich old lady, who lived at Passy. The train
was timed to reach Paris at ten minutes past nine in the
evening, and a maid was to meet her at the station. They
had even settled by letter upon a means of recognition. She
was to wear a black hat with a grey feather in it. But, a little
above Nevers, her train had come upon a goods train which
had run off the rails, its litter of smashed trucks still
obstructing the line. There was quite a series of mishaps
and delays. First an interminable wait in the carriages, which
the passengers had to quit at last, luggage and all, in order to
trudge to the next station, three kilometres distant, where the
authorities had decided to make up another train. By this
time they had lost two hours, and then another two were
lost in the general confusion which the accident had caused
from one end of the line to the other, in such wise that they
reached the Paris terminus four hours behind time, that is,
at one o'clock in the morning.

'Bad luck, indeed,' interrupted Claude, who was still
sceptical, though half disarmed, in his surprise at the neat
way in which the girl arranged the details of her story.

'And, of course, there was no one at the station to meet
you?' he added.

Christine had, indeed, missed Madame Vanzade's maid,
who, no doubt, had grown tired of waiting. She told Claude
of her utter helplessness at the Lyons terminus—that large,
strange, dark station, deserted at that late hour of night.
She had not dared to take a cab at first, but had kept on walking
up and down, carrying her small bag, and still hoping that
somebody would come for her. When at last she made up her
mind there only remained one driver, very dirty and smelling
of drink, who prowled round her, offering his cab in a knowing,
impudent way.

'Yes, I know, a dawdler,' said Claude, getting as interested
as if he were listening to a fairy tale. 'So you got into his
cab?'

Looking up at the ceiling, Christine continued, without shifting her position : 'He made me ; he called me his little dear, and frightened me. When he found out that I was going to Passy, he became very angry, and whipped his horse so hard that I was obliged to hold on by the doors. After that I felt more easy, because the cab trundled along all right through the lighted streets, and I saw people about. At last I recognised the Seine, for though I was never in Paris before, I had often looked at a map. Naturally I thought he would keep along the quay, so I became very frightened again on noticing that we crossed a bridge. Just then it began to rain, and the cab, which had got into a very dark turning, suddenly stopped. The driver got down from his seat, and declared it was raining too hard for him to remain on the box——'

Claude burst out laughing. He no longer doubted. She could not have invented that driver. And as she suddenly stopped, somewhat confused, he said, 'All right, the cabman was having a joke.'

'I jumped out at once by the other door,' resumed Christine. 'Then he began to swear at me, saying that we had arrived at Passy, and that he would tear my hat from my head if I did not pay him. It was raining in torrents, and the quay was absolutely deserted. I was losing my head, and when I had pulled out a five-franc piece, he whipped up his horse and drove off, taking my little bag, which luckily only contained two pocket-handkerchiefs, a bit of cake, and the key of my trunk, which I had been obliged to leave behind in the train.'

'But you ought to have taken his number,' exclaimed the artist indignantly. In fact he now remembered having been brushed against by a passing cab, which had rattled by furiously while he was crossing the Pont Louis Philippe, amid the downpour of the storm. And he reflected how improbable truth often was. The story he had conjured up as being the most simple and logical was utterly stupid beside the natural chain of life's many combinations.

'You may imagine how I felt under the doorway,' concluded Christine. 'I knew well enough that I was not at Passy, and that I should have to spend the night there, in this terrible Paris. And there was the thunder and the lightning—those horrible blue and red flashes, which showed me things that made me tremble.'

She closed her eyelids once more, she shivered, and the colour left her cheeks as, in her fancy, she again beheld the tragic city—that line of quays stretching away' in a furnace-like blaze, the deep moat of the river, with its leaden waters obstructed by huge black masses, lighters looking like lifeless whales, and bristling with motionless cranes which stretched forth gallows-like arms. Was that a welcome to Paris?

Again did silence fall. Claude had resumed his drawing. But she became restless, her arm was getting stiff.

'Just put your elbow a little lower, please,' said Claude. Then, with an air of concern, as if to excuse his curtness : 'Your parents will be very uneasy, if they have heard of the accident.'

'I have no parents.'

'What! neither father nor mother? You are all alone in the world?'

'Yes; all alone.'

She was eighteen years old, and had been born in Strasburg, quite by chance, though, between two changes of garrison, for her father was a soldier, Captain Hallegrain. Just as she entered upon her twelfth year, the captain, a Gascon, hailing from Montauban, had died at Clermont, where he had settled when paralysis of the legs had obliged him to retire from active service. For nearly five years afterwards, her mother, a Parisian by birth, had remained in that dull provincial town, managing as well as she could with her scanty pension, but eking it out by fan-painting, in order that she might bring up her daughter as a lady. She had, however, now been dead for fifteen months, and had left her child penniless and unprotected, without a friend, save the Superior of the Sisters of the Visitation, who had kept her with them. Christine had come straight to Paris from the convent, the Superior having succeeded in procuring her a situation as reader and companion to her old friend, Madame Vanzade, who was almost blind.

At these additional particulars, Claude sat absolutely speechless. That convent, that well-bred orphan, that adventure, all taking so romantic a turn, made him relapse into embarrassment again, into all his former awkwardness of gesture and speech. He had left off drawing, and sat looking, with downcast eyes, at his sketch.

'Is Clermont pretty?' he asked, at last.

'Not very; it's a gloomy town. Besides, I don't know; I scarcely ever went out.'

She was resting on her elbow, and continued, as if talking to herself in a very low voice, still tremulous from the thought of her bereavement.

'Mamma, who wasn't strong, killed herself with work. She spoilt me; nothing was too good for me. I had all sorts of masters, but I did not get on very well; first, because I fell ill, then because I paid no attention. I was always laughing and skipping about like a featherbrain. I didn't care for music, piano playing gave me a cramp in my arms. The only thing I cared about at all was painting.'

He raised his head and interrupted her. 'You can paint?'

'Oh, no; I know nothing, nothing at all. Mamma, who was very talented, made me do a little water-colour, and I sometimes helped her with the backgrounds of her fans. She painted some lovely ones.'

In spite of herself, she then glanced at the startling sketches with which the walls seemed ablaze, and her limpid eyes assumed an uneasy expression at the sight of that rough, brutal style of painting. From where she lay she obtained a topsy-turvy view of the study of herself which the painter had begun, and her consternation at the violent tones she noticed, the rough crayon strokes, with which the shadows were dashed off, prevented her from asking to look at it more closely. Besides, she was growing very uncomfortable in that bed, where she lay broiling; she fidgetted with the idea of going off and putting an end to all these things which, ever since the night before, had seemed to her so much of a dream.

Claude, no doubt, became aware of her discomfort. A sudden feeling of shame brought with it one of compunction.

He put his unfinished sketch aside, and hastily exclaimed: 'Much obliged for your kindness, mademoiselle. Forgive me, I have really abused it. Yes, indeed, pray get up; it's time for you to look for your friends.'

And without appearing to understand why she did not follow his advice, but hid more and more of her bare arm in proportion as he drew nearer, he still insisted upon advising her to rise. All at once, as the real state of things struck him, he swung his arms about like a madman, set the screen in position, and went to the far end of the studio, where he began noisily setting his crockery in order, so that she might jump out and dress herself, without fear of being overheard.

Amidst the din he had thus raised, he failed to hear her hesitating voice, ' Monsieur, monsieur——'

At last he caught her words.

' Monsieur, would you be so kind—I can't find my stockings.'

Claude hurried forward. What had he been thinking of ? What was she to do behind that screen, without her stockings and petticoats, which he had spread out in the sunlight ? The stockings were dry, he assured himself of that by gently rubbing them together, and he handed them to her over the partition ; again noticing her arm, bare, plump and rosy like that of a child. Then he tossed the skirts on to the foot of the bed and pushed her boots forward, leaving nothing but her bonnet suspended from the easel. She had thanked him and that was all ; he scarcely distinguished the rustling of her clothes and the discreet splashing of water. Still he continued to concern himself about her.

' You will find the soap in a saucer on the table. Open the drawer and take a clean towel. Do you want more water ? I'll give you the pitcher.'

Suddenly the idea that he was blundering again exasperated him.

' There, there, I am only worrying you. I will leave you to your own devices. Do as if you were at home.'

And he continued to potter about among the crockery. He was debating with himself whether he should ask her to stay to breakfast. He ought not to let her go like that. On the other hand, if she did stay, he would never get done ; it would mean a loss of his whole morning. Without deciding anything, as soon as he had lighted his spirit lamp, he washed his saucepan and began to make some chocolate. He thought it more *distingué*, feeling rather ashamed of his vermicelli, which he mixed with bread and soused with oil as people do in the South of France. However, he was still breaking the chocolate into bits, when he uttered a cry of surprise, ' What, already ?'

It was Christine, who had pushed back the screen, and who appeared looking neat and correct in her black dress, duly laced and buttoned up, equipped, as it were, in a twinkle. Her rosy face did not even show traces of the water, her thick hair was twisted in a knot at the back of her head, not a single lock out of place. And Claude remained open-mouthed before that miracle of quickness, that proof of feminine skill in dressing well and promptly.

' The deuce, if you go about everything in that way ! ' said he.

He found her taller and handsomer than he had fancied. But what struck him most was her look of quiet decision. She was evidently no longer afraid of him. It seemed as though she had re-donned her armour and become an amazon again. She smiled and looked him straight in the face. Whereupon he said what he was still reluctant to say :

' You'll breakfast with me, won't you ? '

But she refused the offer. ' No, thank you. I am going to the station, where my trunk must have arrived by now, and then I shall drive to Passy.'

It was in vain that he told her that she must be hungry, that it was unreasonable for her to go out without eating something.

' Well, if you won't, I'll go down and fetch you a cab,' he ended by exclaiming.

' Pray don't take such trouble.'

' But you can't go such a distance on foot. Let me at least take you to the cabstand, as you don't know Paris.'

' No, really I do not need you. If you wish to oblige me, let me go away by myself.'

She had evidently made up her mind. She no doubt shrank from the idea of being seen with a man, even by strangers. She meant to remain silent about that strange night, she meant to tell some falsehood, and keep the recollection of her adventure entirely to herself. He made a furious gesture, which was tantamount to sending her to the devil. Good riddance ; it suited him better not to have to go down. But, all the same, he felt hurt at heart, and considered that she was ungrateful.

' As you please, then. I sha'n't resort to force,' he said.

At these words, Christine's vague smile became more accentuated. She did not reply, but took her bonnet and looked round in search of a glass. Failing to find one, she tied the strings as best she could. With her arms uplifted, she leisurely arranged and smoothed the ribbons, her face turned towards the golden rays of the sun. Somewhat surprised, Claude looked in vain for the traits of childish softness that he had just portrayed ; the upper part of her face, her clear forehead, her gentle eyes had become less conspicuous ; and now the lower part stood out, with its somewhat sensual jaw, ruddy mouth, and superb teeth. And still she smiled with that enigmatical, girlish smile, which was, perhaps, an ironical one.

'At any rate,' he said, in a vexed tone, 'I do not think you have anything to reproach me with.'

At which she could not help laughing, with a slight, nervous laugh.

'No, no, monsieur, not in the least.'

He continued staring at her, fighting the battle of inexperience and bashfulness over again, and fearing that he had been ridiculous.   Now that she no longer trembled before him, had she become contemptuously surprised at having trembled at all ?   What ! he had not made the slightest attempt at courtship, not even pressed a kiss on her finger-tips. The young fellow's bearish indifference, of which she had assuredly been conscious, must have hurt her budding womanly feelings.

'You were saying,' she resumed, becoming sedate once more, 'that the cabstand is at the end of the bridge on the opposite quay ? '

'Yes ; at the spot where there is a clump of trees.'

She had finished tying her bonnet strings, and stood ready gloved, with her hands hanging by her side, and yet she did not go, but stared straight in front of her. As her eyes met the big canvas turned to the wall she felt a wish to see it, but did not dare to ask. Nothing detained her ; still she seemed to be looking around as if she had forgotten something there, something which she could not name. At last she stepped towards the door.

Claude was already opening it, and a small loaf placed erect against the post tumbled into the studio.

'You see,' he said, 'you ought to have stopped to breakfast with me. My doorkeeper brings the bread up every morning.'

She again refused with a shake of the head. When she was on the landing she turned round, and for a moment remained quite still. Her gay smile had come back ; she was the first to hold out her hand.

'Thank you, thank you very much.'

He had taken her small gloved hand within his large one, all pastel-stained as it was. Both hands remained like that for a few moments, closely and cordially pressed. The young girl was still smiling at him, and he had a question on the tip of his tongue : 'When shall I see you again?' But he felt ashamed to ask it, and after waiting a while she withdrew her hand.

'Good-bye, monsieur.'

'Good-bye, mademoiselle.'

Christine, without another glance, was already descending the steep ladder-like stairway whose steps creaked, when Claude turned abruptly into his studio, closing the door with a bang, and shouting to himself : 'Ah, those confounded women !'

He was furious—furious with himself, furious with every-one. Kicking about the furniture, he continued to ease his feelings in a loud voice. Was not he right in never allowing them to cross his threshold? They only turned a fellow's head. What proof had he after all that yonder chit with the innocent look, who had just gone, had not fooled him most abominably? And he had been silly enough to believe in her cock-and-bull stories ! All his suspicions revived. No one would ever make him swallow that fairy tale of the general's widow, the railway accident, and especially the cabman. Did such things ever happen in real life? Besides, that mouth of hers told a strange tale, and her looks had been very singular just as she was going. Ah ! if he could only have understood why she had told him all those lies ; but no, they were profitless, inexplicable. It was art for art's sake. How she must be laughing at him by this time.

He roughly folded up the screen and sent it flying into a corner. She had no doubt left all in disorder. And when he found that everything was in its proper place—basin, towel, and soap—he flew into a rage because she had not made the bed. With a great deal of fuss he began to make it himself, lifting the mattress in his arms, banging the pillow about with his fists, and feeling oppressed by the pure scent of youth that rose from everything. Then he had a good wash to cool himself, and in the damp towel he found the same virgin fragrance, which seemed to spread through the studio. Swearing the while, he drank his chocolate from the sauce-pan, so excited, so eager to set to work, as to swallow large mouthfuls of bread without taking breath.

'Why, it's enough to kill one here,' he suddenly exclaimed. 'It must be this confounded heat that's making me ill,'

After all, the sun had shifted, and it was far less hot. But he opened a small window on a level with the roof, and inhaled, with an air of profound relief, the whiff of warm air that entered. Then he took up his sketch of Christine's head and for a long while he lingered looking at it.

II

It had struck twelve, and Claude was working at his picture when there was a loud, familiar knock at the door. With an instinctive yet involuntary impulse, the artist slipped the sketch of Christine's head, by the aid of which he was remodelling the principal figure of his picture, into a portfolio. After which he decided to open the door.

'You, Pierre!' he exclaimed, 'already!'

Pierre Sandoz, a friend of his boyhood, was about twenty-two, very dark, with a round and determined head, a square nose, and gentle eyes, set in energetic features, girt round with a sprouting beard.

'I breakfasted earlier than usual,' he answered, 'in order to give you a long sitting. The devil! you are getting on with it.'

He had stationed himself in front of the picture, and he added almost immediately: 'Hallo! you have altered the character of your woman's features!'

Then came a long pause; they both kept staring at the canvas. It measured about sixteen feet by ten, and was entirely painted over, though little of the work had gone beyond the roughing-out. This roughing-out, hastily dashed off, was superb in its violence and ardent vitality of colour. A flood of sunlight streamed into a forest clearing, with thick walls of verdure; to the left, stretched a dark glade with a small luminous speck in the far distance. On the grass, amidst all the summer vegetation, lay a nude woman with one arm supporting her head, and though her eyes were closed she smiled amidst the golden shower that fell around her. In the background, two other women, one fair, and the other dark, wrestled playfully, setting light flesh tints amidst all the green leaves. And, as the painter had wanted something dark by way of contrast in the foreground, he had contented himself with seating there a gentleman, dressed in a black velveteen jacket. This gentleman had his back turned and the only part of his flesh that one saw was his left hand, with which he was supporting himself on the grass.

'The woman promises well,' said Sandoz, at last ; 'but, dash it, there will be a lot of work in all this.'

Claude, with his eyes blazing in front of his picture, made a gesture of confidence. 'I've lots of time from now till the Salon. One can get through a deal of work in six months. And perhaps this time I'll be able to prove that I am not a brute.'

Thereupon he set up a whistle, inwardly pleased at the sketch he had made of Christine's head, and buoyed up by one of those flashes of hope whence he so often dropped into torturing anguish, like an artist whom passion for nature consumed.

'Come, no more idling,' he shouted. 'As you're here, let us set to.'

Sandoz, out of pure friendship, and to save Claude the cost of a model, had offered to pose for the gentleman in the foreground. In four or five Sundays, the only day of the week on which he was free, the figure would be finished. He was already donning the velveteen jacket, when a sudden reflection made him stop.

'But, I say, you haven't really lunched, since you were working when I came in. Just go down and have a cutlet while I wait here.'

The idea of losing time revolted Claude. 'I tell you I have breakfasted. Look at the saucepan. Besides, you can see there's a crust of bread left. I'll eat it. Come, to work, to work, lazy-bones.'

And he snatched up his palette and caught his brushes, saying, as he did so, 'Dubuche is coming to fetch us this evening, isn't he ? '

'Yes, about five o'clock.'

'Well, that's all right then. We'll go down to dinner directly he comes. Are you ready ? The hand more to the left, and your head a little more forward.'

Having arranged some cushions, Sandoz settled himself on the couch in the required attitude. His back was turned, but all the same the conversation continued for another moment, for he had that very morning received a letter from Plassans, the little Provençal town where he and the artist had known each other when they were wearing out their first pairs of trousers on the eighth form of the local college.

However, they left off talking. The one was working with his mind far away from the world, while the other grew stiff and cramped with the sleepy weariness of protracted immobility.

It was only when Claude was nine years old that a lucky chance had enabled him to leave Paris and return to the little place in Provence, where he had been born. His mother, a hardworking laundress,[1] whom his ne'er-do-well father had scandalously deserted, had afterwards married an honest artisan who was madly in love with her. But in spite of their endeavours, they failed to make both ends meet. Hence they gladly accepted the offer of an elderly and well-to-do townsman to send the lad to school and keep him with him. It was the generous freak of an eccentric amateur of painting, who had been struck by the little figures that the urchin had often daubed. And thus for seven years Claude had remained in the South, at first boarding at the college, and afterwards living with his protector. The latter, however, was found dead in his bed one morning. He left the lad a thousand francs a year, with the faculty of disposing of the principal when he reached the age of twenty-five. Claude, already seized with a passion for painting, immediately left school without even attempting to secure a bachelor's degree, and rushed to Paris whither his friend Sandoz had preceded him.

At the College of Plassans, while still in the lowest form, Claude Lantier, Pierre Sandoz, and another lad named Louis Dubuche, had been three inseparables. Sprung from three different classes of society, by no means similar in character, but simply born in the same year at a few months' interval, they had become friends at once and for aye, impelled thereto by certain secret affinities, the still vague promptings of a common ambition, the dawning consciousness of possessing greater intelligence than the set of dunces who maltreated them. Sandoz's father, a Spaniard, who had taken refuge in France in consequence of some political disturbances in which he had been mixed up, had started, near Plassans, a paper mill with new machinery of his own invention. When he had died, heart-broken by the petty local jealousy that had sought to hamper him in every way, his widow had found herself in so involved a position, and burdened with so many tangled law suits, that the whole of her remaining means were swallowed up. She was a native of Burgundy. Yielding to

---

[1] Gervaise of 'The Dram Shop' (*L'Assommoir*).—ED.

her hatred of the Provençals, and laying at their door even the slow paralysis from which she was suffering, she removed to Paris with her son, who then supported her out of a meagre clerk's salary, he himself haunted by the vision of literary glory. As for Dubuche, he was the son of a baker of Plassans. Pushed by his mother, a covetous and ambitious woman, he had joined his friends in Paris later on. He was attending the courses at the School of Arts as a pupil architect, living as best he might upon the last five-franc pieces that his parents staked on his chances, with the obstinacy of usurers discounting the future at the rate of a hundred per cent.

'Dash it!' at last exclaimed Sandoz, breaking the intense silence that hung upon the room. 'This position isn't at all easy; my wrist feels broken. Can I move for a moment?'

Claude let him stretch himself without answering. He was now working at the velveteen jacket, laying on the colour with thick strokes. However, stepping backward and blinking, he suddenly burst into loud laughter at some reminiscence.

'I say, do you recollect, when we were in the sixth form, how, one day, Pouillaud lighted the candles in that idiot Lalubie's cupboard? And how frightened Lalubie was when, before going to his desk, he opened the cupboard to take his books, and found it transformed into a mortuary chapel? Five hundred lines to every one in the form.'

Sandoz, unable to withstand the contagion of the other's gaiety, flung himself back on the couch. As he resumed his pose, he remarked, 'Ah, that brute of a Pouillaud. You know that in his letter this morning he tells me of Lalubie's forthcoming marriage. The old hack is marrying a pretty girl. But you know her, she's the daughter of Gallissard, the haberdasher— the little fair-haired girl whom we used to serenade!'

Once on the subject of their recollections there was no stopping them, though Claude went on painting with growing feverishness, while Pierre, still turned towards the wall, spoke over his shoulders, shaking every now and then with excitement.

First of all came recollections of the college, the old, dank convent, that extended as far as the town ramparts; the two courtyards with their huge plane trees; the slimy sedge-covered pond, where they had learned to swim, and the class-rooms with dripping plaster walls on the ground floor; then

the refectory, with its atmosphere constantly poisoned by the
fumes of dish-water; the dormitory of the little ones, famous
for its horrors, the linen room, and the infirmary, full of gentle
sisters, nuns in black gowns who looked so sweet beneath their
white coifs. What a to-do there had been when Sister
Angela, she whose Madonna-like face had turned the heads
of all the big fellows, disappeared one morning with Hermeline,
a stalwart first-form lad, who, from sheer love, purposely cut
his hands with his penknife so as to get an opportunity of
seeing and speaking to her while she dressed his self-inflicted
injuries with gold-beater's skin.

Then they passed the whole college staff in review; a
pitiful, grotesque, and terrible procession it was, with such
heads as are seen on meerschaum pipes, and profiles instinct
with hatred and suffering. There was the head master, who
ruined himself in giving parties, in order to marry his
daughters—two tall, elegant girls, the butt of constant and
abominable insults, written and sketched on every wall;
there was the comptroller Pifard, whose wonderful nose
betrayed his presence behind every door, when he went
eavesdropping; and there were all the teachers, each befouled
with some insulting nickname: the severe 'Rbadamantus,'
who had never been seen to smile; 'Filth,' who by the constant rubbing of his head had left his mark on the wall
behind every professional seat he occupied; 'Thou-hast-
deceived-me-Adèle,' the professor of physics, at whom ten
generations of schoolboys had tauntingly flung the name of
his unfaithful wife. There were others still: Spontini, the
ferocious usher, with his Corsican knife, rusty with the blood
of three cousins; little Chantecaille, who was so good-natured
that he allowed the pupils to smoke when out walking; and
also a scullion and a scullery maid, two ugly creatures who
had been nicknamed Paraboulomenos and Paralleluca, and
who were accused of kissing one another over the vegetable
parings.

Then came comical reminiscences; the sudden recollection
of practical jokes, at which they shook with laughter after all
those years. Oh! the morning when they had burned the
shoes of Mimi-la-Mort, *alias* the Skeleton Day Boarder, a
lank lad, who smuggled snuff into the school for the whole
of the form. And then that winter evening when they had
bagged some matches lying near the lamp in the chapel, in
order to smoke dry chestnut leaves in reed pipes. Sandoz,

who had been the ringleader on that occasion, now frankly avowed his terror; the cold perspiration that had come upon him when he had scrambled out of the choir, wrapt in darkness. And again there was the day when Claude had hit upon the sublime idea of roasting some cockchafers in his desk to see whether they were good to eat, as people said they were. So terrible had been the stench, so dense the smoke that poured from the desk, that the usher had rushed to the water pitcher, under the impression that the place was on fire. And then their marauding expeditions; the pillaging of onion beds while they were out walking; the stones thrown at windows, the correct thing being to make the breakage resemble a well-known geographical map. Also the Greek exercises, written beforehand in large characters on the blackboard, so that every dunce might easily read them though the master remained unaware of it; the wooden seats of the courtyard sawn off and carried round the basin like so many corpses, the boys marching in procession and singing funeral dirges. Yes! that had been a capital prank. Dubuche, who played the priest, had tumbled into the basin while trying to scoop some water into his cap, which was to serve as a holy water-pot. But the most comical and amusing of all the pranks had perhaps been that devised by Pouillaud, who one night had fastened all the unmentionable crockery of the dormitory to one long string passed under the beds. At dawn—it was the very morning when the long vacation began—he had pulled the string and skedaddled down the three flights of stairs with this frightful tail of crockery bounding and smashing to pieces behind him.

At the recollection of this last incident, Claude remained grinning from ear to ear, his brush suspended in mid-air. 'That brute of a Pouillaud!' he laughed. 'And so he has written to you. What is he doing now?'

'Why, nothing at all, old man,' answered Sandoz, seating himself more comfortably on the cushions. 'His letter is idiotic. He is just finishing his law studies, and he will inherit his father's practice as a solicitor. You ought to see the style he has already assumed—all the idiotic austerity of a philistine, who has turned over a new leaf.'

They were silent once more until Sandoz added, 'You see, old boy, we have been protected against that sort of thing.'

Then they relapsed again into reminiscences, but such as made their hearts thump; the remembrance of the many happy days they had spent far away from the college, in the open air and the full sunlight. When still very young, and only in the sixth form, the three inseparables had become passionately fond of taking long walks. The shortest holidays were eagerly seized upon to tramp for miles and miles; and, getting bolder as they grew up, they finished by scouring the whole of the country-side, by making journeys that sometimes lasted for days. They slept where they could, in the cleft of a rock, on some threshing-floor, still burning hot, where the straw of the beaten corn made them a soft couch, or in some deserted hut, the ground of which they covered with wild thyme and lavender. Those were flights far from the everyday world, when they became absorbed in healthy mother Nature herself, adoring trees and streams and mountains; revelling in the supreme joy of being alone and free.

Dubuche, who was a boarder, had only joined them on half-holidays and during the long vacation. Besides, his legs were heavy, and he had the quiet nature of a studious lad. But Claude and Sandoz never wearied; they awakened each other every Sunday morning by throwing stones at their respective shutters. In summer, above all, they were haunted by the thought of the Viorne, the torrent, whose tiny stream waters the low-lying pastures of Plassans. When scarcely twelve they already knew how to swim, and it became a passion with them to potter about in the holes where the water accumulated; to spend whole days there, stark naked, drying themselves on the burning sand, and then replunging into the river, living there as it were, on their backs, on their stomachs, searching among the reeds on the banks, immersed up to their ears, and watching the hiding-places of the eels for hours at a stretch. That constant contact of water beneath a burning sun prolonged their childhood, as it were, and lent them the joyous laughter of truant urchins, though they were almost young men, when of an evening they returned to the town amidst the still oppressive heat of a summer sunset. Later on they became very fond of shooting, but shooting such as is carried on in a region devoid of game, where they had to trudge a score of miles to pick off half a dozen pettychaps, or fig-peckers; wonderful expeditions, whence they returned with their bags empty, or with a mere bat, which they had managed to bring down while discharging their guns at the outskirts of the town. Their eyes moistened at the recollection of those happy days; they once more

beheld the white endless roads, covered with layers of dust, as
if there had been a fall of snow. They paced them again and
again in their imagination, happy to hear the fancied creaking
of their heavy shoes. Then they cut across the fields, over
the reddish-brown ferruginous soil, careering madly on and
on ; and there was a sky of molten lead above them, not a
shadow anywhere, nothing but dwarf olive trees and almond
trees with scanty foliage. And then the delicious drowsiness
of fatigue on their return, their triumphant bravado at having
covered yet more ground than on the previous journey, the
delight of being no longer conscious of effort, of advancing
solely by dint of strength acquired, spurring themselves on
with some terrible martial strain which helped to make everything like a dream.

Already at that time Claude, in addition to his powder-
flask and cartridge-belt, took with him an album, in which he
sketched little bits of country, while Sandoz, on his side, always
had some favourite poet in his pocket. They lived in a perfect frenzy of romanticism, winged strophes alternated with
coarse garrison stories, odes were flung upon the burning,
flashing, luminous atmosphere that enwrapt them. And when
perchance they came upon a small rivulet, bordered by half a
dozen willows, casting grey shadows on the soil all ablaze
with colour, they at once went into the seventh heaven. They
there by themselves performed the dramas they knew by
heart, inflating their voices when repeating the speeches of
the heroes, and reducing them to the merest whisper when
they replied as queens and love-sick maidens. On such days
the sparrows were left in peace. In that remote province,
amidst the sleepy stupidity of that small town, they had thus
lived on from the age of fourteen, full of enthusiasm, devoured
by a passion for literature and art. The magnificent scenarios
devised by Victor Hugo, the gigantic phantasies which
fought therein amidst a ceaseless cross-fire of antithesis, had
at first transported them into the fulness of epic glory ; gesticulating, watching the sun decline behind some ruins, seeing
life pass by amidst all the superb but false glitter of a fifth
act. Then Musset had come to unman them with his passion
and his tears ; they heard their own hearts throb in response
to his, a new world opened to them—a world more human—
that conquered them by its cries for pity, and of eternal misery,
which henceforth they were to hear rising from all things.
Besides, they were not difficult to please ; they showed the

voracity of youth, a furious appetite for all kinds of literature, good and bad alike. So eager were they to admire something, that often the most execrable works threw them into a state of exaltation similar to that which the purest masterpieces produce.

And as Sandoz now remarked, it was their great love of bodily exercise, their very revels of literature that had protected them against the numbing influence of their ordinary surroundings. They never entered a café, they had a horror of the streets, even pretending to moult in them like caged eagles, whereas their schoolfellows were already rubbing their elbows over the small marble tables and playing at cards for drinks. Provincial life, which dragged other lads, when still young, within its cogged mechanism, that habit of going to one's club, of spelling out the local paper from its heading to the last advertisement, the everlasting game of dominoes no sooner finished than renewed, the same walk at the self-same hour and ever along the same roads—all that brutifies the mind, like a grindstone crushing the brain, filled them with indignation, called forth their protestations. They preferred to scale the neighbouring hills in search of some unknown solitary spot, where they declaimed verses even amidst drenching showers, without dreaming of shelter in their very hatred of town-life. They had even planned an encampment on the banks of the Viorne, where they were to live like savages, happy with constant bathing, and the company of five or six books, which would amply suffice for their wants. Even womankind was to be strictly banished from that camp. Being very timid and awkward in the presence of the gentler sex, they pretended to the asceticism of superior intellects. For two years Claude had been in love with a 'prentice hattrimmer, whom every evening he had followed at a distance, but to whom he had never dared to address a word. Sandoz nursed dreams of ladies met while travelling, beautiful girls who would suddenly spring up in some unknown wood, charm him for a whole day, and melt into air at dusk. The only love adventure which they had ever met with still evoked their laughter, so silly did it seem to them now. It consisted of a series of serenades which they had given to two young ladies during the time when they, the serenaders, had formed part of the college band. They passed their nights beneath a window playing the clarinet and the cornet-à-piston, and thus raising a discordant din which frightened all the folk of the neighbourhood, until one memorable evening the indignant parents had emptied all the water pitchers of the family over them.

Ah! those were happy days, and how loving was the laughter with which they recalled them. On the walls of the studio hung a series of sketches, which Claude, it so happened, had made during a recent trip southward. Thus it seemed as if they were surrounded by the familiar vistas of bright blue sky overhanging a tawny country-side. Here stretched a plain dotted with little greyish olive trees as far as a rosy network of distant hills. There, between sunburnt russet slopes, the exhausted Viorne was almost running dry beneath the span of an old dust-bepowdered bridge, without a bit of green, nothing save a few bushes, dying for want of moisture. Farther on, the mountain gorge of the Infernets showed its yawning chasm amidst tumbled rocks, struck down by lightning, a huge chaos, a wild desert, rolling stony billows as far as the eye could reach. Then came all sorts of well remembered nooks : the valley of Repentance, narrow and shady, a refreshing oasis amid calcined fields ; the wood of Les Trois Bons-Dieux, with hard, green, varnished pines shedding pitchy tears beneath the burning sun ; the sheep walk of Bouffan, showing white, like a mosque, amidst a far-stretching blood-red plain. And there were yet bits of blinding, sinuous roads ; ravines, where the heat seemed even to wring bubbling perspiration from the pebbles ; stretches of arid, thirsty sand, drinking up rivers drop by drop ; mole hills, goat paths, and hill crests, half lost in the azure sky.

'Hallo!' exclaimed Sandoz, turning towards one sketch, 'what's that ?'

Claude, indignant, waved his palette. 'What! don't you remember ? We were very nigh breaking our necks there. Surely you recollect the day we clambered from the very bottom of Jaumegarde with Dubuche ? The rock was as smooth as your hand, and we had to cling to it with our nails, so that at one moment we could neither get up nor go down again. When we were once atop and about to cook our cutlets, we, you and I, nearly came to blows.'

Sandoz now remembered. 'Yes, yes ; each had to roast his own cutlet on rosemary sticks, and, as mine took fire, you exasperated me by chaffing my cutlet, which was being reduced to cinders.'

They both shook with laughter, until the painter resumed

his work, gravely concluding, ' That's all over, old man.   There is to be no more idling at present.'

He spoke the truth.   Since the three inseparables had realised their dream of meeting together in Paris, which they were bent upon conquering, their life had been terribly hard. They had tried to renew the long walks of old.   On certain Sunday mornings they had started on foot from the Fontainebleau gate, had scoured the copses of Verrières, gone as far as the Bièvre, crossed the woods of Meudon and Bellevue, and returned home by way of Grenelle.   But they taxed Paris with spoiling their legs ; they scarcely ever left the pavement now, entirely taken up as they were with their struggle for fortune and fame.

From Monday morning till Saturday night Sandoz sat fuming and fretting at the municipal building of the fifth Arrondissement in a dark corner of the registry office for births, rooted to his stool by the thought of his mother, whom his salary of a hundred and fifty francs a month helped in some fashion to keep.   Dubuche, anxious to pay his parents the interest of the money placed on his head, was ever on the lookout for some petty jobs among architects, outside his studies at the School of Arts.   As for Claude, thanks to his thousand francs a year, he had his full liberty ; but the latter days of each month were terrible enough, especially if he had to share the fag-end of his allowance.   Luckily he was beginning to sell a little ; disposing of tiny canvases, at the rate of ten and twelve francs a-piece, to Papa Malgras, a wary picture dealer.   After all, he preferred starvation to turning his art into mere commerce by manufacturing portraits of tradesmen and their wives ; concocting conventional religious pictures or daubing blinds for restaurants or sign-boards for accoucheuses.   When first he had returned to Paris, he had rented a very large studio in the Impasse des Bourdonnais ; but he had moved to the Quai de Bourbon from motives of economy.   He lived there like a savage, with an absolute contempt for everything that was not painting.   He had fallen out with his relatives, who disgusted him ; he had even ceased visiting his aunt, who kept a pork-butcher's shop near the Central Markets, because she looked too flourishing and plump.[1]   Respecting the downfall of his mother, who was being eaten out of doors and driven into the streets, he nursed a secret grief.

[1] This aunt is Lisa of ' The Fat and the Thin ' (*Le Ventre de Paris*)' in a few chapters of which Claude figures.— ED.

Suddenly he shouted to Sandoz, 'Will you be kind enough not to tumble to pieces?' But Sandoz declared that he was getting stiff, and jumped from the couch to stretch his legs a bit. They took ten minutes' rest, talking meanwhile about many things. Claude felt condescendingly good-tempered. When his work went smoothly he brightened up and became talkative; he, who painted with his teeth set, and raged inwardly directly he felt that nature was escaping him Hence his friend had scarcely resumed his attitude before he went on chattering, without, however, missing a stroke of his brush.

'It's going on all right, old boy, isn't it? You look all there in it. Oh, the brutes, I'll just see whether they'll refuse me this time. I am more severe for myself than they are for themselves, I'm sure of it; and whenever I pass one of my own pictures, it's more serious than if it had passed before all the hanging committees on earth. You know my picture of the markets, with the two urchins tumbling about on a heap of vegetables? Well, I've scratched it all out, it didn't come right. I found that I had got hold of a beastly machine,[1] a deal too heavy for my strength. But, never you fear, I'll take the subject up again some day, when I know better, and I'll take up others, machines which will knock them all cock-a-hoop with surprise.'

He made a magnificent gesture, as if to sweep a whole crowd away; emptied a tube of cobalt on his palette; and then began to jeer, asking what his first master would say to a picture like this? His first master indeed, Papa Belloque, a retired infantry captain, with one arm, who for a quarter of a century had taught drawing to the youth of Plassans in one of the galleries of the Museum! Then, in Paris, hadn't the celebrated Berthou, the painter of 'Nero in the Circus'— Berthou, whose lessons he had attended for six long months— told him a score of times that he would never be able to do anything? How he now regretted those six months wasted in idiotic efforts, absurd 'studies,' under the iron rule of a man whose ideas differed so much from his own. He at last began to hold forth against working at the Louvre. He would, he said, sooner chop his hand off than return there to spoil his perception of nature by undertaking one of those copies which for ever dim the vision of the world in which one lives.

[1] In familiar conversation, French artists, playwrights, and novelists invariably call their productions by the slang term 'machines.'—[ED.]

Was there aught else in art than the rendering of what one felt within oneself? Was not the whole of art reduced to placing a woman in front of one—and then portraying her according to the feelings that she inspired? Was not a bunch of carrots—yes, a bunch of carrots—studied from nature, and painted unaffectedly, in a personal style, worth all the ever-lasting smudges of the School of Arts, all that tobacco-juice painting, cooked up according to certain given recipes? The day would come when one carrot, originally rendered, would lead to a revolution. It was because of this that he now contented himself with going to the Boutin studio, a free studio, kept by a former model, in the Rue de la Huchette. When he had paid his twenty francs he was put in front of as many men and women as he cared for, and set about his work with a will, never thinking of eating or drinking, but struggling unrestingly with nature, mad almost with the excitement of work, by the side of a pack of dandies who accused him of ignorant laziness, and arrogantly prated about their 'studies,' because they copied noses and mouths, under the eye of a master.

'Listen to this, old man: when one of those whipper-snappers can build up a torso like that one over yonder, he may come up and tell me, and we'll have a talk together.'

With the end of his brush he pointed to a study of the nude, suspended from the wall near the door. It was really magnificent, full of masterly breadth of colouring. By its side were some other admirable bits, a girl's feet exquisite in their delicate truthfulness, and a woman's trunk with quivering satin-like skin. In his rare moments of content he felt proud of those few studies, the only ones which satisfied him, which, as it were, foretold a great painter, admirably gifted, but hampered by sudden and inexplicable fits of impotency.

Dealing sabre-like strokes at the velveteen jacket, he continued lashing himself into excitement with his uncompromising theories which respected nobody:

'They are all so many daubers of penny prints, who have stolen their reputations; a set of idiots or knaves on their knees before public imbecility! Not one among them dares to give the philistines a slap in the face. And, while we are about it, you know that old Ingres turns me sick with his glairy painting. Nevertheless, he's a brick, and a plucky fellow, and I take off my hat to him, for he did not care a curse for anybody, and he used to draw like the very devil.

He ended by making the idiots, who nowadays believe they understand him, swallow that drawing of his. After him there are only two worth speaking of, Delacroix and Courbet. The others are only numskulls. Oh, that old romantic lion, the carriage of him ! He was a decorator who knew how to make the colours blaze. And what a grasp he had ! He would have covered every wall in Paris if they had let him ; his palette boiled, and boiled over. I know very well that it was only so much phantasmagoria. Never mind, I like it for all that, as it was needed to set the School on fire. Then came the other, a stout workman—that one, the truest painter of the century, and altogether classical besides, a fact which not one of the dullards understood. They yelled, of course ; they shouted about profanation and realism, when, after all, the realism was only in the subject. The perception remained that of the old masters, and the execution resumed and continued the best bits of work one can find in our public galleries. Both Delacroix and Courbet came at the proper time. Each made a stride forward. And now—ah, now ! '

He ceased speaking and drew back a few steps to judge of the effect of his picture, becoming absorbed in contemplation for a moment, and then resuming :

' Yes, nowadays we want something different—what, I don't exactly know. If I did, and could do it, I should be clever indeed. No one else would be in the race with me. All I do know and feel is that Delacroix's grand romantic scenes are foundering and splitting, that Courbet's black painting already reeks of the mustiness of a studio which the sun never penetrates. You understand me, don't you ? We, perhaps, want the sun, the open air, a clear, youthful style of painting, men and things such as they appear in the real light. In short, I myself am unable to say what our painting should be ; the painting that our eyes of to-day should execute and behold.'

His voice again fell ; he stammered and found himself unable to explain the formulas of the future that were rising within him. Deep silence came while he continued working at the velveteen jacket, quivering all the time.

Sandoz had been listening to him without stirring from his position. His back was still turned, and he said slowly, as if speaking to the wall in a kind of dream :

' No ; one does not know, and still we ought to know. But each time a professor has wanted to impress a truth upon me, I have mistrustfully revolted, thinking: "He is either deceiving himself or deceiving me." Their ideas exasperate me. It seems to me that truth is larger, more general. How beautiful would it be if one could devote the whole of one's existence to one single work, into which one would endeavour to put everything, the beasts of the field as well as mankind; in short, a kind of immense ark. And not in the order indicated by manuals of philosophy, or according to the idiotic hierarchy on which we pride ourselves, but according to the full current of life; a world in which we should be nothing more than an accident, in which the passing cur, even the stones of the roads, would complete and explain us. In sum, the grand whole, without low or high, or clean or unclean, such as it indeed is in reality. It is certainly to science that poets and novelists ought to address themselves, for it is the only possible source of inspiration to-day. But what are we to borrow from it? How are we to march in its company? The moment I begin to think about that sort of thing I feel that I am floundering. Ah, if I only knew, what a series of books I would hurl at the heads of the crowd!'

He also became silent. The previous winter he had published his first book: a series of little sketches, brought from Plassans, among which only a few rougher notes indicated that the author was a mutineer, a passionate lover of truth and power. And lately he had been feeling his way, questioning himself while all sorts of confused ideas throbbed in his brain. At first, smitten with the thought of undertaking something herculean, he had planned a genesis of the universe, in three phases or parts; the creation narrated according to science; mankind supervening at the appointed hour and playing its part in the chain of beings and events; then the future—beings constantly following one another, and finishing the creation of the world by the endless labour of life. But he had calmed down in presence of the venturesome hypotheses of this third phase; and he was now looking out for a more restricted, more human framework, in which, however, his vast ambition might find room.

'Ah, to be able to see and paint everything,' exclaimed Claude, after a long interval. 'To have miles upon miles of walls to cover, to decorate the railway stations, the markets, the municipal offices, everything that will be built, when architects are no longer idiots. Only strong heads and strong muscles will be wanted, for there will be no lack of subjects

Life such as it runs about the streets, the life of the rich and the poor, in the market places, on the race-courses, on the boulevards, in the populous alleys; and every trade being plied, and every passion portrayed in full daylight, and the peasants, too, and the beasts of the fields and the landscapes —ah! you'll see it all, unless I am a downright brute. My very hands are itching to do it. Yes! the whole of modern life! Frescoes as high as the Pantheon! A series of canvases big enough to burst the Louvre!'

Whenever they were thrown together the painter and the author generally rèached this state of excitement. They spurred each other mutually, they went mad with dreams of glory; and there was such a burst of youth, such a passion for work about their plans, that they themselves often smiled afterwards at those great, proud dreams which seemed to endow them with suppleness, strength, and spirit.

Claude, who had stepped back as far as the wall, remained leaning against it, and gazing at his work. Seeing which, Sandoz, overcome by fatigue, left the couch and joined him. Then both looked at the picture without saying a word. The gentleman in the velveteen jacket was entirely roughed in. His hand, more advanced than the rest, furnished a pretty fresh patch of flesh colour amid the grass, and the dark coat stood out so vigorously that the little silhouettes in the background, the two little women wrestling in the sunlight, seemed to have retreated further into the luminous quivering of the glade. The principal figure, the recumbent woman, as yet scarcely more than outlined, floated about like some aerial creature seen in dreams, some eagerly desired Eve springing from the earth, with her features vaguely smiling and her eyelids closed.

'Well, now, what are you going to call it?' asked Sandoz.

'*The Open Air*,' replied Claude, somewhat curtly.

The title sounded rather technical to the writer, who, in spite of himself, was sometimes tempted to introduce literature into pictorial art.

'*The Open Air!* that doesn't suggest anything.'

'There is no occasion for it to suggest anything. Some women and a man are reposing in a forest in the sunlight. Does not that suffice? Don't fret, there's enough in it to make a masterpiece.'

He threw back his head and muttered between his teeth: 'Dash it all! it's very black still. I can't get Delacroix out of my eye, do what I will. And then the hand, that's Courbet's manner. Everyone of us dabs his brush into the romantic sauce now and then. We had too much of it in our youth, we floundered in it up to our very chins. We need a jolly good wash to get clear of it.'

Sandoz shrugged his shoulders with a gesture of despair. He also bewailed the fact that he had been born at what he called the confluence of Hugo and Balzac. Nevertheless, Claude remained satisfied, full of the happy excitement of a successful sitting. If his friend could give him two or three more Sundays the man in the jacket would be all there. He had enough of him for the present. Both began to joke, for, as a rule, Claude almost killed his models, only letting them go when they were fainting, half dead with fatigue. He himself now very nigh dropped, his legs bending under him, and his stomach empty. And as the cuckoo clock struck five, he snatched at his crust of bread and devoured it. Thoroughly worn out, he broke it with trembling fingers, and scarcely chewed it, again standing before his picture, pursued by his passion to such a degree as to be unconscious even that he was eating.

'Five o'clock,' said Sandoz, as he stretched himself, with his arms upraised. 'Let's go and have dinner. Ah! here comes Dubuche, just in time.'

There was a knock at the door, and Dubuché came in. He was a stout young fellow, dark, with regular but heavy features, close-cropped hair, and moustaches already full-blown. He shook hands with both his friends, and stopped before the picture, looking nonplussed. In reality that harum-scarum style of painting upset him, such was the even balance of his nature, such his reverence as a steady student for the established formulas of art; and it was only his feeling of friendship which, as a rule, prevented him from criticising. But this time his whole being revolted visibly.

'Well, what's the matter? Doesn't it suit you?' asked Sandoz, who was watching him.

'Yes, oh yes, it's very well painted—but——'

'Well, spit it out. What is it that ruffles you?'

'Not much, only the gentleman is fully dressed, and the women are not. People have never seen anything like that before.'

This sufficed to make both the others wild. Why, were there not a hundred pictures in the Louvre composed in precisely the same way? Hadn't all Paris and all the painters and tourists of the world seen them? And besides, if people had never seen anything like it, they would see it now. After all, they didn'tc are a fig for the public!

Not in the least disconcerted by these violent replies, Dubuche repeated quietly : 'The public won't understand—the public will think it indecorous—and so it is!'

'You wretched *bourgeois* philistine!' exclaimed Claude, exasperated. 'They are making a famous idiot of you at the School of Arts. You weren't such a fool formerly.'

These were the current amenities of his two friends since Dubuche had attended the School of Arts. He thereupon beat a retreat, rather afraid of the turn the dispute was taking, and saved himself by belabouring the painters of the School. Certainly his friends were right in one respect, the School painters were real idiots. But as for the architects, that was a different matter. Where was he to get his tuition, if not there? Besides his tuition would not prevent him from having ideas of his own, later on. Wherewith he assumed a very revolutionary air.

'All right,' said Sandoz, 'the moment you apologise, let's go and dine.'

But Claude had mechanically taken up a brush and set to work again. Beside the gentleman in the velveteen jacket the figure of the recumbent woman seemed to be fading away. Feverish and impatient, he traced a bold outline round her so as to bring her forward.

'Are you coming?'

'In a minute; hang it, what's the hurry? Just let me set this right, and I'll be with you.'

Sandoz shook his head and then remarked very quietly, lest he should still further annoy him : 'You do wrong to worry yourself like that, old man. Yes, you are knocked up, and have had nothing to eat, and you'll only spoil your work, as you did the other day.'

But the painter waved him off with a peevish gesture. It was the old story—he did not know when to leave off; he intoxicated himself with work in his craving for an immediate result, in order to prove to himself that he held his masterpiece at last. Doubts had just driven him to despair in the midst of his delight at having terminated a successful sitting. Had he done right, after all, in making the velveteen jacket so prominent, and would he not afterwards fail to secure

the brilliancy which he wished the female figure to show?
Rather than remain in suspense he would have dropped down
dead on the spot. Feverishly drawing the sketch of Christine's
head from the portfolio where he had hidden it, he compared it
with the painting on the canvas, assisting himself, as it were,
by means of this document derived from life.

'Hallo!' exclaimed Dubuche, 'where did you get that
from? Who is it?'

Claude, startled by the questions, did not answer; then,
without reflecting, he who usually told them everything,
brusquely lied, prompted by a delicate impulse to keep silent
respecting the adventure of the night.

'Tell us who it is?' repeated the architect.

'Nobody at all—a model.'

'A model! a very young one, isn't she? She looks very
nice. I wish you would give me her address. Not for myself,
but for a sculptor I know who's on the look-out for a Psyche.
Have you got the address there?'

Thereupon Dubuche turned to a corner of the greyish wall
on which the addresses of several models were written in chalk,
haphazard. The women particularly left their cards in
that way, in awkward, childish handwriting. Zoé Piedefer,
7 Rue Campagne-Première, a big brunette, who was getting
rather too stout, had scrawled her sign manual right across
the names of little Flore Beauchamp, 32 Rue de Laval, and
Judith Vaquez, 69 Rue du Rocher, a Jewess, both of whom
were too thin.

'I say, have you got the address?' resumed Dubuche.

Then Claude flew into a passion. 'Don't pester me! I
don't know and don't care. You're a nuisance, worrying like
that just when a fellow wants to work.'

Sandoz had not said a word. Surprised at first, he had
soon smiled. He was gifted with more penetration than
Dubuche, so he gave him a knowing nod, and they then
began to chaff. They begged Claude's pardon; the moment
he wanted to keep the young person for his personal use,
they would not ask him to lend her. Ha! ha! the scamp
went hunting about for pretty models. And where had he
picked up that one?

More and more embarrassed by these remarks, Claude
went on fidgetting. 'What a couple of idiots you are!' he exclaimed. 'If you only knew what fools you are making of yourselves. That'll do. You really make me sorry for both of you.'

His voice sounded so stern that they both became silent immediately, while he, after once more scratching out the woman's head, drew it anew and began to paint it in, following his sketch of Christine, but with a feverish, unsteady touch which went at random.

'Just give me another ten minutes, will you?' he repeated. 'I will rough in the shoulders to be ready for to-morrow, and then we'll go down.'

Sandoz and Dubuche, knowing that it was of no use to prevent him from killing himself in this fashion, resigned themselves to the inevitable. The latter lighted his pipe, and flung himself on the couch. He was the only one of the three who smoked; the others had never taken kindly to tobacco, always feeling qualmish after a cigar. And when Dubuche was stretched on his back, his eyes turned towards the clouds of smoke he raised, he began to talk about himself in an interminable monotonous fashion. Ah! that confounded Paris, how one had to work one's fingers to the bone in order to get on. He recalled the fifteen months of apprenticeship he had spent with his master, the celebrated Dequersonnière, a former grand-prize man, now architect of the Civil Branch of Public Works, an officer of the Legion of Honour and a member of the Institute, whose chief architectural performance, the church of St. Mathieu, was a cross between a pastry-cook's mould and a clock in the so-called First Empire style. A good sort of fellow, after all, was this Dequersonnière whom Dubuche chaffed, while inwardly sharing his reverence for the old classical formulas. However, but for his fellow-pupils, the young man would not have learnt much at the studio in the Rue du Four, for the master only paid a running visit to the place some three times a week. A set of ferocious brutes, were those comrades of his, who had made his life jolly hard in the beginning, but who, at least, had taught him how to prepare a surface, outline, and wash in a plan. And how often had he had to content himself with a cup of chocolate and a roll for déjeuner in order to pay the necessary five-and-twenty francs to the superintendent! And the sheets of paper he had laboriously smudged, and the hours he had spent in poring over books before he had dared to present himself at the School! And he had narrowly escaped being plucked in spite of all his assiduous endeavours. He lacked imagination, and the drawings he submitted, a caryatide and a summer dining-room, both

extremely mediocre performances, had classed him at the
bottom of the list. Fortunately, he had made up for this in
his oral examination with his logarithms, geometry, and
history of architecture, for he was very strong in the scientific
parts. Now that he was attending the School as a second-
class student, he had to toil and moil in order to secure a
first-class diploma. It was a dog's life, there was no end to
it, said he.

He stretched his legs apart, high upon the cushions, and
smoked vigorously and regularly.

'What with their courses of perspective, of descriptive
geometry, of stereotomy, of building, and of the history of art
—ah! upon my word, they do make one blacken paper with
notes. And every month there is a competitive examination
in architecture, sometimes a simple sketch, at others a complete design. There's no time for pleasure if a fellow wishes
to pass his examinations and secure the necessary honourable
mentions, especially if, besides all that, he has to find time to
earn his bread. As for myself, it's almost killing me.'

One of the cushions having slipped upon the floor, he
fished it up with his feet. 'All the same, I'm lucky. There
are so many of us scouring the town every day without
getting the smallest job. The day before yesterday I
discovered an architect who works for a large contractor.
You can have no idea of such an ignoramus of an architect—
a downright numskull, incapable even of tracing a plan. He
gives me twenty-five sous an hour, and I set his houses
straight for him. It came just in time, too, for my mother
sent me word that she was quite cleared out. Poor mother,
what a lot of money I have to refund her!'

As Dubuche was evidently talking to himself, chewing
the cud of his everyday thoughts—his constant thoughts of
making a rapid fortune—Sandoz did not even trouble to
listen to him. He had opened the little window, and seated
himself on a level with the roof, for he felt oppressed by
the heat in the studio. But all at once he interrupted the
architect.

'I say, are you coming to dinner on Thursday? All the
other fellows will be there—Fagerolles, Mahoudeau, Jory,
Gagnière.'

Every Thursday, quite a band met at Sandoz's: friends
from Plassans and others met in Paris—revolutionaries to a
man, and all animated by the same passionate love of art.

'Next Thursday? No, I think not,' answered Dubuche. 'I am obliged to go to a dance at a family's I know.'

'Where you expect to get hold of a dowry, I suppose?'

'Well, it wouldn't be such a bad spec.'

He shook the ashes from his pipe on to his left palm, and then, suddenly raising his voice—'I almost forgot. I have had a letter from Pouillaud.'

'You, too!—well, I think he's pretty well done for, Pouillaud. Another good fellow gone wrong.'

'Why gone wrong? He'll succeed his father; he'll spend his money quietly down there. He writes rationally enough. I always said he'd show us a thing or two, in spite of all his practical jokes. Ah! that beast of a Pouillaud.'

Sandoz, furious, was about to reply, when a despairing oath from Claude stopped him. The latter had not opened his lips since he had so obstinately resumed his work. To all appearance he had not even listened.

'Curse it—I have failed again. Decidedly, I'm a brute, I shall never do anything.' And in a fit of mad rage he wanted to rush at his picture and dash his fist through it. His friends had to hold him back. Why, it was simply childish to get into such a passion. Would matters be improved when, to his mortal regret, he had destroyed his work? Still shaking, he relapsed into silence, and stared at the canvas with an ardent fixed gaze that blazed with all the horrible agony born of his powerlessness. He could no longer produce anything clear or life-like; the woman's breast was growing pasty with heavy colouring; that flesh which, in his fancy, ought to have glowed, was simply becoming grimy; he could not even succeed in getting a correct focus. What on earth was the matter with his brain that he heard it bursting asunder, as it were, amidst his vain efforts? Was he losing his sight that he was no longer able to see correctly? Were his hands no longer his own that they refused to obey him? And thus he went on winding himself up, irritated by the strange hereditary lesion which sometimes so greatly assisted his creative powers, but at others reduced him to a state of sterile despair, such as to make him forget the first elements of drawing. Ah, to feel giddy with vertiginous nausea, and yet to remain there full of a furious passion to create, when the power to do so fled with everything else, when everything seemed to founder around him—the pride of work, the dreamt-of glory, the whole of his existence!

'Look here, old boy,' said Sandoz at last, 'we don't want to worry you, but it's half-past six, and we are starving. Be reasonable, and come down with us.'

Claude was cleaning a corner of his palette. Then he emptied some more tubes on it, and, in a voice like thunder, replied with one single word, 'No.'

For the next ten minutes nobody spoke; the painter, beside himself, wrestled with his picture, whilst his friends remained anxious at this attack, which they did not know how to allay. Then, as there came a knock at the door, the architect went to open it.

'Hallo, it's Papa Malgras.'

Malgras, the picture-dealer, was a thick-set individual, with close-cropped, brush-like, white hair, and a red splotchy face. He was wrapped in a very dirty old green coat, that made him look like an untidy cabman. In a husky voice, he exclaimed: 'I happened to pass along the quay, on the other side of the way, and I saw that gentleman at the window. So I came up.'

Claude's continued silence made him pause. The painter had turned to his picture again with an impatient gesture. Not that this silence in any way embarrassed the new comer, who, standing erect on his sturdy legs and feeling quite at home, carefully examined the new picture with his bloodshot eyes. Without any ceremony, he passed judgment upon it in one phrase—half ironic, half affectionate: 'Well, well, there's a machine.'

Then, seeing that nobody said anything, be began to stroll round the studio, looking at the paintings on the walls.

Papa Malgras, beneath his thick layer of grease and grime, was really a very cute customer, with taste and scent for good painting. He never wasted his time or lost his way among mere daubers; he went straight, as if from instinct, to individualists, whose talent was contested still, but whose future fame his flaming, drunkard's nose sniffed from afar. Added to this he was a ferocious hand at bargaining, and displayed all the cunning of a savage in his efforts to secure, for a song, the pictures that he coveted. True, he himself was satisfied with very honest profits, twenty per cent., thirty at the most. He based his calculations on quickly turning over his small capital, never purchasing in the morning without knowing where to dispose of his purchase at night. As a superb liar, moreover, he had no equal.

Pausing near the door, before the studies from the nude, painted at the Boutin studio, he contemplated them in silence for a few moments, his eyes glistening the while with the enjoyment of a connoisseur, which his heavy eyelids tried to hide. Assuredly, he thought, there was a great deal of talent and sentiment of life about that big crazy fellow Claude, who wasted his time in painting huge stretches of canvas which ho one would buy. The girl's pretty legs, the admirably painted woman's trunk, filled the dealer with delight. But there was no sale for that kind of stuff, and he had already made his choice—a tiny sketch, a nook of the country round Plassans, at once delicate and violent—which he pretended not to notice. At last he drew near, and said, in an off-hand way :

' What's this ? Ah ! yes, I know, one of the things you brought back with you from the South. It's too crude. I still have the two I bought of you.'

And he went on in mellow, long-winded phrases. ' You'll perhaps not believe me, Monsieur Lantier, but that sort of thing doesn't sell at all—not at all. I've a set of rooms full of them. I'm always afraid of smashing something when I turn round. I can't go on like that, honour bright ; I shall have to go into liquidation, and I shall end my days in the hospital. You know me, eh ? my heart is bigger than my pocket, and there's nothing I like better than to oblige young men of talent like yourself. Oh, for the matter of that, you've got talent, and I keep on telling them so—nay, shouting it to them— but what's the good ? They won't nibble, they won't nibble ! '

He was trying the emotional dodge ; then, with the spirit of a man about to do something rash : ' Well, it sha'n't be said that I came in to waste your time. What do you want for that rough sketch ? '

Claude, still irritated, was painting nervously. He dryly answered, without even turning his head : ' Twenty francs.'

' Nonsense ; twenty francs ! you must be mad. You sold me the others ten francs a-piece—and to-day I won't give a copper more than eight francs.'

As a rule the painter closed with him at once, ashamed and humbled at this miserable chaffering, glad also to get a little money now and then. But this time he was obstinate, and took to insulting the picture-dealer, who, giving tit for tat, all at once dropped the formal ' you ' to assume the glib ' thou,' denied his talent, overwhelmed him with invective, and taxed

him with ingratitude. Meanwhile, however, he had taken
from his pocket three successive five-franc pieces, which, as if
playing at chuck-farthing, he flung from a distance upon the
table, where they rattled among the crockery.

'One, two, three—not one more, dost hear? for there is
already one too many, and I'll take care to get it back; I'll
deduct it from something else of thine, as I live. Fifteen
francs for that! Thou art wrong, my lad, and thou'lt be
sorry for this dirty trick.'

Quite exhausted, Claude let him take down the little
canvas, which disappeared as if by magic in his capacious
green coat. Had it dropped into a special pocket, or was it
reposing on Papa Malgras' ample chest? Not the slightest
protuberance indicated its whereabouts.

Having accomplished his stroke of business, Papa Malgras
abruptly calmed down and went towards the door. But he
suddenly changed his mind and came back. 'Just listen,
Lantier,' he said, in the honeyest of tones; 'I want a lobster
painted. You really owe me that much after fleecing me.
I'll bring you the lobster, you'll paint me a bit of still life from
it, and keep it for your pains. You can eat it with your
friends. It's settled, isn't it?'

At this proposal Sandoz and Dubuche, who had hitherto
listened inquisitively, burst into such loud laughter that the
picture-dealer himself became gay. Those confounded painters,
they did themselves no good, they simply starved. What
would have become of the lazy beggars if he, Papa Malgras,
hadn't brought a leg of mutton now and then, or a nice fresh
plaice, or a lobster, with its garnish of parsley?

'You'll paint me my lobster, eh, Lantier? Much obliged.'
And he stationed himself anew before the large canvas, with
his wonted smile of mingled derision and admiration. And
at last he went off, repeating, 'Well, well, there's a machine.'

Claude wanted to take up his palette and brushes once more.
But his legs refused their service; his arms fell to his side,
stiff, as if pinioned there by some occult force. In the intense
melancholy silence that had followed the din of the dispute he
staggered, distracted, bereft of sight before his shapeless work.

'I'm done for, I'm done for,' he gasped. 'That brute
has finished me off!'

The clock had just struck seven; he had been at work
for eight mortal hours without tasting anything but a crust
of bread, without taking a moment's rest, ever on his legs,

shaken by feverish excitement. And now the sun was setting, shadows began to darken the studio, which in the gloaming assumed a most melancholy aspect. When the light went down like this on the crisis of a bad day's work, it seemed to Claude as if the sun would never rise again, but had for ever carried life and all the jubilant gaiety of colour away.

'Come,' implored Sandoz, with all the gentleness of brotherly compassion. 'Come, there's a good fellow.'

Even Dubuche added, 'You'll see more clearly into it to-morrow. Come and dine.'

For a moment Claude refused to surrender. He stood rooted to the spot, deaf to their friendly voices, and fiercely obstinate.

What did he want to do then, since his tired fingers were no longer able to grasp the brush? He did not know, but, however powerless he might be, he was gnawed by a mad craving to go on working still and to create in spite of everything. Even if he did nothing, he would at least stay there, he would not vacate the spot. All at once, however, he made up his mind, shaken the while as by a big sob. He clutched firmly hold of his broadest palette-knife, and, with one deep, slow sweep, he obliterated the woman's head and bosom. It was veritable murder, a pounding away of human flesh; the whole disappeared in a murky, muddy mash. By the side of the gentleman in the dark jacket, amidst the bright verdure, where the two little wrestlers so lightly tinted were disporting themselves, there remained naught of the nude, headless, breastless woman but a mutilated trunk, a vague cadaverous stump, an indistinct, lifeless patch of visionary flesh.

Sandoz and Dubuche were already descending the stairs with a great clatter, and Claude followed them, fleeing his work, in agony at having to leave it thus scarred with a gaping gash.

III

THE beginning of the week proved disastrous to Claude. He had relapsed into one of those periods of self-doubt that made him hate painting, with the hatred of a lover betrayed, who overwhelms the faithless one with insults although tortured by an uncontrollable desire to worship her yet again. So on the Thursday, after three frightful days of fruitless and solitary battling, he left home as early as eight in the morning, banging his door violently, and feeling so disgusted with himself that he swore he would never take up a brush again. When he was unhinged by one of these attacks there was but one remedy, he had to forget himself, and, to do so, it was needful that he should look up some comrades with whom to quarrel, and, above all, walk about and trudge across Paris, until the heat and odour of battle rising from her paving-stones put heart into him again.

That day, like every other Thursday, he was to dine at Sandoz's, in company with their friends. But what was he to do until the evening ? The idea of remaining by himself, of eating his heart out, disgusted him. He would have gone straight to his friend, only he knew that the latter must be at his office. Then the thought of Dubuche occurred to him, but he hesitated, for their old friendship had lately been cooling down. He felt that the fraternity of the earlier times of effort no longer existed between them. He guessed that Dubuche lacked intelligence, had become covertly hostile, and was occupied with ambitions different from his own. However, he, Claude, must go somewhere. So he made up his mind, and repaired to the Rue Jacob, where the architect rented a small room on the sixth floor of a big frigid-looking house.

Claude was already on the landing of the second floor, when the doorkeeper, calling him back, snappishly told him that M. Dubuche was not at home, and had, in fact, stayed out all night. The young man slowly descended the stairs and found himself in the street, stupefied, as it were, by so prodigious an event as an escapade on the part of Dubuche. It was a piece of inconceivable bad luck. For a moment he strolled along aimlessly ; but, as he paused at the corner of the Rue de Seine, not knowing which way to go, he suddenly recollected what his friend had told him about a certain night spent at the Dequersonnière studio—a night of terrible hard work, the eve of the day on which the pupils' designs had to be deposited at the School of Arts. At once he walked towards the Rue du Four, where the studio was situated. Hitherto he had carefully abstained from calling there for Dubuche, from fear of the yells with which outsiders were greeted. But now he made straight for the place without flinching, his timidity disappearing so thoroughly before the anguish of loneliness that he felt ready to undergo any amount of insult could he but secure a companion in misfortune.

The studio was situated in the narrowest part of the Rue du Four, at the far end of a decrepit, tumble-down building. Claude had to cross two evil-smelling courtyards to reach a third, across which ran a sort of big closed shed, a huge out-house of board and plaster work, which had once served as a packing-case maker's workshop. From outside, through the four large windows, whose panes were daubed with a coating of white lead, nothing could be seen but the bare whitewashed ceiling.

Having pushed the door open, Claude remained motionless on the threshold. The place stretched out before him, with its four long tables ranged lengthwise to the windows—broad double tables they were, which had swarms of students on either side, and were littered with moist sponges, paint saucers, iron candlesticks, water bowls, and wooden boxes, in which each pupil kept his white linen blouse, his compasses, and colours. In one corner, the stove, neglected since the previous winter, stood rusting by the side of a pile of coke that had not been swept away; while at the other end a large iron cistern with a tap was suspended between two towels. And amidst the bare untidiness of this shed, the eye was especially attracted by the walls which, above, displayed a litter of plaster casts ranged in haphazard fashion on shelves, and disappeared lower down behind forests of T-squares and bevels, and piles of drawing boards, tied together with webbing straps. Bit by bit, such parts of the partitions as had remained unoccupied had become covered with inscriptions and drawings, a con-stantly rising flotsam and jetsam of scrawls traced there as on the margin of an ever-open book. There were caricatures of the students themselves, coarse witticisms fit to make a gendarme turn pale, epigrammatic sentences, addition sums, addresses, and so forth; while, above all else, written in big letters, and occupying the most prominent place, appeared this inscription : 'On the 7th of June, Gorfu declared that he didn't care a hang for Rome.—Signed, Godemard.'[1]

Claude was greeted with a growl like that of wild beasts disturbed in their lair. What kept him motionless was the strange aspect of this place on the morning of the 'truck night,' as the embryo architects termed the crucial night of labour. Since the previous evening, the whole studio, some sixty pupils, had been shut up there; those who had no designs to exhibit—'the niggers,' as they were called—

[1] The allusion is to the French Art School at Rome, and the competi-tions into which students enter to obtain admission to it, or to secure the prizes offered for the best exhibits which, during their term of residence, they send to Paris.—ED.

remaining to help the others, the competitors who, being behind time, had to knock off the work of a week in a dozen hours. Already, at midnight, they had stuffed themselves with brawn, saveloys, and similar viands, washed down with cheap wine. Towards one o'clock they had secured the company of some 'ladies'; and, without the work abating, the feast had turned into a Roman orgy, blended with a smoking competition. On the damp, stained floor there remained a great litter of greasy paper and broken bottles; while the atmosphere reeked of burnt tallow, musk, highly seasoned sausages, and cheap bluish wine.

And now many voices savagely yelled: 'Turn him out. Oh, that mug! What does he want, that guy? Turn him out, turn him out.'

For a moment Claude, quite dazed, staggered beneath the violence of the onslaught. But the epithets became viler, for the acme of elegance, even for the more refined among these young fellows, was to rival one's friends in beastly language. He was, nevertheless, recovering and beginning to answer, when Dubuche recognised him. The latter turned crimson, for he detested that kind of adventure. He felt ashamed of his friend, and rushed towards him, amidst the jeers, which were now levelled at himself:

'What, is it you?' he gasped. 'I told you never to come in. Just wait for me a minute in the yard.'

At that moment, Claude, who was stepping back, narrowly escaped being knocked down by a little hand-truck which two big full-bearded fellows brought up at a gallop. It was from this truck that the night of heavy toil derived its name: and for the last week the students who had got behindhand with their work, through taking up petty paid jobs outside, had been repeating the cry,' Oh! I'm in the truck and no mistake.' The moment the vehicle appeared, a clamour arose. It was a quarter to nine o'clock, there was barely time to reach the School of Arts. However, a helter-skelter rush emptied the studio; each brought out his chases, amidst a general jostling; those who obstinately wished to give their designs a last finishing touch were knocked about and carried away with their comrades. In less than five minutes every frame was piled upon the truck, and the two bearded fellows, the most recent additions to the studio, harnessed themselves to it like cattle and drew it along with all their strength, the others vociferating, and pushing from behind. It was like the rush of a sluice; the three courtyards were crossed amidst a torrential crash, and the street was invaded, flooded by the howling throng.

Claude, nevertheless, had set up running by the side of Dubuche, who came at the fag-end, very vexed at not having had another quarter of an hour to finish a tinted drawing more carefully.

'What are you going to do afterwards?' asked Claude.

'Oh! I've errands which will take up my whole day.'

The painter was grieved to see that even this friend escaped him. 'All right, then,' said he; 'in that case I leave you. Shall we see you at Sandoz's to-night?'

'Yes, I think so; unless I'm kept to dinner elsewhere.'

Both were getting out of breath. The band of embryo architects, without slackening their pace, had purposely taken the longest way round for the pleasure of prolonging their uproar. After rushing down the Rue du Four, they dashed across the Place Gozlin and swept into the Rue de l'Echaudé Heading the procession was the truck, drawn and pushed along more and more vigorously, and constantly rebounding over the rough paving-stones, amid the jolting of the frames with which it was laden. Its escort galloped along madly, compelling the passers-by to draw back close to the houses in order to save themselves from being knocked down; while the shop-keepers, standing open-mouthed on their doorsteps, believed in a revolution. The whole neighbourhood seemed topsy-turvy. In the Rue Jacob, such was the rush, so frightful were the yells, that several house shutters were hastily closed. As the Rue Bonaparte was, at last, being reached, one tall, fair fellow thought it a good joke to catch hold of a little servant girl who stood bewildered on the pavement, and drag her along with them, like a wisp of straw caught in a torrent.

'Well,' said Claude, 'good-bye, then; I'll see you to-night.'

'Yes, to-night.'

The painter, out of breath, had stopped at the corner of the Rue des Beaux Arts. The court gates of the Art School stood wide open in front of him, and the procession plunged into the yard.

After drawing breath, Claude retraced his steps to the Rue de Seine. His bad luck was increasing; it seemed ordained that he should not be able to beguile a chum from work that morning. So he went up the street, and slowly walked on as

far as the Place du Pantheon, without any definite aim.
Then it occurred to him that he might just look into the
Municipal Offices, if only to shake hands with Sandoz. That
would, at any rate, mean ten minutes well spent. But he
positively gasped when he was told by an attendant that M.
Sandoz had asked for a day off to attend a funeral. However,
he knew the trick of old. His friend always found the same
pretext whenever he wanted to do a good day's work at home.
He had already made up his mind to join him there, when a
feeling of artistic brotherliness, the scruple of an honest
worker, made him pause ; yes, it would be a crime to go and
disturb that good fellow, and infect him with the discouragement born of a difficult task, at the very moment when he
was, no doubt, manfully accomplishing his own work.

So Claude had to resign himself to his fate. He dragged
his black melancholy along the quays until mid-day, his
head so heavy, so full of thoughts of his lack of power, that
he only espied the well-loved horizons of the Seine through a
mist. Then he found himself once more in the Rue de la
Femme-sans-Tête, where he breakfasted at Gomard's wine
shop, whose sign ' The Dog of Montargis,' inspired him with
interest. Some stonemasons, in their working blouses, bespattered with mortar, were there at table, and, like them, and with
them, he ate his eight sous' ' ordinary '—some beef broth in a
bowl, in which he soaked some bread, followed by a slice of
boiled soup-beef, garnished with haricot beans, and served up
on a plate damp with dish-water. However, it was still too
good, he thought, for a brute unable to earn his bread.
Whenever his work miscarried, he undervalued himself, ranked
himself lower than a common labourer, whose sinewy arms
could at least perform their appointed task. For an hour he
lingered in the tavern brutifying himself by listening to the
conversation at the tables around him. Once outside he
slowly resumed his walk in haphazard fashion.

When he got to the Place de l'Hôtel de Ville, however, a
fresh idea made him quicken his pace. Why had he not thought
of Fagerolles ? Fagerolles was a nice fellow, gay, and by no
means a fool, although he studied at the School of Arts. One
could talk with him, even when he defended bad painting.
If he had lunched at his father's, in the Rue Vieille-du-
Temple, he must certainly still be there.

On entering the narrow street, Claude felt a sensation of
refreshing coolness come over him. In the sun it had grown

very warm, and moisture rose from the pavement, which, however bright the sky, remained damp and greasy beneath the constant tramping of the pedestrians. Every minute, when a push obliged Claude to leave the footwalk, he found himself in danger of being knocked down by trucks or vans. Still the street amused him, with its straggling houses out of line, their flat frontages chequered with signboards up to the very eaves, and pierced with small windows, whence came the hum of every kind of handiwork that can be carried on at home. In one of the narrowest parts of the street a small newspaper shop made him stop. It was betwixt a hairdresser's and a tripeseller's, and had an outdoor display of idiotic prints, romantic balderdash mixed with filthy caricatures fit for a barrack-room. In front of these 'pictures,' a lank hobble-dehoy stood lost in reverie, while two young girls nudged each other and jeered. He felt inclined to slap their faces, but he hurried across the road, for Fagerolles' house happened to be opposite. It was a dark old tenement, standing forward from the others, and was bespattered like them with the mud from the gutters. As an omnibus came up, Claude barely had time to jump upon the foot pavement, there reduced to the proportions of a simple ledge; the wheels brushed against his chest, and he was drenched to his knees.

M. Fagerolles, senior, a manufacturer of artistic zinc-work, had his workshops on the ground floor of the building, and having converted two large front rooms on the first floor into a warehouse, he personally occupied a small, dark, cellar-like apartment overlooking the courtyard. It was there that his son Henri had grown up, like a true specimen of the flora of the Paris streets, at the edge of that narrow pavement constantly struck by the omnibus wheels, always soddened by the gutter water, and opposite the print and newspaper shop, flanked by the barber's and tripeseller's. At first his father had made an ornamental draughtsman of him for personal use. But when the lad had developed higher ambition, taking to painting proper, and talking about the School of Arts, there had been quarrels, blows, a series of separations and reconciliations. Even now, although Henri had already achieved some successes, the manufacturer of artistic zinc-work, while letting him have his will, treated him harshly, like a lad who was spoiling his career.

After shaking off the water, Claude went up the deep archway entrance, to a courtyard, where the light was quite greenish, and where there was a dank, musty smell, like that at the bottom of a tank. There was an overhanging roofing of glass and iron at the foot of the staircase, which was a wide one, with a wrought-iron railing, eaten with rust. As the painter passed the warehouse on the first floor, he glanced through a glass door and noticed M. Fagerolles examining some patterns. Wishing to be polite, he entered, in spite of the artistic disgust he felt for all that zinc, coloured to imitate bronze, and having all the repulsive mendacious prettiness of spurious art.

'Good morning, monsieur. Is Henri still at home?'

The manufacturer, a stout, sallow-looking man, drew himself straight amidst all his nosegay vases and cruets and statuettes. He had in his hand a new model of a thermometer, formed of a juggling girl who crouched and balanced the glass tube on her nose.

'Henri did not come in to lunch,' he answered drily.

This cool reception upset Claude. 'Ah! he did not come back; I beg pardon for having disturbed you, then. Good-day, monsieur.'

'Good-day.'

Once more outside, Claude began to swear to himself. His ill-luck was complete, Fagerolles escaped him also. He even felt vexed with himself for having gone there, and having taken an interest in that picturesque old street; he was infuriated by the romantic gangrene that ever sprouted afresh within him, do what he might. It was his malady, perhaps, the false principle which he sometimes felt like a bar across his skull. And when he had reached the quays again, he thought of going home to see whether his picture was really so very bad. But the mere idea made him tremble all over. His studio seemed a chamber of horrors, where he could no more continue to live, as if, indeed, he had left the corpse of some beloved being there. No, no; to climb the three flights of stairs, to open the door, to shut himself up face to face with 'that,' would have needed strength beyond his courage. So he crossed the Seine and went along the Rue St. Jacques. He felt too wretched and lonely; and, come what might, he would go to the Rue d'Enfer to turn Sandoz from his work.

Sandoz's little fourth-floor flat consisted of a dining-room, a bedroom, and a strip of kitchen. It was tenanted by himself alone; his mother, disabled by paralysis, occupied on the other side of the landing a single room, where she lived in morose and voluntary solitude. The street was a deserted one; the windows of the rooms overlooked the gardens of the Deaf and Dumb Asylum, above which rose the rounded crest of a lofty tree, and the square tower of St. Jacques-du-Haut-Pas.

Claude found Sandoz in his room, bending over his table, busy with a page of ' copy.'

' I am disturbing you ? ' said Claude.

' Not at all. I have been working ever since morning, and I've had enough of it. I've been killing myself for the last hour over a sentence that reads anyhow, and which has worried me all through my lunch.'

The painter made a gesture of despair, and the other, seeing him so gloomy, at once understood matters.

' You don't get on either, eh ? Well, let's go out. A sharp walk will take a little of the rust off us. Shall we go ? '

As he was passing the kitchen, however, an old woman stopped him. It was his charwoman, who, as a rule, came only for two hours in the morning and two hours in the evening. On Thursdays, however, she remained the whole afternoon in order to look after the dinner.

' Then it's decided, monsieur ? ' she asked. ' It's to be a piece of skate and a leg of mutton, with potatoes.'

' Yes, if you like.'

' For how many am I to lay the cloth ? '

' Oh ! as for that, one never knows. Lay for five, at any rate ; we'll see afterwards. Dinner at seven, eh ? we'll try to be home by then.'

When they were on the landing, Sandoz, leaving Claude to wait for him, stole into his mother's room. When he came out again, in the same discreet affectionate manner, they both went downstairs in silence. Outside, having sniffed to right and left, as if to see which way the wind blew, they ended by going up the street, reached the Place de l'Observatoire, and turned down the Boulevard du Montparnasse. This was their ordinary promenade ; they reached the spot instinctively, being fond of the wide expanse of the outer boulevards, where they could roam and lounge at ease. They continued silent, for their heads were heavy still, but the comfort of being together gradually made them more serene. Still it was only when they were opposite the Western Railway Station that Sandoz spoke.

' I say, suppose we go to Mahoudeau's, to see how he's getting on with his big machine. I know that he has given "his gods and saints' the slip to-day."

' All right,' answered Claude. ' Let's go to Mahoudeau's.'

They at once turned into the Rue du Cherche-Midi. There, at a few steps from the boulevard, Mahoudeau, a sculptor, had rented the shop of a fruiterer who had failed in business, and he had installed his studio therein, contenting himself with covering the windows with a layer of whitening. At this point, the street, wide and deserted, has a quiet, provincial aspect, with a somewhat ecclesiastical touch. Large gateways stand wide open showing a succession of deep roomy yards; from a cowkeeper's establishment comes a tepid, pungent smell of litter; and the dead wall of a convent stretches away for a goodly length. It was between this convent and a herbalist's that the shop transformed into a studio was situated. It still bore on its sign-board the inscription, ' Fruit and Vegetables,' in large yellow letters.

Claude and Sandoz narrowly missed being blinded by some little girls who were skipping in the street. On the foot pavement sat several families whose barricades of chairs compelled the friends to step down on to the roadway. However, they were drawing nigh, when the sight of the herbalist's shop delayed them for a moment. Between its windows, decked with enemas, bandages, and similar things, beneath the dried herbs hanging above the doorway, whence came a constant aromatic smell, a thin, dark woman stood taking stock of them, while, behind her, in the gloom of the shop, one saw the vague silhouette of a little sickly-looking man, who was coughing and expectorating. The friends nudged each other, their eyes lighted up with bantering mirth; and then they turned the handle of Mahoudeau's door.

The shop, though tolerably roomy, was almost filled by a mass of clay : a colossal Bacchante, falling back upon a rock. The wooden stays bent beneath the weight of that almost shapeless pile, of which nothing but some huge limbs could as yet be distinguished. Some water had been spilt on the floor, several muddy buckets straggled here and there, while a heap of moistened plaster was lying in a corner. On the shelves, formerly occupied by fruit and vegetables, were scattered some casts from the antique, covered with a tracery of cinder-like dust which had gradually collected there. A wash-house kind of dampness, a stale smell of moist clay, rose from the floor. And the wretchedness of this sculptor's studio and the dirt attendant upon the profession were made still more conspicuous by the wan light that filtered through the shop windows besmeared with whitening.

'What! is it you?' shouted Mahoudeau, who sat before his female figure, smoking a pipe.

He was small and thin, with a bony face, already wrinkled at twenty-seven. His black mane-like hair lay entangled over his very low forehead, and his sallow mask, ugly almost to ferociousness, was lighted up by a pair of childish eyes, bright and empty, which smiled with winning simplicity. The son of a stonemason of Plassans, he had achieved great success at the local art competitions, and had afterwards come to Paris as the town laureate, with an allowance of eight hundred francs per annum, for a period of four years. In the capital, however, he had found himself at sea, defenceless, failing in his competitions at the School of Arts, and spending his allowance to no purpose; so that, at the end of his term, he had been obliged for a livelihood to enter the employment of a dealer in church statues, at whose establishment, for ten hours a day, he scraped away at St. Josephs, St. Rochs, Mary Magdalens, and, in fact, all the saints of the calendar. For the last six months, however, he had experienced a revival of ambition, on finding himself once more among his comrades of Provence, the eldest of whom he was—fellows whom he had known at Geraud's boarding-school for little boys, and who had since grown into savage revolutionaries. At present, through his constant intercourse with impassioned artists, who troubled his brain with all sorts of wild theories, his ambition aimed at the gigantic.

'The devil!' said Claude, 'there's a lump.'

The sculptor, delighted, gave a long pull at his pipe, and blew a cloud of smoke.

'Eh, isn't it? I am going to give them some flesh, and living flesh, too; not the bladders of lard that they turn out.'

'It's a woman bathing, isn't it?' asked Sandoz.

'No; I shall put some vine leaves around her head. A Bacchante, you understand.'

At this Claude flew into a violent passion.

'A Bacchante? Do you want to make fools of people? Does such a thing as a Bacchante exist? A vintaging girl, eh? And quite modern, dash it all. I know she's nude, so let her be a peasant woman who has undressed. And that must be properly conveyed, mind; people must realise that she lives.'

Mahoudeau, taken aback, listened, trembling. He was

afraid of Claude, and bowed to his ideal of strength and truth. So he even improved upon the painter's idea.

'Yes, yes, that's what I meant to say—a vintaging girl. And you'll see whether there isn't a real touch of woman about her.'

At that moment Sandoz, who had been making the tour of the huge block of clay, exclaimed : 'Why, here's that sneak of a Chaîne.'

Behind the pile, indeed, sat Chaîne, a burly fellow who was quietly painting away, copying the fireless rusty stove on a small canvas. It could be told that he was a peasant by his heavy, deliberate manner and his bull-neck, tanned and hardened like leather. His only noticeable feature was his forehead, displaying all the bumps of obstinacy ; for his nose was so small as to be lost between his red cheeks, while a stiff beard hid his powerful jaws. He came from Saint Firmin, a village about six miles from Plassans, where he had been a cow-boy, until he drew for the conscription ; and his misfortunes dated from the enthusiasm that a gentleman of the neighbourhood had shown for the walking-stick handles which he carved out of roots with his knife. From that moment, having become a rustic genius, an embryo great man for this local connoisseur, who happened to be a member of the museum committee, he had been helped by him, adulated and driven crazy with hopes ; but he had successively failed in everything—his studies and competitions—thus missing the town's purse. Nevertheless, he had started for Paris, after worrying his father, a wretched peasant, into premature payment of his heritage, a thousand francs, on which he reckoned to live for a twelvemonth while awaiting the promised victory. The thousand francs had lasted eighteen months. Then, as he had only twenty francs left, he had taken up his quarters with his friend, Mahoudeau. They both slept in the same bed, in the dark back shop ; they both in turn cut slices from the same loaves of bread—of which they bought sufficient for a fortnight at a time, so that it might get very hard, and that they might thus be able to eat but little of it.

'I say, Chaîne,' continued Sandoz, 'your stove is really very exact.'

Chaîne, without answering, gave a chuckle of triumph which lighted up his face like a sunbeam. By a crowning stroke of imbecility, and to make his misfortunes perfect, his

protector's advice had thrown him into painting, in spite of
the real taste that he showed for wood carving. And he
painted like a whitewasher, mixing his colours as a hodman
mixes his mortar, and managing to make the clearest and
brightest of them quite muddy. His triumph consisted, however, in combining exactness with awkwardness; he displayed
all the naïve minuteness of the primitive painters; in fact,
his mind, barely raised from the clods, delighted in petty details.
The stove, with its perspective all awry, was tame and precise,
and in colour as dingy as mire.

Claude approached and felt full of compassion at the
sight of that painting, and though he was as a rule so harsh
towards bad painters, his compassion prompted him to say
a word of praise.

'Ah! one can't say that you are a trickster; you paint, at
any rate, as you feel. Very good, indeed.'

However, the door of the shop had opened, and a good-
looking, fair fellow, with a big pink nose, and large, blue,
short-sighted eyes, entered shouting:

'I say, why does that herbalist woman next door always
stand on her doorstep? What an ugly mug she's got!'

They all laughed, except Mahoudeau, who seemed very
much embarrassed.

'Jory, the King of Blunderers,' declared Sandoz, shaking
hands with the new comer.

'Why? What? Is Mahoudeau interested in her? I
didn't know,' resumed Jory, when he had at length grasped
the situation. 'Well, well, what does it matter? When
everything's said, they are all irresistible.'

'As for you,' the sculptor rejoined, 'I can see you have
tumbled on your lady-love's finger-nails again. She has dug
a bit out of your cheek!'

They all burst out laughing anew, while Jory, in his turn,
reddened. In fact, his face was scratched: there were
even two deep gashes across it. The son of a magistrate
of Plassans, whom he had driven half-crazy by his dissolute
conduct, he had crowned everything by running away with a
music-hall singer under the pretext of going to Paris to
follow the literary profession. During the six months that
they had been camping together in a shady hotel of the
Quartier Latin, the girl had almost flayed him alive each
time she caught him paying attention to anybody else of her
sex. And, as this often happened, he always had some fresh

scar to show—a bloody nose, a torn ear, or a damaged eye, swollen and blackened.

At last they all began to talk, with the exception of Chaîne, who went on painting with the determined expression of an ox at the plough. Jory had at once gone into ecstasies over the roughly indicated figure of the vintaging girl. He worshipped a massive style of beauty. His first writings in his native town had been some Parnassian sonnets celebrating the copious charms of a handsome pork-butcheress. In Paris—where he had fallen in with the whole band of Plassans—he had taken to art criticism, and, for a livelihood, he wrote articles for twenty francs apiece in a small, slashing paper called 'The Drummer.' Indeed, one of these articles, a study on a picture by Claude exhibited at Papa Malgras's, had just caused a tremendous scandal; for Jory had therein run down all the painters whom the public appreciated to extol his friend, whom he set up as the leader of a new school, the school of the 'open air.' Very practical at heart, he did not care in reality a rap about anything that did not conduce to his own pleasures; he simply repeated the theories he heard enunciated by his friends. 'I say, Mahoudeau,' he now exclaimed, 'you shall have an article; I'll launch that woman of yours. What limbs, my boys! She's magnificent!'

Then suddenly changing the conversation: 'By the way,' he said, 'my miserly father has apologised. He is afraid I shall drag his name through the mud, so he sends me a hundred francs a month now. I am paying my debts.'

'Debts! you are too careful to have any,' muttered Sandoz, with a smile.

In fact, Jory displayed a hereditary tightness of fist which much amused his friends. He managed to lead a profligate life without money and without incurring debts; and with the skill he thus displayed was allied constant duplicity, a habit of incessantly lying, which he had contracted in the devout sphere of his family, where his anxiety to hide his vices had made him lie about everything at all hours, and even without occasion. But he now gave a superb reply, the cry of a sage of deep experience.

'Oh, you fellows, you don't know the worth of money!'

This time he was hooted. What a philistine! And the invectives continued, when some light taps on one of the window-panes suddenly made the din cease.

'She is really becoming a nuisance,' said Mahoudeau, with a gesture of annoyance.

'Eh? Who is it? The herbalist woman?' asked Jory. 'Let her come in; it will be great fun.'

The door indeed had already been opened, and Mahoudeau's neighbour, Madame Jabouille, or Mathilde, as she was familiarly called, appeared on the threshold. She was about thirty, with a flat face horribly emaciated, and passionate eyes, the lids of which had a bluish tinge as if they were bruised. It was said that some members of the clergy had brought about her marriage with little Jabouille, at a time when the latter's business was still flourishing, thanks to the custom of all the pious folk of the neighbourhood. The truth was, that one sometimes espied black cassocks stealthily crossing that mysterious shop, where all the aromatic herbs set a perfume of incense. A kind of cloistral quietude pervaded the place; the devotees who came in spoke in low voices, as if in a confessional, slipped their purchases into their bags furtively, and went off with downcast eyes. Unfortunately, some very horrid rumours had got abroad—slander invented by the wine-shop keeper opposite, said pious folks. At any rate, since the widower had re-married, the business had been going to the dogs. The glass jars seemed to have lost all their brightness, and the dried herbs, suspended from the ceiling, were tumbling to dust. Jabouille himself was coughing his life out, reduced to a very skeleton. And although Mathilde professed to be religious, the pious customers gradually deserted her, being of opinion that she made herself too conspicuous with young fellows of the neighbourhood now that Jabouille was almost eaten out of house and home.

For a moment Mathilde remained motionless, blinking her eyes. A pungent smell had spread through the shop, a smell of simples, which she brought with her in her clothes and greasy, tumbled hair; the sickly sweetness of mallow, the sharp odour of elderseed, the bitter effluvia of rhubarb, but, above all, the hot whiff of peppermint, which seemed like her very breath.

She made a gesture of feigned surprise. 'Oh, dear me! you have company—I did not know; I'll drop in again.'

'Yes, do,' said Mahoudeau, looking very vexed. 'Besides, I am going out; you can give me a sitting on Sunday.'

At this Claude, stupefied, fairly stared at the emaciated Mathilde, and then at the huge vintaging woman.

'What!' he cried, 'is it madame who poses for that figure?
The dickens, you exaggerate!'

Then the laughter began again, while the sculptor
stammered his explanations. 'Oh! she only poses for the
head and the hands, and merely just to give me a few indications.'

Mathilde, however, laughed with the others, with a sharp,
brazen-faced laughter, showing the while the gaping holes in
her mouth, where several teeth were wanting.

'Yes,' resumed Mahoudeau. 'I have to go out on some
business now. Isn't it so, you fellows, we are expected
over yonder?'

He had winked at his friends, feeling eager for a good
lounge. They all answered that they were expected, and
helped him to cover the figure of the vintaging girl with some
strips of old linen which were soaking in a pail of water.

However, Mathilde, looking submissive but sad, did not
stir. She merely shifted from one place to another, when they
pushed against her, while Chaîne, who was no longer painting,
glanced at her over his picture. So far, he had not opened
his lips. But as Mahoudeau at last went off with his three
friends, he made up his mind to ask, in his husky voice:

'Shall you come home to-night?'

'Very late. Have your dinner and go to bed. Good-
bye.'

Then Chaîne remained alone with Mathilde in the damp
shop, amidst the heaps of clay and the puddles of water, while
the chalky light from the whitened windows glared crudely
over all the wretched untidiness.

Meantime the four others, Claude and Mahoudeau, Jory
and Sandoz, strolled along, seeming to take up the whole
width of the Boulevard des Invalides. It was the usual
thing, the band was gradually increased by the accession of
comrades picked up on the way, and then came the wild
march of a horde upon the war-path. With the bold assur-
ance of their twenty summers, these young fellows took
possession of the foot pavement. The moment they were
together trumpets seemed to sound in advance of them; they
seized upon Paris and quietly dropped it into their pockets.
There was no longer the slightest doubt about their victory;
they freely displayed their threadbare coats and old shoes,
like destined conquerors of to-morrow who disdained baga-
telles, and had only to take the trouble to become the

masters of all the luxury surrounding them. And all this was attended by huge contempt for everything that was not art—contempt for fortune, contempt for the world at large, and, above all, contempt for politics. What was the good of all such rubbish? Only a lot of incapables meddled with it. A warped view of things, magnificent in its very injustice, exalted them; an intentional ignorance of the necessities of social life, the crazy dream of having none but artists upon earth. They seemed very stupid at times, but, all the same, their passion made them strong and brave.

Claude became excited. Faith in himself revived amidst the glow of common hopes. His worry of the morning had only left a vague numbness behind, and he now once more began to discuss his picture with Sandoz and Mahoudeau, swearing, it is true, that he would destroy it the next day. Jory, who was very short-sighted, stared at all the elderly ladies he met, and aired his theories on artistic work. A man ought to give his full measure at once in the first spurt of inspiration; as for himself, he never corrected anything. And, still discussing, the four friends went on down the boulevard, which, with its comparative solitude, and its endless rows of fine trees, seemed to have been expressly designed as an arena for their disputations. When they reached the Esplanade, the wrangling became so violent that they stopped in the middle of that large open space. Beside himself, Claude called Jory a numskull; was it not better to destroy one's work than to launch a mediocre performance upon the world? Truckling to trade was really disgusting. Mahoudeau and Sandoz, on their side, shouted both together at the same time. Some passers-by, feeling uneasy, turned round to look, and at last gathered round these furious young fellows, who seemed bent on swallowing each other. But they went off vexed, thinking that some practical joke had been played upon them, when they suddenly saw the quartette, all good friends again, go into raptures over a wet-nurse, dressed in light colours, with long cherry-tinted ribbons streaming from her cap. There, now! That was something like—what a tint, what a bright note it set amid the surroundings! Delighted, blinking their eyes, they followed the nurse under the trees, and then suddenly seemed roused and astonished to find they had already come so far. The Esplanade, open on all sides, save on the south, where rose the distant pile of the Hôtel des Invalides, delighted

them—it was so vast, so quiet; they there had plenty of
room for their gestures; and they recovered breath there,
although they were always declaring that Paris was far too
small for them, and lacked sufficient air to inflate their
ambitious lungs.

'Are you going anywhere particular?' asked Sandoz of
Mahoudeau and Jory.

'No,' answered the latter, 'we are going with you.
Where are *you* going?'

Claude, gazing carelessly about him, muttered: 'I don't
know. That way, if you like.'

They turned on to the Quai d'Orsay, and went as far as
the Pont de la Concorde. In front of the Corps Législatif
the painter remarked, with an air of disgust: 'What a
hideous pile!'

'Jules Favre made a fine speech the other day. How he
did rile Rouher,' said Jory.

However, the others left him no time to proceed, the dis-
putes began afresh. 'Who was Jules Favre? Who was
Rouher? Did they exist? A parcel of idiots whom no
one would remember ten years after their death.' The young
men had now begun to cross the bridge, and they shrugged
their shoulders with compassion. Then, on reaching the
Place de la Concorde, they stopped short and relapsed into
silence.

'Well,' opined Claude at last, 'this isn't bad, by any
means.'

It was four o'clock, and the day was waning amidst a
glorious powdery shimmer. To the right and left, towards
the Madeleine and towards the Corps Législatif, lines of
buildings stretched away, showing against the sky, while
in the Tuileries Gardens rose gradients of lofty rounded
chestnut trees. And beyond the verdant borders of the
pleasure walks, the avenue of the Champs Elysées sloped
upward as far as the eye could reach, topped by the colossal
Arc de Triomphe, agape in front of the infinite. A double
current, a twofold stream rolled along—horses showing like
living eddies, vehicles like retreating waves, which the
reflections of a panel or the sudden sparkle of the glass of a
carriage lamp seemed to tip with white foam. Lower down,
the square—with its vast footways, its roads as broad as lakes
—was filled with a constant ebb and flow, crossed in every
direction by whirling wheels, and peopled with black specks of

men, while the two fountains plashed and streamed, exhaling delicious coolness amid all the ardent life.

Claude, quivering with excitement, kept saying: 'Ah! Paris! It's ours. We have only to take it.'

They all grew excited, their eyes opened wide with desire. Was it not glory herself that swept from the summit of that avenue over the whole capital? Paris was there, and they longed to make her theirs.

'Well, we'll take her one day,' said Sandoz, with his obstinate air.

'To be sure we shall,' said Mahoudeau and Jory in the simplest manner.

They had resumed walking; they still roamed about, found themselves behind the Madeleine, and went up the Rue Tronchet. At last, as they reached the Place du Havre, Sandoz exclaimed, 'So we are going to Baudequin's, eh?'

The others looked as if they had dropped from the sky; in fact, it did seem as if they were going to Baudequin's.

'What day of the week is it?' asked Claude. 'Thursday, eh? Then Fagerolles and Gagnière are sure to be there. Let's go to Baudequin s.'

And thereupon they went up the Rue d'Amsterdam. They had just crossed Paris, one of their favourite rambles, but they took other routes at times—from one end of the quays to the other; or from the Porte St. Jacques to the Moulineaux, or else to Père-la-Chaise, followed by a round-about return along the outer boulevards. They roamed the streets, the open spaces, the crossways; they rambled on for whole days, as long as their legs would carry them, as if intent on conquering one district after another by hurling their revolutionary theories at the house-fronts; and the pavement seemed to be their property—all the pavement touched by their feet, all that old battleground whence arose intoxicating fumes which made them forget their lassitude.

The Café Baudequin was situated on the Boulevard des Batignolles, at the corner of the Rue Darcet. Without the least why or wherefore, it had been selected by the band as their meeting-place, though Gagnière alone lived in the neighbourhood. They met there regularly on Sunday nights; and on Thursday afternoons, at about five o'clock, those who were then at liberty had made it a habit to look in for a moment. That day, as the weather was fine and bright, the little tables outside under the awning were occupied by rows of customers, obstructing the footway. But the band hated all elbowing and public exhibition, so they jostled the other people in order to go inside, where all was deserted and cool.

'Hallo, there's Fagerolles by himself,' exclaimed Claude.

He had gone straight to their usual table at the end of the café, on the left, where he shook hands with a pale, thin, young man, whose pert girlish face was lighted up by a pair of winning, satirical grey eyes, which at times flashed like steel. They all sat down and ordered beer, after which the painter resumed:

'Do you know that I went to look for you at your father's; and a nice reception he gave me.'

Fagerolles, who affected a low devil-may-care style, slapped his thighs. 'Oh, the old fellow plagues me! I hooked it this morning, after a row. He wants me to draw some things for his beastly zinc stuff. As if I hadn't enough zinc stuff at the Art School.'

This slap at the professors delighted the young man's friends. He amused them and made himself their idol by dint of alternate flattery and blame. His smile went from one to the other, while, by the aid of a few drops of beer spilt on the table, his long nimble fingers began tracing complicated sketches. His art evidently came very easily to him; it seemed as if he could do anything with a turn of the hand.

'And Gagnière?' asked Mahoudeau; 'haven't you seen him?'

'No; I have been here for the last hour.'

Just then Jory, who had remained silent, nudged Sandoz, and directed his attention to a girl seated with a gentleman at a table at the back of the room. There were only two other customers present, two sergeants, who were playing cards. The girl was almost a child, one of those young Parisian hussies who are as lank as ever at eighteen. She suggested a frizzy poodle—with the shower of fair little locks that fell over her dainty little nose, and her large smiling mouth, set between rosy cheeks. She was turning over the leaves of an illustrated paper, while the gentleman accompanying her gravely sipped a glass of Madeira; but every other minute she darted gay glances from over the newspaper towards the band of artists.

'Pretty, isn't she?' whispered Jory. 'Who is she staring at? Why, she's looking at me.'

But Fagerolles suddenly broke in: 'I say, no nonsense. Don't imagine that I have been here for the last hour merely waiting for you.'

The others laughed; and lowering his voice he told them about the girl, who was named Irma Bécot. She was the daughter of a grocer in the Rue Montorgueil, and had been to school in the neighbourhood till she was sixteen, writing her exercises between two bags of lentils, and finishing off her education on her father's doorstep, lolling about on the pavement, amidst the jostling of the throng, and learning all about life from the everlasting tittle-tattle of the cooks, who retailed all the scandal of the neighbourhood while waiting for five sous' worth of Gruyère cheese to be served them. Her mother having died, her father himself had begun to lead rather a gay life, in such wise that the whole of the grocery stores—tea, coffee, dried vegetables, and jars and drawers of sweetstuff—were gradually devoured. Irma was still going to school, when, one day, the place was sold up. Her father died of a fit of apoplexy, and Irma sought refuge with a poor aunt, who gave her more kicks than halfpence, with the result that she ended by running away, and taking her flight through all the dancing-places of Montmartre and Batignolles.

Claude listened to the story with his usual air of contempt for women. Suddenly, however, as the gentleman rose and went out after whispering in her ear, Irma Bécot, after watching him disappear, bounded from her seat with the impulsiveness of a school girl, in order to join Fagerolles, beside whom she made herself quite at home, giving him a smacking kiss, and drinking out of his glass. And she smiled at the others in a very engaging manner, for she was partial to artists, and regretted that they were generally so miserably poor. As Jory was smoking, she took his cigarette out of his mouth and set it in her own, but without pausing in her chatter, which suggested that of a saucy magpie.

'You are all painters, aren't you? How amusing! But why do those three look as if they were sulking. Just laugh a bit, or I shall make you, you'll see!'

As a matter of fact, Sandoz, Claude, and Mahoudeau, quite taken aback, were watching her most gravely. She herself remained listening, and, on hearing her companion come back, she hastily gave Fagerolles an appointment for the morrow. Then, after replacing the cigarette between Jory's lips, she strode off with her arms raised, and making a very comical grimace ; in such wise that when the gentleman reappeared, looking sedate and somewhat pale, he found her in her former seat, still looking at the same engraving in the newspaper. The whole scene had been acted so quickly, and with such jaunty drollery, that the two sergeants who sat near by, good-natured fellows both of them, almost died of laughter as they shuffled their cards afresh.

In fact, Irma had taken them all by storm. Sandoz declared that her name of Bécot was very well suited for a novel ; Claude asked whether she would consent to pose for a sketch ; while Mahoudeau already pictured her as a Paris *gamin*, a statuette that would be sure to sell. She soon went off, however, and behind the gentleman's back she wafted kisses to the whole party, a shower of kisses which quite upset the impressionable Jory.

It was five o'clock, and the band ordered some more beer. Some of the usual customers had taken possession of the adjacent tables, and these philistines cast sidelong glances at the artists' corner, glances in which contempt was curiously mingled with a kind of uneasy deference. The artists were indeed well known ; a legend was becoming current respecting them. They themselves were now talking on common-place subjects : about the heat, the difficulty of finding room in the omnibus to the Odéon, and the discovery of a wine-shop where real meat was obtainable. One of them wanted to start a discussion about a number of idiotic pictures that had lately been hung in the Luxembourg Museum ; but there was only one opinion on the subject, that the pictures were not worth their frames. Thereupon they left off conversing ; they smoked, merely exchanging a word or a significant smile now and then.

'Well,' asked Claude at last, 'are we going to wait for Gagnière ?'

At this there was a protest. Gagnière was a bore. Besides, he would turn up as soon as he smelt the soup.

'Let's be off, then,' said Sandoz. 'There's a leg of mutton this evening, so let's try to be punctual.'

Each paid his score, and they all went out. Their departure threw the café into a state of emotion. Some young fellows, painters, no doubt, whispered together as they pointed at Claude, much in the same manner as if he were the redoubtable chieftain of a horde of savages. Jory's famous article was producing its effect; the very public was becoming his accomplice, and of itself was soon to found that school of the open air, which the band had so far only joked about. As they gaily said, the Café Baudequin was not aware of the honour they had done it on the day when they selected it to be the cradle of a revolution.

Fagerolles having reinforced the group, they now numbered five, and slowly they took their way across Paris, with their tranquil look of victory. The more numerous they were, the more did they stretch across the pavement, and carry away on their heels the burning life of the streets. When they had gone down the Rue de Clichy, they went straight along the Rue de la Chaussée d'Antin, turned towards the Rue de Richelieu, crossed the Seine by the Pont des Arts, so as to fling their gibes at the Institute, and finally reached the Luxembourg by way of the Rue de Seine, where a poster, printed in three colours, the garish announcement of a travelling circus, made them all shout with admiration. Evening was coming on; the stream of wayfarers flowed more slowly; the tired city was awaiting the shadows of night, ready to yield to the first comer who might be strong enough to take her.

On reaching the Rue d'Enfer, when Sandoz had ushered his four friends into his own apartments, he once more vanished into his mother's room. He remained there for a few moments, and then came out without saying a word, but with the tender, gentle smile habitual to him on such occasions. And immediately afterwards a terrible hubbub, of laughter, argument, and mere shouting, arose in his little flat. Sandoz himself set the example, all the while assisting the charwoman, who burst into bitter language because it was half-past seven, and her leg of mutton was drying up. The five companions, seated at table, were already swallowing their soup, a very good onion soup, when a new comer suddenly appeared.

'Hallo! here's Gagnière,' was the vociferous chorus.

Gagnière, short, slight, and vague looking, with a doll-like startled face, set off by a fair curly beard, stood for a moment on the threshold blinking his green eyes. He belonged to Melun, where his well-to-do parents, who were both dead, had left him two houses; and he had learnt painting, unassisted, in the forest of Fontainebleau. His landscapes were at least conscientiously painted, excellent in intention ; but his real passion was music, a madness for music, a cerebral bonfire which set him on a level with the wildest of the band.

' Am I in the way ? ' he gently asked.

' Not at all ; come in ! ' shouted Sandoz.

The charwoman was already laying an extra knife and fork.

' Suppose she lays a place for Dubuche, while she is about it,' said Claude. ' He told me he would perhaps come.'

But they were all down upon Dubuche, who frequented women in society. Jory said that he had seen him in a carriage with an old lady and her daughter, whose parasols he was holding on his knees.

' Where have you come from to be so late ? ' asked Fage-rolles of Gagnière.

The latter, who was about to swallow his first spoonful of soup, set it in his plate again.

' I was in the Rue de Lancry—you know, where they have chamber music. Oh ! my boy, some of Schumann's machines ! You haven't an idea of them ! They clutch hold of you at the back of your head just as if somebody were breathing down your back. Yes, yes, it's something much more immaterial than a kiss, just a whiff of breath. 'Pon my honour, a fellow feels as if he were going to die.'

His eyes were moistening and he turned pale, as if experiencing some over-acute enjoyment.

' Eat your soup,' said Mahoudeau ; ' you'll tell us all about it afterwards.'

The skate was served, and they had the vinegar bottle put on the table to improve the flavour of the black butter, which seemed rather insipid. They ate with a will, and the hunks of bread swiftly disappeared. There was nothing refined about the repast, and the wine was mere common stuff, which they watered considerably from a feeling of delicacy, in order to lessen their host's expenses. They had just saluted the leg of mutton with a hurrah, and the host had begun to carve it, when the door opened anew. But this time there were furious protests.

' No, no, not another soul ! Turn him out, turn him out.'

Dubuche, out of breath with having run, bewildered at finding himself amidst such howling, thrust his fat, pallid face forward, whilst stammering explanations.

'Really, now, I assure you it was the fault of the omnibuses. I had to wait for five of them in the Champs Elysées.'

'No, no, he's lying!—Let him go, he sha'n't have any of that mutton. Turn him out, turn him out!'

All the same, he ended by coming in, and it was then noticed that he was stylishly attired, all in black, trousers and frock-coat alike, and cravated and booted in the stiff ceremonious fashion of some respectable member of the middle classes going out to dinner.

'Hallo! he has missed his invitation,' chaffed Fagerolles. 'Don't you see that his fine ladies didn't ask him to stay to dinner, and so now he's come to gobble up our leg of mutton, as he doesn't know where else to go?'

At this Dubuche turned red, and stammered: 'Oh! what an idea! How ill-natured you are! And, besides, just attend to your own business.'

Sandoz and Claude, seated next to each other, smiled, and the former, beckoning to Dubuche, said to him: 'Lay your own place, bring a plate and a glass, and sit between us—like that, they'll leave you alone.'

However, the chaff continued all the time that the mutton was being eaten. When the charwoman had brought Dubuche a plate of soup and a piece of skate, he himself fell in with the jokes good-naturedly. He pretended to be famished, greedily mopped out his plate, and related a story about a mother having refused him her daughter because he was an architect. The end of the dinner thus became very boisterous; they all rattled on together. The only dessert, a piece of Brie cheese, met with enormous success. Not a scrap of it was left, and the bread almost ran short. The wine did run short, so they each swallowed a clear draught of water, smacking their lips the while amidst great laughter. And, with faces beaming, and well-filled paunches, they passed into the bedroom with the supreme content of folks who have fared very sumptuously indeed.

Those were Sandoz's jolly evenings. Even at the times when he was hard up he had always had some boiled beef and broth to share with his comrades. He felt delighted at having a number of them around him, all friends, inspired by the same ideas. Though he was of their own age, he beamed with fatherly feelings and satisfied good-nature when he saw them in his rooms, around him, hand in hand, and intoxicated with hope. As he had but two rooms, the bedroom did duty as a drawing-room, and became as much theirs as his. For lack of sufficient chairs, two or three had to seat themselves on the bed. And on those warm summer evenings the window remained wide open to let in the air. From it two black silhouettes were to be seen rising above the houses, against the clear sky—the tower of St. Jacques du Haut-Pas and the tree of the Deaf and Dumb Asylum. When money was plentiful there was beer. Every one brought his own tobacco, the room soon became full of smoke, and without seeing each other they ended by conversing far into the night, amidst the deep mournful silence of that deserted district.

On that particular evening, at about nine o'clock, the charwoman came in.

'Monsieur, I have done. Can I go?'

'Yes, go to bed. You have left the kettle on the fire, haven't you? I'll make the tea myself.'

Sandoz had risen. He went off at the heels of the charwoman, and only returned a quarter of an hour afterwards. He had no doubt been to kiss his mother, whom he tucked up every night before she dozed off.

Meanwhile the voices had risen to a high pitch again. Fagerolles was telling a story.

'Yes, old fellow; at the School they even correct Nature herself. The other day Mazel comes up to me and says: "Those two arms don't correspond"; whereupon I reply: "Look for yourself, monsieur—the model's are like that." It was little Flore Beauchamp, you know. "Well," Mazel furiously replies, "if she has them like that, it's very wrong of her."'

They almost all shrieked, especially Claude, to whom Fagerolles told the story by way of paying court. For some time previously the younger artist had yielded to the elder's influence; and although he continued to paint with purely tricky skill, he no longer talked of anything but substantial, thickly-painted work, of bits of nature thrown on to canvas, palpitating with life, such as they really were. This did not prevent him, though, from elsewhere chaffing the adepts of the open-air school, whom he accused of impasting with a kitchen ladle.

Dubuche, who had not laughed, his sense of rectitude being offended, made so bold as to reply:

'Why do you stop at the School if you think you are being brutified there? It's simple enough, one goes away—— Oh, I know you are all against me, because I defend the School. But, you see, my idea is that, when a fellow wants to carry on a trade, it is not a bad thing for him to begin by learning it.'

Ferocious shouts arose at this, and Claude had need of all his authority to secure a hearing.

'He is right. One must learn one's trade. But it won't do to learn it under the ferule of professors who want to cram their own views forcibly into your nut. That Mazel is a perfect idiot!'

He flung himself backward on the bed, on which he had been sitting, and with his eyes raised to the ceiling, he went on, in an excited tone:

'Ah! life! life! to feel it and portray it in its reality, to love it for itself, to behold in it the only real, lasting, and changing beauty, without any idiotic idea of ennobling it by mutilation. To understand that all so-called ugliness is nothing but the mark of individual character, to create real men and endow them with life—yes, that's the only way to become a god!'

His faith was coming back to him, the march across Paris had spurred him on once more; he was again seized by his passion for living flesh. They listened to him in silence. He made a wild gesture, then calmed down.

'No doubt every one has his own ideas; but the annoyance is that at the Institute they are even more intolerant than we are. The hanging committee of the Salon is in their hands. I am sure that that idiot Mazel will refuse my picture.'

Thereupon they all broke out into imprecations, for this question of the hanging committee was the everlasting subject of their wrath. They demanded reforms; every one had a solution of the problem ready—from universal suffrage, applied to the election of a hanging committee, liberal in the widest sense of the word, down to unrestricted liberty, a Salon open to all exhibitors.[1]

[1] The reader will bear in mind that all these complaints made by Claude and his friends apply to the old Salons, as organised under Government control, at the time of the Second Empire.—Ed.

While the others went on discussing the subject, Gagnière drew Mahoudeau to the open window, where, in a low voice, his eyes the while staring into space, he murmured:

'Oh, it's nothing at all, only four bars; a simple impression jotted down there and then. But what a deal there is in it! To me it's first of all a landscape, dwindling away in the distance; a bit of melancholy road, with the shadow of a tree that one cannot see; and then a woman passes along, scarcely a silhouette; on she goes and you never meet her again, no, never more again.'

Just at that moment, however, Fagerolles exclaimed, 'I say, Gagnière, what are you going to send to the Salon this year?'

Gagnière did not hear, but continued talking, enraptured, as it were.

'In Schumann one finds everything—the infinite. And Wagner, too, whom they hissed again last Sunday!'

But a fresh call from Fagerolles made him start.

'Eh! what? What am I going to send to the Salon? A small landscape, perhaps; a little bit of the Seine. It is so difficult to decide; first of all I must feel pleased with it myself.'

He had suddenly become timid and anxious again. His artistic scruples, his conscientiousness, kept him working for months on a canvas the size of one's hand. Following the track of the French landscape painters, those masters who were the first to conquer nature, he worried about correctness of tone, pondering and pondering over the precise value of tints, till theoretical scruples ended by making his touch heavy. And he often did not dare to chance a bright dash of colour, but painted in a greyish gloomy key which was astonishing, when one remembered his revolutionary passions.

'For my part,' said Mahoudeau, 'I feel delighted at the prospect of making them squint with my woman.'

Claude shrugged his shoulders. 'Oh! you'll get in, the sculptors have broader minds than the painters. And, besides, you know very well what you are about; you have something at your fingers' ends that pleases. There will be plenty of pretty bits about your vintaging girl.'

The compliment made Mahoudeau feel serious. He posed above all for vigour of execution; he was unconscious of his real vein of talent, and despised gracefulness, though it ever invincibly sprung from his big, coarse fingers—the fingers of an untaught working-man—like a flower that obstinately sprouts from the hard soil where the wind has flung its seed.

Fagerolles, who was very cunning, had decided to send nothing, for fear of displeasing his masters ; and he chaffed the Salon, calling it 'a foul bazaar, where all the bad painting made even the good turn musty.' In his inmost heart he was dreaming of one day securing the Rome prize, though he ridiculed it, as he did everything else.

However, Jory stationed himself in the middle of the room, holding up his glass of beer. Sipping every now and then, he declared : 'Well, your hanging committee quite disgusts me ! I say, shall I demolish it ? I'll begin bombarding it in our very next number. You'll give me some notes, eh ? and we'll knock it to pieces. That will be fine fun.'

Claude was at last fully wound up, and general enthusiasm prevailed. Yes, yes, they must start a campaign. They would all be in it, and, pressing shoulder to shoulder, march to the battle together. At that moment there was not one of them who reserved his share of fame, for nothing divided them as yet ; neither the profound dissemblance of their various natures, of which they themselves were ignorant, nor their rivalries, which would some day bring them into collision. Was not the success of one the success of all the others ? Their youth was fermenting, they were brimming over with mutual devotion; they indulged anew in their everlasting dream of gathering into a phalanx to conquer the world, each contributing his individual effort; this one helping that one forward, and the whole band reaching fame at once in one row. Claude, as the acknowledged chief, was already sounding the victory, distributing laurels with such lyrical abundance that he overlooked himself. Fagerolles himself, gibing Parisian though he might be, believed in the necessity of forming an army ; while even Jory, although he had a coarser appetite, with a deal of the provincial still about him, displayed much useful comradeship, catching various artistic phrases as they fell from his companions' lips, and already preparing in his mind the articles which would herald the advent of the band and make them known. And Mahoudeau purposely exaggerated his intentional roughness, and clasped his hands like an ogre kneading human flesh ; while Gagnière, in ecstasy, as if freed from the everlasting

greyishness of his art, sought to refine sensation to the utmost
limits of intelligence ; and Dubuche, with his matter-of-fact
convictions, threw in but a word here and there ; words, however, which were like club-blows in the very midst of the
fray.   Then Sandoz, happy and smiling at seeing them so
united, 'all in one shirt,' as he put it, opened another bottle
of beer.   He would have emptied every one in the house.

'Eh ?' he cried, 'we're agreed, let's stick to it.   It's
really pleasant to come to an understanding among fellows
who have something in their nuts, so may the thunderbolts
of heaven sweep all idiots away ! '

At that same moment a ring at the bell stupefied him.
Amidst the sudden silence of the others, he inquired—'Who,
to the deuce, can that be—at eleven o'clock ? '

He ran to open the door, and they heard him utter a cry
of delight.   He was already coming back again, throwing the
door wide open as he said—'Ah ! it's very kind indeed to
think of us and surprise us like this ! Bongrand, gentlemen.'

The great painter, whom the master of the house
announced in this respectfully familiar way, entered, holding
out both hands.   They all eagerly rose, full of emotion,
delighted with that manly, cordial hand-shake so willingly
bestowed.   Bongrand was then forty-five years old, stout, and
with a very expressive face and long grey hair.   He had
recently become a member of the Institute, and wore the
rosette of an officer of the Legion of Honour in the top button-
hole of his unpretentious alpaca jacket.   He was fond of
young people ; he liked nothing so much as to drop in from
time to time and smoke a pipe among these beginners, whose
enthusiasm warmed his heart.

'I am going to make the tea,' exclaimed Sandoz.

When he came back from the kitchen, carrying the teapot
and cups, he found Bongrand installed astride a chair,
smoking his short cutty, amidst the din which had again
arisen.   Bongrand himself was holding forth in a stentorian
voice.   The grandson of a farmer of the Beauce region, the
son of a man risen to the middle classes, with peasant blood in
his veins, indebted for his culture to a mother of very artistic
tastes, he was rich, had no need to sell his pictures, and retained
many tastes and opinions of Bohemian life.

'The hanging committee ? Well, I'd sooner hang myself
than belong to it ! ' said he, with sweeping gestures. 'Am I

an executioner to kick poor devils, who often have to earn their
bread, out of doors?'

'Still, you might render us great service by defending our
pictures before the committee,' observed Claude.

'Oh, dear, no! I should only make matters worse for you
—I don't count; I'm nobody.'

There was a chorus of protestations; Fagerolles objected,
in a shrill voice:

'Well, if the painter of "The Village Wedding" does not
count——'

But Bongrand was getting angry; he had risen, his cheeks
afire.

'Eh? Don't pester me with "The Wedding"; I warn you
I am getting sick of that picture. It is becoming a perfect night-
mare to me ever since it has been hung in the Luxembourg
Museum.'

This 'Village Wedding'—a party of wedding guests roaming
through a corn-field, peasants studied from life, with an epic
look of the heroes of Homer about them—had so far remained
his masterpiece. The picture had brought about an evolution
in art, for it had inaugurated a new formula. Coming after
Delacroix, and parallel with Courbet, it was a piece of romanticism tempered by logic, with more correctness of observation,
more perfection in the handling. And though it did not
squarely tackle nature amidst the crudity of the open air, the
new school claimed connection with it.

'There can be nothing more beautiful,' said Claude, 'than
the two first groups, the fiddler, and then the bride with the
old peasant.'

'And the strapping peasant girl, too,' added Mahoudeau;
'the one who is turning round and beckoning! I had a great
mind to take her for the model of a statue.'

'And that gust of wind among the corn,' added Gagnière,
'and the pretty bit of the boy and girl skylarking in the
distance.'

Bongrand sat listening with an embarrassed air, and a
smile of inward suffering; and when Fagerolles asked him
what he was doing just then, he answered, with a shrug of his
shoulders:

'Well, nothing; some little things. But I sha'n't exhibit
this time. I should like to find a telling subject. Ah, you
fellows are happy at still being at the bottom of the hill. A
man has good legs then, he feels so plucky when it's a question

of getting up. But when once he is a-top, the deuce take it ! the worries begin. A real torture, fisticuffs, efforts which must be constantly renewed, lest one should slip down too quickly. Really now, one would prefer being below, for the pleasure of still having everything to do—— Ah, you may laugh, but you'll see it all for yourselves some day ! '

They were indeed laughing, thinking it a paradox, or a little piece of affectation, which they excused. To be hailed, like Bongrand, with the name of master—was that not the height of bliss ? He, with his arms resting on the back of his chair, listened to them in silence, leisurely puffing his pipe, and renouncing the idea of trying to make them understand him.

Meanwhile, Dubuche, who had rather domesticated tastes, helped Sandoz to hand the tea round, and the din continued. Fagerolles related a story about Daddy Malgras and a female cousin by marriage, whom the dealer offered as a model on conditions that he was given a presentment of her in oils. Then they began to talk of models. Mahoudeau waxed furious, because the really well-built female models were disappearing. It was impossible to find one with a decent figure now. Then suddenly the tumult increased again ; Gagnière was being congratulated about a connoisseur whose acquaintance he had made in the Palais Royal one afternoon, while the band played, an eccentric gentleman living on a small income, who never indulged in any other extravagance than that of buying pictures. The other artists laughed and asked for the gentleman's address. Then they fell foul of the picture dealers, dirty black- guards, who preyed on artists and starved them. It was really a pity that connoisseurs mistrusted painters to such a degree as to insist upon a middleman under the impression that they would thus make a better bargain. This question of bread and butter excited them yet more, though Claude showed magnificent contempt for it all. The artist was robbed, no doubt, but what did that matter, if he had painted a masterpiece, and had some water to drink ? Jory, having again expressed some low ideas about lucre, aroused general indignation. Out with the journalist ! He was asked stringent questions. Would he sell his pen ? Would he not sooner chop off his wrist than write anything against his convictions ? But they scarcely waited for his answer, for the excitement was on the increase ; it became the superb madness of early manhood, contempt for the whole world, an absorbing passion for good work, freed from all human weaknesses, soaring in the sky like a very sun. Ah! how strenuous was their desire to lose themselves, consume themselves, in that brazier of their own kindling!

Bongrand, who had not stirred the while, made a vague gesture of suffering at the sight of that boundless confidence, that boisterous joy at the prospect of attack. He forgot the hundred paintings which had brought him his glory, he was thinking of the work which he had left roughed out on his easel now. Taking his cutty from between his lips, he murmured, his eyes glistening with kindliness, 'Oh, youth, youth!'

Until two in the morning, Sandoz, who seemed ubiquitous, kept on pouring fresh supplies of hot water into the teapot. From the neighbourhood, now asleep, one now only heard the miawing of an amorous tabby. They all talked at random, intoxicated by their own words, hoarse with shouting, their eyes scorched, and when at last they made up their minds to go, Sandoz took the lamp to show them a light over the banisters, saying very softly:

'Don't make a noise, my mother is asleep.'

The hushed tread of their boots on the stairs died away at last, and deep silence fell upon the house.

It struck four. Claude, who had accompanied Bongrand, still went on talking to him in the deserted streets. He did not want to go to bed; he was waiting for daylight, with impatient fury, so that he might set to work at his picture again. This time he felt certain of painting a masterpiece, exalted as he was by that happy day of good-fellowship, his mind pregnant with a world of things. He had discovered at last what painting meant, and he pictured himself re-entering his studio as one returns into the presence of a woman one adores, his heart throbbing violently, regretting even this one day's absence, which seemed to him endless desertion. And he would go straight to his canvas, and realise his dream in one sitting. However, at every dozen steps or so, amidst the flickering light of the gaslamps, Bongrand caught him by a button of his coat, to repeat to him that, after all, painting was an accursed trade. Sharp as he, Bongrand, was supposed to be, he did not understand it yet. At each new work he undertook, he felt as if he were making a *début*; it was enough to make one smash one's head against the wall. The sky was now brightening, some market gardeners' carts began rolling down towards the central markets; and the pair continued chattering, each talking for himself, in a loud voice, beneath the paling stars.

IV

Six weeks later, Claude was painting one morning amidst a flood of sunshine that streamed through the large window of his studio. Constant rain had made the middle of August very dull, but his courage for work returned with the blue sky. His great picture did not make much progress, albeit he worked at it throughout long, silent mornings, like the obstinate, pugnacious fellow he was.

All at once there came a knock at his door. He thought that Madame Joseph, the doorkeeper, was bringing up his lunch, and as the key was always in the door, he simply called: 'Come in!'

The door had opened; there was a slight rustle, and then all became still. He went on painting without even turning his head. But the quivering silence, and the consciousness of some vague gentle breathing near him, at last made him fidgety. He looked up, and felt amazed; a woman stood there clad in a light gown, her features half-hidden by a white veil, and he did not know her, and she was carrying a bunch of roses, which completed his bewilderment.

All at once he recognised her.

'You, mademoiselle? Well, I certainly didn't expect you!'

It was Christine. He had been unable to restrain that somewhat unamiable exclamation, which was a cry from the heart itself. At first he had certainly thought of her; then, as the days went by for nearly a couple of months without sign of life from her, she had become for him merely a fleeting, regretted vision, a charming silhouette which had melted away in space, and would never be seen again.

'Yes, monsieur, it's I. I wished to come. I thought it was wrong not to come and thank you——'

She blushed and stammered, at a loss for words. She was out of breath, no doubt through climbing the stairs, for her heart was beating fast. What! was this long-debated visit out of place after all? It had ended by seeming quite natural to her. The worst was that, in passing along the quay, she had bought that bunch of roses with the delicate intention of thereby showing her gratitude to the young fellow, and the flowers now dreadfully embarrassed her. How was she to give them to him? What would he think of her? The impropriety of the whole proceeding had only struck her as she opened the door.

But Claude, more embarrassed still, resorted to exaggerated politeness. He had thrown aside his palette and was turning the studio upside down in order to clear a chair.

'Pray be seated, mademoiselle. This is really a surprise. You are too kind.'

Once seated, Christine recovered her equanimity. He looked so droll with his wild sweeping gestures, and she felt so conscious of his shyness that she began to smile, and bravely held out the bunch of roses.

'Look here; I wished to show you that I am not ungrateful.'

At first he said nothing, but stood staring at her, thunder-struck. When he saw, though, that she was not making fun of him, he shook both her hands, with almost sufficient energy to dislocate them. Then he at once put the flowers in his water-jug, repeating:

'Ah! now you are a good fellow, you really are. This is the first time I pay that compliment to a woman, honour bright.'

He came back to her, and, looking straight into her eyes, he asked:

'Then you have not altogether forgotten me?'

'You see that I have not,' she replied, laughing.

'Why, then, did you wait two months before coming to see me?'

Again she blushed. The falsehood she was about to tell revived her embarrassment for a moment.

'But you know that I am not my own mistress,' she said. 'Oh, Madame Vanzade is very kind to me, only she is a great invalid, and never leaves the house. But she grew anxious as to my health and compelled me to go out to breathe a little fresh air.'

She did not allude to the shame which she had felt during the first few days after her adventure on the Quai de Bourbon. Finding herself in safety, beneath the old lady's roof, the recollection of the night she had spent in Claude's room had filled her with remorse; but she fancied at last that she had succeeded in dismissing the matter from her mind. It was no longer anything but a bad dream, which grew more indistinct each day. Then, how it was she could not tell, but

amidst the profound quietude of her existence, the image of
that young man who had befriended her had returned to her
once more, becoming more and more precise, till at last it
occupied her daily thoughts. Why should she forget him?
She had nothing to reproach him with; on the contrary, she
felt she was his debtor. The thought of seeing him again,
dismissed at first, struggled against later on, at last became
an all-absorbing craving. Each evening the temptation to go
and see him came strong upon her in the solitude of her own
room. She experienced an uncomfortable irritating feeling,
a vague desire which she could not define, and only calmed
down somewhat on ascribing this troubled state of mind to a
wish to evince her gratitude. She was so utterly alone, she
felt so stifled in that sleepy abode, the exuberance of youth
seethed so strongly within her, her heart craved so desperately for friendship!

'So I took advantage of my first day out,' she continued.
'And besides, the weather was so nice this morning after all
the dull rain.'

Claude, feeling very happy and standing before her, also
confessed himself, but *he* had nothing to hide.

'For my part,' said he, 'I dared not think of you any
more. You are like one of the fairies of the story-books, who
spring from the floor and disappear into the walls at the
very moment one least expects it; aren't you now? I said
to myself, "It's all over: it was perhaps only in my fancy
that I saw her come to this studio." Yet here you are. Well,
I am pleased at it, very pleased indeed.'

Smiling, but embarrassed, Christine averted her head,
pretending to look around her. But her smile soon died
away. The ferocious-looking paintings which she again
beheld, the glaring sketches of the South, the terrible
anatomical accuracy of the studies from the nude, all chilled
her as on the first occasion. She became really afraid again,
and she said gravely, in an altered voice:

'I am disturbing you; I am going.'

'Oh! not at all, not at all,' exclaimed Claude, preventing
her from rising. 'It does me good to have a talk with you,
for I was working myself to death. Oh! that confounded
picture; it's killing me as it is.'

Thereupon Christine, lifting her eyes, looked at the large
picture, the canvas that had been turned to the wall on
the previous occasion, and which she had vainly wished to see.

The background—the dark glade pierced by a flood of sunlight—was still only broadly brushed in. But the two little wrestlers—the fair one and the dark—almost finished by now, showed clearly in the light. In the foreground, the gentleman in the velveteen jacket, three times begun afresh, had now been left in distress. The painter was more particularly working at the principal figure, the woman lying on the grass. He had not touched the head again. He was battling with the body, changing his model every week, so despondent at being unable to satisfy himself that for a couple of days he had been trying to improve the figure from imagination, without recourse to nature, although he boasted that he never invented.

Christine at once recognised herself. Yes, that nude girl sprawling on the grass, one arm behind her head, smiling with lowered eyelids, was herself, for she had her features. The idea absolutely revolted her, and she was wounded too by the wildness of the painting, so brutal indeed that she considered herself abominably insulted. She did not understand that kind of art; she thought it execrable, and felt a hatred against it, the instinctive hatred of an enemy. She rose at last, and curtly repeated, ' I must be going.'

Claude watched her attentively, both grieved and surprised by her sudden change of manner.

' Going already ? '

' Yes, they are waiting for me. Good-bye.'

And she had already reached the door before he could take her hand, and venture to ask her :

' When shall I see you again ? '

She allowed her hand to remain in his. For a moment she seemed to hesitate.

' I don't know. I am so busy.'

Then she withdrew her hand and went off, hastily, saying : ' One of these days, when I can. Good-bye.'

Claude remained stock-still on the threshold. He wondered what had come over her again to cause her sudden coolness, her covert irritation. He closed the door, and walked about, with dangling arms, and without understanding, seeking vainly for the phrase, the gesture that could have offended her. And he in his turn became angry, and launched an oath into space, with a terrific shrug of the shoulders, as if to rid himself of this silly worry. Did a man ever understand women ? However, the sight of the roses, overlapping the water-jug, pacified him; they smelt so sweet. Their scent pervaded the whole studio, and silently he resumed his work amidst the perfume.

Two more months passed by. During the earlier days Claude, at the slightest stir of a morning, when Madame Joseph brought him up his breakfast or his letters, quickly turned his head, and could not control a gesture of disappointment. He no longer went out until after four, and the doorkeeper having told him one evening, on his return home, that a young person had called to see him at about five, he had only grown calm on ascertaining that the visitor was merely a model, Zoé Piédefer. Then, as the days went by, he was seized with a furious fit of work, becoming unapproachable to every one, indulging in such violent theories that even his friends did not venture to contradict him. He swept the world from his path with one gesture; there was no longer to be anything but painting left. One might murder one's parents, comrades, and women especially, and it would all be a good riddance. After this terrible fever he fell into abominable despondency, spending a week of impotence and doubt, a whole week of torture, during which he fancied himself struck silly. But he was getting over it, he had resumed his usual life, his resigned solitary struggle with his great picture, when one foggy morning, towards the end of October, he started and hastily set his palette aside. There had been no knock, but he had just recognised the footfall coming up the stairs. He opened the door and she walked in. She had come at last.

Christine that day wore a large cloak of grey material which enveloped her from head to foot. Her little velvet hat was dark, and the fog outside had pearled her black lace veil. But he thought her looking very cheerful, with the first slight shiver of winter upon her. She at once began to make excuses for having so long delayed her return. She smiled at him in her pretty candid manner, confessed that she had hesitated, and that she had almost made up her mind to come no more. Yes, she had her own opinions about things, which she felt sure he understood. As it happened, he did not understand at all—he had no wish to understand, seeing that she was there. It was quite sufficient that she was not vexed with him, that she would consent to look in now and then like a chum. There were no explanations; they kept their respective torments and the

struggles of recent times to themselves. For nearly an hour
they chatted together right pleasantly, with nothing hidden
nor antagonistic remaining between them ; it was as if an
understanding had been arrived at, unknown to themselves,
and while they were far apart. She did not even appear to
notice the sketches and studies on the walls. For a moment
she looked fixedly at the large picture, at the figure of the
woman lying on the grass under the blazing golden sun.
No, it was not like herself, that girl had neither her face nor
her body. How silly to have fancied that such a horrid mess
of colour was herself ! And her friendship for the young
fellow was heightened by a touch of pity ; he could not even
convey a likeness. When she went off, it was she who on
the threshold cordially held out her hand.

'You know, I shall come back again—— '

'Yes, in two months' time.'

'No, next week. You'll see, next Thursday.'

On the Thursday she punctually returned, and after that
she did not miss a week. At first she had no particular day
for calling, simply taking advantage of her opportunities ; but
subsequently she selected Monday, the day allowed her by
Madame Vanzade in order that she might have a walk in
the fresh, open air of the Bois de Boulogne. She had to be
back home by eleven, and she walked the whole way very
quickly, coming in all aglow from the run, for it was a long
stretch from Passy to the Quai de Bourbon. During four
winter months, from October to February, she came in this
fashion, now in drenching rain, now among the mists from
the Seine, now in the pale sunlight that threw a little
warmth over the quays. Indeed, after the first month, she
at times arrived unexpectedly, taking advantage of some
errand in town to look in, and then she could only stay for a
couple of minutes ; they had barely had time enough to say
'How do you do ?' when she was already scampering down
the stairs again, exclaiming 'Good-bye.'

And now Claude learned to know Christine. With his
everlasting mistrust of woman a suspicion had remained to
him, the suspicion of some love adventure in the provinces ;
but the girl's soft eyes and bright laughter had carried all
before them ; he felt that she was as innocent as a big child.
As soon as she arrived, quite unembarrassed, feeling fully at
her ease, as with a friend, she began to indulge in a ceaseless
flow of chatter. She had told him a score of times about

her childhood at Clermont, and she constantly reverted to it.
On the evening that her father, Captain Hallegrain, had
suddenly died, she and her mother had been to church. She
perfectly remembered their return home and the horrible
night that had followed ; the captain, very stout and muscular, lying stretched on a mattress, with his lower jaw
protruding to such a degree that in her girlish memory she
could not picture him otherwise. She also had that same jaw,
and when her mother had not known how to master her, she
had often cried : 'Ah, you Punch, you'll eat your heart's
blood out like your father.' Poor mother ! how she, Christine,
had worried her with her love of horseplay, with her mad
turbulent fits. As far back as she could remember, she
pictured her mother ever seated at the same window, quietly
painting fans, a slim little woman with very soft eyes, the only
thing she had inherited of her. When people wanted to
please her mother they told her, 'she has got your eyes.'
And then she smiled, happy in the thought of having contributed at least that touch of sweetness to her daughter's
features. After the death of her husband, she had worked so
late as to endanger her eyesight. But how else could she
have lived ? Her widow's pension—five hundred francs per
annum—barely sufficed for the needs of her child. For five
years Christine had seen her mother grow thinner and paler,
wasting away a little bit each day until she became a
mere shadow. And now she felt remorseful at not having
been more obedient, at having driven her mother to despair
by lack of application. She had begun each week with magnificent intentions, promising that she would soon help her to earn
money ; but her arms and legs got the fidgets, in spite of
her efforts ; the moment she became quiet she fell ill. Then
one morning her mother had been unable to get up, and had
died ; her voice too weak to make itself heard, her eyes full of
big tears. Ever did Christine behold her thus dead, with her
weeping eyes wide open and fixed on her.

At other times, Christine, when questioned by Claude
about Clermont, forgot those sorrows to recall more cheerful memories. She laughed gaily at the idea of their encampment, as she called it, in the Rue de l'Éclache ; she born
in Strasburg, her father a Gascon, her mother a Parisian,
and all three thrown into that nook of Auvergne, which
they detested. The Rue de l'Éclache, sloping down to the
Botanical Gardens, was narrow and dank, gloomy, like a

vault. Not a shop, never a passer-by—nothing but melancholy frontages, with shutters always closed. At the back,
however, their windows, overlooking some courtyards, were
turned to the full sunlight. The dining-room opened even
on to a spacious balcony, a kind of wooden gallery, whose
arcades were hung with a giant wistaria which almost
smothered them with foliage. And the girl had grown up
there, at first near her invalid father, then cloistered, as it
were, with her mother, whom the least exertion exhausted.
She had remained so complete a stranger to the town and its
neighbourhood, that Claude and herself burst into laughter
when she met his inquiries with the constant answer, 'I don't
know.' The mountains? Yes, there were mountains on one
side, they could be seen at the end of the streets; while on
the other side of the town, after passing along other streets,
there were flat fields stretching far away; but she never went
there, the distance was too great. The only height she remembered was the Puy de Dôme, rounded off at the summit
like a hump. In the town itself she could have found her
way to the cathedral blindfold; one had to turn round by the
Place de Jaude and take the Rue des Gras; but more than
that she could not tell him; the rest of the town was an en-
tanglement, a maze of sloping lanes and boulevards; a town
of black lava ever dipping downward, where the rain of
the thunderstorms swept by torrentially amidst formidable
flashes of lightning. Oh! those storms; she still shuddered
to think of them. Just opposite her room, above the roofs,
the lightning conductor of the museum was always on fire.
In the sitting-room she had her own window—a deep recess
as big as a room itself—where her work-table and personal
nick-nacks stood. It was there that her mother had taught
her to read; it was there that, later on, she had fallen asleep
while listening to her masters, so greatly did the fatigue of
learning daze her. And now she made fun of her own
ignorance; she was a well-educated young lady, and no mistake,
unable even to repeat the names of the Kings of France, with
the dates of their accessions; a famous musician too, who had
never got further than that elementary pianoforte exercise,
'The little boats'; a prodigy in water-colour painting, who
scamped her trees because foliage was too difficult to imitate.
Then she skipped, without any transition, to the fifteen
months she had spent at the Convent of the Visitation after
her mother's death—a large convent, outside the town, with

magnificent gardens.   There was no end to her stories about
the good sisters, their jealousies, their foolish doings, their
simplicity, that made one start.   She was to have taken the
veil, but she felt stifled the moment she entered a church.   It
had seemed to be all over with her, when the Superior, by
whom she was treated with great affection, diverted her from
the cloister by procuring her that situation at Madame
Vanzade's.   She had not yet got over the surprise.   How had
Mother des Saints Anges been able to read her mind so clearly ?
For, in fact, since she had been living in Paris she had
dropped into complete indifference about religion.

When all the reminiscences of Clermont were exhausted,
Claude wanted to hear about her life at Madame Vanzade's,
and each week she gave him fresh particulars.   The life led
in the little house at Passy, silent and shut off from the
outer world, was a very regular one, with no more noise
about it than the faint tic-tac of an old-fashioned timepiece.
Two antiquated domestics, a cook and a man servant, who
had been with the family for forty years, alone glided in
their slippers about the deserted rooms, like a couple of ghosts.
Now and then, at very long intervals, there came a visitor :
some octogenarian general, so desiccated, so slight of build
that he scarcely pressed on the carpet.   The house was also
the home of shadows ; the sun filtered with the mere gleam
of a night light through the Venetian blinds.   Since madame
had become paralysed in the knees and stone blind, so that
she no longer left her room, she had had no other recreation
than that of listening to the reading of religious books.   Ah !
those endless readings, how they weighed upon the girl at
times !   If she had only known a trade, how gladly she
would have cut out dresses, concocted bonnets, or goffered
the petals of artificial flowers.   And to think that she was
capable of nothing, when she had been taught everything,
and that there was only enough stuff in her to make a
salaried drudge, a semi-domestic !   She suffered horribly, too,
in that stiff, lonely dwelling which smelt of the tomb.   She
was seized once more with the vertigo of her childhood, as
when she had striven to compel herself to work, in order
to please her mother ; her blood rebelled ; she would have
liked to shout and jump about, in her desire for life.   But
madame treated her so gently, sending her away from her
room, and ordering her to take long walks, that she felt full
of remorse when, on her return to the Quai de Bourbon, she

was obliged to tell a falsehood; to talk of the Bois de Boulogne or invent some ceremony at church where she now never set foot. Madame seemed to take to her more and more every day; there were constant presents, now a silk dress, now a tiny gold watch, even some underlinen. She herself was very fond of Madame Vanzade; she had wept one day when the latter had called her daughter; she had sworn never to leave her, such was her heart-felt pity at seeing her so old and helpless.

'Well,' said Claude one morning, 'you'll be rewarded; she'll leave you her money.'

Christine looked astonished. 'Do you think so? It is said that she is worth three millions of francs. No, no, I have never dreamt of such a thing, and I won't. What would become of me?'

Claude had averted his head, and hastily replied, 'Well, you'd become rich, that's all. But no doubt she'll first of all marry you off——'

On hearing this, Christine could hold out no longer, but burst into laughter. 'To one of her old friends, eh? perhaps the general who has a silver chin. What a good joke!'

So far they had gone no further than chumming like old friends. He was almost as new to life as she, having had nothing but chance adventures, and living in an ideal world of his own, fanciful amid romantic amours. To see each other in secret like this, from pure friendship, without anything more tender passing between them than a cordial shake of the hand at her arrival, and another one when she left, seemed to them quite natural. Still for her part she scented that he was shy, and at times she looked at him fixedly, with the wondering perturbation of unconscious passion. But as yet nothing ardent or agitating spoilt the pleasure they felt in being together. Their hands remained cool; they spoke cheerfully on all subjects; they sometimes argued like friends, who feel sure they will not fall out. Only, this friendship grew so keen that they could no longer live without seeing one another.

The moment Christine came, Claude took the key from outside the door. She herself insisted upon this, lest somebody might disturb them. After a few visits she had taken absolute possession of the studio. She seemed to be at home there. She was tormented by a desire to make the place a little more tidy, for such disorder worried her and made her uncomfortable. But it was not an easy matter. The painter had strictly forbidden Madame Joseph to sweep up things, lest the dust should get on the fresh paint. So, on the first occasions when his companion attempted to clean up a bit, he watched her with anxious entreating eyes. What was the good of changing the place of things? Didn't it suffice to have them at hand? However, she exhibited such gay determination, she seemed so happy at playing the housewife, that he let her have her own way at last. And now, the moment she had arrived and taken off her gloves, she pinned up her dress to avoid soiling it, and set the big studio in order in the twinkling of an eye. There was no longer a pile of cinders before the stove; the screen hid the bedstead and the washstand; the couch was brushed, the wardrobe polished; the deal table was cleared of the crockery, and had not a stain of paint; and above the chairs, which were symmetrically arranged, and the spanned easels propped against the walls, the big cuckoo clock, with full-blown pink flowers on its dial, seemed to tick more sonorously. Altogether it was magnificent; one would not have recognised the place. He, stupefied, watched her trotting to and fro, twisting about and singing as she went. Was this then the lazybones who had such dreadful headaches at the least bit of work? But she laughed; at headwork, yes; but exertion with her hands and feet did her good, seemed to straighten her like a young sapling. She confessed, even as she would have confessed some depraved taste, her liking for lowly household cares; a liking which had greatly worried her mother, whose educational ideal consisted of accomplishments, and who would have made her a governess with soft hands, touching nothing vulgar. How Christine had been chided indeed whenever she was caught, as a little girl, sweeping, dusting, and playing delightedly at being cook! Even nowadays, if she had been able to indulge in a bout with the dust at Madame Vanzade's, she would have felt less bored. But what would they have said to that? She would no longer have been considered a lady. And so she came to satisfy her longings at the Quai de Bourbon, panting with the exercise, all aglow, her eyes glistening with a woman's delight at biting into forbidden fruit.

Claude by this time grew conscious of having a woman's care around him. In order to make her sit down and chat quietly, he would ask her now and then to sew a torn cuff or coat-tail. She herself had offered to look over his linen; but it was no longer with the ardour of a housewife, eager to be up and doing. First of all, she hardly knew how to work; she held her needle like a girl brought up in contempt of sewing. Besides, the enforced quiescence and the attention that had to be given to such work, the small stitches which had to be looked to one by one, exasperated her. Thus the studio was bright with cleanliness like a drawing-room, but Claude himself remained in rags, and they both joked about it, thinking it great fun.

How happy were those months that they spent together, those four months of frost and rain whiled away in the studio, where the red-hot stove roared like an organ-pipe! The winter seemed to isolate them from the world still more. When the snow covered the adjacent roofs, when the sparrows fluttered against the window, they smiled at feeling warm and cosy, at being lost, as it were, amidst the great silent city. But they did not always confine themselves to that one little nook, for she allowed him at last to see her home. For a long while she had insisted upon going away by herself, feeling ashamed of being seen in the streets on a man's arm. Then, one day when the rain fell all of a sudden, she was obliged to let him come downstairs with an umbrella. The rain having ceased almost immediately, she sent him back when they reached the other side of the Pont Louis-Philippe. They only remained a few moments beside the parapet, looking at the Mail, and happy at being together in the open air. Down below, large barges, moored against the quay, and full of apples, were ranged four rows deep, so close together that the planks thrown across them made a continuous path for the women and children running to and fro. They were amused by the sight of all that fruit, those enormous piles littering the banks, the round baskets which were carried hither and thither, while a strong odour, suggestive of cider in fermentation, mingled with the moist gusts from the river.

A week later, when the sun again showed itself, and Claude extolled the solitude of the quays round the Isle Saint Louis, Christine consented to take a walk. They strolled up the Quai de Bourbon and the Quai d'Anjou, pausing at every few steps and growing interested in the various scenes of river life; the dredger whose buckets grated against their chains, the floating wash-house, which resounded with the hubbub of

a quarrel, and the steam cranes busy unloading the lighters.
She did not cease to wonder at one thought which came to her.
Was it possible that yonder Quai des Ormes, so full of life
across the stream, that this Quai Henri IV., with its broad
embankment and lower shore, where bands of children and
dogs rolled over in the sand, that this panorama of an active,
densely-populated capital was the same accursed scene that
had appeared to her for a moment in a gory flash on the
night of her arrival? They went round the point of the
island, strolling more leisurely still to enjoy the solitude and
tranquillity which the old historic mansions seem to have
implanted there. They watched the water seething between the
wooden piles of the Estacade, and returned by way of the
Quai de Béthune and the Quai d'Orléans, instinctively drawn
closer to each other by the widening of the stream, keeping
elbow to elbow at sight of the vast flow, with their eyes fixed on
the distant Halle aux Vins and the Jardin des Plantes. In
the pale sky, the cupolas of the public buildings assumed a
bluish hue. When they reached the Pont St. Louis, Claude
had to point out Notre-Dame by name, for Christine did not
recognise the edifice from the rear, where it looked like a
colossal creature crouching down between its flying buttresses,
which suggested sprawling paws, while above its long
leviathan spine its towers rose like a double head. Their
real find that day, however, was at the western point of the
island, that point like the prow of a ship always riding at
anchor, afloat between two swift currents, in sight of Paris,
but ever unable to get into port. They went down some very
steep steps there, and discovered a solitary bank planted with
lofty trees. It was a charming refuge—a hermitage in the
midst of a crowd. Paris was rumbling around them, on the
quays, on the bridges, while they at the water's edge tasted
the delight of being alone, ignored by the whole world.
From that day forth that bank became a little rustic coign
of theirs, a favourite open-air resort, where they took
advantage of the sunny hours, when the great heat of the
studio, where the red-hot stove kept roaring, oppressed them
too much, filling their hands with a fever of which they were
afraid.

Nevertheless, Christine had so far objected to be accompanied farther than the Mail. At the Quai des Ormes she
always bade Claude go back, as if Paris, with her crowds and
possible encounters, began at the long stretch of quays which

she had to traverse on her way home. But Passy was so far
off, and she felt so dull at having to go such a distance alone,
that gradually she gave way. She began by allowing Claude
to see her as far as the Hôtel de Ville; then as far as the
Pont-Neuf; at last as far as the Tuileries. She forgot the
danger; they walked arm in arm like a young married couple;
and that constantly repeated promenade, that leisurely journey
over the self-same ground by the river side, acquired an
infinite charm, full of a happiness such as could scarcely be
surpassed in after-times. They truly belonged to each other,
though they had not erred. It seemed as if the very soul of
the great city, rising from the river, wrapped them around
with all the love that had throbbed behind the grey stone walls
through the long lapse of ages.

Since the nipping colds of December, Christine only came
in the afternoon, and it was about four o'clock, when the sun
was sinking, that Claude escorted her back on his arm. On
days when the sky was clear, they could see the long line
of quays stretching away into space directly they had crossed
the Pont Louis-Philippe. From one end to the other the
slanting sun powdered the houses on the right bank with
golden dust, while, on the left, the islets, the buildings, stood
out in a black line against the blazing glory of the sunset.
Between the sombre and the brilliant margin, the spangled
river sparkled, cut in twain every now and then by the long
bars of its bridges; the five arches of the Pont Notre-Dame
showing under the single span of the Pont d'Arcole; then the
Pont-au-Change and the Pont-Neuf, beyond each of whose
shadows appeared a luminous patch, a sheet of bluish satiny
water, growing paler here and there with a mirror-like reflection. And while the dusky outlines on the left terminated in
the silhouettes of the pointed towers of the Palais de Justice,
sharply and darkly defined against the sky, a gentle curve
undulated on the right, stretching away so far that the
Pavillon de Flore, who stood forth like a citadel at the curve's
extreme end, seemed a fairy castle, bluey, dreamlike and
vague, amidst the rosy mist on the horizon. But Claude and
Christine, with the sunlight streaming on them, athwart the
leafless plane trees, turned away from the dazzlement, preferring to gaze at certain spots, one above all—a block of old
houses just above the Mail. Below, there was a series of
one-storied tenements, little huckster and fishing-tackle shops,
with flat terrace roofs, ornamented with laurel and Virginia

creeper. And in the rear rose loftier, but decrepit, dwellings, with linen hung out to dry at their windows, a collection of fantastic structures, a confused mass of woodwork and masonry, overtoppling walls, and hanging gardens, in which coloured glass balls shone out like stars. They walked on, leaving behind them the big barracks and the Hôtel de Ville, and feeling much more interest in the Cité which appeared across the river, pent between lofty smooth embankments rising from the water. Above the darkened houses rose the towers of Notre-Dame, as resplendent as if they had been newly gilt. Then the second-hand bookstalls began to invade the quays. Down below a lighter full of charcoal struggled against the strong current beneath an arch of the Pont Notre-Dame. And then, on the days when the flower market was held, they stopped, despite the inclement weather, to inhale the scent of the first violets and the early gillyflowers. On their left a long stretch of bank now became visible; beyond the pepper-caster turrets of the Palais de Justice, the small, murky tenements of the Quai de l'Horloge showed as far as the clump of trees midway across the Pont-Neuf; then, as they went farther on, other quays emerged from the mist, in the far distance: the Quai Voltaire, the Quai Malaquais, the dome of the Institute of France, the square pile of the Mint, a long grey line of frontages of which they could not even distinguish the windows, a promontory of roofs, which, with their stacks of chimney-pots, looked like some rugged cliff, dipping down into a phosphorescent sea. In front, however, the Pavillon de Flore lost its dreamy aspect, and became solidified in the final sun blaze. Then right and left, on either bank of the river, came the long vistas of the Boulevard de Sebastopol and the Boulevard du Palais; the handsome new buildings of the Quai de la Mégisserie, with the new Prefecture of Police across the water; and the old Pont-Neuf, with its statue of Henri IV. looking like a splash of ink. The Louvre, the Tuileries followed, and beyond Grenelle there was a far-stretching panorama of the slopes of Sèvres, the country steeped in a stream of sun rays. Claude never went farther. Christine always made him stop just before they reached the Pont Royal, near the fine trees beside Vigier's swimming baths; and when they turned round to shake hands once more in the golden sunset now flushing into crimson, they looked back and, on the horizon, espied the Isle Saint Louis, whence they had come, the indistinct distance of the city upon which night was already descending from the slate-hued eastern sky.

Ah! what splendid sunsets they beheld during those weekly strolls. The sun accompanied them, as it were, amid the throbbing gaiety of the quays, the river life, the dancing ripples of the currents; amid the attractions of the shops, as warm as conservatories, the flowers sold by the seed merchants, and the noisy cages of the bird fanciers; amid all the din of sound and wealth of colour which ever make a city's waterside its youthful part. As they proceeded, the ardent blaze of the western sky turned to purple on their left, above the dark line of houses, and the orb of day seemed to wait for them, falling gradually lower, slowly rolling towards the distant roofs when once they had passed the Pont Notre-Dame in front of the widening stream. In no ancient forest, on no mountain road, beyond no grassy plain will there ever be such triumphal sunsets as behind the cupola of the Institute. It is there one sees Paris retiring to rest in all her glory. At each of their walks the aspect of the conflagration changed; fresh furnaces added their glow to the crown of flames. One evening, when a shower had surprised them, the sun, showing behind the downpour, lit up the whole rain cloud, and upon their heads there fell a spray of glowing water, irisated with pink and azure. On the days when the sky was clear, however, the sun, like a fiery ball, descended majestically in an unruffled sapphire lake; for a moment the black cupola of the Institute seemed to cut away part of it and make it look like the waning moon; then the globe assumed a violet tinge and at last became submerged in the lake, which had turned blood-red. Already, in February, the planet described a wider curve, and fell straight into the Seine, which seemed to seethe on the horizon as at the contact of red-hot iron. However, the grander scenes, the vast fairy pictures of space only blazed on cloudy evenings. Then, according to the whim of the wind, there were seas of sulphur splashing against coral reefs; there were palaces and towers, marvels of architecture, piled upon one another, burning and crumbling, and throwing torrents of lava from their many gaps; or else the orb which had disappeared, hidden by a veil of clouds, suddenly transpierced that veil with such a press of light that shafts of sparks shot forth from one horizon to the other, showing as plainly as a volley of golden arrows. And then the twilight fell, and they said good-bye to each other, while their eyes were still full of the final dazzlement. They felt that triumphal Paris was the accomplice of the joy which they could not exhaust, the joy of ever resuming together that walk beside the old stone parapets.

One day, however, there happened what Claude had always secretly feared. Christine no longer seemed to believe in the possibility of meeting anybody who knew her. In fact, was there such a person ? She would always pass along like this, remaining altogether unknown. He, however, thought of his own friends, and at times felt a kind of tremor when he fancied he recognised in the distance the back of some acquaintance. He was troubled by a feeling of delicacy ; the idea that somebody might stare at the girl, approach them, and perhaps begin to joke, gave him intolerable worry. And that very evening, as she was close beside him on his arm, and they were approaching the Pont des Arts, he fell upon Sandoz and Dubuche, who were coming down the steps of the bridge. It was impossible to avoid them, they were almost face to face ; besides, his friends must have seen him, for they smiled. Claude, very pale, kept advancing, and he thought it all up on seeing Dubuche take a step towards him ; but Sandoz was already holding the architect back, and leading him away. They passed on with an indifferent air and disappeared into the courtyard of the Louvre without as much as turning round. They had both just recognised the original of the crayon sketch, which the painter hid away with all the jealousy of a lover. Christine, who was chattering, had noticed nothing. Claude, with his heart throbbing, answered her in monosyllables, moved to tears, brimming over with gratitude to his old chums for their discreet behaviour.

A few days later, however, he had another shock. He did not expect Christine, and had therefore made an appointment with Sandoz. Then, as she had run up to spend an hour—it was one of those surprises that delighted them—they had just withdrawn the key, as usual, when there came a familiar knock with the fist on the door. Claude at once recognised the rap, and felt so upset at the mishap that he overturned a chair. After that it was impossible to pretend to be out. But Christine turned so pale, and implored him with such a wild gesture, that he remained rooted to the spot, holding his breath. The knocks continued, and a voice called, ' Claude, Claude ! ' He still remained quite still, debating with himself, however, with ashen lips and downcast eyes. Deep silence reigned, and then footsteps were heard, making the stairs creak as they went down. Claude's breast heaved with intense sadness; he felt it bursting with remorse at the sound of each retreating step, as if he had denied the friendship of his whole youth.

However, one afternoon there came another knock, and Claude had only just time to whisper despairingly, 'The key has been left in the door.'

In fact, Christine had forgotten to take it out. She became quite scared and darted behind the screen, with her handkerchief over her mouth to stifle the sound of her breathing.

The knocks became louder, there was a burst of laughter, and the painter had to reply, 'Come in.'

He felt more uncomfortable still when he saw Jory, who gallantly ushered in Irma Bécot, whose acquaintance he had made through Fagerolles, and who was flinging her youth about the Paris studios.

'She insisted upon seeing your studio, so I brought her,' explained the journalist.

The girl, however, without waiting, was already walking about and making remarks, with perfect freedom of manner. 'Oh! how funny it is here. And what funny painting. Come, there's a good fellow, show me everything. I want to see everything.'

Claude, apprehensively anxious, was afraid that she might push the screen aside. He pictured Christine behind it, and felt distracted already at what she might hear.

'You know what she has come to ask of you?' resumed Jory cheerfully. 'What, don't you remember? You promised that she might pose for something. And she'll do so if you like.'

'Of course I will,' said Irma.

'The fact is,' replied Claude, in an embarrassed tone, 'my picture here will take up all my time till the Salon. I have a figure in it that gives me a deal of trouble. It's impossible to perfect it with those confounded models.'

Irma had stationed herself in front of the picture, and looked at it with a knowing air. 'Oh! I see,' she said, 'that woman in the grass, eh? Do you think I could be of any use to you?'

Jory flared up in a moment, warmly approving the idea, but Claude with the greatest energy replied, 'No, no madame

wouldn't suit. She is not at all what I want for this picture;
not at all.'

Then he went on stammering excuses. He would be only
too pleased later on, but just now he was afraid that another
model would quite complete his confusion over that picture;
and Irma responded by shrugging her shoulders, and looking
at him with an air of smiling contempt.

Jory, however, now began to chat about their friends.
Why had not Claude come to Sandoz's on the previous
Thursday? One never saw him now. Dubuche asserted all
sorts of things about him. There had been a row between
Fagerolles and Mahoudeau on the subject whether evening
dress was a thing to be reproduced in sculpture. Then on
the previous Sunday Gagnière had returned home from a
Wagner concert with a black eye. He, Jory, had nearly had
a duel at the Café Baudequin on account of one of his last
articles in 'The Drummer.' The fact was he was giving it
hot to the twopenny-halfpenny painters, the men with the
usurped reputations! The campaign against the hanging
committee of the Salon was making a deuce of a row; not a
shred would be left of those guardians of the ideal, who wanted
to prevent nature from entering their show.

Claude listened to him with impatient irritation. He had
taken up his palette and was shuffling about in front of his
picture. The other one understood at last.

'You want to work, I see; all right, we'll leave you.'

Irma, however, still stared at the painter, with her vague
smile, astonished at the stupidity of this simpleton, who did
not seem to appreciate her, and seized despite herself with a
whim to please him. His studio was ugly, and he himself
wasn't handsome; but why should he put on such bugbear
airs? She chaffed him for a moment, and on going off again
offered to sit for him, emphasising her offer by warmly pressing his hand.

'Whenever you like,' were her parting words.

They had gone at last, and Claude was obliged to pull
the screen aside, for Christine, looking very white, remained
seated behind it, as if she lacked the strength to rise. She did
not say a word about the girl, but simply declared that she
had felt very frightened; and—trembling lest there should
come another knock—she wanted to go at once, carrying away
with her, as her startled looks testified, the disturbing thought
of many things which she did not mention.

In fact, for a long time that sphere of brutal art, that studio full of glaring pictures, had caused her a feeling of discomfort. Wounded in all her feelings, full of repugnance, she could not get used to it all. She had grown up full of affectionate admiration for a very different style of art—her mother's fine water-colours, those fans of dreamy delicacy, in which lilac-tinted couples floated about in bluish gardens—and she quite failed to understand Claude's work. Even now she often amused herself by painting tiny girlish landscapes, two or three subjects repeated over and over again—a lake with a ruin, a water-mill beating a stream, a chalet and some pine trees, white with snow. And she felt surprised that an intelligent young fellow should paint in such an unreasonable manner, so ugly and so untruthful besides. For she not only thought Claude's realism monstrously ugly, but considered it beyond every permissible truth. In fact, she thought at times that he must be mad.

One day Claude absolutely insisted upon seeing a small sketch-book which she had brought away from Clermont, and which she had spoken about. After objecting for a long while, she brought it with her, flattered at heart and feeling very curious to know what he would say. He turned over the leaves, smiling all the while, and as he did not speak, she was the first to ask :

' You think it very bad, don't you ? '

' Not at all,' he replied. ' It's innocent.'

The reply hurt her, despite Claude's indulgent tone, which aimed at making it amiable.

' Well, you see I had so few lessons from mamma. I like painting to be well done, and pleasing.'

Thereupon he burst into frank laughter.

' Confess now that my painting makes you feel ill! I have noticed it. You purse your lips and open your eyes wide with fright. Certainly it is not the style of painting for ladies, least of all for young girls. But you'll get used to it ; it's only a question of educating your eyes and you'll end by seeing that what I am doing is very honest and healthy.'

Indeed, Christine slowly became used to it. But, at first, artistic conviction had nothing to do with the change, especially as Claude, with his contempt for female opinion, did not take the trouble to indoctrinate her. On the contrary, in her company he avoided conversing about art, as if he wished to retain for himself that passion of his life, apart from the new passion which was gradually taking possession of him. Still, Christine glided into the habit of the thing, and became familiarised with it; she began to feel interested in those abominable pictures, on noticing the important place they held in the artist's existence. This was the first stage on the road to conversion; she felt greatly moved by his rageful eagerness to be up and doing, the whole-heartedness with which he devoted himself to his work. Was it not very touching? Was there not something very creditable in it? Then, on noticing his joy or suffering, according to the success or the failure of the day's work, she began to associate herself with his efforts. She felt saddened when she found him sad, she grew cheerful when he received her cheerfully; and from that moment her worry was—had he done a lot of work? was he satisfied with what he had done since they had last seen each other? At the end of the second month she had been gained over; she stationed herself before his pictures to judge whether they were progressing or not. She no longer felt afraid of them. She still did not approve particularly of that style of painting, but she began to repeat the artistic expressions which she had heard him use; declared this bit to be ' vigorous in tone,' ' well built up,' or ' just in the light it should be.' He seemed to her so good-natured, and she was so fond of him, that after finding excuses for him for daubing those horrors, she ended by discovering qualities in them in order that she might like them a little also.

Nevertheless, there was one picture, the large one, the one intended for the Salon, to which for a long while she was quite unable to reconcile herself. She already looked without dislike at the studies made at the Boutin studio and the sketches of Plassans, but she was still irritated by the sight of the woman lying in the grass. It was like a personal grudge, the shame of having momentarily thought that she could detect in it a likeness of herself, and silent embarrassment, too, for that big figure continued to wound her feelings, although she now found less and less of a resemblance in it. At first she had protested by averting her eyes. Now she remained for several minutes looking at it fixedly, in mute contemplation. How was it that the likeness to herself had disappeared? The more vigorously that Claude struggled on, never satisfied, touching up the same bit a hundred times over, the more did that likeness to herself gradually fade away. And, without being able to account for it, without daring to admit as much to herself, she, whom the painting had so greatly offended when she had first seen it, now felt a growing sorrow at noticing that nothing of herself remained.

Indeed it seemed to her as if their friendship suffered from this obliteration ; she felt herself further away from him as trait after trait vanished.   Didn't he care for her that he thus allowed her to be effaced from his work ?   And who was the new woman, whose was the unknown indistinct face that appeared from beneath hers ?

Claude, in despair at having spoilt the figure's head, did not know exactly how to ask her for a few hours' sitting. She would merely have had to sit down, and he would only have taken some hints.   But he had previously seen her so pained that he felt afraid of irritating her again.   Moreover, after resolving in his own mind to ask her this favour in a gay, off-hand way, he had been at a loss for words, feeling all at once ashamed at the notion.

One afternoon he quite upset her by one of those bursts of anger which he found it impossible to control, even in her presence.   Everything had gone wrong that week ; he talked of scraping his canvas again, and he paced up and down, beside himself, and kicking the furniture about.   Then all of a sudden he caught her by the shoulders, and made her sit down on the couch.

' I beg of you, do me this favour, or it'll kill me, I swear it will.'

She did not understand him.

' What—what is it you want ? '

Then as soon as she saw him take up his brushes, she added, without heeding what she said, ' Ah, yes !   Why did not you ask me before ? '

And of her own accord she threw herself back on a cushion and slipped her arm under her neck.   But surprise and confusion at having yielded so quickly made her grave, for she did not know that she was prepared for this kind of thing ; indeed, she could have sworn that she would never serve him as a model again.   Her compliance already filled her with remorse, as if she were lending herself to something wrong by letting him impart her own countenance to that big creature, lying refulgent under the sun.

However, in two sittings, Claude worked in the head all right.   He exulted with delight, and exclaimed that it was the best bit of painting he had ever done ; and he was right, never had he thrown such a play of real light over such a life-like face. Happy at seeing him so pleased, Christine also became gay, going as far as to express approval of her head, which, though not extremely like her, had a wonderful expression. They stood for a long while before the picture, blinking at it, and drawing back as far as the wall.

'And now,' he said at last, ' I'll finish her off with a model. Ah ! so I've got her at last.'

In a burst of childish glee, he took the girl round the waist, and they performed ' a triumphant war dance,' as he called it. She laughed very heartily, fond of romping as she was, and no longer feeling aught of her scruples and discomfort.

But the very next week Claude became gloomy again. He had chosen Zoé Piédefer as a model, but she did not satisfy him. Christine's delicate head, as he expressed it, did not set well on the other's shoulders. He, nevertheless, persisted, scratched out, began anew, and worked so hard that he lived in a constant state of fever. Towards the middle of January, seized with despair, he abandoned his picture and turned it against the wall, swearing that he would not finish it. But a fortnight later, he began to work at it again with another model, and then found himself obliged to change the whole tone of it. Thus matters got still worse ; so he sent for Zoé again ; became altogether at sea, and quite ill with uncertainty and anguish. And the pity of it was, that the central figure alone worried him, for he was well satisfied with the rest of the painting, the trees of the background, the two little women and the gentleman in the velvet coat, all finished and vigorous. February was drawing to a close ; he had only a few days left to send his picture to the Salon ; it was quite a disaster.

One evening, in Christine's presence, he began swearing, and all at once a cry of fury escaped him : ' After all, by the thunder of heaven, is it possible to stick one woman's head on another's shoulders ? I ought to chop my hand off.'

From the depths of his heart a single idea now rose to his brain : to obtain her consent to pose for the whole figure. It had slowly sprouted, first as a simple wish, quickly discarded as absurd ; then had come a silent, constantly-renewed debate with himself ; and at last, under the spur of necessity, keen and definite desire. The recollection of the morning after the storm, when she had accepted his hospitality, haunted and tortured him. It was she whom he needed; she alone could enable him to realise his dream, and he beheld her again in all her youthful freshness, beaming and indispensable. If he could not get her to pose, he might as well give up his picture, for no one else would ever satisfy him. At times, while he remained seated for hours, distracted in front of the unfinished canvas, so utterly powerless that he no longer knew where to give a stroke of the brush, he formed heroic resolutions. The moment she came in he would throw himself at her feet; he would tell her of his distress in such touching words that she would perhaps consent. But as soon as he beheld her, he lost all courage, he averted his eyes, lest she might decipher his thoughts in his instinctive glances. Such a request would be madness. One could not expect such a service from a friend; he would never have the audacity to ask.

Nevertheless, one evening as he was getting ready to accompany her, and as she was putting on her bonnet, with her arms uplifted, they remained for a moment looking into each other's eyes, he quivering, and she suddenly becoming so grave, so pale, that he felt himself detected. All along the quays they scarcely spoke; the matter remained unmentioned between them while the sun set in the coppery sky. Twice afterwards he again read in her looks that she was aware of his all-absorbing thought. In fact, since he had dreamt about it, she had begun to do the same, in spite of herself, her attention roused by his involuntary allusions. They scarcely affected her at first, though she was obliged at last to notice them; still the question seemed to her to be beyond the range of possibility, to be one of those unavowable ideas which people do not even speak of. The fear that he would dare to ask her did not even occur to her; she knew him well by now; she could have silenced him with a gesture, before he had stammered the first words, and in spite of his sudden bursts of anger. It was simple madness. Never, never !

Days went by, and between them that fixed idea grew in intensity. The moment they were together they could not help thinking of it. Not a word was spoken on the subject, but their very silence was eloquent; they no longer made a movement, no longer exchanged a smile without stumbling upon that thought, which they found impossible to put into words, though it filled their minds. Soon nothing but that remained in their fraternal intercourse. And the perturbation of heart and senses which they had so far avoided in the course of their familiar intimacy, came at last, under the influence of the all-besetting thought. And then the anguish which they left unmentioned, but which they could not hide from one another, racked and stifled them, left them heaving distressfully with painful sighs.

Towards the middle of March, Christine, at one of her visits, found Claude seated before his picture, overcome with sorrow. He had not even heard her enter. He remained motionless, with vacant, haggard eyes staring at his unfinished work. In another three days the delay for sending in exhibits for the Salon would expire.

'Well,' she inquired gently, after standing for a long time behind him, grief-stricken at seeing him in such despair.

He started and turned round.

'Well, it's all up. I sha'n't exhibit anything this year. Ah! I who relied so much upon this Salon!'

Both relapsed into despondency—a despondency and agitation full of confused thoughts. Then she resumed, thinking aloud as it were:

'There would still be time.'

'Time? Oh! no indeed. A miracle would be needed. Where am I to find a model so late in the day? Do you know, since this morning I have been worrying, and for a moment I thought I had hit upon an idea: Yes, it would be to go and fetch that girl, that Irma who came while you were here. I know well enough that she is short and not at all such as I thought of, and so I should perhaps have to change everything once more; but all the same it might be possible to make her do. Decidedly, I'll try her——'

He stopped short. The glowing eyes with which he gazed at her clearly said: 'Ah! there's you! ah! it would be the hoped-for miracle, and triumph would be certain, if you were to make this supreme sacrifice for me. I beseech you, I ask you devoutly, as a friend, the dearest, the most beauteous, the most pure.'

She, erect, looking very pale, seemed to hear each of those words, though all remained unspoken, and his ardently beseeching eyes overcame her. She herself did not speak. She simply did as she was desired, acting almost like one in a dream. Beneath it all there lurked the thought that he must not ask elsewhere, for she was now conscious of her earlier jealous disquietude and wished to share his affections with none.   Yet it was in silence and all chastity that she stretched herself on the couch, and took up the pose, with one arm under her head, her eyes closed.

And Claude ? Startled, full of gratitude, he had at last found again the sudden vision that he had so often evoked. But he himself did not speak ; he began to paint in the deep solemn silence that had fallen upon them both.   For two long hours he stood to his work with such manly energy that he finished right off a superb roughing out of the whole figure. Never before had he felt such enthusiasm in his art.   It seemed to him as if he were in the presence of some saint ; and at times he wondered at the transfiguration of Christine's face, whose somewhat massive jaws seemed to have receded beneath the gentle placidity which her brow and cheeks displayed.   During those two hours she did not stir, she did not speak, but from time to time she opened her clear eyes, fixing them on some vague, distant point, and remaining thus for a moment, then closing them again, and relapsing into the lifelessness of fine marble, with the mysterious fixed smile required by the pose.

It was by a gesture that Claude apprized her he had finished. He turned away, and when they stood face to face again, she ready to depart, they gazed at one another, overcome by emotion which still prevented them from speaking. Was it sadness, then, unconscious, unnameable sadness ? For their eyes filled with tears, as if they had just spoilt their lives and dived to the depths of human misery.   Then, moved and grieved, unable to find a word, even of thanks, he kissed her religiously upon the brow.

V

On the 15th May, a Friday, Claude, who had returned at three o'clock in the morning from Sandoz's, was still asleep at nine, when Madame Joseph brought him up a large bouquet of white lilac which a commissionaire had just left downstairs. He understood at once.   Christine had wished to be beforehand in celebrating the success of his painting. For this was a great day for him, the opening day of the

'Salon of the Rejected,' which was first instituted that year,[1] and at which his picture—refused by the hanging committee of the official Salon—was to be exhibited.

That delicate attention on Christine's part, that fresh and fragrant lilac, affected him greatly, as if presaging a happy day. Still in his nightshirt, with his feet bare, he placed the flowers in his water-jug on the table. Then, with his eyes still swollen with sleep, almost bewildered, he dressed, scolding himself the while for having slept so long. On the previous night he had promised Dubuche and Sandoz to call for them at the latter's place at eight o'clock, in order that they might all three go together to the Palais de l'Industrie, where they would find the rest of the band. And he was already an hour behind time.

Then, as luck would have it, he could not lay his hands upon anything in his studio, which had been turned topsy-turvy since the despatch of the big picture. For more than five minutes he hunted on his knees for his shoes, among a quantity of old chases. Some particles of gold leaf flew about, for, not knowing where to get the money for a proper frame, he had employed a joiner of the neighbourhood to fit four strips of board together, and had gilded them himself, with the assistance of his friend Christine, who, by the way, had proved a very unskilful gilder. At last, dressed and shod, and having his soft felt hat bespangled with yellow sparks of the gold, he was about to go, when a superstitious thought brought him back to the nosegay, which had remained alone on the centre of the table. If he did not kiss the lilac he was sure to suffer an affront. So he kissed it and felt perfumed by its strong springtide aroma.

Under the archway, he gave his key as usual to the door-keeper. 'Madame Joseph,' he said, 'I shall not be home all day.'

In less than twenty minutes he was in the Rue d'Enfer, at Sandoz's. But the latter, whom he feared would have already gone, was equally late in consequence of a sudden indisposition which had come upon his mother. It was nothing serious. She had merely passed a bad night, but it had for a while quite upset him with anxiety. Now, easy in mind again, Sandoz told Claude that Dubuche had written saying that they were not to wait for him, and giving an

---

[1] This was in 1863.—Ed.

appointment at the Palais. They therefore started off, and as it was nearly eleven, they decided to lunch in a deserted little *crèmerie* in the Rue St. Honoré, which they did very leisurely, seized with laziness amidst all their ardent desire to see and know; and enjoying, as it were, a kind of sweet, tender sadness from lingering awhile and recalling memories of their youth.

One o'clock was striking when they crossed the Champs Elysées. It was a lovely day, with a limpid sky, to which the breeze, still somewhat chilly, seemed to impart a brighter azure. Beneath the sun, of the hue of ripe corn, the rows of chestnut trees showed new foliage of a delicate and seemingly freshly varnished green; and the fountains with their leaping sheafs of water, the well-kept lawns, the deep vistas of the pathways, and the broad open spaces, all lent an air of luxurious grandeur to the panorama. A few carriages, very few at that early hour, were ascending the avenue, while a stream of bewildered, bustling people, suggesting a swarm of ants, plunged into the huge archway of the Palais de l'Industrie.

When they were inside, Claude shivered slightly while crossing the gigantic vestibule, which was as cold as a cellar, with a damp pavement which resounded beneath one's feet, like the flagstones of a church. He glanced right and left at the two monumental stairways, and asked contemptuously: 'I say, are we going through their dirty Salon?'

'Oh! no, dash it!' answered Sandoz. 'Let's cut through the garden. The western staircase over there leads to "the Rejected."'

Then they passed disdainfully between the two little tables of the catalogue vendors. Between the huge red velvet curtains and beyond a shady porch appeared the garden, roofed in with glass. At that time of day it was almost deserted; there were only some people at the buffet under the clock, a throng of people lunching. The crowd was in the galleries on the first floor, and the white statues alone edged the yellow-sanded pathways which with stretches of crude colour intersected the green lawns. There was a whole nation of motionless marble there steeped in the diffuse light falling from the glazed roof on high. Looking southwards, some holland screens barred half of the nave, which showed ambery in the sunlight and was speckled at both ends by the dazzling blue and crimson of stained-glass windows. Just a few visitors, tired already, occupied the brand-new chairs and seats, shiny with fresh paint; while the flights of sparrows, who dwelt above, among the iron girders, swooped down, quite at home, raking up the sand and twittering as they pursued each other.

Claude and Sandoz made a show of walking very quickly without giving a glance around them. A stiff classical bronze statue, a Minerva by a member of the Institute, had exasperated them at the very door. But as they hastened past a seemingly endless line of busts, they recognised Bongrand, who, all alone, was going slowly round a colossal, overflowing, recumbent figure, which had been placed in the middle of the path. With his hands behind his back, quite absorbed, he bent his wrinkled face every now and then over the plaster.

'Hallo, it's you?' he said, as they held out their hands to him. 'I was just looking at our friend Mahoudeau's figure, which they have at least had the intelligence to admit, and to put in a good position.' Then, breaking off: 'Have you been upstairs?' he asked.

'No, we have just come in,' said Claude.

Thereupon Bongrand began to talk warmly about the Salon of the Rejected. He, who belonged to the Institute, but who lived apart from his colleagues, made very merry over the affair; the everlasting discontent of painters; the campaign conducted by petty newspapers like 'The Drummer'; the protestations, the constant complaints that had at last disturbed the Emperor, and the artistic *coup d'état* carried out by that silent dreamer, for this Salon of the Rejected was entirely his work. Then the great painter alluded to all the hubbub caused by the flinging of such a paving-stone into that frog's pond, the official art world.

'No,' he continued, 'you can have no idea of the rage and indignation among the members of the hanging committee. And remember I'm distrusted, they generally keep quiet when I'm there. But they are all furious with the realists. It was to them that they systematically closed the doors of the temple; it is on account of them that the Emperor has allowed the public to revise their verdict; and finally it is they, the realists, who triumph. Ah! I hear some nice things said; I wouldn't give a high price for your skins, youngsters.'

He laughed his big, joyous laugh, stretching out his arms

the while as if to embrace all the youthfulness that he divined rising around him.

'Your disciples are growing,' said Claude, simply.

But Bongrand, becoming embarrassed, silenced him with a wave of his hand. He himself had not sent anything for exhibition, and the prodigious mass of work amidst which he found himself—those pictures, those statues, all those proofs of creative effort—filled him with regret. It was not jealousy, for there lived not a more upright and better soul; but as a result of self-examination, a gnawing fear of impotence, an unavowed dread haunted him.

'And at "the Rejected,"' asked Sandoz; 'how goes it there?'

'Superb; you'll see.'

Then turning towards Claude, and keeping both the young man's hands in his own, 'You, my good fellow, you are a trump. Listen! they say I am clever: well, I'd give ten years of my life to have painted that big hussy of yours.'

Praise like that, coming from such lips, moved the young painter to tears. Victory had come at last, then? He failed to find a word of thanks, and abruptly changed the conversation, wishing to hide his emotion.

'That good fellow Mahoudeau!' he said, 'why, his figure's capital! He has a deuced fine temperament, hasn't he?'

Sandoz and Claude had begun to walk round the plaster figure. Bongrand replied with a smile.

'Yes, yes; there's too much fulness and massiveness in parts. But just look at the articulations, they are delicate and really pretty. Come, good-bye, I must leave you. I'm going to sit down a while. My legs are bending under me.'

Claude had raised his head to listen. A tremendous uproar, an incessant crashing that had not struck him at first, careered through the air; it was like the din of a tempest beating against a cliff, the rumbling of an untiring assault, dashing forward from endless space.

'Hallo, what's that?' he muttered.

'That,' said Bongrand, as he walked away, 'that's the crowd upstairs in the galleries.'

And the two young fellows, having crossed the garden, then went up to the Salon of the Rejected.

It had been installed in first-rate style. The officially-received pictures were not lodged more sumptuously: lofty hangings of old tapestry at the doors; 'the line' set off with

green baize; seats of crimson velvet; white linen screens
under the large sky-lights of the roof. And all along the suite
of galleries the first impression was the same—there were the
same gilt frames, the same bright colours on the canvases.
But there was a special kind of cheerfulness, a sparkle of
youth which one did not altogether realise at first. The
crowd, already compact, increased every minute, for the official
Salon was being deserted. People came stung by curiosity,
impelled by a desire to judge the judges, and, above all, full
of the conviction that they were going to see some very
diverting things. It was very hot; a fine dust arose from
the flooring; and certainly, towards four o'clock people would
stifle there.

'Hang it!' said Sandoz, trying to elbow his way, 'it will
be no easy job to move about and find your picture.'

A burst of fraternal feverishness made him eager to get to it.
That day he only lived for the work and glory of his old
chum.

'Don't worry!' exclaimed Claude; 'we shall get to it all
right. My picture won't fly off.'

And he affected to be in no hurry, in spite of the almost
irresistible desire that he felt to run. He raised his head
and looked around him; and soon, amidst the loud voices of
the crowd that had bewildered him, he distinguished some
restrained laughter, which was almost drowned by the tramp
of feet and the hubbub of conversation. Before certain pictures
the public stood joking. This made him feel uneasy, for
despite all his revolutionary brutality he was as sensitive and
as credulous as a woman, and always looked forward to
martyrdom, though he was ever grieved and stupefied at
being repulsed and railed at.

'They seem gay here,' he muttered.

'Well, there's good reason,' remarked Sandoz. 'Just look
at those extravagant jades!'

At the same moment, while still lingering in the first
gallery, Fagerolles ran up against them without seeing them.
He started, being no doubt annoyed by the meeting. However, he recovered his composure immediately, and behaved
very amiably.

'Hallo! I was just thinking of you. I have been here for
the last hour.'

'Where have they put Claude's picture?' asked Sandoz.

Fagerolles, who had just remained for twenty minutes in

front of that picture studying it and studying the impression
which it produced on the public, answered without wincing,
' I don't know ; I haven't been able to find it. We'll look for
it together if you like.'

And he joined them. Terrible wag as he was, he no
longer affected low-bred manners to the same degree as
formerly ; he already began to dress well, and although
with his mocking nature he was still disposed to snap at
everybody as of old, he pursed his lips into the serious
expression of a fellow who wants to make his way in the
world. With an air of conviction he added : ' I must say that
I now regret not having sent anything this year ! I should be
here with all the rest of you, and have my share of success.
And there are really some astonishing things, my boys !
those horses, for instance.'

He pointed to a huge canvas in front of them, before
which the crowd was gathering and laughing. It was, so
people said, the work of an erstwhile veterinary surgeon, and
showed a number of life-size horses in a meadow, fantastic
horses, blue, violet, and pink, whose astonishing anatomy
transpierced their sides.

' I say, don't you humbug us,' exclaimed Claude, sus-
piciously.

But Fagerolles pretended to be enthusiastic. ' What do
you mean ? The picture's full of talent. The fellow who
painted it understands horses devilish well. No doubt he
paints like a brute. But what's the odds if he's original, and
contributes a document ? '

As he spoke Fagerolles' delicate girlish face remained
perfectly grave, and it was impossible to tell whether he was
joking. There was but the slightest yellow twinkle of spite-
fulness in the depths of his grey eyes. And he finished with
a sarcastic allusion, the drift of which was as yet patent to him
alone. ' Ah, well ! if you let yourself be influenced by the
fools who laugh, you'll have enough to do by and by.'

The three friends had gone on again, only advancing,
however, with infinite difficulty amid that sea of surging
shoulders. On entering the second gallery they gave a
glance round the walls, but the picture they sought was not
there. In lieu thereof they perceived Irma Bécot on the arm
of Gagnière, both of them pressed against a hand-rail, he busy
examining a small canvas, while she, delighted at being hustled
about, raised her pink little mug and laughed at the crowd.

'Hallo!' said Sandoz, surprised, 'here she is with Gagnière now!'

'Oh, just a fancy of hers!' exclaimed Fagerolles quietly. 'She has a very swell place now. Yes, it was given her by that young idiot of a marquis, whom the papers are always talking about. She's a girl who'll make her way; I've always said so! But she seems to retain a weakness for painters, and every now and then drops into the Café Baudequin to look up old friends!'

Irma had now seen them, and was making gestures from afar. They could but go to her. When Gagnière, with his light hair and little beardless face, turned round, looking more grotesque than ever, he did not show the least surprise at finding them there.

'It's wonderful,' he muttered.

'What's wonderful?' asked Fagerolles.

'This little masterpiece—and withal honest and naïf, and full of conviction.'

He pointed to a tiny canvas before which he had stood absorbed, an absolutely childish picture, such as an urchin of four might have painted; a little cottage at the edge of a little road, with a little tree beside it, the whole out of drawing, and girt round with black lines. Not even a corkscrew imitation of smoke issuing from the roof was forgotten.

Claude made a nervous gesture, while Fagerolles repeated phlegmatically:

'Very delicate, very delicate. But your picture, Gagnière, where is it?'

'My picture, it is there.'

In fact, the picture he had sent happened to be very near the little masterpiece. It was a landscape of a pearly grey, a bit of the Seine banks, painted carefully, pretty in tone, though somewhat heavy, and perfectly ponderated without a sign of any revolutionary splash.

'To think that they were idiotic enough to refuse that!' said Claude, who had approached with an air of interest. 'But why, I ask you, why?'

'Because it's realistic,' said Fagerolles, in so sharp a voice that one could not tell whether he was gibing at the jury or at the picture.

Meanwhile, Irma, of whom no one took any notice, was looking fixedly at Claude with the unconscious smile which the savage loutishness of that big fellow always brought to her lips. To think that he had not even cared to see her again. She found him so much altered since the last time she had seen him, so funny, and not at all prepossessing, with his hair standing on end, and his face wan and sallow, as if he had had a severe fever. Pained that he did not seem to notice her, she wanted to attract his attention, and touched his arm with a familiar gesture.

'I say, isn't that one of your friends over there, looking for you?'

It was Dubuche, whom she knew from having seen him on one occasion at the Café Baudequin. He was, with difficulty, elbowing his way through the crowd, and staring vaguely at the sea of heads around him. But all at once, when Claude was trying to attract his notice by dint of gesticulations, the other turned his back to bow very low to a party of three—the father short and fat, with a sanguine face; the mother very thin, of the colour of wax, and devoured by anæmia; and the daughter so physically backward at eighteen, that she retained all the lank scragginess of childhood.

'All right!' muttered the painter. 'There he's caught now. What ugly acquaintances the brute has! Where can he have fished up such horrors?'

Gagnière quietly replied that he knew the strangers by sight. M. Margaillan was a great masonry contractor, already a millionaire five or six times over, and was making his fortune out of the great public works of Paris, running up whole boulevards on his own account. No doubt Dubuche had become acquainted with him through one of the architects he worked for.

However, Sandoz, compassionating the scragginess of the girl, whom he kept watching, judged her in one sentence.

'Ah! the poor little flayed kitten. One feels sorry for her.'

'Let them alone!' exclaimed Claude, ferociously. 'They have all the crimes of the middle classes stamped on their faces; they reek of scrofula and idiocy. It serves them right. But hallo! our runaway friend is making off with them. What grovellers architects are! Good riddance. He'll have to look for us when he wants us!'

Dubuche, who had not seen his friends, had just offered his arm to the mother, and was going off, explaining the pictures with gestures typical of exaggerated politeness.

'Well, let's proceed then,' said Fagerolles; and, addressing

Gagnière, heasked, ' Do you know where they have put
Claude's picture ? '

'I ? no, I was looking for it—I am going with you.'

He accompanied them, forgetting Irma Bécot against the
' line.' It was she who had wanted to visit the Salon on his
arm, and he was so little used to promenading a woman
about, that he had constantly lost her on the way, and was
each time stupefied to find her again beside him, no longer
knowing how or why they were thus together. She ran after
them, and took his arm once more in order to follow Claude,
who was already passing into another gallery with Fagerolles
and Sandoz.

Then the five roamed about in Indian file, with their
noses in the air, now separated by a sudden crush, now
reunited by another, and ever carried along by the stream.
An abomination of Chaîne's, a ' Christ pardoning the Woman
taken in Adultery,' made them pause ; it was a group of dry
figures that looked as if cut out of wood, very bony of build,
and seemingly painted with mud. But close by they admired
a very fine study of a woman, seen from behind, with her
head turned sideways. The whole show was a mixture of
the best and the worst, all styles were mingled together, the
drivellers of the historical school elbowed the young lunatics
of realism, the pure simpletons were lumped together with
those who bragged about their originality. A dead Jezabel,
that seemed to have rotted in the cellars of the School of Arts,
was exhibited near a lady in white, the very curious conception
of a future great artist[1] ; then a huge shepherd looking at the
sea, a weak production, faced a little painting of some Spaniards
playing at rackets, a dash of light of splendid intensity.
Nothing execrable was wanting, neither military scenes full of
little leaden soldiers, nor wan antiquity, nor the middle ages,
smeared, as it were, with bitumen. But from amidst the
incoherent *ensemble*, and especially from the landscapes, all of
which were painted in a sincere, correct key, and also from the
portraits, most of which were very interesting in respect to
workmanship, there came a good fresh scent of youth, bravery
and passion. If there were fewer bad pictures in the official
Salon, the average there was assuredly more commonplace and
mediocre. Here one found the smell of battle, of cheerful
battle, given jauntily at daybreak, when the bugle sounds, and

---

[1] Edouard Manet. Ed.

when one marches to meet the enemy with the certainty of beating him before sunset.

Claude, whose spirits had revived amidst that martial odour, grew animated and pugnacious as he listened to the laughter of the public. He looked as defiant, indeed, as if he had heard bullets whizzing past him. Sufficiently discreet at the entrance of the galleries, the laughter became more boisterous, more unrestrained, as they advanced. In the third room the women ceased concealing their smiles behind their handkerchiefs, while the men openly held their sides the better to ease themselves. It was the contagious hilarity of people who had come to amuse themselves, and who were growing gradually excited, bursting out at a mere trifle, diverted as much by the good things as by the bad. Folks laughed less before Chaîne's Christ than before the back view of the nude woman, who seemed to them very comical indeed. The 'Lady in White' also stupefied people and drew them together; folks nudged each other and went into hysterics almost; there was always a grinning group in front of it. Each canvas thus had its particular kind of success; people hailed each other from a distance to point out something funny, and witticisms flew from mouth to mouth; to such a degree indeed that, as Claude entered the fourth gallery, lashed into fury by the tempest of laughter that was raging there as well, he all but slapped the face of an old lady whose chuckles exasperated him.

'What idiots!' he said, turning towards his friends. 'One feels inclined to throw a lot of masterpieces at their heads.'

Sandoz had become fiery also, and Fagerolles continued praising the most dreadful daubs, which only tended to increase the laughter, while Gagnière, at sea amid the hubbub, dragged on the delighted Irma, whose skirts somehow wound round the legs of all the men.

But of a sudden Jory stood before them. His fair handsome face absolutely beamed. He cut his way through the crowd, gesticulated, and exulted, as if over a personal victory. And the moment he perceived Claude, he shouted:

'Here you are at last! I have been looking for you this hour. A success, old fellow, oh! a success——'

'What success?'

'Why, the success of your picture. Come, I must show it you. You'll see, it's stunning.'

Claude grew pale. A great joy choked him, while he

pretended to receive the news with composure. Bongrand's words came back to him. He began to believe that he possessed genius.

'Hallo, how are you?' continued Jory, shaking hands with the others.

And, without more ado, he, Fagerolles and Gagnière surrounded Irma, who smiled on them in a good-natured way.

'Perhaps you'll tell us where the picture is,' said Sandoz, impatiently. 'Take us to it.'

Jory assumed the lead, followed by the band. They had to fight their way into the last gallery. But Claude, who brought up the rear, still heard the laughter that rose on the air, a swelling clamour, the roll of a tide near its full. And as he finally entered the room, he beheld a vast, swarming, closely packed crowd pressing eagerly in front of his picture. All the laughter arose, spread, and ended there. And it was his picture that was being laughed at.

'Eh!' repeated Jory, triumphantly, 'there's a success for you.'

Gagnière, intimidated, as ashamed as if he himself had been slapped, muttered: 'Too much of a success—I should prefer something different.'

'What a fool you are,' replied Jory, in a burst of exalted conviction. 'That's what I call success. Does it matter a curse if they laugh? We have made our mark; to-morrow every paper will talk about us.'

'The idiots,' was all that Sandoz could gasp, choking with grief.

Fagerolles, disinterested and dignified like a family friend following a funeral procession, said nothing. Irma alone remained gay, thinking it all very funny. And, with a caressing gesture, she leant against the shoulder of the derided painter, and whispered softly in his ear: 'Don't fret, my boy. It's all humbug, be merry all the same.'

But Claude did not stir. An icy chill had come over him. For a moment his heart had almost ceased to beat, so cruel had been the disappointment And with his eyes enlarged, attracted and fixed by a resistless force, he looked at his picture. He was surprised, and scarcely recognised it; it certainly was not such as it had seemed to be in his studio. It had grown yellow beneath the livid light of the linen screens; it seemed, moreover, to have become smaller; coarser

and more laboured also ; and whether it was the effect of
the light in which it now hung, or the contrast of the
works beside it, at all events he now at the first glance saw
all its defects, after having remained blind to them, as it
were, for months. With a few strokes of the brush he, in
thought, altered the whole of it, deepened the distances, set
a badly drawn limb right, and modified a tone. Decidedly,
the gentleman in the velveteen jacket was worth nothing at
all, he was altogether pasty and badly seated ; the only
really good bit of work about him was his hand. In the
background the two little wrestlers—the fair and the dark
one—had remained too sketchy, and lacked substance ; they
were amusing only to an artist's eye. But he was pleased
with the trees, with the sunny glade ; and the nude woman
—the woman lying on the grass appeared to him superior to
his own powers, as if some one else had painted her, and as if
he had never yet beheld her in such resplendency of life.

He turned to Sandoz, and said simply :

'They do right to laugh ; it's incomplete. Never mind,
the woman is all right ! Bongrand was not hoaxing me.'

His friend wished to take him away, but he became
obstinate, and drew nearer instead. Now that he had judged
his work, he listened and looked at the crowd. The explosion
continued—culminated in an ascending scale of mad laughter.
No sooner had visitors crossed the threshold than he saw
their jaws part, their eyes grow small, their entire faces expand ; and he heard the tempestuous puffing of the fat men,
the rusty grating jeers of the lean ones, amidst all the shrill,
flute-like laughter of the women. Opposite him, against the
hand-rails, some young fellows went into contortions, as if
somebody had been tickling them. One lady had flung herself on a seat, stifling and trying to regain breath with her
handkerchief over her mouth. Rumours of this picture, which
was so very, very funny, must have been spreading, for there
was a rush from the four corners of the Salon, bands of
people arrived, jostling each other, and all eagerness to share
the fun. 'Where is it ? ' 'Over there.' 'Oh, what a joke ! '
And the witticisms fell thicker than elsewhere. It was
especially the subject that caused merriment ; people failed
to understand it, thought it insane, comical enough to make
one ill with laughter. ' You see the lady feels too hot, while
the gentleman has put on his velveteen jacket for fear of
catching cold.' ' Not at all ; she is already blue ; the gentle-

man has pulled her out of a pond, and he is resting at a distance, holding his nose.' 'I tell you it's a young ladies' school out for a ramble. Look at the two playing at leap-frog.' 'Hallo! washing day; the flesh is blue; the trees are blue; he's dipped his picture in the blueing tub!'

Those who did not laugh flew into a rage: that bluish tinge, that novel rendering of light seemed an insult to them. Some old gentlemen shook their sticks. Was art to be out-raged like this? One grave individual went away very wroth, saying to his wife that he did not like practical jokes. But another, a punctilious little man, having looked in the catalogue for the title of the work, in order to tell his daughter, read out the words, '*In the Open Air*,' whereupon there came a formidable renewal of the clamour, hisses and shouts, and what not else besides. The title sped about; it was repeated, commented on. '*In the Open Air!* ah, yes, the open air, the nude woman in the air, everything in the air, tra la la laire.' The affair was becoming a scandal. The crowd still increased. People's faces grew red with congestion in the growing heat. Each had the stupidly gaping mouth of the ignoramus who judges painting, and between them they indulged in all the asinine ideas, all the preposterous reflec-tions, all the stupid spiteful jeers that the sight of an original work can possibly elicit from *bourgeois* imbecility.

At that moment, as a last blow, Claude beheld Dubuche reappear, dragging the Margaillans along. As soon as he came in front of the picture, the architect, ill at ease, over-taken by cowardly shame, wished to quicken his pace and lead his party further on, pretending that he saw neither the canvas nor his friends. But the contractor had already drawn himself up on his short, squat legs, and was staring at the picture, and asking aloud in his thick hoarse voice:

'I say, who's the blockhead that painted this?'

That good-natured bluster, that cry of a millionaire parvenu resuming the average opinion of the assembly, in-creased the general merriment; and he, flattered by his success, and tickled by the strange style of the painting, started laughing in his turn, so sonorously that he could be heard above all the others. This was the hallelujah, a final outburst of the great organ of opinion.

'Take my daughter away,' whispered pale-faced Madame Margaillan in Dubuche's ear.

He sprang forward, and freed Régine, who had lowered her

eyelids, from the crowd ; displaying in doing so as much muscular energy as if it had been a question of saving the poor creature from imminent death. Then having taken leave of the Margaillans at the door, with a deal of handshaking and bows, he came towards his friends, and said straightway to Sandoz, Fagerolles, and Gagnière :

'What would you have ? It isn't my fault—I warned him that the public would not understand him. It's improper ; yes, you may say what you like, it's improper.'

'They hissed Delacroix,' broke in Sandoz, white with rage, and clenching his fists. 'They hissed Courbet. Oh, the race of enemies ! Oh, the born idiots ! '

Gagnière, who now shared this artistic vindictiveness, grew angry at the recollection of his Sunday battles at the Pasdeloup Concerts in favour of real music.

'And they hiss Wagner too ; they are the same crew. I recognise them. You see that fat fellow over there——'

Jory had to hold him back. The journalist for his part would rather have urged on the crowd. He kept on repeating that it was famous, that there was a hundred thousand francs' worth of advertisements in it. And Irma, left to her own devices once more, went up to two of her friends, young Bourse men who were among the most persistent scoffers, but whom she began to indoctrinate, forcing them, as it were, into admiration, by rapping them on the knuckles.

Fagerolles, however, had not opened his lips. He kept on examining the picture, and glancing at the crowd. With his Parisian instinct and the elastic conscience of a skilful fellow, he at once fathomed the misunderstanding. He was already vaguely conscious of what was wanted for that style of painting to make the conquest of everybody—a little trickery perhaps, some attenuations, a different choice of subject, a milder method of execution. In the main, the influence that Claude had always had over him persisted in making itself felt ; he remained imbued with it ; it had set its stamp upon him for ever. Only he considered Claude to be an arch-idiot to have exhibited such a thing as that. Wasn't it stupid to believe in the intelligence of the public ? What was the meaning of that nude woman beside that gentleman who was fully dressed ? And what did those two little wrestlers in the background mean ? Yet the picture showed many of the qualities of a master. There wasn't another bit of painting like it in the Salon ! And he felt a great contempt for that artist, so admirably endowed, who through lack of tact made all Paris roar as if he had been the worst of daubers.

This contempt became so strong that he was unable to hide it. In a moment of irresistible frankness he exclaimed:

'Look here, my dear fellow, it's your own fault, you are too stupid.'

Claude, turning his eyes from the crowd, looked at him in silence. He had not winced, he had only turned pale amidst the laughter, and if his lips quivered it was merely with a slight nervous twitching; nobody knew him, it was his work alone that was being buffeted. Then for a moment he glanced again at his picture, and slowly inspected the other canvases in the gallery. And amidst the collapse of his illusions, the bitter agony of his pride, a breath of courage, a whiff of health and youth came to him from all that gaily-brave painting which rushed with such headlong passion to beat down classical conventionality. He was consoled and inspirited by it all; he felt no remorse nor contrition, but, on the contrary, was impelled to fight the popular taste still more. No doubt there was some clumsiness and some puerility of effort in his work, but on the other hand what a pretty general tone, what a play of light he had thrown into it, a silvery grey light, fine and diffuse, brightened by all the dancing sunbeams of the open air. It was as if a window had been suddenly opened amidst all the old bituminous cookery of art, amidst all the stewing sauces of tradition, and the sun came in and the walls smiled under that invasion of springtide. The light note of his picture, the bluish tinge that people had been railing at, flashed out among the other paintings also. Was this not the expected dawn, a new aurora rising on art? He perceived a critic who stopped without laughing, some celebrated painters who looked surprised and grave, while Papa Malgras, very dirty, went from picture to picture with the pout of a wary connoisseur, and finally stopped short in front of his canvas, motionless, absorbed. Then Claude turned round to Fagerolles, and surprised him by this tardy reply:

'A fellow can only be an idiot according to his own lights, my dear chap, and it looks as if I were going to remain one. So much the better for you if you are clever!'

Fagerolles at once patted him on the shoulder, like a chum who had only been in fun, and Claude allowed Sandoz to take his arm. They led him off at last. The whole band left the Salon of the Rejected, deciding that they would pass on their way through the gallery of architecture; for a design for a museum by Dubuche had been accepted, and for some few minutes he had been fidgeting and begging them with so humble a look, that it seemed difficult indeed to deny him this satisfaction.

'Ah!' said Jory, jocularly, on entering the gallery, 'what an ice-well! One can breathe here.'

They all took off their hats and wiped their foreheads, with a feeling of relief, as if they had reached some big shady trees after a long march in full sunlight. The gallery was empty. From the roof, shaded by a white linen screen, there fell a soft, even, rather sad light, which was reflected like quiescent water by the well-waxed, mirror-like floor. On the four walls, of a faded red, hung the plans and designs in large and small chases, edged with pale blue borders. Alone—absolutely alone—amidst this desert stood a very hirsute gentleman, who was lost in the contemplation of the plan of a charity home. Three ladies who appeared became frightened and fled across the gallery with hasty steps.

Dubuche was already showing and explaining his work to his comrades. It was only a drawing of a modest little museum gallery, which he had sent in with ambitious haste, contrary to custom and against the wishes of his master, who, nevertheless, had used his influence to have it accepted, thinking himself pledged to do so.

'Is your museum intended for the accommodation of the paintings of the "open air" school?' asked Fagerolles, very gravely.

Gagnière pretended to admire the plan, nodding his head, but thinking of something else; while Claude and Sandoz examined it with sincere interest.

'Not bad, old boy,' said the former. 'The ornamentation is still bastardly traditional; but never mind; it will do.'

Jory, becoming impatient at last, cut him short.

'Come along, let's go, eh? I'm catching my death of cold here.'

The band resumed its march. The worst was that to make a short cut they had to go right through the official Salon, and they resigned themselves to doing so, notwithstanding the oath they had taken not to set foot in it, as a matter of protest. Cutting their way through the crowd, keeping rigidly erect, they followed the suite of galleries, casting indignant

glances to right and left. There was none of the gay
scandal of their Salon, full of fresh tones and an exaggeration of
sunlight, here. One after the other came gilt frames full of
shadows; black pretentious things, nude figures showing
yellowish in a cellar-like light, the frippery of so-called classical art, historical, genre and landscape painting, all showing
the same conventional black grease. The works reeked of
uniform mediocrity, they were characterised by a muddy
dinginess of tone, despite their primness—the primness of
impoverished, degenerate blood. And the friends quickened
their steps : they ran to escape from that reign of bitumen,
condemning everything in one lump with their superb sec-
tarian injustice, repeating that there was nothing in the
place worth looking at—nothing, nothing at all !

At last they emerged from the galleries, and were going
down into the garden when they met Mahoudeau and Chaîne.
The former threw himself into Claude's arms.

'Ah, my dear fellow, your picture ; what artistic temperament it shows ! '

The painter at once began to praise the 'Vintaging Girl.'

'And you, I say, you have thrown a nice big lump at their
heads ! '

But the sight of Chaîne, to whom no one spoke about the
'Woman taken in Adultery,' and who went silently wandering
around, awakened Claude's compassion. He thought there was
something very sad about that execrable painting, and the
wasted life of that peasant who was a victim of middle-class
admiration. He always gave him the delight of a little praise ;
so now he shook his hand cordially, exclaiming :

'Your machine's very good too. Ah, my fine fellow,
draughtsmanship has no terrors for you ! '

'No, indeed,' declared Chaîne, who had grown purple with
vanity under his black bushy beard.

He and Mahoudeau joined the band, and the latter asked
the others whether they had seen Chambouvard's 'Sower.'
It was marvellous ; the only piece of statuary worth looking
at in the Salon. Thereupon they all followed him into the
garden, which the crowd was now invading.

'There,' said Mahoudeau, stopping in the middle of the
central path : 'Chambouvard is standing just in front of his
"Sower."'

In fact, a portly man stood there, solidly planted on his
fat legs, and admiring his handiwork. With his head sunk

between his shoulders, he had the heavy, handsome features of a Hindu idol. He was said to be the son of a veterinary surgeon of the neighbourhood of Amiens. At forty-five he had already produced twenty masterpieces: statues all simplicity and life, flesh modern and palpitating, kneaded by a workman of genius, without any pretension to refinement; and all this was chance production, for he furnished work as a field bears harvest, good one day, bad the next, in absolute ignorance of what he created. He carried the lack of critical acumen to such a degree that he made no distinction between the most glorious offspring of his hands and the detestably grotesque figures which now and then he chanced to put together. Never troubled by nervous feverishness, never doubting, always solid and convinced, he had the pride of a god.

'Wonderful, the " Sower " ! ' whispered Claude. 'What a figure ! and what an attitude ! '

Fagerolles, who had not looked at the statue, was highly amused by the great man, and the string of young, open-mouthed disciples whom as usual he dragged at his tail.

'Just look at them, one would think they are taking the sacrament, 'pon my word—and he himself, eh ? What a fine brutish face he has ! '

Isolated, and quite at his ease, amidst the general curiosity, Chambouvard stood there wondering, with the stupefied air of a man who is surprised at having produced such a masterpiece. He seemed to behold it for the first time, and was unable to get over his astonishment. Then an expression of delight gradually stole over his broad face, he nodded his head, and burst into soft, irresistible laughter, repeating a dozen times, 'It's comical, it's really comical ! '

His train of followers went into raptures, while he himself could find nothing more forcible to express how much he worshipped himself. All at once there was a slight stir. Bongrand, who had been walking about with his hands behind his back, glancing vaguely around him, had just stumbled on Chambouvard, and the public, drawing back, whispered, and watched the two celebrated artists shaking hands ; the one short and of a sanguine temperament, the other tall and restless. Some expressions of good-fellowship were overheard. 'Always fresh marvels.' 'Of course ! And you, nothing this year ? ' 'No, nothing ; I am resting, seeking—— ' 'Come, you joker ! There's no need to seek, the thing comes by itself.'

'Good-bye.' 'Good-bye.' And Chambouvard, followed by his court, was already moving slowly away among the crowd, with the glances of a king, who enjoys life, while Bongrand, who had recognised Claude and his friends, approached them with outstretched feverish hands, and called attention to the sculptor with a nervous jerk of the chin, saying, 'There's a fellow I envy! Ah! to be confident of always producing masterpieces!'

He complimented Mahoudeau on his 'Vintaging Girl'; showed himself paternal to all of them, with that broad-minded good-nature of his, the free and easy manner of an old Bohemian of the romantic school, who had settled down and was decorated. Then, turning to Claude:

'Well, what did I tell you? Did you see upstairs? You have become the chief of a school.'

'Ah! yes,' replied Claude. 'They are giving it me nicely. You are the master of us all.'

But Bongrand made his usual gesture of vague suffering and went off, saying, 'Hold your tongue! I am not even my own master.'

For a few moments longer the band wandered through the garden. They had gone back to look at the 'Vintaging Girl,' when Jory noticed that Gagnière no longer had Irma Bécot on his arm. Gagnière was stupefied; where the deuce could he have lost her? But when Fagerolles had told him that she had gone off in the crowd with two gentlemen, he recovered his composure, and followed the others, lighter of heart now that he was relieved of that girl who had bewildered him.

People now only moved about with difficulty. All the seats were taken by storm; groups blocked up the paths, where the promenaders paused every now and then, flowing back around the successful bits of bronze and marble. From the crowded buffet there arose a loud buzzing, a clatter of saucers and spoons which mingled with the throb of life pervading the vast nave. The sparrows had flown up to the forest of iron girders again, and one could hear their sharp little chirps, the twittering with which they serenaded the setting sun, under the warm panes of the glass roof. The atmosphere, moreover, had become heavy, there was a damp greenhouse-like warmth; the air, stationary as it was, had an odour as of humus, freshly turned over. And rising above the garden throng, the din of the first-floor galleries, the tramping of feet on their iron-girdered flooring still rolled on with the clamour of a tempest beating against a cliff.

Claude, who had a keen perception of that rumbling storm, ended by hearing nothing else ; it had been let loose and was howling in his ears. It was the merriment of the crowd whose jeers and laughter swept hurricane-like past his picture. With a weary gesture he exclaimed :

' Come, what are we messing about here for ? I sha'n't take anything at the refreshment bar, it reeks of the Institute. Let's go and have a glass of beer outside, eh ? '

They all went out, with sinking legs and tired faces, expressive of contempt. Once outside, on finding themselves again face to face with healthy mother Nature in her spring-tide season, they breathed noisily with an air of delight. It had barely struck four o'clock, the slanting sun swept along the Champs Elysées and everything flared : the serried rows of carriages, like the fresh foliage of the trees, and the sheaf-like fountains which spouted up and whirled away in golden dust. With a sauntering step they went hesitatingly down the central avenue, and finally stranded in a little café, the Pavillon de la Concorde, on the left, just before reaching the Place. The place was so small that they sat down outside it at the edge of the footway, despite the chill which fell from a vault of leaves, already fully grown and gloomy. But beyond the four rows of chestnut-trees, beyond the belt of verdant shade, they could see the sunlit roadway of the main avenue where Paris passed before them as in a nimbus, the carriages with their wheels radiating like stars, the big yellow omni-buses, looking even more profusely gilded than triumphal chariots, the horsemen whose steeds seemed to raise clouds of sparks, and the foot passengers whom the light enveloped in splendour.

And during nearly three hours, with his beer untasted before him, Claude went on talking and arguing amid a growing fever, broken down as he was in body, and with his mind full of all the painting he had just seen. It was the usual winding up of their visit to the Salon, though this year they were more impassioned on account of the liberal measure of the Emperor.

' Well, and what of it, if the public does laugh ? ' cried Claude. ' We must educate the public, that's all. In reality it's a victory. Take away two hundred grotesque canvases, and our Salon beats theirs. We have courage and audacity—

we are the future. Yes, yes, you'll see it later on ; we shall
kill their Salon. We shall enter it as conquerors, by dint of
producing masterpieces. Laugh, laugh, you big stupid Paris—
laugh until you fall on your knees before us ! '

And stopping short, he pointed prophetically to the triumphal avenue, where the luxury and happiness of the city went
rolling by in the sunlight. His arms stretched out till they
embraced even the Place de la Concorde, which could be seen
slantwise from where they sat under the trees—the Place de
la Concorde, with the plashing water of one of its fountains,
a strip of balustrade, and two of its statues—Rouen, with
the gigantic bosom, and Lille, thrusting forward her huge
bare foot.

' " In the open air "—it amuses them, eh ? ' he resumed.
' All right, since they are bent on it, the " open air " then, the
school of the " open air ! " Eh ! it was a thing strictly between
us, it didn't exist yesterday beyond the circle of a few painters.
But now they throw the word upon the winds, and they found
the school. Oh ! I'm agreeable. Let it be the school of the
" open air ! " '

Jory slapped his thighs.

' Didn't I tell you ? I felt sure of making them bite with
those articles of mine, the idiots that they are. Ah ! how
we'll plague them now.'

Mahoudeau also was singing victory, constantly dragging
in his ' Vintaging Girl,' the daring points of which he explained
to the silent Chaîne, the only one who listened to him ; while
Gagnière, with the sternness of a timid man waxing wroth
over questions of pure theory, spoke of guillotining the
Institute ; and Sandoz, with the glowing sympathy of a hard
worker, and Dubuche, giving way to the contagion of revolutionary friendship, became exasperated, and struck the table,
swallowing up Paris with each draught of beer. Fagerolles,
very calm, retained his usual smile. He had accompanied
them for the sake of amusement, for the singular pleasure
which he found in urging his comrades into farcical affairs
that were bound to turn out badly. At the very moment when
he was lashing their spirit of revolt, he himself formed the
firm resolution to work in future for the Prix de Rome. That
day had decided him ; he thought it idiotic to compromise his
prospects any further.

The sun was declining on the horizon, there was now only
a returning stream of carriages, coming back from the Bois in

the pale golden shimmer of the sunset. And the exodus from the Salon must have been nearly over; a long string of pedestrians passed by, gentlemen who looked like critics, each with a catalogue under his arm.

But all at once Gagnière became enthusiastic: 'Ah! Courajod, there was one who had his share in inventing landscape painting! Have you seen his "Pond of Gagny" at the Luxembourg?'

'A marvel!' exclaimed Claude. 'It was painted thirty years ago, and nothing more substantial has been turned out since. Why is it left at the Luxembourg? It ought to be in the Louvre.'

'But Courajod isn't dead,' said Fagerolles.

'What! Courajod isn't dead! No one ever sees him or speaks of him now.'

There was general stupefaction when Fagerolles assured them that the great landscape painter, now seventy years of age, lived somewhere in the neighbourhood of Montmartre, in a little house among his fowls, ducks, and dogs. So one might outlive one's own glory! To think that there were such melancholy instances of old artists disappearing before their death! Silence fell upon them all; they began to shiver when they perceived Bongrand pass by on a friend's arm, with a congestive face and a nervous air as he waved his hand to them; while almost immediately behind him, surrounded by his disciples, came Chambouvard, laughing very loudly, and tapping his heels on the pavement with the air of absolute mastery that comes from confidence in immortality.

'What! are you going?' said Mahoudeau to Chaîne, who was rising from his chair.

The other mumbled some indistinct words in his beard, and went off after distributing hand-shakes among the party.

'I know,' said Jory to Mahoudeau. 'I believe he has a weakness for your neighbour, the herbalist woman. I saw his eyes flash all at once; it comes upon him like toothache. Look how he's running over there.'

The sculptor shrugged his shoulders amidst the general laughter.

But Claude did not hear. He was now discussing architecture with Dubuche. No doubt, that plan of a museum gallery which he exhibited wasn't bad; only there was nothing new in it. It was all so much patient marquetry of the school formulas. Ought not all the arts to advance in one line of battle ? Ought not the evolution that was transforming literature, painting, even music itself, to renovate architecture as well ? If ever the architecture of a period was to have a style of its own, it was assuredly the architecture of the period they would soon be entering, a new period when they would find the ground freshly swept, ready for the rebuilding of everything. Down with the Greek temples ! there was no reason why they should continue to exist under our sky, amid our society ! down with the Gothic cathedrals, since faith in legend was dead ! down with the delicate colonnades, the lace-like work of the Renaissance—that revival of the antique grafted on mediævalism—precious art-jewellery, no doubt, but in which democracy could not dwell. And he demanded, he called with violent gestures for an architectural formula suited to democracy ; such work in stone as would express its tenets ; edifices where it would really be at home ; something vast and strong, great and simple at the same time ; the something that was already being indicated in the new railway stations and markets, whose ironwork displayed such solid elegance, but purified and raised to a standard of beauty, proclaiming the grandeur of the intellectual conquests of the age.

'Ah ! yes, ah ! yes,' repeated Dubuche, catching Claude's enthusiasm ; 'that's what I want to accomplish, you'll see some day. Give me time to succeed, and when I'm my own master—ah ! when I'm my own master.'

Night was coming on apace, and Claude was growing more and more animated and passionate, displaying a fluency, an eloquence which his comrades had not known him to possess. They all grew excited in listening to him, and ended by becoming noisily gay over the extraordinary witticisms he launched forth. He himself, having returned to the subject of his picture, again discussed it with a deal of gaiety, caricaturing the crowd he had seen looking at it, and imitating the imbecile laughter. Along the avenue, now of an ashy hue, one only saw the shadows of infrequent vehicles dart by. The sidewalk was quite black ; an icy chill fell from the trees. Nothing broke the stillness but the sound of song coming from a clump of verdure behind the café ; there was some rehearsal at the Concert de l'Horloge, for one-heard the sentimental voice of a girl trying a love-song.

'Ah ! how they amused me, the idiots ! ' exclaimed Claude, in a last burst. 'Do you know, I wouldn't take a hundred thousand francs for my day's pleasure ! '

Then he relapsed into silence, thoroughly exhausted. Nobody had any saliva left; silence reigned; they all shivered in the icy gust that swept by. And they separated in a sort of bewilderment, shaking hands in a tired fashion. Dubuche was going to dine out; Fagerolles had an appointment; in vain did Jory, Mahoudeau, and Gagnière try to drag Claude to Foucart's, a twenty-five sous' restaurant; Sandoz was already taking him away on his arm, feeling anxious at seeing him so excited.

'Come along, I promised my mother to be back for dinner. You'll take a bit with us. It will be nice; we'll finish the day together.'

They both went down the quay, past the Tuileries, walking side by side in fraternal fashion. But at the Pont des Saints-Pères the painter stopped short.

'What, are you going to leave me?' exclaimed Sandoz. 'Why, I thought you were going to dine with me?'

'No, thanks; I've too bad a headache—I'm going home to bed.'

And he obstinately clung to this excuse.

'All right, old man,' said Sandoz at last, with a smile. 'One doesn't see much of you nowadays. You live in mystery. Go on, old boy, I don't want to be in your way.'

Claude restrained a gesture of impatience; and, letting his friend cross the bridge, he went his way along the quays by himself. He walked on with his arms hanging beside him, with his face turned towards the ground, seeing nothing, but taking long strides like a somnambulist who is guided by instinct. On the Quai de Bourbon, in front of his door, he looked up, full of surprise on seeing a cab waiting at the edge of the foot pavement, and barring his way. And it was with the same automatical step that he entered the doorkeeper's room to take his key.

'I have given it to that lady,' called Madame Joseph from the back of the room. 'She is upstairs.'

'What lady?' he asked in bewilderment.

'That young person. Come, you know very well, the one who always comes.'

He had not the remotest idea whom she meant. Still, in his utter confusion of mind, he decided to go upstairs. The key was in the door, which he slowly opened and closed again.

For a moment Claude stood stock still. Darkness had invaded the studio; a violet dimness, a melancholy gloom fell from the large window, enveloping everything. He could no longer plainly distinguish either the floor, or the furniture, or the sketches; everything that was lying about seemed to be melting in the stagnant waters of a pool. But on the edge of the couch there loomed a dark figure, stiff with waiting, anxious and despairing amid the last gasp of daylight. It was Christine; he recognised her.

She held out her hands, and murmured in a low, halting voice:

'I have been here for three hours; yes, for three hours, all alone, and listening. I took a cab on leaving there, and I only wanted to stay a minute, and get back as soon as possible. But I should have stayed all night; I could not go away without shaking hands with you.'

She continued, and told him of her mad desire to see the picture; her prank of going to the Salon, and how she had tumbled into it amidst the storm of laughter, amidst the jeers of all those people. It was she whom they had hissed like that; it was on herself that they had spat. And seized with wild terror, distracted with grief and shame, she had fled, as if she could feel that laughter lashing her like a whip, until the blood flowed. But she now forgot about herself in her concern for him, upset by the thought of the grief he must feel, for her womanly sensibility magnified the bitterness of the repulse, and she was eager to console.

'Oh, friend, don't grieve! I wished to see and tell you that they are jealous of it all, that I found the picture very nice, and that I feel very proud and happy at having helped you— at being, if ever so little, a part of it.'

Still, motionless, he listened to her as she stammered those tender words in an ardent voice, and suddenly he sank down at her feet, letting his head fall upon her knees, and bursting into tears. All his excitement of the afternoon, all the bravery he had shown amidst the jeering, all his gaiety and violence now collapsed, in a fit of sobs which well nigh choked him. From the gallery where the laughter had buffeted him, he heard it pursuing him through the Champs Elysées, then along the banks of the Seine, and now in his very studio. His strength was utterly spent; he felt weaker than a child; and rolling his head from one side to another he repeated in a stifled voice:

'My God! how I do suffer!'

Then she, with both hands, raised his face to her lips in a

transport of passion. She kissed him, and with her warm breath she blew to his very heart the words: 'Be quiet, be quiet, I love you!'

They adored each other; it was inevitable. Near them, on the centre of the table, the lilac she had sent him that morning embalmed the night air, and, alone shiny with lingering light, the scattered particles of gold leaf, wafted from the frame of the big picture, twinkled like a swarming of stars.

VI

THE very next morning, at seven o'clock, Christine was at the studio, her face still flushed by the falsehood which she had told Madame Vanzade about a young friend from Clermont whom she was to meet at the station, and with whom she should spend the day.

Claude, overjoyed by the idea of spending a whole day with her, wanted to take her into the country, far away under the glorious sunlight, so as to have her entirely to himself. She was delighted; they scampered off like lunatics, and reached the St. Lazare Station just in time to catch the Havre train. He knew, beyond Mantes, a little village called Bennecourt, where there was an artists' inn which he had at times invaded with some comrades; and careless as to the two hours' rail, he took her to lunch there, just as he would have taken her to Asnières. She made very merry over this journey, to which there seemed no end. So much the better if it were to take them to the end of the world! It seemed to them as if evening would never come.

At ten o'clock they alighted at Bonnières; and there they took the ferry—an old ferry-boat that creaked and grated against its chain—for Bennecourt is situated on the opposite bank of the Seine. It was a splendid May morning, the rippling waters were spangled with gold in the sunlight, the young foliage showed delicately green against the cloudless azure. And, beyond the islets situated at this point of the river, how delightful it was to find the country inn, with its little grocery business attached, its large common room smelling of soapsuds, and its spacious yard full of manure, on which the ducks disported themselves.

'Hallo, Faucheur! we have come to lunch. An omelette, some sausages, and some cheese, eh?'

'Are you going to stay the night, Monsieur Claude?'

'No, no; another time. And some white wine; eh? you know that pinky wine, that grates a bit in the throat.'

Christine had already followed mother Faucheur to the barn-yard, and when the latter came back with her eggs, she asked Claude with her artful peasant's laugh:

'And so now you're married?'

'Well,' replied the painter without hesitation, 'it looks like it since I'm with my wife.'

The lunch was exquisite: the omelette overdone, the sausages too greasy, and the bread so hard that he had to cut it into fingers for Christine lest she should hurt her wrist. They emptied two bottles of wine, and began a third, becoming so gay and noisy that they ended by feeling bewildered in the long room, where they partook of the meal all alone. She, with her cheeks aflame, declared that she was tipsy; it had never happened to her before, and she thought it very funny. Oh! so funny, and she burst into uncontrollable laughter.

'Let us get a breath of air,' she said at last.

'Yes, let's take a stroll. We must start back at four o'clock; so we have three hours before us.'

They went up the village of Bennecourt, whose yellow houses straggle along the river bank for about a couple of thousand yards. All the villagers were in the fields; they only met three cows, led by a little girl. He, with an outstretched arm, told her all about the locality; seemed to know whither he was going, and when they had reached the last house—an old building, standing on the bank of the Seine, just opposite the slopes of Jeufos—sehe turned round it, and entered a wood of oak trees. It was like the end of the world, roofed in with foliage, through which the sun alone penetrated in narrow tongues of flame. And there they could stroll and talk and kiss in freedom.

When at last it became necessary for them to retrace their steps, they found a peasant standing at the open doorway of the house by the wood-side. Claude recognised the man and called to him:

'Hallo, Porrette! Does that shanty belong to you?'

At this the old fellow, with tears in his eyes, related that it did, and that his tenants had gone away without paying him, leaving their furniture behind. And he invited them inside.

'There's no harm in looking; you may know somebody who would like to take the place. There are many Parisians who'd be glad of it. Three hundred francs a year, with the furniture; it's for nothing, eh?'

They inquisitively followed him inside. It was a rambling old place that seemed to have been cut out of a barn. Downstairs they found an immense kitchen and a dining-room, in which one might have given a dance; upstairs were two rooms also, so vast that one seemed lost in them. As for the furniture, it consisted of a walnut bedstead in one of the rooms, and of a table and some household utensils in the kitchen. But in front of the house the neglected garden was planted with magnificent apricot trees, and overgrown with large rose-bushes in full bloom; while at the back there was a potato field reaching as far as the oak wood, and surrounded by a quick-set hedge.

'I'd leave the potatoes as they are,' said old Porrette.

Claude and Christine looked at each other with one of those sudden cravings for solitude and forgetfulness common to lovers. Ah! how sweet it would be to love one another there in the depths of that nook, so far away from everybody else! But they smiled. Was such a thing to be thought of? They had barely time to catch the train that was to take them back to Paris. And the old peasant, who was Madame Faucheur's father, accompanied them along the river bank, and as they were stepping into the ferry-boat, shouted to them, after quite an inward struggle:

'You know, I'll make it two hundred and fifty francs— send me some people.'

On reaching Paris, Claude accompanied Christine to Madame Vanzade's door. They had grown very sad. They exchanged a long handshake, silent and despairing, not daring to kiss each other there.

A life of torment then began. In the course of a fortnight she was only able to call on three occasions; and she arrived panting, having but a few minutes at her disposal, for it so happened that the old lady had just then become very exacting. Claude questioned her, feeling uneasy at seeing her look so pale and out of sorts, with her eyes bright with fever. Never had that pious house, that vault, without air or light, where she died of boredom, caused her so much suffering. Her fits of giddiness had come upon her again; the want of exercise made the blood throb in her temples.

She owned to him that she had fainted one evening in her room, as if she had been suddenly strangled by a leaden hand. Still she did not say a word against her employer; on the contrary, she softened on speaking of her: the poor creature, so old and so infirm, and so kind-hearted, who called her daughter! She felt as if she were committing a wicked act each time that she forsook her to hurry to her lover's.

Two more weeks went by, and the falsehoods with which Christine had to buy, as it were, each hour of liberty became intolerable to her. She loved, she would have liked to proclaim it aloud, and her feelings revolted at having to hide her love like a crime, at having to lie basely, like a servant afraid of being sent away.

At last, one evening in the studio, at the moment when she was leaving, she threw herself with a distracted gesture into Claude's arms, sobbing with suffering and passion. 'Ah! I cannot, I cannot—keep me with you; prevent me from going back.'

He had caught hold of her, and was almost smothering her with kisses.

'You really love me, then! Oh, my darling! But I am so very poor, and you would lose everything. Can I allow you to forego everything like this?'

She sobbed more violently still; her halting words were choked by her tears.

'The money, eh? which she might leave me? Do you think I calculate? I have never thought of it, I swear it to you! Ah! let her keep everything and let me be free! I have no ties, no relatives; can't I be allowed to do as I like?'

Then, in a last sob of agony: 'Ah, you are right; it's wrong to desert the poor woman. Ah! I despise myself. I wish I had the strength. But I love you too much, I suffer too much; surely you won't let me die?'

'Oh!' he cried in a passionate transport. 'Let others die, there are but we two on earth.'

It was all so much madness. Christine left Madame Vanzade in the most brutal fashion. She took her trunk away the very next morning. She and Claude had at once remembered the deserted old house at Bennecourt, the giant rose-bushes, the immense rooms. Ah! to go away, to go away without the loss of an hour, to live at the world's end, in all the bliss of their passion! She clapped her hands for very joy. He, still smarting from his defeat at the Salon, and anxious to recover from it, longed for complete rest in the country; yonder he would find the real 'open air,' he would work away with grass up to his neck and bring back master-pieces. In a couple of days everything was ready, the studio relinquished, the few household chattels conveyed to the rail-way station. Besides, they met with a slice of luck, for Papa Malgras gave some five hundred francs for a score of sketches, selected from among the waifs and strays of the removal. Thus they would be able to live like princes. Claude still had his income of a thousand francs a year; Christine, too, had saved some money, besides having her outfit and dresses. And away they went; it was perfect flight, friends avoided and not even warned by letter, Paris despised and forsaken amid laughter expressive of relief.

June was drawing to a close, and the rain fell in torrents during the week they spent in arranging their new home. They discovered that old Porrette had taken away half the kitchen utensils before signing the agreement. But that matter did not affect them. They took a delight in dabbling about amidst the showers; they made journeys three leagues long, as far as Vernon, to buy plates and saucepans, which they brought back with them in triumph. At last they got shipshape, occupying one of the upstairs rooms, abandoning the other to the mice, and transforming the dining-room into a studio; and, above all, as happy as children at taking their meals in the kitchen off a deal table, near the hearth where the soup sang in the pot. To wait upon them they engaged a girl from the village, who came every morning and went home at night. She was called Mélie, she was a niece of the Faucheurs, and her stupidity delighted them. In fact, one could not have found a greater idiot in the whole region.

The sun having shown itself again, some delightful days followed, the months slipping away amid monotonous felicity. They never knew the date, they were for ever mixing up the days of the week. Every day, after the second breakfast, came endless strolls, long walks across the tableland planted with apple trees, over the grassy country roads, along the banks of the Seine through the meadows as far as La Roche-Guyon; and there were still more distant explorations, perfect journeys on the opposite side of the river, amid the cornfields of Bonnières and Jeufosse. A person who was obliged to leave the neighbourhood sold them an old boat for thirty francs, so that they also had the river at their disposal, and, like savages, became seized with a passion for it, living on its waters for days together, rowing about, discovering new countries, and lingering for hours under the willows on the banks, or in little creeks, dark with shade. Betwixt the eyots scattered along the stream there was a shifting and mysterious city, a network of passages along which, with the lower branches of the trees caressingly brushing against them, they softly glided, alone, as it were, in the world, with the ringdoves and the kingfishers. He at times had to spring out upon the sand, with bare legs, to push off the skiff. She bravely plied the oars, bent on forcing her way against the strongest currents, and exulting in her strength. And in the evening they ate cabbage soup in the kitchen, laughing at Mélie's stupidity, as they had laughed at it the day before ; to begin the morrow just in the same fashion.

Every evening, however, Christine said to Claude :

' Now, my dear, you must promise me one thing—that you'll set to work to-morrow.'

' Yes, to-morrow ; I give you my word.'

' And you know if you don't, I shall really get angry this time. Is it I who prevent you ? '

' You ! what an idea. Since I came here to work—dash it all ! you'll see to-morrow.'

On the morrow they started off again in the skiff ; she looked at him with an embarrassed smile when she saw that he took neither canvas nor colours. Then she kissed him, laughing, proud of her power, moved by the constant sacrifice he made to her. And then came fresh affectionate remonstrances : ' To-morrow, ah ! to-morrow she would tie him to his easel ! '

However, Claude did make some attempts at work. He began a study of the slopes of Jeufosse, with the Seine in the foreground ; but Christine followed him to the islet where he had installed himself, and sat down on the grass close to him with parted lips, her eyes watching the blue sky. And she looked so pretty there amidst the verdure, in that solitude, where nothing broke the silence but the rippling of the water, that every minute he relinquished his palette to nestle by her side. On another occasion, he was altogether charmed by an old farmhouse, shaded by some antiquated apple trees which had grown to the size of oaks. He came thither two days in succession, but on the third Christine took him to the market at Bonnières to buy some hens. The next day was also lost; the canvas had dried; then he grew impatient in trying to work at it again, and finally abandoned it altogether. Throughout the warm weather he thus made but a pretence to work—barely roughing out little bits of painting, which he laid aside on the first pretext, without an effort at perseverance. His passion for toil, that fever of former days that had made him rise at daybreak to battle with his rebellious art, seemed to have gone; a reaction of indifference and laziness had set in, and he vegetated delightfully, like one who is recovering from some severe illness.

But Christine lived indeed. All the latent passion of her nature burst into being. She was indeed an amorosa, a child of nature and of love.

Thus their days passed by and solitude did not prove irksome to them. No desire for diversion, of paying or receiving visits, as yet made them look beyond themselves. Such hours as she did not spend near him, she employed in household cares, turning the house upside down with great cleanings, which Mélie executed under her supervision, and falling into fits of reckless activity, which led her to engage in personal combats with the few saucepans in the kitchen. The garden especially occupied her; provided with pruning shears, careless of the thorns which lacerated her hands, she reaped harvests of roses from the giant rose-bushes; and she gave herself a thorough back-ache in gathering the apricots, which she sold for two hundred francs to some of the Englishmen who scoured the district every year. She was very proud of her bargain, and seriously talked of living upon the garden produce. Claude cared less for gardening; he had placed his couch in the large dining-room, transformed into a studio; and he stretched himself upon it, and through the open window watched her sow and plant. There was profound peace, the certainty that nobody would come, that no ring at the bell would disturb them at any moment of the day. Claude carried this fear of coming into contact with people so far as to avoid passing Faucheur's inn, for he dreaded lest he might run against some party of chums from Paris. Not a soul came, however, throughout the livelong summer. And every night as they went upstairs, he repeated that, after all, it was deuced lucky.

There was, however, a secret sore in the depths of his happiness. After their flight from Paris, Sandoz had learnt their address, and had written to ask whether he might go to see Claude, but the latter had not answered the letter, and so coolness had followed, and the old friendship seemed dead. Christine was grieved at this, for she realised well enough that he had broken off all intercourse with his comrades for her sake. She constantly reverted to the subject; she did not want to estrange him from his friends, and indeed she insisted that he should invite them. But, though he promised to set matters right, he did nothing of the kind. It was all over; what was the use of raking up the past?

However, money having become scarce towards the latter days of July, he was obliged to go to Paris to sell Papa Malgras half a dozen of his old studies, and Christine, on accompanying him to the station, made him solemnly promise that he would go to see Sandoz. In the evening she was there again, at the Bonnières Station, waiting for him.

'Well, did you see him? did you embrace each other?'

He began walking by her side in silent embarrassment. Then he answered in a husky voice:

'No; I hadn't time.'

Thereupon, sorely distressed, with two big tears welling to her eyes, she replied:

'You grieve me very much indeed.'

Then, as they were walking under the trees, he kissed her, crying also, and begging her not to make him sadder still. 'Could people alter life? Did it not suffice that they were happy together?'

During the earlier months they only once met some strangers. This occurred a little above Bennecourt, in the direction of La Roche-Guyon. They were strolling along a deserted, wooded lane, one of those delightful dingle paths of the region, when, at a turning, they came upon three middle-class people out for a walk—father, mother, and daughter. It precisely happened that, believing themselves to be quite alone, Claude and Christine had passed their arms round each other's waists; she, bending towards him, was offering her lips; while he laughingly protruded his; and their surprise was so sudden that they did not change their attitude, but, still clasped together, advanced at the same slow pace. The amazed family remained transfixed against one of the side banks, the father stout and apoplectic, the mother as thin as a knife-blade, and the daughter, a mere shadow, looking like a sick bird moulting—all three of them ugly, moreover, and but scantily provided with the vitiated blood of their race. They looked disgraceful amidst the throbbing life of nature, beneath the glorious sun. And all at once the sorry girl, who with stupefied eyes thus watched love passing by, was pushed off by her father, dragged along by her mother, both beside themselves, exasperated by the sight of that embrace, and asking whether there was no longer any country police, while, still without hurrying, the lovers went off triumphantly in their glory.

Claude, however, was wondering and searching his memory. Where had he previously seen those heads, so typical of *bourgeois* degeneracy, those flattened, crabbed faces reeking of millions earned at the expense of the poor ? It was assuredly in some important circumstance of his life. And all at once he remembered ; they were the Margaillans, the man was that building contractor whom Dubuche had promenaded through the Salon of the Rejected, and who had laughed in front of his picture with the roaring laugh of a fool. A couple of hundred steps further on, as he and Christine emerged from the lane and found themselves in front of a large estate, where a big white building stood, girt with fine trees, they learnt from an old peasant woman that La Richaudière, as it was called, had belonged to the Margaillans for three years past. They had paid fifteen hundred thousand francs for it, and had just spent more than a million in improvements.

' That part of the country won't see much of us in future,' said Claude, as they returned to Bennecourt. ' Those monsters spoil the landscape.'

Towards the end of the summer, an important event changed the current of their lives. Christine was *enceinte*. At first, both she and Claude felt amazed and worried. Now for the first time they seemed to dread some terrible complications in their life. Later on, however, they gradually grew accustomed to the thought of what lay before them and made all necessary preparations. But the winter proved a terribly inclement one, and Christine was compelled to remain indoors, whilst Claude went walking all alone over the frost-bound, clanking roads. And he, finding himself in solitude during these walks, after months of constant companionship, wondered at the way his life had turned, against his own will, as it were. He had never wished for home life even with her ; had he been consulted, he would have expressed his horror of it ; it had come about, however, and could not be undone, for—without mentioning the child—he was one of those who lack the courage to break off. This fate had evidently been in store for him, he felt ; he had been destined to succumb to the first woman who did not feel ashamed of him. The hard ground resounded beneath his wooden-soled shoes, and the blast froze the current of his reverie, which lingered on vague thoughts, on his luck of having, at any rate, met with a good and honest girl, on how cruelly he would have suffered had it been otherwise. And then his love came back to him ; he hurried home to take Christine in his trembling arms as if he had been in danger of losing her.

The child, a boy, was born about the middle of February, and at once began to revolutionise the home, for Christine, who had shown herself such an active housewife, proved to be a very awkward nurse. She failed to become motherly, despite her kind heart and her distress at the sight of the slightest pimple. She soon grew weary, gave in, and called for Mélie, who only made matters worse by her gaping stupidity. The father had to come to the rescue, and proved still more awkward than the two women. The discomfort which needlework had caused Christine of old, her want of aptitude as regards the usual occupations of her sex, revived amid the cares that the baby required. The child was ill-kept, and grew up anyhow in the garden, or in the large rooms left untidy in sheer despair, amidst broken toys, uncleanliness and destruction. And when matters became too bad altogether, Christine could only throw herself upon the neck of the man she loved. She was pre-eminently an amorosa and would have sacrificed her son for his father twenty times over.

It was at this period, however, that Claude resumed work a little. The winter was drawing to a close ; he did not know how to spend the bright sunny mornings, since Christine could no longer go out before mid-day on account of Jacques, whom they had named thus after his maternal grandfather, though they neglected to have him christened. Claude worked in the garden, at first, in a random way : made a rough sketch of the lines of apricot trees, roughed out the giant rose-bushes, composed some bits of ' still life,' out of four apples, a bottle, and a stoneware jar, disposed on a table-napkin. This was only to pass his time. But afterwards he warmed to his work ; the idea of painting a figure in the full

sunlight ended by haunting him; and from that moment his
wife became his victim, she herself agreeable enough, offering
herself, feeling happy at affording him pleasure, without as
yet understanding what a terrible rival she was giving herself in art. He painted her a score of times, dressed in white,
in red, amidst the verdure, standing, walking, or reclining on
the grass, wearing a wide-brimmed straw hat, or bare-headed,
under a parasol, the cherry-tinted silk of which steeped her
features in a pinky glow. He never felt wholly satisfied; he
scratched out the canvases after two or three sittings, and at
once began them afresh, obstinately sticking to the same
subject. Only a few studies, incomplete, but charmingly
indicated in a vigorous style, were saved from the palette-
knife, and hung against the walls of the dining-room.

And after Christine it became Jacques' turn to pose.
They stripped him to the skin, like a little St. John the
Baptist, on warm days, and stretched him on a blanket, where
he was told not to stir. But devil a bit could they make
him keep still. Getting frisky, in the sunlight, he crowed
and kicked with his tiny pink feet in the air, rolling about
and turning somersaults. The father, after laughing, became
angry, and swore at the tiresome mite, who would not keep
quiet for a minute. Who ever heard of trifling with painting?
Then the mother made big eyes at the little one, and held
him while the painter quickly sketched an arm or a leg.
Claude obstinately kept at it for weeks, tempted as he felt by
the pretty tones of that childish skin. It was not as a father,
but as an artist, that he gloated over the boy as the subject
for a masterpiece, blinking his eyes the while, and dreaming
of some wonderful picture he would paint. And he renewed
the experiment again and again, watching the lad for days,
and feeling furious when the little scamp would not go to
sleep at times when he, Claude, might so well have painted
him.

One day, when Jacques was sobbing, refusing to keep still,
Christine gently remarked:

' My dear, you tire the poor pet.'

At this Claude burst forth, full of remorse:

' After all! you are right; I'm a fool with this painting of
mine. Children are not intended for that sort of thing.'

The spring and summer sped by amidst great quietude.
They went out less often; they had almost given up the boat,
which finished rotting against the bank, for it was quite a job

to take the little one with them among the islets. But they
often strolled along the banks of the Seine, without, however,
going farther afield than a thousand yards or so. Claude,
tired of the everlasting views in the garden, now attempted
some sketches by the river-side, and on such days Christine
went to fetch him with the child, sitting down to watch him
paint, until they all three returned home with flagging steps,
beneath the ashen dusk of waning daylight. One afternoon
Claude was surprised to see Christine bring with her the old
album which she had used as a young girl. She joked about
it, and explained that to sit behind him like that had roused
in her a wish to work herself. Her voice was a little unsteady as she spoke ; the truth was that she felt a longing to
share his labour, since this labour took him away from her
more and more each day. She drew and ventured to wash in
two or three water-colours in the careful style of a school-
girl. Then, discouraged by his smiles, feeling that no community of ideas would be arrived at on that ground, she once
more put her album aside, making him promise to give her
some lessons in painting whenever he should have time.

Besides, she thought his more recent pictures very pretty.
After that year of rest in the open country, in the full sunlight, he painted with fresh and clearer vision, as it were, with
a more harmonious and brighter colouring. He had never
before been able to treat reflections so skilfully, or possessed
a more correct perception of men and things steeped in
diffuse light. And henceforth, won over by that feast of
colours, she would have declared it all capital if he would
only have condescended to finish his work a little more, and if
she had not remained nonplussed now and then before a
mauve ground or a blue tree, which upset all her precon-
ceived notions of colour. One day when she ventured upon a
bit of criticism, precisely about an azure-tinted poplar, he
made her go to nature and note for herself the delicate bluish-
ness of the foliage. It was true enough, the tree was blue ;
but in her inmost heart she did not surrender, and
condemned reality ; there ought not to be any blue trees in
nature.

She no longer spoke but gravely of the studies hanging in
the dining-room. Art was returning into their lives, and it
made her muse. When she saw him go off with his bag, his
portable easel, and his sunshade, it often happened that she
flung herself upon his neck, asking :

' You love me, say ? '

' How silly you are ! Why shouldn't I love you ? '

' Then kiss me, since you love me, kiss me a great deal, a great deal.'

Then accompanying him as far as the road, she added :

' And mind you work ; you know that I have never prevented you from working. Go, go ; I am very pleased when you work.'

Anxiety seemed to seize hold of Claude, when the autumn of the second year tinged the leaves yellow, and ushered in the cold weather. The season happened to be abominable ; a fortnight of pouring rain kept him idle at home ; and then fog came at every moment, hindering his work. He sat in front of the fire, out of sorts ; he never spoke of Paris, but the city rose up over yonder, on the horizon, the winter city, with its gaslamps flaring already at five o'clock, its gatherings of friends, spurring each other on to emulation, and its life of ardent production, which even the frosts of December could not slacken. He went there thrice in one month, on the pretext of seeing Malgras, to whom he had, again, sold a few small pictures. He no longer avoided passing in front of Faucheur's inn ; he even allowed himself to be waylaid at times by old Porrette, and to accept a glass of white wine at the inn, and his glance scoured the room as if, despite the season, he had been looking for some comrades of yore, who had arrived there, perchance, that morning. He lingered as if awaiting them ; then, in despair at his solitude, he returned home, stifling with all that was fermenting within him, ill at having nobody to whom he might shout the thoughts which made his brain almost burst.

However, the winter went by, and Claude had the consolation of being able to paint some lovely snow scenes. A third year was beginning, when, towards the close of May, an unexpected meeting filled him with emotion. He had that morning climbed up to the plateau to find a subject, having at last grown tired of the banks of the Seine ; and at the bend of a road he stopped short in amazement on seeing Dubuche, in a silk hat, and carefully-buttoned frock coat, coming towards him, between the double row of elder hedges.

' What ! is it you ? '

The architect stammered from sheer vexation :

' Yes, I am going to pay a visit. It's confoundedly idiotic in the country, eh ? But it can't be helped. There are certain

things one's obliged to do. And you live near here, eh? I
knew—that is to say, I didn't. I had been told something
about it, but I thought it was on the opposite side, farther
down.'

Claude, very much moved at seeing him, helped him out
of his difficulty.

'All right, all right, old man, there is no need to apologise.
I am the most guilty party. Ah! it's a long while since we
saw one another! If you knew what a thump my heart gave
when I saw your nose appear from behind the leaves!'

Then he took his arm and accompanied him, giggling with
pleasure, while the other, in his constant worry about his
future, which always made him talk about himself, at once
began speaking of his prospects. He had just become a
first-class pupil at the School, after securing the regulation
'honourable mentions,' with infinite trouble. But his
success left him as perplexed as ever. His parents no longer
sent him a penny, they wailed about their poverty so much
that he might have to support them in his turn. He had given
up the idea of competing for the Prix de Rome, feeling certain
of being beaten in the effort, and anxious to earn his living.
And he was weary already; sick at scouring the town, at
earning twenty-five sous an hour from ignorant architects,
who treated him like a hodman. What course should he
adopt? How was he to guess at the shortest route? He
might leave the School; he would get a lift from his master,
the influential Dequersonnière, who liked him for his docility
and diligence; only what a deal of trouble and uncertainty
there would still be before him! And he bitterly complained
of the Government schools, where one slaved away for years,
and which did not even provide a position for all those whom
they cast upon the pavement.

Suddenly he stopped in the middle of the path. The
elder hedges were leading to an open plain, and La Richaudière appeared amid its lofty trees.

'Hold hard! of course,' exclaimed Claude, 'I hadn't
thought about it—you're going to that shanty. Oh! the
baboons; there's a lot of ugly mugs, if you like!'

Dubuche, looking vexed at this outburst of artistic feeling,
protested stiffly. 'All the same, Papa Margaillan, idiot as he
seems to you, is a first-rate man of business. You should see
him in his building-yards, among the houses he runs up, as
active as the very fiend, showing marvellous good management,

and a wonderful scent as to the right streets to build and what materials to buy! Besides, one does not earn millions without becoming a gentleman. And then, too, it would be very silly of me not to be polite to a man who can be useful to me.'

While talking, he barred the narrow path, preventing his friend from advancing further—no doubt from a fear of being compromised by being seen in his company, and in order to make him understand that they ought to separate there.

Claude was on the point of inquiring about their comrades in Paris, but he kept silent. Not even a word was said respecting Christine, and he was reluctantly deciding to quit Dubuche, holding out his hand to take leave, when, in spite of himself, this question fell from his quivering lips:

'And is Sandoz all right?'

'Yes, he's pretty well. I seldom see him. He spoke to me about you last month. He is still grieved at your having shown us the door.'

'But I didn't show you the door,' exclaimed Claude, beside himself. 'Come and see me, I beg of you. I shall be so glad!'

'All right, then, we'll come. I'll tell him to come, I give you my word—good-bye, old man, good-bye; I'm in a hurry.'

And Dubuche went off towards La Richaudière, whilst Claude watched his figure dwindle as he crossed the cultivated plain, until nothing remained but the shiny silk of his hat and the black spot of his coat. The young man returned home slowly, his heart bursting with nameless sadness. However, he said nothing about this meeting to Christine.

A week later she had gone to Faucheur's to buy a pound of vermicelli, and was lingering on her way back, gossiping with a neighbour, with her child on her arm, when a gentleman who alighted from the ferry-boat approached and asked her:

'Does not Monsieur Claude Lantier live near here?'

She was taken aback, and simply answered:

'Yes, monsieur; if you'll kindly follow me——'

They walked on side by side for about a hundred yards. The stranger, who seemed to know her, had glanced at her with a good-natured smile; but as she hurried on, trying to hide her embarrassment by looking very grave, he remained silent. She opened the door and showed the visitor into the studio, exclaiming:

'Claude, here is somebody for you.'

Then a loud cry rang out; the two men were already in each other's arms.

'Oh, my good old Pierre! how kind of you to come! And Dubuche?'

'He was prevented at the last moment by some business, and he sent me a telegram to go without him.'

'All right, I half expected it; but you are here. By the thunder of heaven, I am glad!'

And, turning towards Christine, who was smiling, sharing their delight:

'It's true, I didn't tell you. But the other day I met Dubuche, who was going up yonder, to the place where those monsters live——'

But he stopped short again, and then with a wild gesture shouted:

'I'm losing my wits, upon my word. You have never spoken to each other, and I leave you there like that. My dear, you see this gentleman? He's my old chum, Pierre Sandoz, whom I love like a brother. And you, my boy; let me introduce my wife. And you have got to give each other a kiss.'

Christine began to laugh outright, and tendered her cheek heartily. Sandoz had pleased her at once with his good-natured air, his sound friendship, the fatherly sympathy with which he looked at her. Tears of emotion came to her eyes as he kept both her hands in his, saying:

'It is very good of you to love Claude, and you must love each other always, for love is, after all, the best thing in life.'

Then, bending to kiss the little one, whom she had on her arm, he added: 'So there's one already!'

While Christine, preparing lunch, turned the house upside down, Claude retained Sandoz in the studio. In a few words he told him the whole of the story, who she was, how they had met each other, and what had led them to start housekeeping together, and he seemed to be surprised when his friend asked him why they did not get married. In faith, why? Because they had never even spoken about it, because they would certainly be neither more nor less happy; in short, it was a matter of no consequence whatever.

'Well,' said the other, 'it makes no difference to me; but, if she was a good and honest girl when she came to you, you ought to marry her.'

'Why, I'll marry her whenever she likes, old man. Surely I don't mean to leave her in the lurch!'

Sandoz then began to marvel at the studies hanging on the walls. Ha, the scamp had turned his time to good account! What accuracy of colouring! What a dash of real sunlight! And Claude, who listened to him, delighted, and laughing proudly, was just going to question him about the comrades in Paris, about what they were all doing, when Christine reappeared, exclaiming: 'Make haste, the eggs are on the table.'

They lunched in the kitchen, and an extraordinary lunch it was; a dish of fried gudgeons after the boiled eggs; then the beef from the soup of the night before, arranged in salad fashion, with potatoes, and a red herring. It was delicious; there was the pungent and appetising smell of the herring which Mélie had upset on the live embers, and the song of the coffee, as it passed, drop by drop, into the pot standing on the range; and when the dessert appeared—some strawberries just gathered, and a cream cheese from a neighbour's dairy—they gossiped and gossiped with their elbows squarely set on the table. In Paris? Well, to tell the truth, the comrades were doing nothing very original in Paris. And yet they were fighting their way, jostling each other in order to get first to the front. Of course, the absent ones missed their chance; it was as well to be there if one did not want to be altogether forgotten. But was not talent always talent? Wasn't a man always certain to get on with strength and will? Ah! yes, it was a splendid dream to live in the country, to accumulate master-pieces, and then, one day, to crush Paris by simply opening one's trunks.

In the evening, when Claude accompanied Sandoz to the station, the latter said to him:

'That reminds me, I wanted to tell you something. I think I am going to get married.'

The painter burst out laughing.

'Ah, you wag, now I understand why you gave me a lecture this morning.'

While waiting for the train to arrive, they went on chatting. Sandoz explained his ideas on marriage, which, in middle-class fashion, he considered an indispensable condition for good work, substantial orderly labour, among great modern producers. The theory of woman being a destructive creature—one who killed an artist, pounded his heart, and fed upon his brain—was a romantic idea against which facts protested. Besides, as for himself, he needed an affection that would prove the guardian of his tranquillity, a loving home, where he might shut himself up, so as to devôte his whole life to the huge work which he ever dreamt of. And he added that everything depended upon a man's choice—that he believed he had found what he had been looking for, an orphan, the daughter of petty tradespeople, without a penny, but handsome and intelligent. For the last six months, after resigning his clerkship, he had embraced journalism, by which he gained a larger income. He had just moved his mother to a small house at Batignolles, where the three would live together—two women to love him, and he strong enough to provide for the household.

'Get married, old man,' said Claude. 'One should act according to one's feelings. And good-bye, for here's your train. Don't forget your promise to come and see us again.'

Sandoz returned very often. He dropped in at odd times whenever his newspaper work allowed him, for he was still free, as he was not to be married till the autumn. Those were happy days, whole afternoons of mutual confidences when all their old determination to secure fame revived.

One day, while Sandoz was alone with Claude on an island of the Seine, both of them lying there with their eyes fixed on the sky, he told the painter of his vast ambition, confessed himself aloud.

'Journalism, let me tell you, is only a battle-ground. A man must live, and he has to fight to do so. Then, again, that wanton, the Press, despite the unpleasant phases of the profession, is after all a tremendous power, a resistless weapon in the hands of a fellow with convictions. But if I am obliged to avail myself of journalism, I don't mean to grow grey in it ! Oh, dear no ! And, besides, I've found what I wanted, a machine that'll crush one with work, something I'm going to plunge into, perhaps never to come out of it.'

Silence reigned amid the foliage, motionless in the dense heat. He resumed speaking more slowly and in jerky phrases :

'To study man as he is, not man the metaphysical puppet, but physiological man, whose nature is determined by his surroundings, and to show all his organism in full play. That's my idea! Is it not farcical that some should constantly and exclusively study the functions of the brain on the pretext that the brain alone is the noble part of our organism? Thought, thought, confound it all! thought is the product of the whole body. Let them try to make a brain think by itself alone; see what becomes of the nobleness of the brain when the stomach is ailing! No, no, it's idiotic; there is no philosophy nor science in it! We are positivists, evolutionists, and yet we are to stick to the literary lay-figures of classic times, and continue disentangling the tangled locks of pure reason! He who says psychologist says traitor to truth. Besides, psychology, physiology, it all signifies nothing. The one has become blended with the other, and both are but one nowadays, the mechanism of man leading to the sum total of his functions. Ah, the formula is there, our modern revolution has no other basis; it means the certain death of old society, the birth of a new one, and necessarily the upspringing of a new art in a new soil. Yes, people will see what literature will sprout forth for the coming century of science and democracy.'

His cry uprose and was lost in the immense vault of heaven. Not a breath stirred; there was nought but the silent ripple of the river past the willows. And Sandoz turned abruptly towards his companion, and said to him, face to face:

'So I have found what I wanted for myself. Oh, it isn't much, a little corner of study only, but one that should be sufficient for a man's life, even when his ambition is over-vast. I am going to take a family, and I shall study its members, one by one, whence they come, whither they go, how they re-act one upon another—in short, I shall have mankind in a small compass, the way in which mankind grows and behaves. On the other hand, I shall set my men and women in some given period of history, which will provide me with the necessary surroundings and circumstances,—you understand, eh? a series of books, fifteen, twenty books, episodes that will cling together, although each will have a separate framework, a series of novels with which I shall be able to build myself a house for my old days, if they don't crush me!'

He fell on his back again, spread out his arms on the grass, as if he wanted to sink into the earth, laughing and joking all the while.

'Oh, beneficent earth, take me unto thee, thou who art our

common mother, our only source of life! thou the eternal,
the immortal one, in whom circulates the soul of the world,
the sap that spreads even into the stones, and makes the trees
themselves our big, motionless brothers! Yes, I wish to
lose myself in thee; it is thou that I feel beneath my limbs,
clasping and inflaming me; thou alone shalt appear in my
work as the primary force, the means and the end, the
immense ark in which everything becomes animated with
the breath of every being!'

Though begun as mere pleasantry, with all the bombast of
lyrical emphasis, the invocation terminated in a cry of ardent
conviction, quivering with profound poetical emotion, and
Sandoz's eyes grew moist; and, to hide how much he felt
moved, he added, roughly, with a sweeping gesture that took
in the whole scene around:

'How idiotic it is! a soul for every one of us, when there
is that big soul there!'

Claude, who had disappeared amid the grass, had not
stirred. After a fresh spell of silence he summed up everything:

'That's it, old boy! Run them through, all of them.
Only you'll get trounced.'

'Oh,' said Sandoz, rising up and stretching himself, 'my
bones are too hard. They'll smash their own wrists. Let's
go back; I don't want to miss the train.'

Christine had taken a great liking to him, seeing him so
robust and upright in his doings, and she plucked up courage
at last to ask a favour of him: that of standing godfather to
Jacques. True, she never set foot in church now, but why
shouldn't the lad be treated according to custom? What
influenced her above all was the idea of giving the boy a
protector in this godfather, whom she found so serious and
sensible, even amidst the exuberance of his strength. Claude
expressed surprise, but gave his consent with a shrug of the
shoulders. And the christening took place; they found a
godmother, the daughter of a neighbour, and they made a
feast of it, eating a lobster, which was brought from Paris.

That very day, as they were saying good-bye, Christine
took Sandoz aside, and said, in an imploring voice:

'Do come again soon, won't you? He is bored.'

In fact, Claude had fits of profound melancholy. He
abandoned his work, went out alone, and prowled in spite of
himself about Faucheur's inn, at the spot where the ferry-boat

landed its passengers, as if ever expecting to see all Paris come ashore there. He had Paris on the brain; he went there every month and returned desolate, unable to work. Autumn came, then winter, a very wet and muddy winter, and he spent it in a state of morose torpidity, bitter even against Sandoz, who, having married in October, could no longer come to Bennecourt so often. Claude only seemed to wake up at each of the other's visits; deriving a week's excitement from them, and never ceasing to comment feverishly about the news brought from yonder. He, who formerly had hidden his regret of Paris, nowadays bewildered Christine with the way in which he chatted to her from morn till night about things she was quite ignorant of, and people she had never seen. When Jacques fell asleep, there were endless comments between the parents as they sat by the fireside. Claude grew passionate, and Christine had to give her opinion and to pronounce judgment on all sorts of matters.

Was not Gagnière an idiot for stultifying his brain with music, he who might have developed so conscientious a talent as a landscape painter? It was said that he was now taking lessons on the piano from a young lady—the idea, at his age! What did she, Christine, think of it? And Jory had been trying to get into the good graces of Irma Bécot again, ever since she had secured that little house in the Rue de Moscou! Christine knew those two; two jades who well went together, weren't they? But the most cunning of the whole lot was Fagerolles, to whom he, Claude, would tell a few plain truths and no mistake, when he met him. What! the turn-coat had competed for the Prix de Rome, which, of course, he had managed to miss. To think of it. That fellow did nothing but jeer at the School, and talked about knocking everything down, yet took part in official competitions! Ah, there was no doubt but that the itching to succeed, the wish to pass over one's comrades and be hailed by idiots, impelled some people to very dirty tricks. Surely Christine did not mean to stick up for him, eh? She was not sufficiently a philistine to defend him. And when she had agreed with everything Claude said, he always came back with nervous laughter to the same story—which he thought exceedingly comical—the story of Mahoudeau and Chaîne, who, between them, had killed little Jabouille, the husband of Mathilde, that dreadful herbalist woman. Yes, killed the poor consumptive fellow with kindness one evening when he had had a fainting fit, and when, on being called in by the woman, they had taken to rubbing him with so much vigour that he had remained dead in their hands.

And if Christine failed to look amused at all this, Claude rose up and said, in a churlish voice : ' Oh, you ; nothing will make you laugh—let's go to bed.'

He still adored her, but she no longer sufficed. Another torment had invincibly seized hold of him—the passion for art, the thirst for fame.

In the spring, Claude, who, with an affectation of disdain, had sworn he would never again exhibit, began to worry a great deal about the Salon. Whenever he saw Sandoz he questioned him about what the comrades were going to send. On the opening day he went to Paris and came back the same evening, stern and trembling. There was only a bust by Mahoudeau, said he, good enough, but of no importance. A small landscape by Gagnière, admitted among the ruck, was also of a pretty sunny tone. Then there was nothing else, nothing but Fagerolles' picture—an actress in front of her looking-glass painting her face. He had not mentioned it at first ; but he now spoke of it with indignant laughter. What a trickster that Fagerolles was ! Now that he had missed his prize he was no longer afraid to exhibit—he threw the School overboard ; but you should have seen how skilfully he managed it, what compromises he effected, painting in a style which aped the audacity of truth without possessing one original merit. And it would be sure to meet with success, the *bourgeois* were only too fond of being titillated while the artist pretended to hustle them. Ah ! it was time indeed for a true artist to appear in that mournful desert of a Salon, amid all the knaves and the fools. And, by heavens, what a place might be taken there !

Christine, who listened while he grew angry, ended by faltering :

' If you liked, we might go back to Paris.'

' Who was talking of that ? ' he shouted. ' One can never say a word to you but you at once jump to false conclusions.'

Six weeks afterwards he heard some news that occupied his mind for a week. His friend Dubuche was going to marry Mademoiselle Régine Margaillan, the daughter of the owner of La Richaudière. It was an intricate story, the details of which surprised and amused him exceedingly.

First of all, that cur Dubuche had managed to hook a medal for a design of a villa in a park, which he had exhibited ; that of itself was already sufficiently amusing, as it was said that the drawing had been set on its legs by his master, Dequersonnière, who had quietly obtained this medal for him from the jury over which he presided. Then the best of it was that this long-awaited reward had decided the marriage. Ah ! it would be nice trafficking if medals were now awarded to settle needy pupils in rich families ! Old Margaillan, like all parvenus, had set his heart upon having a son-in-law who could help him, by bringing authentic diplomas and fashionable clothes into the business ; and for some time past he had had his eyes on that young man, that pupil of the School of Arts, whose notes were excellent, who was so persevering, and so highly recommended by his masters. The medal aroused his enthusiasm ; he at once gave the young fellow his daughter and took him as a partner, who would soon increase his millions now lying idle, since he knew all that was needful in order to build properly. Besides, by this arrangement poor Régine, always low-spirited and ailing, would at least have a husband in perfect health.

'Well, a man must be fond of money to marry that wretched flayed kitten,' repeated Claude.

And as Christine compassionately took the girl's part, he added :

'But I am not down upon her. So much the better if the marriage does not finish her off. *She* is certainly not to be blamed, if her father, the ex-stonemason, had the stupid ambition to marry a girl of the middle-classes. Her father, you know, has the vitiated blood of generations of drunkards in his veins, and her mother comes of a stock in the last stages of degeneracy. Ah ! they may coin money, but that doesn't prevent them from being excrescences on the face of the earth ! '

He was growing ferocious, and Christine had to clasp him in her arms and kiss him, and laugh, to make him once more the good-natured fellow of earlier days. Then, having calmed down, he professed to understand things, saying that he approved of the marriages of his old chums. It was true enough, all three had taken wives unto themselves. How funny life was !

Once more the summer drew to an end ; it was the fourth spent at Bennecourt. In reality they could never be happier than now; life was peaceful and cheap in the depths of that village. Since they had been there they had never lacked money. Claude's thousand francs a year and the proceeds of the few pictures he had sold had sufficed for their wants; they had even put something by, and had bought some house linen. On the other hand, little Jacques, by now two years and a half old, got on admirably in the country. From morning till night he rolled about the garden, ragged and dirt-begrimed, but growing as he listed in robust ruddy health. His mother often did not know where to take hold of him when she wished to wash him a bit. However, when she saw him eat and sleep well she did not trouble much; she reserved her anxious affection for her big child of an artist, whose despondency filled her with anguish. The situation grew worse each day, and although they lived on peacefully without any cause for grief, they, nevertheless, drifted to melancholy, to a discomfort that showed itself in constant irritation.

It was all over with their first delights of country life. Their rotten boat, staved in, had gone to the bottom of the Seine. Besides, they did not even think of availing themselves of the skiff that the Faucheurs had placed at their disposal. The river bored them; they had grown too lazy to row. They repeated their exclamations of former times respecting certain delightful nooks in the islets, but without ever being tempted to return and gaze upon them. Even the walks by the river-side had lost their charm—one was broiled there in summer, and one caught cold there in winter. And as for the plateau, the vast stretch of land planted with apple trees that overlooked the village, it became like a distant country, something too far off for one to be silly enough to risk one's legs there. Their house also annoyed them—that barracks where they had to take their meals amid the greasy refuse of the kitchen, where their room seemed a meeting-place for the winds from every point of the compass. As a finishing stroke of bad luck, the apricots had failed that year, and the finest of the giant rose-bushes, which were very old, had been smitten with some canker or other and died. How sorely time and habit wore everything away! How eternal nature herself seemed to age amidst that satiated weariness. But the worst was that the painter himself was getting disgusted with the country, no longer finding a single subject to arouse his enthusiasm, but scouring the fields with a mournful tramp, as if the whole place were a void, whose life he had exhausted without leaving as much as an overlooked tree, an unforeseen effect of light to interest him. No, it was over, frozen, he should never again be able to paint anything worth looking at in that confounded country!

October came with its rain-laden sky. On one of the first wet evenings Claude flew into a passion because dinner was not ready. He turned that goose of a Mélie out of the house and clouted Jacques, who got between his legs. Whereupon, Christine, crying, kissed him and said:

'Let's go, oh, let us go back to Paris.'

He disengaged himself, and cried in an angry voice:

'What, again! Never! do you hear me?'

'Do it for my sake,' she said, warmly. 'It's I who ask it of you, it's I that you'll please.'

'Why, are you tired of being here, then?'

'Yes, I shall die if we stay here much longer; and, besides, I want you to work. I feel quite certain that your place is there. It would be a crime for you to bury yourself here any longer.'

'No, leave me!'

He was quivering. On the horizon Paris was calling him, the Paris of winter-tide which was being lighted up once more. He thought he could hear from where he stood the great efforts that his comrades were making, and, in fancy, he returned thither in order that they might not triumph without him, in order that he might become their chief again, since not one of them had strength or pride enough to be such. And amid this hallucination, amid the desire he felt to hasten to Paris, he yet persisted in refusing to do so, from a spirit of involuntary contradiction, which arose, though he could not account for it, from his very entrails. Was it the fear with which the bravest quivers, the mute struggle of happiness seeking to resist the fatality of destiny?

'Listen,' said Christine, excitedly. 'I shall get our boxes ready, and take you away.'

Five days later, after packing and sending their chattels to the railway, they started for Paris.

Claude was already on the road with little Jacques, when Christine fancied that she had forgotten something. She returned alone to the house; and finding it quite bare and empty, she burst out crying. It seemed as if something were being torn from her, as if she were leaving something of herself behind—what, she could not say. How willingly would she have remained! how ardent was her wish to live there always—she who had just insisted on that departure, that return to the city of passion where she scented the presence of a rival. However, she continued searching for what she lacked, and in front of the kitchen she ended by plucking a rose, a last rose, which the cold was turning brown. And then she slowly closed the gate upon the deserted garden.

VII

When Claude found himself once more on the pavement of Paris he was seized with a feverish longing for hubbub and motion, a desire to gad about, scour the whole city, and see his chums. He was off the moment he awoke, leaving Christine to get things shipshape by herself in the studio which they had taken in the Rue de Douai, near the Boulevard de Clichy. In this way, on the second day of his arrival, he dropped in at Mahoudeau's at eight o'clock in the morning, in the chill, grey November dawn which had barely risen.

However, the shop in the Rue du Cherche-Midi, which the sculptor still occupied, was open, and Mahoudeau himself, half asleep, with a white face, was shivering as he took down the shutters.

'Ah! it's you. The devil! you've got into early habits in the country. So it's settled—you are back for good?'

'Yes; since the day before yesterday.'

'That's all right. Then we shall see something of each other. Come in; it's sharp this morning.'

But Claude felt colder in the shop than outside. He kept the collar of his coat turned up, and plunged his hands deep into his pockets; shivering before the dripping moisture of the bare walls, the muddy heaps of clay, and the pools of water soddening the floor. A blast of poverty had swept into the place, emptying the shelves of the casts from the antique, and smashing stands and buckets, which were now held together with bits of rope. It was an abode of dirt and disorder, a mason's cellar going to rack and ruin. On the window of the door, besmeared with whitewash, there appeared in mockery, as it were, a large beaming sun, roughly drawn with thumb-strokes, and ornamented in the centre with a face, the mouth of which, describing a semicircle, seemed likely to burst with laughter.

'Just wait,' said Mahoudeau, 'a fire's being lighted. These confounded workshops get chilly directly, with the water from the covering cloths.'

At that moment, Claude, on turning round, noticed Chaîne on his knees near the stove, pulling the straw from the seat of an old stool to light the coals with. He bade him good-morning, but only elicited a muttered growl, without succeeding in making him look up.

'And what are you doing just now, old man?' he asked the sculptor.

'Oh! nothing of much account. It's been a bad year—worse than the last one, which wasn't worth a rap. There's a crisis in the church-statue business. Yes, the market for holy wares is bad, and, dash it, I've had to tighten my belt! Look, in the meanwhile, I'm reduced to this.'

He thereupon took the linen wraps off a bust, showing a long face still further elongated by whiskers, a face full of conceit and infinite imbecility.

'It's an advocate who lives near by. Doesn't he look repugnant, eh? And the way he worries me about being very careful with his mouth. However, a fellow must eat, mustn't he?'

He certainly had an idea for the Salon; an upright figure, a girl about to bathe, dipping her foot in the water, and shivering at its freshness with that slight shiver that renders a woman so adorable. He showed Claude a little model of it, which was already cracking, and the painter looked at it in silence, surprised and displeased at certain concessions he noticed in it: a sprouting of prettiness from beneath a persistent exaggeration of form, a natural desire to please, blended with a lingering tendency to the colossal. However, Mahoudeau began lamenting; an upright figure was no end of a job. He would want iron braces that cost money, and a modelling frame, which he had not got; in fact, a lot of appliances. So he would, no doubt, decide to model the figure in a recumbent attitude beside the water.

'Well, what do you say—what do you think of it?' he asked.

'Not bad,' answered the painter at last. 'A little bit senti-mental, in spite of the strapping limbs; but it'll all depend upon the execution. And put her upright, old man; upright, for there would be nothing in it otherwise.'

The stove was roaring, and Chaîne, still mute, rose up.

He prowled about for a minute, entered the dark back shop, where stood the bed that he shared with Mahoudeau, and then reappeared, his hat on his head, but more silent, it seemed, than ever. With his awkward peasant fingers he leisurely took up a stick of charcoal and then wrote on the wall: 'I am going to buy some tobacco; put some more coals in the stove.' And forthwith he went out.

Claude, who had watched him writing, turned to the other in amazement.

'What's up?'

'We no longer speak to one another; we write,' said the sculptor, quietly.

'Since when?'

'Since three months ago.'

'And you sleep together?'

'Yes.'

Claude burst out laughing. Ah! dash it all! they must have hard nuts. But what was the reason of this falling-out? Then Mahoudeau vented his rage against that brute of a Chaîne! Hadn't he, one night on coming home unexpectedly, found him treating Mathilde, the herbalist woman, to a pot of jam? No, he would never forgive him for treating himself in that dirty fashion to delicacies on the sly, while he, Mahoudeau, was half starving, and eating dry bread. The deuce! one ought to share and share alike.

And the grudge had now lasted for nearly three months without a break, without an explanation. They had arranged their lives accordingly; they had reduced their strictly necessary intercourse to a series of short phrases charcoaled on the walls. As for the rest, they lived as before, sharing the same bed in the back shop. After all, there was no need for so much talk in life, people managed to understand one another all the same.

While filling the stove, Mahoudeau continued to relieve his mind.

'Well, you may believe me if you like, but when a fellow's almost starving it isn't disagreeable to keep quiet. Yes, one gets numb amidst silence; it's like an inside coating that stills the gnawing of the stomach a bit. Ah, that Chaîne! You haven't a notion of his peasant nature. When he had spent his last copper without earning the fortune he expected by painting, he went into trade, a petty trade, which was to enable him to finish his studies. Isn't the fellow a sharp 'un, eh? And just listen to his plan. He had some olive oil sent to him from Saint-Firmin, his village, and then he tramped the streets and found a market for the oil among well-to-do families from Provence living in Paris. Unfortunately, it did not last. He is such a clod hopper that they showed him the door on all sides. And as there was a jar of oil left which nobody would buy, well, old man, we live upon it. Yes, on the days when we happen to have some bread we dip our bread into it.'

Thereupon he pointed to the jar standing in a corner of the shop. Some of the oil having been spilt, the wall and the floor were darkened by large greasy stains.

Claude left off laughing. Ah! misery, how discouraging it was! how could he show himself hard on those whom it crushed? He walked about the studio, no longer vexed at finding models weakened by concessions to middle-class taste; he even felt tolerant with regard to that hideous bust. But, all at once, he came across a copy that Chaîne had made at the Louvre, a Mantegna, which was marvellously exact in its dryness.

'Oh, the brute,' he muttered, 'it's almost the original; he's never done anything better than that. Perhaps his only fault is that he was born four centuries too late.'

Then, as the heat became too great, he took off his overcoat, adding:

'He's a long while fetching his tobacco.'

'Oh! his tobacco! I know what that means,' said Mahoudeau, who had set to work at his bust, finishing the whiskers; 'he has simply gone next door.'

'Oh! so you still see the herbalist?'

'Yes, she comes in and out.'

He spoke of Mathilde and Chaîne without the least show of anger, simply saying that he thought the woman crazy. Since little Jabouille's death she had become devout again, though this did not prevent her from scandalising the neighbourhood. Her business was going to wreck, and bankruptcy seemed impending. One night, the gas company having cut off the gas in default of payment, she had come to borrow some of their olive oil, which, after all, would not burn in the lamps. In short, it was quite a disaster; that mysterious shop, with its fleeting shadows of priests' gowns, its discreet confessional-like whispers, and its odour of sacristy incense, was gliding to the abandonment of ruin. And the wretchedness had reached such a point that the dried herbs suspended from the ceiling swarmed with spiders, while defunct leeches, which had already turned green, floated on the tops of the glass jars.

'Hallo, here he comes!' resumed the sculptor. 'You'll see her arrive at his heels.'

In fact, Chaîne came in. He made a great show of drawing a screw of tobacco from his pocket, then filled his pipe, and began to smoke in front of the stove, remaining obstinately silent, as if there were nobody present. And immediately afterwards Mathilde made her appearance like a neighbour who comes in to say 'Good morning.' Claude thought that she had grown still thinner, but her eyes were all afire, and her mouth was seemingly enlarged by the loss of two more teeth. The smell of aromatic herbs which she always carried in her uncombed hair seemed to have become rancid. There was no longer the sweetness of camomile, the freshness of aniseed; she filled the place with a horrid odour of peppermint that seemed to be her very breath.

'Already at work!' she exclaimed. 'Good morning.' And, without minding Claude, she kissed Mahoudeau. Then, after going to shake hands with the painter in her brazen way, she continued:

'What do you think? I've found a box of mallow root, and we will treat ourselves to it for breakfast. Isn't that nice of me now! We'll share.'

'Thanks,' said the sculptor, 'it makes my mouth sticky. I prefer to smoke a pipe.'

And, seeing that Claude was putting on his overcoat again, he asked: 'Are you going?'

'Yes. I want to get the rust off, and breathe the air of Paris a bit.'

All the same, he stopped for another few minutes watching Chaîne and Mathilde, who stuffed themselves with mallow root, each taking a piece by turns. And though he had been warned, he was again amazed when he saw Mahoudeau take up the stick of charcoal and write on the wall: 'Give me the tobacco you have shoved into your pocket.'

Without a word, Chaîne took out the screw and handed it to the sculptor, who filled his pipe.

'Well, I'll see you again soon,' said Claude.

'Yes, soon—at any rate, next Thursday, at Sandoz's.'

Outside, Claude gave an exclamation of surprise on jostling

a gentleman, who stood in front of the herbalist's peering into the shop.

'What, Jory! What are you doing there?'

Jory's big pink nose gave a sniff.

'I? Nothing. I was passing and looked in,' said he in dismay.

Then he decided to laugh, and, as if there were any one to overhear him, lowered his voice to ask:

'She is next door with our friends, isn't she? All right; let's be off, quick!'

And he took the painter with him, telling him all manner of strange stories of that creature Mathilde.

'But you used to say that she was frightful,' said Claude, laughing.

Jory made a careless gesture. Frightful? No, he had not gone as far as that. Besides, there might be something attractive about a woman even though she had a plain face. Then he expressed his surprise at seeing Claude in Paris, and, when he had been fully posted, and learned that the painter meant to remain there for good, he all at once exclaimed:

'Listen, I am going to take you with me. You must come to lunch with me at Irma's.'

The painter, taken aback, refused energetically, and gave as a reason that he wasn't even wearing a frock-coat.

'What does that matter? On the contrary, it makes it more droll. She'll be delighted. I believe she has a secret partiality for you. She is always talking about you to us. Come, don't be a fool. I tell you she expects me this morning, and we shall be received like princes.'

He did not relax his hold on Claude's arm, and they both continued their way towards the Madeleine, talking all the while. As a rule, Jory kept silent about his many love adventures, just as a drunkard keeps silent about his potations. But that morning he brimmed over with revelations, chaffed himself and owned to all sorts of scandalous things. After all he was delighted with existence, his affairs went apace. His miserly father had certainly cut off the supplies once more, cursing him for obstinately pursuing a scandalous career, but he did not care a rap for that now; he earned between seven and eight thousand francs a year by journalism, in which he was making his way as a gossipy leader writer and art critic. The noisy days of 'The Drummer,' the articles at a louis apiece, had been left far behind. He was getting steady, wrote for two widely circulated papers, and although, in his inmost heart he remained a sceptical voluptuary, a worshipper of success at any price, he was acquiring importance, and readers began to look upon his opinions as fiats. Swayed by hereditary meanness, he already invested money every month in petty speculations, which were only known to himself, for never had his vices cost him less than nowadays.

As he and Claude reached the Rue de Moscou, he told the painter that it was there that Irma Bécot now lived. ' Oh ! she is rolling in wealth,' said he, ' paying twenty thousand francs a year rent and talking of building a house which would cost half a million.' Then suddenly pulling up he exclaimed : ' Come, here we are ! In with you, quick ! '

But Claude still objected. His wife was waiting for him to lunch ; he really couldn't. And Jory was obliged to ring the bell, and then push him inside the hall, repeating that his excuse would not do ; for they would send the valet to the Rue de Douai to tell his wife. A door opened and they found themselves face to face with Irma Bécot, who uttered a cry of surprise as soon as she perceived the painter.

' What ! is it you, savage ? ' she said.

She made him feel at home at once by treating him like an old chum, and, in fact, he saw well enough that she did not even notice his old clothes. He himself was astonished, for he barely recognised her. In the course of four years she had become a different being ; her head was ' made up ' with all an actress's skill, her brow hidden beneath a mass of curly hair, and her face elongated, by a sheer effort of will, no doubt. And from a pale blonde she had become flaringly carrotty ; so that a Titianesque creature seemed to have sprung from the little urchin-like girl of former days. Her house, with all its show of luxury, still had its bald spots. What struck the painter were some good pictures on the walls, a Courbet, and, above all, an unfinished study by Delacroix. So this wild, wilful creature was not altogether a fool, although there was a frightful cat in coloured *biscuit* standing on a console in the drawing-room.

When Jory spoke of sending the valet to his friend's place, she exclaimed in great surprise :

' What ! you are married ? '

' Why, yes,' said Claude, simply.

She glanced at Jory, who smiled ; then she understood, and added

'Ah! But why did people tell me that you were a woman-hater? I'm awfully vexed, you know. I frightened you, don't you remember, eh? You still think me very ugly, don't you? Well, well, we'll talk about it all some other day.'

It was the coachman who went to the Rue de Douai with a note from Claude, for the valet had opened the door of the dining-room, to announce that lunch was served. The repast, a very delicate one, was partaken of in all propriety, under the icy stare of the servant. They talked about the great building works that were revolutionising Paris; and then discussed the price of land, like middle-class people with money to invest. But at dessert, when they were all three alone with the coffee and liqueurs, which they had decided upon taking there, without leaving the table, they gradually became animated, and dropped into their old familiar ways, as if they had met each other at the Café Baudequin.

'Ah, my lads,' said Irma, 'this is the only real enjoyment, to be jolly together and to snap one's fingers at other people.'

She was twisting cigarettes; she had just placed the bottle of chartreuse near her, and had begun to empty it, looking the while very flushed, and lapsing once more to her low street drollery.

'So,' continued Jory, who was apologising for not having sent her that morning a book she wanted, 'I was going to buy it last night at about ten o'clock, when I met Fagerolles——'

'You are telling a lie,' said she, interrupting him in a clear voice. And to cut short his protestations—'Fagerolles was here,' she added, 'so you see that you are telling a lie.'

Then, turning to Claude, 'No, it's too disgusting. You can't conceive what a liar he is. He tells lies like a woman, for the pleasure of it, for the merest trifle. Now, the whole of his story amounts simply to this: that he didn't want to spend three francs to buy me that book. Each time he was to have sent me a bouquet, he had dropped it under the wheels of a carriage, or there were no flowers to be had in all Paris. Ah! there's a fellow who only cares for himself, and no mistake.'

Jory, without getting in the least angry, tilted back his chair and sucked his cigar, merely saying with a sneer:

'Oh! if you see Fagerolles now——'

'Well, what of it?' she cried, becoming furious. 'It's no business of yours. I snap my fingers at your Fagerolles, do you hear? He knows very well that people don't quarrel with me. We know each other; we sprouted in the same crack between the paving-stones. Look here, whenever I like, I have only to hold up my finger, and your Fagerolles will be there on the floor, licking my feet.'

She was growing animated, and Jory thought it prudent to beat a retreat.

'*My* Fagerolles,' he muttered; '*my* Fagerolles.'

'Yes, *your* Fagerolles. Do you think that I don't see through you both? He is always patting you on the back, as he hopes to get articles out of you, and you affect generosity and calculate the advantage you'll derive if you write up an artist liked by the public.'

This time Jory stuttered, feeling very much annoyed on account of Claude being there. He did not attempt to defend himself, however, preferring to turn the quarrel into a joke. Wasn't she amusing, eh? when she blazed up like that, with her lustrous wicked eyes, and her twitching mouth, eager to indulge in vituperation?

'But remember, my dear, this sort of thing cracks your Titianesque "make-up,"' he added.

She began to laugh, mollified at once.

Claude, basking in physical comfort, kept on sipping small glasses of cognac one after another, without noticing it. During the two hours they had been there a kind of intoxication had stolen over them, the hallucinatory intoxication produced by liqueurs and tobacco smoke. They changed the conversation; the high prices that pictures were fetching came into question. Irma, who no longer spoke, kept a bit of extinguished cigarette between her lips, and fixed her eyes on the painter. At last she abruptly began to question him about his wife.

Her questions did not appear to surprise him; his ideas were going astray: 'She had just come from the provinces,' he said. 'She was in a situation with a lady, and was a very good and honest girl.'

'Pretty?'

'Why, yes, pretty.'

For a moment Irma relapsed into her reverie, then she said, smiling: 'Dash it all! How lucky you are!'

Then she shook herself, and exclaimed, rising from the table: 'Nearly three o'clock! Ah! my children, I must turn you out of the house. Yes, I have an appointment with an architect; I am going to see some ground near the Parc

Monceau, you know, in the new quarter which is being built.
I have scented a stroke of business in that direction.'

They had returned to the drawing-room. She stopped
before a looking-glass, annoyed at seeing herself so flushed.

'It's about that house, isn't it?' asked Jory. 'You have
found the money, then?'

She brought her hair down over her brow again, then
with her hands seemed to efface the flush on her cheeks;
elongated the oval of her face, and rearranged her tawny head,
which had all the charm of a work of art; and finally, turning
round, she merely threw Jory these words by way of reply:
'Look! there's my Titianesque effect back again.'

She was already, amidst their laughter, edging them
towards the hall, where once more, without speaking, she
took Claude's hands in her own, her glance yet again diving
into the depths of his eyes. When he reached the street he
felt uncomfortable. The cold air dissipated his intoxication;
he remorsefully reproached himself for having spoken of
Christine in that house, and swore to himself that he would
never set foot there again.

Indeed, a kind of shame deterred Claude from going home,
and when his companion, excited by the luncheon and feeling
inclined to loaf about, spoke of going to shake hands with
Bongrand, he was delighted with the idea, and both made their
way to the Boulevard de Clichy.

For the last twenty years Bongrand had there occupied a
very large studio, in which he had in no wise sacrificed to the
tastes of the day, to that magnificence of hangings and nick-
nacks with which young painters were then beginning to
surround themselves. It was the bare, greyish studio of
the old style, exclusively ornamented with sketches by the
master, which hung there unframed, and in close array like
the votive offerings in a chapel. The only tokens of elegance
consisted of a cheval glass, of the First Empire style, a large
Norman wardrobe, and two arm-chairs upholstered in Utrecht
velvet, and threadbare with usage. In one corner, too, a
bearskin which had lost nearly all its hair covered a large
couch. However, the artist had retained since his youthful
days, which had been spent in the camp of the Romanticists,
the habit of wearing a special costume, and it was in flowing
trousers, in a dressing-gown secured at the waist by a silken
cord, and with his head covered with a priest's skull-cap, that
he received his visitors.

He came to open the door himself, holding his palette and brushes.

'So here you are! It was a good idea of yours to come! I was thinking about you, my dear fellow. Yes, I don't know who it was that told me of your return, but I said to myself that it wouldn't be long before I saw you.'

The hand that he had free grasped Claude's in a burst of sincere affection. He then shook Jory's, adding:

'And you, young pontiff; I read your last article, and thank you for your kind mention of myself. Come in, come in, both of you! You don't disturb me; I'm taking advantage of the daylight to the very last minute, for there's hardly time to do anything in this confounded month of November.'

He had resumed his work, standing before his easel, on which there was a small canvas, which showed two women, mother and daughter, sitting sewing in the embrasure of a sunlit window. The young fellows stood looking behind him.

'Exquisite,' murmured Claude, at last.

Bongrand shrugged his shoulders without turning round.

'Pooh! A mere nothing at all. A fellow must occupy his time, eh? I did this from life at a friend's house, and I am cleaning it a bit.'

'But it's perfect—it is a little gem of truth and light,' replied Claude, warming up. 'And do you know, what over-comes me is its simplicity, its very simplicity.'

On hearing this the painter stepped back and blinked his eyes, looking very much surprised.

'You think so? It really pleases you? Well, when you came in I was just thinking it was a foul bit of work. I give you my word, I was in the dumps, and felt convinced that I hadn't a scrap of talent left.'

His hands shook, his stalwart frame trembled as with the agony of travail. He rid himself of his palette, and came back towards them, his arms sawing the air, as it were; and this artist, who had grown old amidst success, who was assured of ranking in the French School, cried to them:

'It surprises you, eh? but there are days when I ask myself whether I shall be able to draw a nose correctly. Yes, with every one of my pictures I still feel the emotion of a beginner; my heart beats, anguish parches my mouth—in fact, I funk abominably. Ah! you youngsters, you think you know what funk means; but you haven't as much as a notion of it, for if you fail with one work, you get quits by trying to do something better. Nobody is down upon you; whereas we, the veterans, who have given our measure, who are obliged to keep up to the level previously attained, if not to surpass it, we mustn't weaken under penalty of rolling down into the common grave. And so, Mr. Celebrity, Mr. Great Artist, wear out your brains, consume yourself in striving to climb higher, still higher, ever higher, and if you happen to kick your heels on the summit, think yourself lucky! Wear your heels out in kicking them up as long as possible, and if you feel that you are declining, why, make an end of yourself by rolling down amid the death rattle of your talent, which is no lor ver suited to the period; roll down forgetful of such of your works as are destined to immortality, and in despair at your powerless efforts to create still further!'

His full voice had risen to a final outburst like thunder, and his broad flushed face wore an expression of anguish. He strode about, and continued, as if carried away, in spite of himself, by a violent whirlwind:

'I have told you a score of times that one was for ever beginning one's career afresh, that joy did not consist in having reached the summit, but in the climbing, in the gaiety of scaling the heights. Only, you don't understand, you cannot understand; a man must have passed through it. Just remember! You hope for everything, you dream of everything; it is the hour of boundless illusions, and your legs are so strong that the most fatiguing roads seem short; you are consumed with such an appetite for glory, that the first petty successes fill your mouth with a delicious taste. What a feast it will be when you are able to gratify ambition to satiety! You have nearly reached that point, and you look right cheerfully on your scratches! Well, the thing is accomplished; the summit has been gained; it is now a question of remaining there. Then a life of abomination begins; you have exhausted intoxication, and you have discovered that it does not last long enough, that it is not worth the struggle it has cost, and that the dregs of the cup taste bitter. There is nothing left to be learnt, no new sensation to be felt; pride has had its allowance of fame; you know that you have produced your greatest works; and you are surprised that they did not bring keener enjoyment with them. From that moment the horizon becomes void; no fresh hope inflames you; there is nothing left but to die.

And yet you still cling on, you won't admit that it's all up
with you, you obstinately persist in trying to produce—just
as old men cling to love with painful, ignoble efforts. Ah !
a man ought to have the courage and the pride to strangle
himself before his last masterpiece ! '

While he spoke he seemed to have increased in stature,
reaching to the elevated ceiling of the studio, and shaken by
such keen emotion that the tears started to his eyes. And
he dropped into a chair before his picture, asking with
the anxious look of a beginner who has need of encourage-
ment :

'Then this really seems to you all right ? I myself no
longer dare to believe anything. My unhappiness springs
from the possession of both too much and not enough critical
acumen. The moment I begin a sketch I exalt it, then, if
it's not successful, I torture myself. It would be better not
to know anything at all about it, like that brute Chambouvard, or else to see very clearly into the business and
then give up painting. . . . Really now, you like this little
canvas ? '

Claude and Jory remained motionless, astonished and embarrassed by those tokens of the intense anguish of art in its
travail. Had they come at a moment of crisis, that this
master thus groaned with pain, and consulted them like
comrades ? The worst was that they had been unable to dis-
guise some hesitation when they found themselves under the
gaze of the ardent, dilated eyes with which he implored them
—eyes in which one could read the hidden fear of decline.
They knew current rumours well enough ; they agreed with
the opinion that since his ' Village Wedding ' the painter had
produced nothing equal to that famous picture. Indeed,
after maintaining something of that standard of excellence in
a few works, he was now gliding into a more scientific, drier
manner. Brightness of colour was vanishing ; each work
seemed to show a decline. However, these were things not
to be said ; so Claude, when he had recovered his composure,
exclaimed :

' You never painted anything so powerful ! '

Bongrand looked at him again, straight in the eyes.
Then he turned to his work, in which he became absorbed,
making a movement with his herculean arms, as if he were
breaking every bone of them to lift that little canvas which
was so very light. And he muttered to himself : ' Confound it !

how heavy it is! Never mind, I'll die at it rather than show a falling-off.'

He took up his palette and grew calm at the first stroke of the brush, while bending his manly shoulders and broad neck, about which one noticed traces of peasant build remaining amid the *bourgeois* refinement contributed by the crossing of classes of which he was the outcome.

Silence had ensued, but Jory, his eyes still fixed on the picture, asked:

'Is it sold?'

Bongrand replied leisurely, like the artist who works when he likes without care of profit:

'No; I feel paralysed when I've a dealer at my back.'

And, without pausing in his work, he went on talking, growing waggish.

'Ah! people are beginning to make a trade of painting now. Really and truly I have never seen such a thing before, old as I am getting. For instance, you, Mr. Amiable Journalist, what a quantity of flowers you fling to the young ones in that article in which you mentioned me! There were two or three youngsters spoken of who were simply geniuses, nothing less.'

Jory burst out laughing.

'Well, when a fellow has a paper, he must make use of it. Besides, the public likes to have great men discovered for it.'

'No doubt, public stupidity is boundless, and I am quite willing that you should trade on it. Only I remember the first starts that we old fellows had. Dash it! We were not spoiled like that, I can tell you. We had ten years' labour and struggle before us ere we could impose on people a picture the size of your hand; whereas nowadays the first hobbledehoy who can stick a figure on its legs makes all the trumpets of publicity blare. And what kind of publicity is it? A hullabaloo from one end of France to the other, sudden reputations that shoot up of a night, and burst upon one like thunderbolts, amid the gaping of the throng. And I say nothing of the works themselves, those works announced with salvoes of artillery, awaited amid a delirium of impatience, maddening Paris for a week, and then falling into everlasting oblivion!'

'This is an indictment against journalism,' said Jory, who had stretched himself on the couch and lighted another cigar.

'There is a great deal to be said for and against it, but devil a bit, a man must keep pace with the times.'

Bongrand shook his head, and then started off again, amid a tremendous burst of mirth :

'No! no! one can no longer throw off the merest daub without being hailed as a young "master." Well, if you only knew how your young masters amuse me!'

But as if these words had led to some other ideas, he cooled down, and turned towards Claude to ask this question : 'By the way, have you seen Fagerolles' picture?'

'Yes,' said the young fellow, quietly.

They both remained looking at each other : a restless smile had risen to their lips, and Bongrand eventually added :

'There's a fellow who pillages you right and left.'

Jory, becoming embarrassed, had lowered his eyes, asking himself whether he should defend Fagerolles. He, no doubt, concluded that it would be profitable to do so, for he began to praise the picture of the actress in her dressing-room, an engraving of which was then attracting a great deal of notice in the print-shops. Was not the subject a really modern one? Was it not well painted, in the bright clear tone of the new school? A little more vigour might, perhaps, have been desirable ; but every one ought to be left to his own temperament. And besides, refinement and charm were not so common by any means, nowadays.

Bending over his canvas, Bongrand, who, as a rule, had nothing but paternal praise for the young ones, shook and made a visible effort to avoid an outburst. The explosion took place, however, in spite of himself.

'Just shut up, eh? about your Fagerolles! Do you think us greater fools than we really are? There! you see the great painter here present. Yes; I mean the young gentleman in front of you. Well, the whole trick consists in pilfering his originality, and dishing it up with the wishy-washy sauce of the School of Arts! Quite so! you select a modern subject, and you paint in the clear bright style, only you adhere to correctly commonplace drawing, to all the habitual pleasing style of composition—in short, to the formula which is taught over yonder for the pleasure of the middle-classes. And you souse all that with deftness, that execrable deftness of the fingers which would just as well carve cocoanuts, the flowing, pleasant deftness that begets success, and which ought to be punished with penal servitude, do you hear?'

He brandished his palette and brushes aloft, in his clenched fists.

'You are severe,' said Claude, feeling embarrassed. 'Fagerolles shows delicacy in his work.'

'I have been told,' muttered Jory, mildly, 'that he has just signed a very profitable agreement with Naudet.'

That name, thrown haphazard into the conversation, had the effect of once more soothing Bongrand, who repeated, shrugging his shoulders :

'Ah! Naudet—ah! Naudet.'

And he greatly amused the young fellows by telling them about Naudet, with whom he was well acquainted. He was a dealer, who, for some few years, had been revolutionising the picture trade. There was nothing of the old fashion about his style—the greasy coat and keen taste of Papa Malgras, the watching for the pictures of beginners, bought at ten francs, to be resold at fifteen, all the little humdrum comedy of the connoisseur, turning up his nose at a coveted canvas in order to depreciate it, worshipping painting in his inmost heart, and earning a meagre living by quickly and prudently turning over his petty capital. No, no ; the famous Naudet had the appearance of a nobleman, with a fancy-pattern jacket, a diamond pin in his scarf, and patent-leather boots ; he was well pomaded and brushed, and lived in fine style, with a livery-stable carriage by the month, a stall at the opera, and his particular table at Bignon's. And he showed himself wherever it was the correct thing to be seen. For the rest, he was a speculator, a Stock Exchange gambler, not caring one single rap about art. But he unfailingly scented success, he guessed what artist ought to be properly started, not the one who seemed likely to develop the genius of a great painter, furnishing food for discussion, but the one whose deceptive talent, set off by a pretended display of audacity, would command a premium in the market. And that was the way in which he revolutionised that market, giving the amateur of taste the cold shoulder, and only treating with the moneyed amateur, who knew nothing about art, but who bought a picture as he might buy a share at the Stock Exchange, either from vanity or with the hope that it would rise in value.

At this stage of the conversation Bongrand, very jocular by nature, and with a good deal of the mummer about him, began to enact the scene. Enter Naudet in Fagerolles' studio.

'" You've real genius, my dear fellow. Your last picture is sold, then? For how much?"

'" For five hundred francs."

'" But you must be mad; it was worth twelve hundred. And this one which you have by you—how much?"

'" Well, my faith, I don't know. Suppose we say twelve hundred?"

'" What are you talking about? Twelve hundred francs! You don't understand me, then, my boy; it's worth two thousand. I take it at two thousand. And from this day forward you must work for no one but myself—for me, Naudet. Good-bye, good-bye, my dear fellow; don't overwork yourself —your fortune is made. I have taken it in hand." Wherewith he goes off, taking the picture with him in his carriage. He trots it round among his amateurs, among whom he has spread the rumour that he has just discovered an extraordinary painter. One of the amateurs bites at last, and asks the price.

'" Five thousand."

'" What, five thousand francs for the picture of a man whose name hasn't the least notoriety? Are you playing the fool with me?"

'" Look here, I'll make you a proposal; I'll sell it you for five thousand francs, and I'll sign an agreement to take it back in a twelvemonth at six thousand, if you no longer care for it."

'Of course the amateur is tempted. What does he risk after all? In reality it's a good speculation, and so he buys. After that Naudet loses no time, but disposes in a similar manner of nine or ten paintings by the same man during the course of the year. Vanity gets mingled with the hope of gain, the prices go up, the pictures get regularly quoted, so that when Naudet returns to see his amateur, the latter, instead of returning the picture, buys another one for eight thousand francs. And the prices continue to go up, and painting degenerates into something shady, a kind of gold mine situated on the heights of Montmartre, promoted by a number of bankers, and around which there is a constant battle of bank-notes.'

Claude was growing indignant, but Jory thought it all very clever, when there came a knock at the door. Bongrand, who went to open it, uttered a cry of surprise.

'Naudet, as I live! We were just talking about you.'

Naudet, very correctly dressed, without a speck of mud on him, despite the horrible weather, bowed and came in with the reverential politeness of a man of society entering a church.

'Very pleased—feel flattered, indeed, dear master. And you only spoke well of me, I'm sure of it.'

'Not at all, Naudet, not at all,' said Bongrand, in a quiet tone. 'We were saying that your manner of trading was giving us a nice generation of artists—tricksters crossed with dishonest business-men.'

Naudet smiled, without losing his composure.

'The remark is harsh, but so charming! Never mind, never mind, dear master, nothing that you say offends me.'

And, dropping into ecstasy before the picture of the two little women at needlework :

'Ah! Good heavens, I didn't know this, it's a little marvel! Ah! that light, that broad substantial treatment! One has to go back to Rembrandt for anything like it; yes, to Rembrandt! Look here, I only came in to pay my respects, but I thank my lucky star for having brought me here. Let us do a little bit of business. Let me have this gem. Anything you like to ask for it—I'll cover it with gold.'

One could see Bongrand's back shake, as if his irritation were increasing at each sentence. He curtly interrupted the dealer.

'Too late ; it's sold.'

'Sold, you say. And you cannot annul your bargain? Tell me, at any rate, to whom it's sold? I'll do everything, I'll give anything. Ah! What a horrible blow! Sold, are you quite sure of it? Suppose you were offered double the sum?'

'It's sold, Naudet. That's enough, isn't it?

However, the dealer went on lamenting. He remained for a few minutes longer, going into raptures before other sketches, while making the tour of the studio with the keen glances of a speculator in search of luck. When he realised that his time was badly chosen, and that he would be able to take nothing away with him, he went off, bowing with an air of gratitude, and repeating remarks of admiration as far as the landing.

As soon as he had gone, Jory, who had listened to the conversation with surprise, ventured to ask a question :

'But you told us, I thought—— It isn't sold, is it?'

Without immediately answering, Bongrand went back to his picture. Then, in his thundering voice, resuming in one cry all his hidden suffering, the whole of the nascent struggle within him which he dared not avow, he said :

' He plagues me. He shall never have anything of mine ! Let him go and buy of Fagerolles ! '

A quarter of an hour later, Claude and Jory also said good-bye, leaving Bongrand struggling with his work in the waning daylight. Once outside, when the young painter had left his companion, he did not at once return home to the Rue de Douai, in spite of his long absence. He still felt the want of walking about, of surrendering himself up to that great city of Paris, where the meetings of one single day sufficed to fill his brain ; and this need of motion made him wander about till the black night had fallen, through the frozen mud of the streets, beneath the gas-lamps, which, lighted up one by one, showed like nebulous stars amidst the fog.

Claude impatiently awaited the Thursday when he was to dine at Sandoz's, for the latter, immutable in his habits, still invited his cronies to dinner once a week. All those who chose could come, their covers were laid. His marriage, his change of life, the ardent literary struggle into which he had thrown himself, made no difference ; he kept to his day ' at home,' that Thursday which dated from the time he had left college, from the time they had all smoked their first pipes. As he himself expressed it, alluding to his wife, there was only one chum more.

' I say, old man,' he had frankly said to Claude, ' I'm greatly worried——'

' What about ? '

' Why, about inviting Madame Christine. There are a lot of idiots, a lot of philistines watching me, who would say all manner of things——'

' You are quite right, old man. But Christine herself would decline to come. Oh ! we understand the position very well. I'll come alone, depend upon it.'

At six o'clock, Claude started for Sandoz's place in the Rue Nollet, in the depths of Batignolles, and he had no end of trouble in finding the small pavilion which his friend had rented. First of all he entered a large house facing the street, and applied to the doorkeeper, who made him cross three successive courtyards ; then he went down a passage, between two other buildings, descended some steps, and tumbled upon the iron gate of a small garden. That was the spot, the pavilion was there at the end of a path. But it was so dark, and he had nearly broken his legs coming down the steps, that he dared not venture any further, the more so as a huge dog was barking furiously. At last he heard the voice of Sandoz, who was coming forward and trying to quiet the dog.

'Ah, it's you! We are quite in the country, aren't we? We are going to set up a lantern, so that our company may not break their necks. Come in, come in! Will you hold your noise, you brute of a Bertrand? Don't you see that it's a friend, fool?'

Thereupon the dog accompanied them as far as the pavilion, wagging his tail and barking joyously. A young servant-girl had come out with a lantern, which she fastened to the gate, in order to light up the breakneck steps. In the garden there was simply a small central lawn, on which there stood a large plum tree, diffusing a shade around that rotted the grass; and just in front of the low house, which showed only three windows, there stretched an arbour of Virginia creeper, with a brand-new seat shining there as an ornament amid the winter showers, pending the advent of the summer sun.

'Come in,' repeated Sandoz.

On the right-hand side of the hall he ushered Claude into the parlour, which he had turned into a study. The dining-room and kitchen were on the left. Upstairs, his mother, who was now altogether bedridden, occupied the larger room, while he and his wife contented themselves with the other one, and a dressing-room that parted the two. That was the whole place, a real cardboard box, with rooms like little drawers separated by partitions as thin as paper. Withal, it was the abode of work and hope, vast in comparison with the ordinary garrets of youth, and already made bright by a beginning of comfort and luxury.

'There's room here, eh?' he exclaimed. 'Ah! it's a jolly sight more comfortable than the Rue d'Enfer. You see that I've a room to myself. And I have bought myself an oaken writing-table, and my wife made me a present of that dwarf palm in that pot of old Rouen ware. Isn't it swell, eh?'

His wife came in at that very moment. Tall, with a pleasant, tranquil face and beautiful brown hair, she wore a large white apron over her plainly made dress of black poplin; for although they had a regular servant, she saw to the cooking, for she was proud of certain of her dishes, and she put the household on a footing of middle-class cleanliness and love of cheer.

She and Claude became old chums at once.

'Call him Claude, my darling. And you, old man, call her Henriette. No madame nor monsieur, or I shall fine you five sous each time.'

They laughed, and she scampered away, being wanted in the kitchen to look after a southern dish, a *bouillabaisse*, with which she wished to surprise the Plassans friend. She had obtained the recipe from her husband himself, and had become marvellously deft at it, so he said.

'Your wife is charming,' said Claude, 'and I see she spoils you.'

But Sandoz, seated at his table, with his elbows among such pages of the book he was working at as he had written that morning, began to talk of the first novel of his series, which he had published in October. Ah! they had treated his poor book nicely! It had been a throttling, a butchering, all the critics yelling at his heels, a broadside of imprecations, as if he had murdered people in a wood. He himself laughed at it, excited rather than otherwise, for he had sturdy shoulders and the quiet bearing of a toiler who knows what he's after. Mere surprise remained to him at the profound lack of intelligence shown by those fellows the critics, whose articles, knocked off on the corner of some table, bespattered him with mud, without appearing as much as to guess at the least of his intentions. Everything was flung into the same slop-pail of abuse: his studies of physiological man; the important part he assigned to circumstances and surroundings; his allusions to nature, ever and ever creating; in short, life—entire, universal life—existent through all the animal world without there really being either high or low, beauty or ugliness; he was insulted, too, for his boldness of language, for the conviction he expressed that all things ought to be said, that there are abominable expressions which become necessary, like branding irons, and that a language emerges enriched from such strength-giving baths. He easily granted their anger, but he would at least have liked them to do him the honour of understanding him and getting angry at his audacity, not at the idiotic, filthy designs of which he was accused.

'Really,' he continued, 'I believe that the world still contains more idiots than downright spiteful people. They are enraged with me on account of the form I give to my productions, the written sentences, the similes, the very life of my style. Yes, the middle-classes fairly split with hatred of literature ! '

Then he became silent, having grown sad.

' Never mind,' said Claude, after an interval, ' you are happy, you at least work, you produce——'

Sandoz had risen from his seat with a gesture of sudden pain.

' True, I work. I work out my books to their last pages— But if you only knew, if I told you amidst what discouragement, amidst what torture ! Won't those idiots take it into their heads to accuse me of pride ! I, whom the imperfection of my work pursues even in my sleep—I, who never look over the pages of the day before, lest I should find them so execrable that I might afterwards lack the courage to continue. Oh, I work, no doubt, I work ! I go on working, as I go on living, because I am born to it, but I am none the gayer on account of it. I am never satisfied ; there is always a great collapse at the end.'

He was interrupted by a loud exclamation outside, and Jory appeared, delighted with life, and relating that he had just touched up an old article in order to have the evening to himself. Almost immediately afterwards Gagnière and Mahoudeau, who had met at the door, came in conversing together. The former, who had been absorbed for some months in a theory of colours, was ex   ining his system to the other.

' I paint my shade in,' he continued, as if in a dream ' The red of the flag loses its brightness and becomes yellowish because it stands out against the blue of the sky, the complementary shade of which—orange—blends with red——'

Claude, interested at once, was already questioning him when the servant brought in a telegram.

' All right,' said Sandoz, ' it's from Dubuche, who apologises ; he promises to come and surprise us at about eleven o'clock.'

At this moment Henriette threw the door wide open, and personally announced that dinner was ready. She had doffed her white apron, and cordially shook hands, as hostess, with all of them. ' Take your seats ! take your seats ! ' was her cry. It was half-past seven already, the *bouillabaisse* could not wait. Jory, having observed that Fagerolles had sworn to him that he would come, they would not believe it. Fagerolles was getting ridiculous with his habit of aping the great artist overwhelmed with work!

The dining-room into which they passed was so small that, in order to make room for a piano, a kind of alcove had been made out of a dark closet which had formerly served for the accommodation of crockery. However, on grand occasions half a score of people still gathered round the table, under the white porcelain hanging lamp, but this was only accomplished by blocking up the sideboard, so that the servant could not even pass to take a plate from it. However, it was the mistress of the house who carved, while the master took his place facing her, against the blockaded sideboard, in order to hand round whatever things might be required.

Henriette had placed Claude on her right hand, Mahoudeau on her left, while Gagnière and Jory were seated next to Sandoz.

'Françoise,' she called, 'give me the slices of toast. They are on the range.'

And the girl having brought the toast, she distributed two slices to each of them, and was beginning to ladle the *bouillabaisse* into the plates, when the door opened once more.

'Fagerolles at last!' she said. 'I have given your seat to Mahoudeau. Sit down there, next to Claude.'

He apologised with an air of courtly politeness, by alleging a business appointment. Very elegantly dressed, tightly buttoned up in clothes of an English cut, he had the carriage of a man about town, relieved by the retention of a touch of artistic free-and-easiness. Immediately on sitting down he grasped his neighbour's hand, affecting great delight.

'Ah, my old Claude! I have for such a long time wanted to see you. A score of times I intended going after you into the country; but then, you know, circumstances——'

Claude, feeling uncomfortable at these protestations, endeavoured to meet them with a like cordiality. But Henriette, who was still serving, saved the situation by growing impatient.

'Come, Fagerolles, just answer me. Do you wish two slices of toast?'

'Certainly, madame, two, if you please. I am very fond of *bouillabaisse*. Besides, yours is delicious, a marvel!'

In fact, they all went into raptures over it, especially Jory

and Mahoudeau, who declared they had never tasted anything
better at Marseilles ; so much so, that the young wife, delighted
and still flushed with the heat of the kitchen, her ladle in her
hand, had all she could do to refill the plates held out to her ;
and, indeed, she rose up and ran in person to the kitchen to
fetch the remains of the soup, for the servant-girl was losing
her wits.

'Come, eat something,' said Sandoz to her. 'We'll wait
well enough till you have done.'

But she was obstinate and remained standing.

'Never mind me. You had better pass the bread—yes,
there, behind you on the sideboard. Jory prefers crumb, which
he can soak in the soup.'

Sandoz rose in his turn and assisted his wife, while the
others chaffed Jory on his love for sops. And Claude, moved
by the pleasant cordiality of his hosts, and awaking, as it were,
from a long sleep, looked at them all, asking himself whether
he had only left them on the previous night, or whether four
years had really elapsed since he had dined with them one
Thursday. They were different, however ; he felt them to be
changed : Mahoudeau soured by misery, Jory wrapt up in his
own pleasures, Gagnière more distant, with his thoughts
elsewhere. And it especially seemed to him that Fagerolles
was chilly, in spite of his exaggerated cordiality of manner.
No doubt their features had aged somewhat amid the wear
and tear of life ; but it was not only that which he noticed, it
seemed to him also as if there was a void between them ; he
beheld them isolated and estranged from each other, although
they were seated elbow to elbow in close array round the
table. Then the surroundings were different ; nowadays,
a woman brought her charm to bear on them, and calmed
them by her presence. Then why did he, face to face with
the irrevocable current of things, which die and are renewed,
experience that sensation of beginning something over again
—why was it that he could have sworn that he had been
seated at that same place only last Thursday ? At last he
thought he understood. It was Sandoz who had not changed,
who remained as obstinate as regards his habits of friendship,
as regards his habits of work, as radiant at being able to
receive his friends at the board of his new home as he had
formerly been, when sharing his frugal bachelor fare with
them. A dream of eternal friendship made him changeless.
Thursdays similar one to another followed and followed on

until the furthest stages of their lives. All of them were eternally together, all started at the self-same hour, and participated in the same triumph!

Sandoz must have guessed the thought that kept Claude mute, for he said to him across the table, with his frank, youthful smile:

' Well, old man, here you are again! Ah, confound it! we missed you sorely. But, you see, nothing is changed; we are all the same—aren't we, all of you?'

They answered by nodding their heads—no doubt, no doubt!

' With this difference,' he went on, beaming—' with this difference, that the cookery is somewhat better than in the Rue d'Enfer! What a lot of messes I did make you swallow!'

After the *bouillabaisse* there came a *civet* of hare; and a roast fowl and salad terminated the dinner. But they sat for a long time at table, and the dessert proved a protracted affair, although the conversation lacked the fever and violence of yore. Every one spoke of himself and ended by relapsing into silence on perceiving that the others did not listen to him. With the cheese, however, when they had tasted some burgundy, a sharp little growth, of which the young couple had ordered a cask out of the profits of Sandoz's first novel, their voices rose to a higher key, and they all grew animated.

' So you have made an arrangement with Naudet, eh?' asked Mahoudeau, whose bony cheeks seemed to have grown yet more hollow. ' Is it true that he guarantees you fifty thousand francs for the first year?'

Fagerolles replied, with affected carelessness, ' Yes, fifty thousand francs. But nothing is settled; I'm thinking it over. It is hard to engage oneself like that. I am not going to do anything precipitately.'

' The deuce!' muttered the sculptor; ' you are hard to please. For twenty francs a day I'd sign whatever you like.'

They all now listened to Fagerolles, who posed as being wearied by his budding success. He still had the same good-looking, disturbing hussy-like face, but the fashion in which he wore his hair and the cut of his beard lent him an appearance of gravity. Although he still came at long intervals to Sandoz's, he was separating from the band; he showed himself on the boulevards, frequented the cafés and newspaper offices—all the places where a man can advertise himself and make useful acquaintances. These were tactics of his own, a determination to carve his own victory apart from the others; the smart idea that if he wished to triumph he ought to have nothing more in common with those revolutionists, neither dealer, nor connections, nor habits. It was even said that he had interested the female element of two or three drawing-rooms in his success, not in Jory's style, but like a vicious fellow who rises superior to his passions, and is content to adulate superannuated baronesses.

Just then Jory, in view of lending importance to himself, called Fagerolles' attention to a recently published article; he pretended that he had made Fagerolles just as he pretended that he had made Claude. ' I say, have you read that article of Vernier's about yourself? There's another fellow who repeats my ideas!'

' Ah, he does get articles, and no mistake!' sighed Mahoudeau.

Fagerolles made a careless gesture, but he smiled with secret contempt for all those poor beggars who were so utterly deficient in shrewdness that they clung, like simpletons, to their crude style, when it was so easy to conquer the crowd. Had it not sufficed for him to break with them, after pillaging them, to make his own fortune? He benefited by all the hatred that folks had against them; his pictures, of a sof-tened, attenuated style, were held up in praise, so as to deal the death-blow to their ever obstinately violent works.

' Have you read Vernier's article?' asked Jory of Gagnière. ' Doesn't he say exactly what I said?'

For the last few moments Gagnière had been absorbed in contemplating his glass, the wine in which cast a ruddy reflection on the white tablecloth. He started:

' Eh, what, Vernier's article?'

' Why, yes; in fact, all those articles which appear about Fagerolles.'

Gagnière in amazement turned to the painter.

' What, are they writing articles about you? I know nothing about them, I haven't seen them. Ah! they are writing articles about you, but whatever for?'

There was a mad roar of laughter. Fagerolles alone grinned with an ill grace, for he fancied himself the butt of some spiteful joke. But Gagnière spoke in absolute good faith. He felt surprised at the success of a painter who did not even observe the laws regulating the value of tints. Success for that trickster! Never! For in that case what would become of conscientiousness?

This boisterous hilarity enlivened the end of the dinner. They all left off eating, though the mistress of the house still insisted upon filling their plates.

'My dear, do attend to them,' she kept saying to Sandoz, who had grown greatly excited amidst the din. 'Just stretch out your hand; the biscuits are on the sideboard.'

They all declined anything more, and rose up. As the rest of the evening was to be spent there, round the table, drinking tea, they leaned back against the walls and continued chatting while the servant cleared away. The young couple assisted, Henriette putting the salt-cellars in a drawer, and Sandoz helping to fold the cloth.

'You can smoke,' said Henriette. 'You know that it doesn't inconvenience me in the least.'

Fagerolles, who had drawn Claude into the window recess, offered him a cigar, which was declined.

'True, I forgot; you don't smoke. Ah! I say, I must go to see what you have brought back with you. Some very interesting things, no doubt. You know what I think of your talent. You are the cleverest of us all.'

He showed himself very humble, sincere at heart, and allowing his admiration of former days to rise once more to the surface; indeed, he for ever bore the imprint of another's genius, which he admitted, despite the complex calculations of his cunning mind. But his humility was mingled with a certain embarrassment very rare with him—the concern he felt at the silence which the master of his youth preserved respecting his last picture. At last he ventured to ask, with quivering lips:

'Did you see my actress at the Salon? Do you like it? Tell me candidly.'

Claude hesitated for a moment; then, like the good-natured fellow he was, said:

'Yes; there are some very good bits in it.'

Fagerolles already repented having asked that stupid question, and he ended by altogether floundering; he tried to excuse himself for his plagiarisms and his compromises. When with great difficulty he had got out of the mess, enraged with himself for his clumsiness, he for a moment became the joker of yore again, made even Claude laugh till he cried, and amused them all. At last he held out his hand to take leave of Henriette.

' What, going so soon ? '

' Alas ! yes, dear madame. This evening my father is entertaining the head of a department at one of the ministries, an official whom he's trying to influence in view of obtaining a decoration ; and, as I am one of his titles to that distinction, I had to promise that I would look in.'

When he was gone, Henriette, who had exchanged a few words in a low voice with Sandoz, disappeared ; and her light footfall was heard on the first floor. Since her marriage it was she who tended the old, infirm mother, absenting herself in this fashion several times during the evening, just as the son had done formerly.

Not one of the guests, however, had noticed her leave the room. Mahoudeau and Gagnière were now talking about Fagerolles ; showing themselves covertly bitter, without openly attacking him. As yet they contented themselves with ironical glances and shrugs of the shoulders—all the silent contempt of fellows who don't wish to slash a chum. Then they fell back on Claude ; they prostrated themselves before him, overwhelmed him with the hopes they set in him. Ah ! it was high time for him to come back, for he alone, with his great gifts, his vigorous touch, could become the master, the recognised chief. Since the Salon of the Rejected the 'school of the open air ' had increased in numbers ; a growing influence was making itself felt ; but unfortunately, the efforts were frittered away ; the new recruits contented themselves with producing sketches, impressions thrown off with a few strokes of the brush ; they were awaiting the necessary man of genius, the one who would incarnate the new formula in masterpieces. What a position to take ! to master the multitude, to open up a century, to create a new art ! Claude listened to them, with his eyes turned to the floor and his face very pale. Yes, that indeed was his unavowed dream, the ambition he dared not confess to himself. Only, with the delight that the flattery caused him, there was mingled a strange anguish, a dread of the future, as he heard them raising him to the position of dictator, as if he had already triumphed.

' Don't,' he exclaimed at last ; ' there are others as good as myself. I am still seeking my real line.'

Jory, who felt annoyed, was smoking in silence. Suddenly, as the others obstinately kept at it, he could not refrain from remarking :

'All this, my boys, is because you are vexed at Fagerolles' success.'

They energetically denied it; they burst out in protestations. Fagerolles, the young master! What a good joke!

'Oh, you are turning your back upon us, we know it,' said Mahoudeau. 'There's no fear of your writing a line about us nowadays.'

'Well, my dear fellow,' answered Jory, vexed, 'everything I write about you is cut out. You make yourselves hated everywhere. Ah! if I had a paper of my own!'

Henriette came back, and Sandoz's eyes having sought hers, she answered him with a glance and the same affectionate, quiet smile that he had shown when leaving his mother's room in former times. Then she summoned them all. They sat down again round the table while she made the tea and poured it out. But the gathering grew sad, benumbed, as it were, with lassitude. Sandoz vainly tried a diversion by admitting Bertrand, the big dog, who grovelled at sight of the sugar-basin, and ended by going to sleep near the stove, where he snored like a man. Since the discussion on Fagerolles there had been intervals of silence, a kind of bored irritation, which fell heavily upon them amidst the dense tobacco smoke. And, in fact, Gagnière felt so out of sorts that he left the table for a moment to seat himself at the piano, murdering some passages from Wagner in a subdued key, with the stiff fingers of an amateur who tries his first scale at thirty.

Towards eleven o'clock Dubuche, arriving at last, contributed the finishing touch to the general frost. He had made his escape from a ball to fulfil what he considered a remaining duty towards his old comrades; and his dress-coat, his white necktie, his fat, pale face, all proclaimed his vexation at having come, the importance he attached to the sacrifice, and the fear he felt of compromising his new position. He avoided mentioning his wife, so that he might not have to bring her to Sandoz's. When he had shaken hands with Claude, without showing more emotion than if he had met him the day before, he declined a cup of tea and spoke slowly—puffing out his cheeks the while—of his worry in settling in a brand-new house, and of the work that had overwhelmed him since he had attended to the business of his father-in-law, who was building a whole street near the Parc Monceau.

Then Claude distinctly felt that something had snapped.

Had life then already carried away the evenings of former days, those evenings so fraternal in their very violence, when nothing had as yet separated them, when not one of them had thought of keeping his part of glory to himself ? Nowadays the battle was beginning. Each hungry one was eagerly biting. And a fissure was there, a scarcely perceptible crack that had rent the old, sworn friendships, and some day would make them crumble into a thousand pieces.

However, Sandoz, with his craving for perpetuity, had so far noticed nothing; he still beheld them as they had been in the Rue d'Enfer, all arm in arm, starting off to victory. Why change what was well ? Did not happiness consist in one pleasure selected from among all, and then enjoyed for ever afterwards ? And when, an hour later, the others made up their minds to go off, wearied by the dull egotism of Dubuche, who had not left off talking about his own affairs; when they had dragged Gagnière, in a trance, away from the piano, Sandoz, followed by his wife, absolutely insisted, despite the coldness of the night, on accompanying them all to the gate at the end of the garden. He shook hands all round, and shouted after them :

' Till Thursday, Claude ; till next Thursday, all of you, eh ? Mind you all come ! '

' Till Thursday ! ' repeated Henriette, who had taken the lantern and was holding it aloft so as to light the steps.

And, amid the laughter, Gagnière and Mahoudeau replied, jokingly : ' Till Thursday, young master ! Good-night, young master ! '

Once in the Rue Nollet, Dubuche immediately hailed a cab, in which he drove away. The other four walked together as far as the outer boulevards, scarcely exchanging a word, looking dazed, as it were, at having been in each other's company so long. At last Jory decamped, pretending that some proofs were waiting for him at the office of his newspaper. Then Gagnière mechanically stopped Claude in front of the Café Baudequin, the gas of which was still blazing away. Mahoudeau refused to go in, and went off alone, sadly ruminating, towards the Rue du Cherche-Midi.

Without knowing how, Claude found himself seated at their old table, opposite Gagnière, who was silent. The café had not changed. The friends still met there of a Sunday, showing a deal of fervour, in fact, since Sandoz had lived in the neighbourhood ; but the band was now lost amid a flood of new-comers; it was slowly being submerged by the increasing triteness of the young disciples of the 'open air.' At that hour of night, however, the establishment was getting empty. Three young painters, whom Claude did not know, came to shake hands with him as they went off; and then there merely remained a petty retired tradesman of the neighbourhood, asleep in front of a saucer.

Gagnière, quite at his ease, as if he had been at home, absolutely indifferent to the yawns of the solitary waiter, who was stretching his arms, glanced towards Claude, but without seeing him, for his eyes were dim.

'By the way,' said the latter, 'what were you explaining to Mahoudeau this evening? Yes, about the red of a flag turning yellowish amid the blue of the sky. That was it, eh? You are studying the theory of complementary colours.'

But the other did not answer. He took up his glass of beer, set it down again without tasting its contents, and with an ecstatic smile ended by muttering:

'Haydn has all the gracefulness of a rhetorician—his is a gentle music, quivering like the voice of a great-grandmother in powdered hair. Mozart, he's the precursory genius—the first who endowed an orchestra with an individual voice; and those two will live mostly because they created Beethoven. Ah, Beethoven! power and strength amidst serene suffering, Michael Angelo at the tomb of the Medici! A heroic logician, a kneader of human brains; for the symphony, with choral accompaniments, was the starting-point of all the great ones of to-day!'

The waiter, tired of waiting, began to turn off the gas, wearily dragging his feet along as he did so. Mournfulness pervaded the deserted room, dirty with saliva and cigar ends, and reeking of spilt drink; while from the hushed boulevard the only sound that came was the distant blubbering of some drunkard.

Gagnière, still in the clouds, however, continued to ride his hobby-horse.

'Weber passes by us amid a romantic landscape, conducting the ballads of the dead amidst weeping willows and oaks with twisted branches. Schumann follows him, beneath the pale moonlight, along the shores of silvery lakes. And behold, here comes Rossini, incarnation of the musical gift, so gay, so natural, without the least concern for expression, caring nothing for the public, and who isn't my man by a long way

—ah! certainly not—but then, all the same, he astonishes one by his wealth of production, and the huge effects he derives from an accumulation of voices and an ever-swelling repetition of the same strain. These three led to Meyerbeer, a cunning fellow who profited by everything, introducing symphony into opera after Weber, and giving dramatic expression to the unconscious formulas of Rossini. Oh! the superb bursts of sound, the feudal pomp, the martial mysticism, the quivering of fantastic legends, the cry of passion ringing out through history! And such finds!—each instrument endowed with a personality, the dramatic *recitativos* accompanied symphoniously by the orchestra—the typical musical phrase on which an entire work is built! Ah! he was a great fellow—a very great fellow indeed!'

'I am going to shut up, sir,' said the waiter, drawing near.

And, seeing that Gagnière did not as much as look round, he went to awaken the petty retired tradesman, who was still dozing in front of his saucer.

'I am going to shut up, sir.'

The belated customer rose up, shivering, fumbled in the dark corner where he was seated for his walking-stick, and when the waiter had picked it up for him from under the seats he went away.

And Gagnière rambled on:

'Berlioz has mingled literature with his work. He is the musical illustrator of Shakespeare, Virgil, and Goethe. But what a painter!—the Delacroix of music, who makes sound blaze forth amidst effulgent contrasts of colour. And withal he has romanticism in his brain, a religious mysticism that carries him away, an ecstasy that soars higher than mountain summits. A bad builder of operas, but marvellous in detached pieces, asking too much at times of the orchestra which he tortures, having pushed the personality of instruments to its furthest limits; for each instrument represents a character to him. Ah! that remark of his about clarionets: "They typify beloved women." Ah! it has always made a shiver run down my back. And Chopin, so dandified in his Byronism; the dreamy poet of those who suffer from neurosis! And Mendelssohn, that faultless chiseller! a Shakespeare in dancing pumps, whose "songs without words" are gems for women of intellect! And after that—after that—a man should go down on his knees.'

There was now only one gas-lamp alight just above his

head, and the waiter standing behind him stood waiting amid
the gloomy, chilly void of the room. Gagnière's voice had come
to a reverential *tremolo*. He was reaching devotional fervour
as he approached the inner tabernacle, the holy of holies.

'Oh! Schumann, typical of despair, the voluptuousness of
despair! Yes, the end of everything, the last song of saddened
purity hovering above the ruins of the world! Oh! Wagner,
the god in whom centuries of music are incarnated! His work
is the immense ark, all the arts blended in one; the real
humanity of the personages at last expressed, the orchestra
itself living apart the life of the drama. And what a
massacre of conventionality, of inept formulas! what a revolutionary emancipation amid the infinite! The overture of
"Tannhauser," ah! that's the sublime hallelujah of the new
era. First of all comes the chant of the pilgrims, the
religious strain, calm, deep and slowly throbbing; then the
voices of the sirens gradually drown it; the voluptuous
pleasures of Venus, full of enervating delight and languor,
grow more and more imperious and disorderly; and soon the
sacred air gradually returns, like the aspiring voice of space,
and seizes hold of all other strains and blends them in one
supreme harmony, to waft them away on the wings of a
triumphal hymn!'

'I am going to shut up, sir,' repeated the waiter.

Claude, who no longer listened, he also being absorbed in
his own passion, emptied his glass of beer and cried:

'Eh, old man, they are going to shut up.'

Then Gagnière trembled. A painful twitch came over his
ecstatic face, and he shivered as if he had dropped from the
stars. He gulped down his beer, and once on the pavement
outside, after pressing his companion's hand in silence, he
walked off into the gloom.

It was nearly two o'clock in the morning when Claude
returned to the Rue de Douai. During the week that he had
been scouring Paris anew, he had each time brought back with
him the feverish excitement of the day. But he had never
before returned so late, with his brain so hot and smoky.
Christine, overcome with fatigue, was asleep under the lamp,
which had gone out, her brow resting on the edge of the
table.

VIII

At last Christine gave a final stroke with her feather-broom, and they were settled. The studio in the Rue de Douai, small and inconvenient, had only one little room, and a kitchen, as big as a cupboard, attached to it. They were obliged to take their meals in the studio; they had to live in it, with the child always tumbling about their legs. And Christine had a deal of trouble in making their few sticks suffice, as she wished to do, in order to save expense. After all, she was obliged to buy a second-hand bedstead; and yielded to the temptation of having some white muslin curtains, which cost her seven sous the mètre. The den then seemed charming to her, and she began to keep it scrupulously clean, resolving to do everything herself, and to dispense with a servant, as living would be a difficult matter.

During the first months Claude lived in ever-increasing excitement. His peregrinations through the noisy streets; his feverish discussions on the occasion of his visits to friends; all the rage and all the burning ideas he thus brought home from out of doors, made him hold forth aloud even in his sleep. Paris had seized hold of him again; and in the full blaze of that furnace, a second youth, enthusiastic ambition to see, do, and conquer, had come upon him. Never had he felt such a passion for work, such hope, as if it sufficed for him to stretch out his hand in order to create masterpieces that should set him in the right rank, which was the first. While crossing Paris he discovered subjects for pictures everywhere; the whole city, with its streets, squares, bridges, and panoramas of life, suggested immense frescoes, which he, however, always found too small, for he was intoxicated with the thought of doing something colossal. Thus he returned home quivering, his brain seething with projects; and of an evening threw off sketches on bits of paper, in the lamp-light, without being able to decide by what he ought to begin the series of grand productions that he dreamt about.

One serious obstacle was the smallness of his studio. If he had only had the old garret of the Quai de Bourbon, or even the huge dining-room of Bennecourt! But what could he do in that oblong strip of space, that kind of passage, which the landlord of the house impudently let to painters for four hundred francs a year, after roofing it in with glass ? The worst was that the sloping glazed roof looked to the north, between two high walls, and only admitted a greenish cellar-like light. He was therefore obliged to postpone his ambitious projects, and he decided to begin with average-sized canvases, wisely saying to himself that the dimensions of a picture are not a proper test of an artist's genius.

The moment seemed to him favourable for the success of a courageous artist who, amidst the breaking up of the old schools, would at length bring some originality and sincerity into his work. The formulas of recent times were already shaken. Delacroix had died without leaving any disciples. Courbet had barely a few clumsy imitators behind him ; their best pieces would merely become so many museum pictures, blackened by age, tokens only of the art of a certain period. It seemed easy to foresee the new formula that would spring from theirs, that rush of sunshine, that limpid dawn which was rising in new works under the nascent influence of the 'open air' school. It was undeniable ; those light-toned paintings over which people had laughed so much at the Salon of the Rejected were secretly influencing many painters, and gradually brightening every palette. Nobody, as yet, admitted it, but the first blow had been dealt, and an evolution was beginning, which became more perceptible at each succeeding Salon. And what a stroke it would be if, amidst the unconscious copies of impotent essayists, amidst the timid artful attempts of tricksters, a master were suddenly to reveal himself, giving body to the new formula by dint of audacity and power, without compromise, showing it such as it should be, substantial, entire, so that it might become the truth of the end of the century !

In that first hour of passion and hope, Claude, usually so harassed by doubts, believed in his genius. He no longer experienced any of those crises, the anguish of which had driven him for days into the streets in quest of his vanished courage. A fever stiffened him, he worked on with the blind obstinacy of an artist who dives into his entrails, to drag therefrom the fruit that tortures him. His long rest in the country had endowed him with singular freshness of visual perception, and joyous delight in execution ; he seemed to have been born anew to his art, and endowed with a facility and balance of power he had never hitherto possessed. He also felt certain of progress, and experienced great satisfaction at some successful bits of work, in which his former sterile efforts at last culminated. As he had said at Bennecourt, he had got hold of his ' open air,' that carolling gaiety of tints which astonished his comrades when they came to see him. They all admired, convinced that he would only have to show his work to take a very high place with it, such was its individuality of style, for the first time showing nature flooded with real light, amid all the play of reflections and the constant variations of colours.

Thus, for three years, Claude struggled on, without weakening, spurred to further efforts by each rebuff, abandoning nought of his ideas, but marching straight before him, with all the vigour of faith.

During the first year he went forth amid the December snows to place himself for four hours a day behind the heights of Montmartre, at the corner of a patch of waste land whence as a background he painted some miserable, low, tumble-down buildings, overtopped by factory chimneys, whilst in the foreground, amidst the snow, he set a girl and a ragged street rough devouring stolen apples. His obstinacy in painting from nature greatly complicated his work, and gave rise to almost insuperable difficulties. However, he finished this picture out of doors ; he merely cleaned and touched it up a bit in his studio. When the canvas was placed beneath the wan daylight of the glazed roof, he himself was startled by its brutality. It showed like a scene beheld through a doorway open on the street. The snow blinded one. The two figures, of a muddy grey in tint, stood out, lamentable. He at once felt that such a picture would not be accepted, but he did not try to soften it ; he sent it to the Salon, all the same. After swearing that he would never again try to exhibit, he now held the view that one should always present something to the hanging committee if merely to accentuate its wrong-doing. Besides, he admitted the utility of the Salon, the only battlefield on which an artist might come to the fore at one stroke. The hanging committee refused his picture.

The second year Claude sought a contrast. He selected a bit of the public garden of Batignolles in May ; in the background were some large chestnut trees casting their shade around a corner of greensward and several six-storied houses ;

while in front, on a seat of a crude green hue, some nurses and petty cits of the neighbourhood sat in a line watching three little girls making sand pies. When permission to paint there had been obtained, he had needed some heroism to bring his work to a successful issue amid the bantering crowd. At last he made up his mind to go there at five in the morning, in order to paint in the background ; reserving the figures, he contented himself with making mere sketches of them from nature, and finishing them in his studio. This time his picture seemed to him less crude ; it had acquired some of the wan, softened light which descended through the glass roof. He thought his picture accepted, for all his friends pronounced it to be a masterpiece, and went about saying that it would revolutionise the Salon. There was stupefaction and indignation when a fresh refusal of the hanging committee was rumoured. The committee's intentions could not be denied : it was a question of systematically strangling an original artist. He, after his first burst of passion, vented all his anger upon his work, which he stigmatised as false, dishonest, and execrable. It was a well-deserved lesson, which he should remember : ought he to have relapsed into that cellar-like studio light ? Was he going to revert to the filthy cooking of imaginary figures ? When the picture came back, he took a knife and ripped it from top to bottom.

And so during the third year he obstinately toiled on a work of revolt. He wanted the blazing sun, that Paris sun which, on certain days, turns the pavement to a white heat in the dazzling reflection from the house frontages. Nowhere is it hotter ; even people from burning climes mop their faces ; you would say you were in some region of Africa beneath the heavily raining glow of a sky on fire. The subject Claude chose was a corner of the Place du Carrousel, at one o'clock in the afternoon, when the sunrays fall vertically. A cab was jolting along, its driver half asleep, its horse steaming, with drooping head, vague amid the throbbing heat. The passers-by seemed, as it were, intoxicated, with the one exception of a young woman, who, rosy and gay under her parasol, walked on with an easy queen-like step, as if the fiery element were her proper sphere. But what especially rendered this picture terrible was a new interpretation of the effects of light, a very accurate decomposition of the sunrays, which ran counter to all the habits of eyesight, by emphasising blues, yellows and reds, where nobody had been accustomed to see any. In the background the Tuileries vanished in a golden shimmer; the paving-stones bled, so to say; the figures were only so many indications, sombre patches eaten into by the vivid glare. This time his comrades, while still praising, looked embarrassed, all seized with the same apprehensions. Such painting could only lead to martyrdom. He, amidst their praises, understood well enough the rupture that was taking place, and when the hanging committee had once more closed the Salon against him, he dolorously exclaimed, in a moment of lucidity:

'All right; it's an understood thing—I'll die at the task.'

However, although his obstinate courage seemed to increase, he now and then gradually relapsed into his former doubts, consumed by the struggle he was waging with nature. Every canvas that came back to him seemed bad to him— above all incomplete, not realising what he had aimed at. It was this idea of impotence that exasperated him even more than the refusals of the hanging committee. No doubt he did not forgive the latter; his works, even in an embryo state, were a hundred times better than all the trash which was accepted. But what suffering he felt at being ever unable to show himself in all his strength, in such a master-piece as he could not bring his genius to yield! There were always some superb bits in his paintings. He felt satisfied with this, that, and the other. Why, then, were there sudden voids? Why were there inferior bits, which he did not perceive while he was at work, but which afterwards utterly killed the picture like ineffaceable defects? And he felt quite unable to make any corrections; at certain moments a wall rose up, an insuperable obstacle, beyond which he was forbidden to venture. If he touched up the part that displeased him a score of times, so a score of times did he aggravate the evil, till everything became quite muddled and messy.

He grew anxious, and failed to see things clearly; his brush refused to obey him, and his will was paralysed. Was it his hands or his eyes that ceased to belong to him amid those progressive attacks of the hereditary disorder that had already made him anxious? Those attacks became more frequent; he once more lapsed into horrible weeks, wearing himself out, oscillating bewixt uncertainty and hope; and his only support during those terrible hours, which he spent in a desperate hand-to-hand struggle with his rebellious work, was the consoling dream of his future masterpiece, the one with which he would at last be fully satisfied, in painting which his hands would show all the energy and deftness of true creative skill. By some ever-recurring phenomenon, his longing to create outstripped the quickness of his fingers ; he never worked at one picture without planning the one that was to follow. Then all that remained to him was an eager desire to rid himself of the work on which he was engaged, for it brought him torture ; no doubt it would be good for nothing ; he was still making fatal concessions, having recourse to trickery, to everything that a true artist should banish from his conscience. But what he meant to do after that—ah ! what he meant to do—he beheld it superb and heroic, above attack and indestructible. All this was the everlasting mirage that goads on the condemned disciples of art, a falsehood that comes in a spirit of tenderness and compassion, and without which production would become impossible to those who die of their failure to create life.

In addition to those constantly renewed struggles with himself, Claude's material difficulties now increased. Was it not enough that he could not give birth to what he felt existing within him ? Must he also battle with every-day cares ? Though he refused to admit it, painting from nature in the open air became impossible when a picture was beyond a certain size. How could he settle himself in the streets amidst the crowd?—how obtain from each person the necessary number of sittings ? That sort of painting must evidently be confined to certain determined subjects, landscapes, small corners of the city, in which the figures would be but so many silhouettes, painted in afterwards. There were also a thousand and one difficulties connected with the weather ; the wind which threatened to carry off the easel, the rain which obliged one to interrupt one's work. On such days Claude came home in a rage, shaking his fist at the sky and accusing nature of resisting him in order that he might not take and vanquish her. He also complained bitterly of being poor ; for his dream was to have a movable studio, a vehicle in Paris, a boat on the Seine, in both of which he would have lived like an artistic gipsy. But nothing came to his aid, everything conspired against his work.

And Christine suffered with Claude. She had shared his hopes very bravely, brightening the studio with her house-

wifely activity; but now she sat down, discouraged, when
she saw him powerless. At each picture which was refused
she displayed still deeper grief, hurt in her womanly self-
love, taking that pride in success which all women have.
The painter's bitterness soured her also; she entered into
his feelings and passions, identified herself with his tastes,
defended his painting, which had become, as it were, part of
herself, the one great concern of their lives—indeed, the only
important one henceforth, since it was the one whence she
expected all her happiness. She understood well enough
that art robbed her more and more of her lover each day, but
the real struggle between herself and art had not yet begun.
For the time she yielded, and let herself be carried away with
Claude, so that they might be but one—one only in the self-
same effort. From that partial abdication of self there sprang,
however, a sadness, a dread of what might be in store for her
later on. Every now and then a shudder chilled her to the
very heart. She felt herself growing old, while intense
melancholy upset her, an unreasoning longing to weep, which
she satisfied in the gloomy studio for hours together, when
she was alone there.

At that period her heart expanded, as it were, and a
mother sprang from the loving woman. That motherly
feeling for her big artist child was made up of all the vague
infinite pity which filled her with tenderness, of the illogical
fits of weakness into which she saw him fall each hour, of the
constant pardons which she was obliged to grant him. He
was beginning to make her unhappy, his caresses were few
and far between, a look of weariness constantly overspread
his features. How could she love him then if not with that
other affection of every moment, remaining in adoration
before him, and unceasingly sacrificing herself? In her
inmost being insatiable passion still lingered; she was still the
sensuous woman with thick lips set in obstinately prominent
jaws. Yet there was a gentle melancholy, in being merely a
mother to him, in trying to make him happy amid that life of
theirs which now was spoilt.

Little Jacques was the only one to suffer from that
transfer of tenderness. She neglected him more; the man,
his father, became her child, and the poor little fellow remained as mere testimony of their great passion of yore.
As she saw him grow up, and no longer require so much care,
she began to sacrifice him, without intentional harshness, but

merely because she felt like that. At meal-times she only
gave him the inferior bits; the cosiest nook near the stove
was not for his little chair; if ever the fear of an accident
made her tremble now and then, her first cry, her first protecting movement was not for her helpless child. She ever
relegated him to the background, suppressed him, as it were:
'Jacques, be quiet; you tire your father. Jacques, keep still;
don't you see that your father is at work?'

The urchin suffered from being cooped up in Paris. He,
who had had the whole country-side to roll about in, felt
stifled in the narrow space where he now had to keep quiet.
His rosy cheeks became pale, he grew up puny, serious, like a
little man, with eyes which stared at things in wonder. He
was five by now, and his head by a singular phenomenon had
become disproportionately large, in such wise as to make his
father say, 'He has a great man's nut!' But the child's intelligence seemed, on the contrary, to decrease in proportion as
his skull became larger. Very gentle and timid, he became
absorbed in thought for hours, incapable of answering a
question. And when he emerged from that state of immobility
he had mad fits of shouting and jumping, like a young
animal giving rein to instinct. At such times warnings 'to
keep quiet' rained upon him, for his mother failed to understand his sudden outbursts, and became uneasy at seeing
the father grow irritated as he sat before his easel. Getting
cross herself, she would then hastily seat the little fellow in
his corner again. Quieted all at once, giving the startled
shudder of one who has been too abruptly awakened, the
child would after a time doze off with his eyes wide open,
so careless of enjoying life that his toys, corks, pictures,
and empty colour-tubes dropped listlessly from his hands.
Christine had already tried to teach him his alphabet, but he
had cried and struggled, so they had decided to wait another
year or two before sending him to school, where his masters
would know how to make him learn.

Christine at last began to grow frightened at the prospect
of impending misery. In Paris, with that growing child
beside them, living proved expensive, and the end of each
month became terrible, despite her efforts to save in every
direction. They had nothing certain but Claude's thousand
francs a year; and how could they live on fifty francs a
month, which was all that was left to them after deducting
four hundred francs for the rent? At first they had got out

of embarrassment, thanks to the sale of a few pictures, Claude
having found Gagnière's old amateur, one of those detested
bourgeois who possess the ardent souls of artists, despite the
monomaniacal habits in which they are confined. This one,
M. Hue, a retired chief clerk in a public department, was
unfortunately not rich enough to be always buying, and he
could only bewail the purblindness of the public, which once
more allowed a genius to die of starvation; for he himself,
convinced, struck by grace at the first glance, had selected
Claude's crudest works, which he hung by the side of his
Delacroix, predicting equal fortune for them. The worst was
that Papa Malgras had just retired after making his fortune.
It was but a modest competence after all, an income of
about ten thousand francs, upon which he had decided to live
in a little house at Bois Colombes, like the careful man he
was.

It was highly amusing to hear him speak of the famous
Naudet, full of disdain for the millions turned over by that
speculator, 'millions that would some day fall upon his nose,'
said Malgras. Claude, having casually met him, only succeeded
in selling him a last picture, one of his sketches from the nude
made at the Boutin studio, that superb study of a woman's
trunk which the erstwhile dealer had not been able to see
afresh without feeling a revival of his old passion for it. So
misery was imminent; outlets were closing instead of new ones
opening; disquieting rumours were beginning to circulate
concerning the young painter's works, so constantly rejected
at the Salon; and besides, Claude's style of art, so revolutionary
and imperfect, in which the startled eye found nought of
admitted conventionality, would of itself have sufficed to drive
away wealthy buyers. One evening, being unable to settle
his bill at his colour shop, the painter had exclaimed that he
would live upon the capital of his income rather than lower
himself to the degrading production of trade pictures. But
Christine had violently opposed such an extreme measure; she
would retrench still further; in short, she preferred anything
to such madness, which would end by throwing them into the
streets without even bread to eat.

After the rejection of Claude's third picture, the summer
proved so wonderfully fine that the painter seemed to derive
new strength from it. There was not a cloud; limpid light
streamed day after day upon the giant activity of Paris.
Claude had resumed his peregrinations through the city,

determined to find a masterstroke, as he expressed it, something huge, something decisive, he did not exactly know what. September came, and still he had found nothing that satisfied him; he simply went mad for a week about one or another subject, and then declared that it was not the thing after all. His life was spent in constant excitement; he was ever on the watch, on the point of setting his hand on the realisation of his dream, which always flew away. In reality, beneath his intractable realism lay the superstition of a nervous woman; he believed in occult and complex influences; everything, luck or ill-luck, must depend upon the view selected.

One afternoon—it was one of the last fine days of the season—Claude took Christine out with him, leaving little Jacques in the charge of the doorkeeper, a kind old woman, as was their wont when they wanted to go out together. That day the young painter was possessed by a sudden whim to ramble about and revisit in Christine's company the nooks beloved in other days; and behind this desire of his there lurked a vague hope that she would bring him luck. And thus they went as far as the Pont Louis-Philippe, and remained for a quarter of an hour on the Quai des Ormes, silent, leaning against the parapet, and looking at the old Hôtel du Martoy, across the Seine, where they had first loved each other. Then, still without saying a word, they went their former round; they started along the quays, under the plane trees, seeing the past rise up before them at every step. Everything spread out again: the bridges with their arches opening upon the sheeny water; the Cité, enveloped in shade, above which rose the flavescent towers of Notre-Dame; the great curve of the right bank flooded with sunlight, and ending in the indistinct silhouette of the Pavillon de Flore, together with the broad avenues, the monuments and edifices on both banks, and all the life of the river, the floating washhouses, the baths, and the lighters.

As of old, the orb in its decline followed them, seemingly rolling along the distant housetops, and assuming a crescent shape, as it appeared from behind the dome of the Institute. There was a dazzling sunset, they had never beheld a more magnificent one, such a majestic descent amidst tiny cloudlets that changed into purple network, between the meshes of which a shower of gold escaped. But of the past that thus rose up before their eyes there came to them nought but invincible sadness—a sensation that things escaped them, and that it was impossible for them to retrace their way up stream and live their life over again. All those old stones remained cold. The constant current beneath the bridges, the water that had ever flowed onward and onward, seemed to have borne away something of their own selves, the delight of early desire and the joyfulness of hope. Now that they belonged to one another, they no longer tasted the simple happiness born of feeling the warm pressure of their arms as they strolled on slowly, enveloped by the mighty vitality of Paris.

On reaching the Pont des Saints-Pères, Claude, in sheer despair, stopped short. He had relinquished Christine's arm, and had turned his face towards the point of the Cité. She no doubt felt the severance that was taking place and became very sad. Seeing that he lingered there obliviously, she wished to regain her hold upon him.

'My dear,' said she, 'let us go home; it's time. Jacques will be waiting for us, you know.'

But he went half way across the bridge, and she had to follow him. Then once more he remained motionless, with his eyes still fixed on the Cité, on that island which ever rode at anchor, the cradle and heart of Paris, where for centuries all the blood of her arteries had converged amid the constant growth of faubourgs invading the plain. And a glow came over Claude's face, his eyes sparkled, and at last he made a sweeping gesture :

'Look ! Look ! '

In the immediate foreground beneath them was the port of St. Nicolas, with the low shanties serving as offices for the inspectors of navigation, and the large paved river-bank sloping down, littered with piles of sand, barrels, and sacks, and edged with a row of lighters, still full, in which busy lumpers swarmed beneath the gigantic arm of an iron crane. Then on the other side of the river, above a cold swimming-bath, resounding with the shouts of the last bathers of the season, the strips of grey linen that served as a roofing flapped in the wind. In the middle, the open stream flowed on in rippling, greenish wavelets tipped here and there with white, blue, and pink. And then there came the Pont des Arts, standing back, high above the water on its iron girders, like black lace-work, and animated by a ceaseless procession of foot-passengers, who looked like ants careering over the narrow line of the horizontal plane. Below, the Seine flowed away to the far distance ; you saw the old arches of the Pont-Neuf, browny with stone-rust; on the left, as far as the Isle of St. Louis, came a mirror-like gap; and the other arm of the river curved sharply, the lock gates of the Mint shutting out the view with a bar of foam. Along the Pont-Neuf passed big yellow omnibuses, motley vehicles of all kinds, with the mechanical regularity of so many children's toys. The whole of the background was inframed within the perspective of the two banks; on the right were houses on the quays, partly hidden by a cluster of lofty trees, from behind which on the horizon there emerged a corner of the Hôtel de Ville, together with the square clock tower of St. Gervais, both looking as indistinct as if they had stood far away in the suburbs. And on the left bank there was a wing of the Institute, the flat frontage of the Mint, and yet another enfilade of trees.

But the centre of the immense picture, that which rose most prominently from the stream and soared to the sky, was the Cité, showing like the prow of an antique vessel, ever burnished by the setting sun. Down below, the poplars on the strip of ground that joins the two sections of the Pont-Neuf hid the statue of Henri IV. with a dense mass of green foliage. Higher up, the sun set the two lines of frontages in contrast, wrapping the grey buildings of the Quai de l'Horloge in shade, and illumining with a blaze those of the Quai des Orfèvres, rows of irregular houses which stood out so clearly that one distinguished the smallest details, the shops, the signboards, even the curtains at the windows. Higher up, amid the jagged outlines of chimney stacks, behind a slanting chess-board of smaller roofs, the pepper-caster turrets of the Palais de Justice and the garrets of the Prefecture of Police displayed sheets of slate, intersected by a colossal advertisement painted in blue upon a wall, with gigantic letters which, visible to all Paris, seemed like some efflorescence of the feverish life of modern times sprouting on the city's brow. Higher, higher still, betwixt the twin towers of Notre-Dame, of the colour of old gold, two arrows darted upwards, the spire of the cathedral itself, and to the left that of the Sainte-Chapelle, both so elegantly slim that they seemed to quiver in the breeze, as if they had been the proud topmasts of the ancient vessel rising into the brightness of the open sky.

'Are you coming, dear?' asked Christine, gently.

Claude did not listen to her; this, the heart of Paris, had

taken full possession of him. The splendid evening seemed to widen the horizon. There were patches of vivid light, and of clearly defined shadow; there was a brightness in the precision of each detail, a transparency in the air, which throbbed with gladness. And the river life, the turmoil of the quays, all the people, streaming along the streets, rolling over the bridges, arriving from every side of that huge cauldron, Paris, steamed there in visible billows, with a quiver that was apparent in the sunlight. There was a light breeze, high aloft a flight of small cloudlets crossed the paling azure sky, and one could hear a slow but mighty palpitation, as if the soul of Paris here dwelt around its cradle.

But Christine, frightened at seeing Claude so absorbed, and seized herself with a kind of religious awe, took hold of his arm and dragged him away, as if she had felt that some great danger was threatening him.

'Let us go home. You are doing yourself harm. I want to get back.'

At her touch he started like a man disturbed in sleep. Then, turning his head to take a last look, he muttered:

'Ah! heavens! Ah! heavens, how beautiful!'

He allowed himself to be led away. But throughout the evening, first at dinner, afterwards beside the stove, and until he went to bed, he remained like one dazed, so deep in his cogitations that he did not utter half a dozen sentences. And Christine, failing to draw from him any answer to her questions, at last became silent also. She looked at him anxiously; was it the approach of some serious illness, had he inhaled some bad air whilst standing midway across the bridge yonder? His eyes stared vaguely into space, his face flushed as if with some inner straining. One would have thought it the mute travail of germination, as if something were springing into life within him.

The next morning, immediately after breakfast, he set off, and Christine spent a very sorrowful day, for although she had become more easy in mind on hearing him whistle some of his old southern tunes as he got up, she was worried by another matter, which she had not mentioned to him for fear of damping his spirits again. That day they would for the first time lack everything; a whole week separated them from the date when their little income would fall due, and she had spent her last copper that morning. She had nothing left for the evening, not even the wherewithal to buy a loaf.

To whom could she apply? How could she manage to hide
the truth any longer from him when he came home hungry?
She made up her mind to pledge the black silk dress which
Madame Vanzade had formerly given her, but it was with a
heavy heart; she trembled with fear and shame at the idea
of the pawnshop, that familiar resort of the poor which she
had never as yet entered. And she was tortured by such
apprehension about the future, that from the ten francs
which were lent her she only took enough to make a sorrel
soup and a stew of potatoes. On coming out of the pawn-
office, a meeting with somebody she knew had given her the
finishing stroke.

As it happened, Claude came home very late, gesticulating
merrily, and his eyes very bright, as if he were excited by
some secret joy; he was very hungry, and grumbled because
the cloth was not laid. Then, having sat down between
Christine and little Jacques, he swallowed his soup and
devoured a plateful of potatoes.

'Is that all?' he asked, when he had finished. 'You
might as well have added a scrap of meat. Did you have
to buy some boots again?'

She stammered, not daring to tell him the truth, but hurt
at heart by this injustice. He, however, went on chaffing
her about the coppers she juggled away to buy herself things
with; and getting more and more excited, amid the egotism
of feelings which he seemingly wished to keep to himself, he
suddenly flew out at Jacques.

'Hold your noise, you brat!—you drive one mad.'

The child, forgetting all about his dinner, had been
tapping the edge of his plate with his spoon, his eyes full of
mirthful delight at this music.

'Jacques, be quiet,' scoldingly said his mother, in her
turn. 'Let your father have his dinner in peace.'

Then the little one, abashed, at once became very quiet,
and relapsed into gloomy stillness, with his lustreless eyes
fixed on his potatoes, which, however, he did not eat.

Claude made a show of stuffing himself with cheese,
while Christine, quite grieved, offered to fetch some cold
meat from a ham and beef shop; but he declined, and
prevented her going by words that pained her still more.
Then, the table having been cleared, they all sat round the
lamp for the evening, she sewing, the little one turning over
a picture-book in silence, and Claude drumming on the table

with his fingers, his mind the while wandering back to the spot whence he had come. Suddenly he rose, sat down again with a sheet of paper and a pencil, and began sketching rapidly, in the vivid circle of light that fell from under the lamp-shade. And such was his longing to give outward expression to the tumultuous ideas beating in his skull, that soon this sketch did not suffice for his relief. On the contrary, it goaded him on, and he finished by unburthening his mind in a flood of words. He would have shouted to the walls; and if he addressed himself to his wife it was because she happened to be there.

'Look, that's what we saw yesterday. It's magnificent. I spent three hours there to-day. I've got hold of what I want—something wonderful, something that'll knock everything else to pieces. Just look! I station myself under the bridge; in the immediate foreground I have the Port of St. Nicolas, with its crane, its lighters which are being unloaded, and its crowd of labourers. Do you see the idea—it's Paris at work—all those brawny fellows displaying their bare arms and chests? Then on the other side I have the swimming-baths—Paris at play—and some skiff there, no doubt, to occupy the centre of the composition; but of that I am not as yet certain. I must feel my way. As a matter of course, the Seine will be in the middle, broad, immense.'

While talking, he kept on indicating outlines with his pencil, thickening his strokes over and over again, and tearing the paper in his very energy. She, in order to please him, bent over the sketch, pretending to grow very interested in his explanations. But there was such a labyrinth of lines, such a confusion of summary details, that she failed to distinguish anything.

'You are following me, aren't you?'

'Yes, yes, very beautiful indeed.'

'Then I have the background, the two arms of the river with their quays, the Cité, rising up triumphantly in the centre, and standing out against the sky. Ah! that background, what a marvel! People see it every day, pass before it without stopping; but it takes hold of one all the same; one's admiration accumulates, and one fine afternoon it bursts forth. Nothing in the world can be grander; it is Paris herself, glorious in the sunlight. Ah! what a fool I was not to think of it before! How many times I have looked at it without seeing! However, I stumbled on it after that ramble along the quays! And, do you remember, there's a dash of shadow on that side; while here the sunrays fall quite straight. The towers are yonder; the spire of the Sainte-Chapelle tapers upward, as slim as a needle pointing to the sky. But no, it's more to the right. Wait, I'll show you.'

He began again, never wearying, but constantly retouching the sketch, and adding innumerable little characteristic details which his painter's eye had noticed; here the red signboard of a distant shop vibrated in the light; closer by was a greenish bit of the Seine, on whose surface large patches of oil seemed to be floating; and then there was the delicate tone of a tree, the gamut of greys supplied by the house frontages, and the luminous cast of the sky. She complaisantly approved of all he said and tried to look delighted.

But Jacques once again forgot what he had been told. After long remaining silent before his book, absorbed in the contemplation of a wood-cut depicting a black cat, he began to hum some words of his own composition: 'Oh, you pretty cat; oh, you ugly cat; oh, you pretty, ugly cat,' and so on, *ad infinitum*, ever in the same lugubrious manner.

Claude, who was made fidgety by the buzzing noise, did not at first understand what was upsetting him. But after a time the child's harassing phrase fell clearly upon his ear.

'Haven't you done worrying us with your cat?' he shouted furiously.

'Hold your tongue, Jacques, when your father is talking!' repeated Christine.

'Upon my word, I do believe he is becoming an idiot. Just look at his head, if it isn't like an idiot's. It's dreadful. Just say; what do you mean by your pretty and ugly cat?'

The little fellow, turning pale and wagging his big head, looked stupid, and replied: 'Don't know.'

Then, as his father and mother gazed at each other with a discouraged air, he rested his cheek on the open picture-book, and remained like that, neither stirring nor speaking, but with his eyes wide open.

It was getting late; Christine wanted to put him to bed, but Claude had already resumed his explanations. He now told her that, the very next morning, he should go and make a sketch on the spot, just in order to fix his ideas. And, as he rattled on, he began to talk of buying a small camp easel, a thing upon which he had set his heart for months. He

kept harping on the subject, and spoke of money matters.
till she at last became embarrassed, and ended by telling him
of everything—the last copper she had spent that morning,
and the silk dress she had pledged in order to dine that evening. Thereupon he became very remorseful and affectionate ;
he kissed her and asked her forgiveness for having complained
about the dinner. She would excuse him, surely ; he would
have killed father and mother, as he kept on repeating, when
that confounded painting got hold of him. As for the pawnshop, it made him laugh ; he defied misery.

'I tell you that we are all right,' he exclaimed. 'That
picture means success.'

She kept silent, thinking about her meeting of the morning, which she wished to hide from him ; but without apparent
cause or transition, in the kind of torpor that had come over
her, the words she would have kept back rose invincibly to
her lips.

'Madame Vanzade is dead,' she said.

He looked surprised. Ah ! really ? How did she, Christine, know it ?

'I met the old man-servant. Oh, he's a gentleman by
now, looking very sprightly, in spite of his seventy years. I
did not know him again. It was he who spoke to me. Yes,
she died six weeks ago. Her millions have gone to various
charities, with the exception of an annuity to the old servants,
upon which they are living snugly like people of the middle-
classes.'

He looked at her, and at last murmured, in a saddened voice :
'My poor Christine, you are regretting things now, aren't you ?
She would have given you a marriage portion, have found
you a husband ! I told you so in days gone by. She would,
perhaps, have left you all her money, and you wouldn't now
be starving with a crazy fellow like myself.'

She then seemed to wake from her dream. She drew her
chair to his, caught hold of one of his arms and nestled against
him, as if her whole being protested against his words :

'What are you saying ? Oh ! no ; oh ! no. It would
have been shameful to have thought of her money. I would
confess it to you if it were the case, and you know that I never
tell lies ; but I myself don't know what came over me when I
heard the news. I felt upset and saddened, so sad that I
imagined everything was over for me. It was no doubt
remorse ; yes, remorse at having deserted her so brutally,

poor invalid that she was, the good old soul who called me her daughter! I behaved very badly, and it won't bring me luck. Ah! don't say "No," I feel it well enough; henceforth there's an end to everything for me.'

Then she wept, choked by those confused regrets, the significance of which she failed to understand, regrets mingling with the one feeling that her life was spoilt, and that she now had nothing but unhappiness before her.

'Come, wipe your eyes,' said Claude, becoming affectionate once more. 'Is it possible that you, who were never nervous, can conjure up chimeras and worry yourself in this way? Dash it all, we shall get out of our difficulties! First of all, you know that it was through you that I found the subject for my picture. There cannot be much of a curse upon you, since you bring me luck.'

He laughed, and she shook her head, seeing well enough that he wanted to make her smile. She was suffering on account of his picture already; for on the bridge he had completely forgotten her, as if she had ceased to belong to him! And, since the previous night, she had realised that he was farther and farther removed from her, alone in a world to which she could not ascend. But she allowed him to soothe her, and they exchanged one of their kisses of yore, before rising from the table to retire to rest.

Little Jacques had heard nothing. Benumbed by his stillness, he had fallen asleep, with his cheek on his picture-book; and his big head, so heavy at times that it bent his neck, looked pale in the lamplight. Poor little offspring of genius, which, when it begets at all, so often begets idiocy or physical imperfection! When his mother put him to bed Jacques did not even open his eyes.

It was only at this period that the idea of marrying Christine came to Claude. Though yielding to the advice of Sandoz, who expressed his surprise at the prolongation of an irregular situation which no circumstances justified, he more particularly gave way to a feeling of pity, to a desire to show himself kind to his mistress, and to win forgiveness for his delinquencies. He had seen her so sad of late, so uneasy with respect to the future, that he did not know how to revive her spirits. He himself was growing soured, and relapsing into his former fits of anger, treating her, at times, like a servant, to whom one flings a week's notice. Being his lawful wife, she would, no doubt, feel herself more in her rightful home, and would suffer less from his rough behaviour. She herself, for that matter, had never again spoken of marriage. She seemed to care nothing for earthly things, but entirely reposed upon him; however, he understood well enough that it grieved her that she was not able to visit at Sandoz's. Besides, they no longer lived amid the freedom and solitude of the country; they were in Paris, with its thousand and one petty spites, everything that is calculated to wound a woman in an irregular position. In reality, he had nothing against marriage save his old prejudices, those of an artist who takes life as he lists. Since he was never to leave her, why not afford her that pleasure? And, in fact, when he spoke to her about it, she gave a loud cry and threw her arms round his neck, surprised at experiencing such great emotion. During a whole week it made her feel thoroughly happy. But her joy subsided long before the ceremony.

Moreover, Claude did not hurry over any of the formalities, and they had to wait a long while for the necessary papers. He continued getting the sketches for his picture together, and she, like himself, did not seem in the least impatient. What was the good? It would assuredly make no difference in their life. They had decided to be married merely at the municipal offices, not in view of displaying any contempt for religion, but to get the affair over quickly and simply. That would suffice. The question of witnesses embarrassed them for a moment. As she was absolutely unacquainted with anybody, he selected Sandoz and Mahoudeau to act for her. For a moment he had thought of replacing the latter by Dubuche, but he never saw the architect now, and he feared to compromise him. He, Claude, would be content with Jory and Gagnière. In that way the affair would pass off among friends, and nobody would talk of it.

Several weeks had gone by; they were in December, and the weather proved terribly cold. On the day before the wedding, although they barely had thirty-five francs left them, they agreed that they could not send their witnesses away with a mere shake of the hand; and, rather than have a lot of trouble in the studio, they decided to offer them lunch at a small restaurant on the Boulevard de Clichy, after which they would all go home.

In the morning, while Christine was tacking a collar to a grey linsey gown which, with the coquetry of woman, she had made for the occasion, it occurred to Claude, who was already wearing his frock-coat and kicking his heels impatiently, to go and fetch Mahoudeau, for the latter, he asserted, was quite capable of forgetting all about the appointment. Since autumn, the sculptor had been living at Montmartre, in a small studio in the Rue des Tilleuls. He had moved thither in consequence of a series of affairs that had quite upset him. First of all, he had been turned out of the fruiterer's shop in the Rue du Cherche-Midi for not paying his rent; then had come a definite rupture with Chaîne, who, despairing of being able to live by his brush, had rushed into commercial enterprise, betaking himself to all the fairs around Paris as the manager of a kind of 'fortune's wheel' belonging to a widow; while last of all had come the sudden flight of Mathilde, her herbalist's business sold up, and she herself disappearing, it seemed, with some mysterious admirer. At present Mahoudeau lived all by himself in greater misery than ever, only eating when he secured a job at scraping some architectural ornaments, or preparing work for some more prosperous fellow-sculptor.

'I am going to fetch him, do you hear?' Claude repeated to Christine. 'We still have a couple of hours before us. And, if the others come, make them wait. We'll go to the municipal offices all together.'

Once outside, Claude hurried along in the nipping cold which loaded his moustache with icicles. Mahoudeau's studio was at the end of a conglomeration of tenements— 'rents,' so to say—and he had to cross a number of small gardens, white with rime, and showing the bleak, stiff melancholy of cemeteries. He could distinguish his friend's place from afar on account of the colossal plaster statue of the 'Vintaging Girl,' the once successful exhibit of the Salon, for which there had not been sufficient space in the narrow ground-floor studio. Thus it was rotting out in the open like so much rubbish shot from a cart, a lamentable spectacle, weather-bitten, riddled by the rain's big, grimy tears. The key was in the door, so Claude went in.

'Hallo! have you come to fetch me?' said Mahoudeau, in surprise. 'I've only got my hat to put on. But wait a bit, I was asking myself whether it wouldn't be better to light a little fire. I am uneasy about my woman there.'

Some water in a bucket was ice-bound. So cold was the studio that it froze inside as hard as it did out of doors, for, having been penniless for a whole week, Mahoudeau had gingerly eked out the little coal remaining to him, only lighting the stove for an hour or two of a morning. His studio was a kind of tragic cavern, compared with which the shop of former days evoked reminiscences of snug comfort, such was the tomb-like chill that fell on one's shoulders from the creviced ceiling and the bare walls. In the various corners some statues, of less bulky dimensions than the 'Vintaging Girl,' plaster figures which had been modelled with passion and exhibited, and which had then come back for want of buyers, seemed to be shivering with their noses turned to the wall, forming a melancholy row of cripples, some already badly damaged, showing mere stumps of arms, and all dust-begrimed and clay-bespattered. Under the eyes of their artist creator, who had given them his heart's blood, those wretched nudities dragged out years of agony. At first, no doubt, they were preserved with jealous care, despite the lack of room, but then they lapsed into the grotesque horror of all lifeless things, until a day came when, taking up a mallet, he himself finished them off, breaking them into mere lumps of plaster, so as to be rid of them.

'You say we have got two hours, eh?' resumed Mahoudeau. 'Well, I'll just light a bit of fire; it will be the wiser perhaps.'

Then, while lighting the stove, he began bewailing his fate in an angry voice. What a dog's life a sculptor's was! The most bungling stonemason was better off. A figure which the Government bought for three thousand francs cost well nigh two thousand, what with its model, clay, marble or bronze, all sorts of expenses, indeed, and for all that it remained buried in some official cellar on the pretext that there was no room for it elsewhere. The niches of the public buildings remained empty, pedestals were awaiting statues in the public gardens. No matter, there was never any room! And there were no possible commissions from private people; at best one received an order for a few busts, and at very rare intervals one for a memorial statue, subscribed for by the public and hurriedly executed at reduced terms. Sculpture was the noblest of arts, the most manly, yes, but the one which led the most surely to death by starvation!

'Is your machine progressing?' asked Claude.

'Without this confounded cold, it would be finished,' answered Mahoudeau. 'I'll show it you.'

He rose from his knees after listening to the snorting of

the stove. In the middle of the studio, on a packing-case, strengthened by cross-pieces, stood a statue swathed in linen wraps which were quite rigid, hard frozen, draping the figure with the whiteness of a shroud. This statue embodied Mahoudeau's old dream, unrealised until now from lack of means—it was an upright figure of that bathing girl of whom more than a dozen small models had been knocking about his place for years. In a moment of impatient revolt he himself had manufactured trusses and stays out of broom-handles, dispensing with the necessary iron work in the hope that the wood would prove sufficiently solid. From time to time he shook the figure to try it, but as yet it had not budged.

'The devil!' he muttered; 'some warmth will do her good. These wraps seem glued to her—they form quite a breastplate.'

The linen was crackling between his fingers, and splinters of ice were breaking off. He was obliged to wait until the heat produced a slight thaw, and then with great care he stripped the figure, baring the head first, then the bosom, and then the hips, well pleased at finding everything intact, and smiling like a lover at a woman fondly adored.

'Well, what do you think of it?'

Claude, who had only previously seen a little rough model of the statue, nodded his head, in order that he might not have to answer immediately. Decidedly, that good fellow Mahoudeau was turning traitor, and drifting towards grace-fulness, in spite of himself, for pretty things ever sprang from under his big fingers, former stonecutter though he was. Since his colossal 'Vintaging Girl,' he had gone on reducing and reducing the proportions of his figures without appearing to be aware of it himself, always ready to stick out ferociously for the gigantic, which agreed with his temperament, but yielding to the partiality of his eyes for sweetness and grace-fulness. And indeed real nature broke at last through inflated ambition. Exaggerated still, his 'Bathing Girl' was already possessed of great charm, with her quivering shoulders and her tightly-crossed arms that supported her breast.

'Well, you don't like her?' he asked, looking annoyed.

'Oh, yes, I do! I think you are right to tone things down a bit, seeing that you feel like that. You'll have a great success with this. Yes, it's evident it will please people very much.'

Mahoudeau, whom such praises would once have thrown into consternation, seemed delighted. He explained that he wished to conquer public opinion without relinquishing a tithe of his convictions.

' Ah ! dash it ! it takes a weight off my mind to find you pleased,' said he, ' for I should have destroyed it if you had told me to do so, I give you my word ! Another fortnight's work, and I'll sell my skin to no matter whom in order to pay the moulder. I say, I shall have a fine show at the Salon, perhaps get a medal.'

He laughed, waved his arms about, and then, breaking off :

' As we are not in a hurry, sit down a bit. I want to get the wraps quite thawed.'

The stove, which was becoming red hot, diffused great heat. The figure, placed close by, seemed to revive under the warm air that now crept up her from her shins to her neck. And the two friends, who had sat down, continued looking the statue full in the face, chatting about it and noting each detail. The sculptor especially grew excited in his delight, and indulged in caressing gestures.

All at once, however, Claude fancied he was the victim of some hallucination. To him the figure seemed to be moving ; a quiver like the ripple of a wavelet crossed her stomach, and her left hip became straightened, as if the right leg were about to step out.

' Have you noticed the smooth surface just about the loins ? ' Mahoudeau went on, without noticing anything. ' Ah, my boy, I took great pains over that ! '

But by degrees the whole statue was becoming animated. The loins swayed and the bosom swelled, as with a deep sigh, between the parted arms. And suddenly the head drooped, the thighs bent, and the figure came forward like a living being, with all the wild anguish, the grief-inspired spring of a woman who is flinging herself down.

Claude at last understood things, when Mahoudeau uttered a terrible cry. ' By heavens, she's breaking to pieces ! —she is coming down ! '

The clay, in thawing, had snapped the weak wooden trusses. There came a cracking noise, as if bones indeed were splitting ; and Mahoudeau, with the same passionate gesture with which he had caressed the figure from afar, working himself into a fever, opened both arms, at the risk of being killed by the fall. For a moment the bathing girl swayed to and fro, and then with one crash came down on her face, broken in twain at the ankles, and leaving her feet sticking to the boards.

Claude had jumped up to hold his friend back.

'Dash it! you'll be smashed!' he cried.

But dreading to see her finish herself off on the floor, Mahoudeau remained with hands outstretched. And the girl seemed to fling herself on his neck. He caught her in his arms, winding them tightly around her. Her bosom was flattened against his shoulder and her thighs beat against his own, while her decapitated head rolled upon the floor. The shock was so violent that Mahoudeau was carried off his legs and thrown over, as far back as the wall; and there, without relaxing his hold on the girl's trunk, he remained as if stunned, lying beside her.

'Ah! confound it!' repeated Claude, furiously, believing that his friend was dead.

With great difficulty Mahoudeau rose to his knees, and burst into violent sobs. He had only damaged his face in the fall. Some blood dribbled down one of his cheeks, mingling with his tears.

'Ah! curse poverty!' he said. 'It's enough to make a fellow drown himself not to be able to buy a couple of rods! And there she is, there she is!'

His sobs grew louder; they became an agonising wail; the painful shrieking of a lover before the mutilated corpse of his affections. With unsteady hands he touched the limbs lying in confusion around him; the head, the torso, the arms that had snapped in twain; above aught else the bosom, now caved in. That bosom, flattened, as if it had been operated upon for some terrible disease, suffocated him, and he unceasingly returned to it, probing the sore, trying to find the gash by which life had fled, while his tears, mingled with blood, flowed freely, and stained the statue's gaping wounds with red.

'Do help me!' he gasped. 'One can't leave her like this.'

Claude was overcome also, and his own eyes grew moist from a feeling of artistic brotherliness. He hastened to his comrade's side, but the sculptor, after claiming his assistance, persisted in picking up the remains by himself, as if dreading the rough handling of anybody else. He slowly crawled about on his knees, took up the fragments one by one, and put them together on a board. The figure soon lay there in its entirety, as if it had been one of those girls who, committing suicide from love, throw themselves from some monument and are shattered by their fall, and put together again, looking both grotesque and lamentable, to be carried to the Morgue. Mahoudeau, seated on the floor before his statue, did not take his eyes from it, but became absorbed in heart-rending contemplation. However, his sobs subsided, and at last he said with a long-drawn sigh : ' I shall have to model her lying down ! There's no other way ! Ah, my poor old woman, I had such trouble to set her on her legs, and I thought her so grand like that ! '

But all at once Claude grew uneasy. What about his wedding ? Mahoudeau must change his clothes. As he had no other frock-coat than the one he was wearing, he was obliged to make a jacket do. Then, the figure having been covered with linen wraps once more, like a corpse over which a sheet has been pulled, they both started off at a run. The stove was roaring away, the thaw filled the whole studio with water, and slush streamed from the old dust-begrimed plaster casts.

When they reached the Rue de Douai there was no one there except little Jacques, in charge of the doorkeeper. Christine, tired of waiting, had just started off with the three others, thinking that there had been some mistake—that Claude might have told her that he would go straight to the mayor's offices with Mahoudeau. The pair fell into a sharp trot, but only overtook Christine and their comrades in the Rue Drouot in front of the municipal edifice. They all went upstairs together, and as they were late they met with a very cool reception from the usher on duty. The wedding was got over in a few minutes, in a perfectly empty room. The mayor mumbled on, and the bride and bridegroom curtly uttered the binding ' Yes,' while their witnesses were marvelling at the bad taste of the appointments of the apartment. Once outside, Claude took Christine's arm again, and that was all.

It was pleasant walking in the clear frosty weather. Thus the party quietly went back on foot, climbing the Rue des Martyrs to reach the restaurant on the Boulevard de Clichy. A small private room had been engaged ; the lunch was a very friendly affair, and not a word was said about the simple formality that had just been gone through ; other subjects were spoken of all the while, as at one of their customary gatherings.

It was thus that Christine, who in reality was very affected despite her pretended indifference, heard her husband and his friends excite themselves for three mortal hours about Mahoudeau's unfortunate statue. Since the others had been made acquainted with the story, they kept harping on every particular of it. Sandoz thought the whole thing very wonderful ; Jory and Gagnière discussed the strength of stays and trusses ; the former mainly concerned about the monetary loss involved, and the other demonstrating with a chair that the statue might have been kept up. As for Mahoudeau, still very shaky and growing dazed, he complained of a stiffness which he had not felt before ; his limbs began to hurt him, he had strained his muscles and bruised his skin as if he had been caught in the embrace of a stone siren. Christine washed the scratch on his cheek, which had begun to bleed again, and it seemed to her as if the mutilated bathing girl had sat down to table with them, as if she alone was of any importance that day ; for she alone seemed to interest Claude, whose narrative, repeated a score of times, was full of endless particulars about the emotion he had felt on seeing that bosom and those hips of clay shattered at his feet.

However, at dessert there came a diversion, for Gagnière all at once remarked to Jory :

' By the way, I saw you with Mathilde the day before yesterday. Yes, yes, in the Rue Dauphine.'

Jory, who had turned very red, tried to deny it ; ' Oh, a mere accidental meeting—honour bright ! ' he stammered. ' I don't know where she hangs out, or I would tell you.'

' What ! is it you who are hiding her ? ' exclaimed Mahoudeau. ' Well, nobody wants to see her again ! '

The truth was that Jory, throwing to the winds all his habits of prudence and parsimony, was now secretly providing for Mathilde. She had gained an ascendency over him by his vices.

They still lingered at table, and night was falling when they escorted Mahoudeau to his own door. Claude and Christine, on reaching home, took Jacques from the door-keeper, and found the studio quite chilly, wrapped in such dense gloom that they had to grope about for several minutes before they were able to light the lamp. They also had to light the stove again, and it struck seven o'clock before they were able to draw breath at their ease. They were not hungry, so they merely finished the remains of some boiled beef, mainly by way of encouraging the child to eat his soup ; and when they had put him to bed, they settled themselves with the lamp betwixt them, as was their habit every evening.

However, Christine had not put out any work, she felt too much moved to sew. She sat there with her hands resting idly on the table, looking at Claude, who on his side had at once become absorbed in a sketch, a bit of his picture, some workmen of the Port Saint Nicolas, unloading plaster. Invincible dreaminess came over the young woman, all sorts of recollections and regrets became apparent in the depths of her dim eyes ; and by degrees growing sadness, great mute grief took absolute possession of her, amid the indifference, the boundless solitude into which she seemed to be drifting, although she was so near to Claude. He was, indeed, on the other side of the table, yet how far away she felt him to be ! He was yonder before that point of the Cité, he was even farther still, in the infinite inaccessible regions of art ; so far, indeed, that she would now never more be able to join him ! She several times tried to start a conversation, but without eliciting any answer. The hours went by, she grew weary and numb with doing nothing, and she ended by taking out her purse and counting her money.

'Do you know how much we have to begin our married life with ? '

Claude did not even raise his head.

'We've nine *sous*. Ah ! talk of poverty——'

He shrugged his shoulders, and finally growled : 'We shall be rich some day ; don't fret.'

Then the silence fell again, and she did not even attempt to break it, but gazed at her nine coppers laid in a row upon the table. At last, as it struck midnight, she shivered, ill with waiting and chilled by the cold.

'Let's go to bed, dear,' she murmured ; 'I'm dead tired.'

He, however, was working frantically, and did not even hear her.

'The fire's gone out,' she began again, 'we shall make ourselves ill ; let's go to bed.'

Her imploring voice reached him at last, and made him start with sudden exasperation.

'Oh! go if you like! You can see very well that I want to finish something!'

She remained there for another minute, amazed by his sudden anger, her face expressive of deep sorrow. Then, feeling that he would rather be without her, that the very presence of a woman doing nothing upset him, she rose from the table and went off, leaving the door wide open. Half an hour, three-quarters went by, nothing stirred, not a sound came from her room; but she was not asleep, her eyes were staring into the gloom; and at last she timidly ventured upon a final appeal, from the depths of the dark alcove.

An oath was the only reply she received. And nothing stirred after that. She perhaps dozed off. The cold in the studio grew keener, and the wick of the lamp began to carbonise and burn red, while Claude, still bending over his sketch, did not seem conscious of the passing minutes.

At two o'clock, however, he rose up, furious to find the lamp going out for lack of oil. He only had time to take it into the other room, so that he might not have to undress in the dark. But his displeasure increased on seeing that Christine's eyes were wide open. He felt inclined to complain of it. However, after some random remarks, he suddenly exclaimed:

'The most surprising thing is that her trunk wasn't hurt!'

'What do you mean?' asked Christine, in amazement.

'Why, Mahoudeau's girl,' he answered.

At this she shook nervously, turned and buried her face in the pillow; and he was quite surprised on hearing her burst into sobs.

'What! you are crying?' he exclaimed.

She was choking, sobbing with heart-rending violence.

'Come, what's the matter with you?—I've said nothing to you. Come, darling, what's the matter?'

But, while he was speaking, the cause of her great grief dawned upon him. No doubt, on a day like that, he ought to have shown more affection; but his neglect was unintentional enough; he had not even given the matter a thought. She surely knew him, said he; he became a downright brute when he was at work. Then he bent over and embraced her. But it was as if something irreparable had taken place, as if something had for ever snapped, leaving a void between them. The formality of marriage seemed to have killed love.

IX

As Claude could not paint his huge picture in the small
studio of the Rue de Douai, he made up his mind to rent some
shed that would be spacious enough, elsewhere; and strolling
one day on the heights of Montmartre, he found what he
wanted half way down the slope of the Rue Tourlaque, a street
that descends abruptly behind the cemetery, and whence one
overlooks Clichy as far as the marshes of Gennevilliers. It
had been a dyer's drying shed, and was nearly fifty feet long
and more than thirty broad, with walls of board and plaster
admitting the wind from every point of the compass. The
place was let to him for three hundred francs. Summer was
at hand; he would soon work off his picture and then quit.

This settled, feverish with hope, Claude decided to go to
all the necessary expenses; as fortune was certain to come in
the end, why trammel its advent by unnecessary scruples?
Taking advantage of his right, he broke in upon the principal
of his income, and soon grew accustomed to spend money without
counting. At first he kept the matter from Christine, for she
had already twice stopped him from doing so; and when he
was at last obliged to tell her, she also, after a week of
reproaches and apprehension, fell in with it, happy at the
comfort in which she lived, and yielding to the pleasure of
always having a little money in her purse. Thus there came
a few years of easy unconcern.

Claude soon became altogether absorbed in his picture.
He had furnished the huge studio in a very summary style: a
few chairs, the old couch from the Quai de Bourbon, and a
deal table bought second-hand for five francs sufficed him. In
the practice of his art he was entirely devoid of that vanity
which delights in luxurious surroundings. The only real
expense to which he went was that of buying some steps on
castors, with a platform and a movable footboard. Next
he busied himself about his canvas, which he wished to be
six and twenty feet in length and sixteen in height. He
insisted upon preparing it himself; ordered a framework and
bought the necessary seamless canvas, which he and a

couple of friends had all the work in the world to stretch properly by the aid of pincers. Then he just coated the canvas with ceruse, laid on with a palette-knife, refusing to size it previously, in order that it might remain absorbent, by which method he declared that the painting would be bright and solid. An easel was not to be thought of. It would not have been possible to move a canvas of such dimensions on it. So he invented a system of ropes and beams, which held it slightly slanting against the wall in a cheerful light. And backwards and forwards in front of the big white surface rolled the steps, looking like an edifice, like the scaffolding by means of which a cathedral is to be reared.

But when everything was ready, Claude once more experienced misgivings. An idea that he had perhaps not chosen the proper light in which to paint his picture fidgeted him. Perhaps an early morning effect would have been better? Perhaps, too, he ought to have chosen a dull day, and so he went back to the Pont des Saint-Pères, and lived there for another three months.

The Cité rose up before him, between the two arms of the river, at all hours and in all weather. After a late fall of snow he beheld it wrapped in ermine, standing above mud-coloured water, against a light slatey sky. On the first sun-shiny days he saw it cleanse itself of everything that was wintry and put on an aspect of youth, when verdure sprouted from the lofty trees which rose from the ground below the bridge. He saw it, too, on a somewhat misty day recede to a distance and almost evaporate, delicate and quivering, like a fairy palace. Then, again, there were pelting rains, which submerged it, hid it as with a huge curtain drawn from the sky to the earth; storms, with lightning flashes which lent it a tawny hue, the opaque light of some cut-throat place half destroyed by the fall of the huge copper-coloured clouds; and there were winds that swept over it tempestuously, sharpening its angles and making it look hard, bare, and beaten against the pale blue sky. Then, again, when the sunbeams broke into dust amidst the vapours of the Seine, it appeared steeped in diffused brightness, without a shadow about it, lighted up equally on every side, and looking as charmingly delicate as a cut gem set in fine gold. He insisted on beholding it when the sun was rising and transpiercing the morning mists, when the Quai de l'Horloge flushes and the Quai des Orfèvres remains wrapt in gloom; when, up in the pink sky, it is already full of life, with the bright awakening of its towers and spires, while night, similar to a falling cloak, slides slowly from its lower buildings. He beheld it also at noon, when the sunrays fall on it vertically, when a crude glare bites into it, and it becomes discoloured and mute like a dead city, retaining nought but the life of heat, the quiver that darts over its distant housetops. He beheld it, moreover, beneath the setting sun, surrendering itself to the night which was slowly rising from the river, with the salient edges of its buildings still fringed with a glow as of embers, and with final conflagrations rekindling in its windows, from whose panes leapt tongue-like flashes. But in presence of those twenty different aspects of the Cité, no matter what the hour or the weather might be, he ever came back to the Cité that he had seen the first time, at about four o'clock one fine September afternoon, a Cité all serenity under a gentle breeze, a Cité which typified the heart of Paris beating in the limpid atmosphere, and seemingly enlarged by the vast stretch of sky which a flight of cloudlets crossed.

Claude spent his time under the Pont des Saints-Pères, which he had made his shelter, his home, his roof. The constant din of the vehicles overhead, similar to the distant rumbling of thunder, no longer disturbed him. Settling himself against the first abutment, beneath the huge iron arches, he took sketches and painted studies. The *employés* of the river navigation service, whose offices were hard by, got to know him, and, indeed, the wife of an inspector, who lived in a sort of tarred cabin with her husband, two children, and a cat, kept his canvases for him, to save him the trouble of carrying them to and fro each day. It became his joy to remain in that secluded nook beneath Paris, which rumbled in the air above him, whose ardent life he ever felt rolling overhead. He at first became passionately interested in Port St. Nicolas, with its ceaseless bustle suggesting that of a distant genuine seaport. The steam crane, *The Sophia*, worked regularly, hauling up blocks of stone ; tumbrels arrived to fetch loads of sand ; men and horses pulled, panting for breath on the big paving-stones, which sloped down as far as the water, to a granite margin, alongside which two rows of lighters and barges were moored. For weeks Claude worked hard at a study of some lightermen unloading a cargo of plaster, carrying white sacks on their shoulders, leaving a white pathway behind them, and bepowdered with white themselves, whilst hard by the coal removed from another barge had stained the waterside with a huge inky smear. Then he sketched the silhouette of a swimming-bath on the left bank, together with a floating wash-house somewhat in the rear, showing the windows open and the washerwomen kneeling in a row, on a level with the stream, and beating their dirty linen. In the middle of the river, he studied a boat which a waterman sculled over the stern ; then, farther behind, a steamer of the towing service straining its chain, and dragging a series of rafts loaded with barrels and boards up stream. The principal backgrounds had been sketched a long while ago, still he did several bits over again—the two arms of the Seine, and a sky all by itself, into which rose only towers and spires gilded by the sun. And under the hospitable bridge, in that nook as secluded as some far-off cleft in a rock, he was rarely disturbed by anybody. Anglers passed by with contemptuous unconcern. His only companion was virtually the overseer's cat, who cleaned herself in the sunlight, ever placid beneath the tumult of the world overhead.

At last Claude had all his materials ready. In a few days he threw off an outline sketch of the whole, and the great work was begun. However, the first battle between himself and his huge canvas raged in the Rue Tourlaque throughout the summer ; for he obstinately insisted upon personally attending to all the technical calculations of his composition, and he failed to manage them, getting into constant muddles about the slightest deviation from mathematical accuracy, of which he had no experience. It made him indignant with himself. So he let it go, deciding to make what corrections might be necessary afterwards. He covered his canvas with a rush—in such a fever as to live all day on his steps, brandishing huge brushes, and expending as much muscular force as if he were anxious to move mountains. And when evening came he reeled about like a drunken man, and fell asleep as soon as he had swallowed his last mouthful of food. His wife even had to put him to bed like a child. From those heroic efforts, however, sprang a masterly first draught in which genius blazed forth amidst the somewhat chaotic masses of colour. Bongrand, who came to look at it, caught the painter in his big arms, and stifled him with embraces, his eyes full of tears. Sandoz, in his enthusiasm, gave a dinner ; the others, Jory, Mahoudeau and Gagnière, again went about announcing a masterpiece. As for Fagerolles, he

remained motionless before the painting for a moment, then
burst into congratulations, pronouncing it too beautiful.

And, in fact, subsequently, as if the irony of that successful
trickster had brought him bad luck, Claude only spoilt his
original draught. It was the old story over again. He spent
himself in one effort, one magnificent dash ; he failed to bring
out all the rest ; he did not know how to finish. He fell into
his former impotence ; for two years he lived before that
picture only, having no feeling for anything else. At times
he was in a seventh heaven of exuberant joy ; at others flung
to earth, so wretched, so distracted by doubt, that dying men
gasping in their beds in a hospital were happier than himself.
Twice already had he failed to be ready for the Salon, for
invariably, at the last moment, when he hoped to have
finished in a few sittings, he found some void, felt his composition crack and crumble beneath his fingers. When the third
Salon drew nigh, there came a terrible crisis ; he remained
for a fortnight without going to his studio in the Rue
Tourlaque, and when he did so, it was as to a house desolated
by death. He turned the huge canvas to the wall and
rolled his steps into a corner ; he would have smashed and
burned everything if his faltering hands had found strength
enough. Nothing more existed ; amid a blast of anger he
swept the floor clean, and spoke of setting to work at little
things, since he was incapable of perfecting paintings of any
size.

In spite of himself, his first idea of a picture on a smaller
scale took him back to the Cité. Why should not he paint a
simple view, on a moderate sized canvas ? But a kind of shame,
mingled with strange jealousy, prevented him from settling
himself in his old spot under the Pont des Saints-Pères. It
seemed to him as if that spot were sacred now ; that he ought
not to offer any outrage to his great work, dead as it was.
So he stationed himself at the end of the bank, above the
bridge. This time, at any rate, he would work directly from
nature ; and he felt happy at not having to resort to any
trickery, as was unavoidable with works of a large size. The
small picture, very carefully painted, more highly finished
than usual, met, however, with the same fate as the others
before the hanging committee, who were indignant with this
style of painting, executed with a tipsy brush, as was said at
the time in the studios. The slap in the face which Claude
thus received was all the more severe, as a report had spread

of concessions, of advances made by him to the School of Arts, in order that his work might be received. And when the picture came back to him, he, deeply wounded, weeping with rage, tore it into narrow shreds, which he burned in his stove. It was not sufficient that he should kill that one with a knife-thrust, it must be annihilated.

Another year went by for Claude in desultory toil. He worked from force of habit, but finished nothing ; he himself saying, with a dolorous laugh, that he had lost himself, and was trying to find himself again. In reality, tenacious consciousness of his genius left him a hope which nothing could destroy, even during his longest crises of despondency. He suffered like some one damned, for ever rolling the rock which slipped back and crushed him ; but the future remained, with the certainty of one day seizing that rock in his powerful arms and flinging it upward to the stars. His friends at last beheld his eyes light up with passion once more. It was known that he again secluded himself in the Rue Tourlaque. He who formerly had always been carried beyond the work on which he was engaged, by some dream of a picture to come, now stood at bay before that subject of the Cité. It had become his fixed idea—the bar that closed up his life. And soon he began to speak freely of it again in a new blaze of enthusiasm, exclaiming, with childish delight, that he had found his way and that he felt certain of victory.

One day Claude, who, so far, had not opened his door to his friends, condescended to admit Sandoz. The latter tumbled upon a study with a deal of dash in it, thrown off without a model, and again admirable in colour. The subject had remained the same—the Port St. Nicolas on the left, the swimming-baths on the right, the Seine and Cité in the background. But Sandoz was amazed at perceiving, instead of the boat sculled by a waterman, another large skiff taking up the whole centre of the composition—a skiff occupied by three women. One, in a bathing costume, was rowing ; another sat over the edge with her legs dangling in the water, her costume partially unfastened, showing her bare shoulder ; while the third stood erect and nude at the prow, so bright in tone that she seemed effulgent, like the sun.

'Why, what an idea!' muttered Sandoz. 'What are those women doing there?'

'Why, they are bathing,' Claude quietly answered. 'Don't you see that they have come out of the swimming-baths? It supplies me with a motive for the nude; it's a real find, eh? Does it shock you?'

His old friend, who knew him well by now, dreaded lest he should give him cause for discouragement.

'I? Oh, no! Only I am afraid that the public will again fail to understand. That nude woman in the very midst of Paris—it's improbable.'

Claude looked naïvely surprised.

'Ah! you think so? Well, so much the worse. What's the odds, as long as the woman is well painted? Besides, I need something like that to get my courage up.'

On the following occasions, Sandoz gently reverted to the strangeness of the composition, pleading, as was his nature, the cause of outraged logic. How could a modern painter who prided himself on painting merely what was real—how could he so bastardise his work as to introduce fanciful things into it? It would have been so easy to choose another subject, in which the nude would have been necessary. But Claude became obstinate, and resorted to lame and violent explanations, for he would not avow his real motive: an idea which had come to him and which he would have been at a loss to express clearly. It was, however, a longing for some secret symbolism. A recrudescence of romanticism made him see an incarnation of Paris in that nude figure; he pictured the city bare and impassioned, resplendent with the beauty of woman.

Before the pressing objections of his friend he pretended to be shaken in his resolutions.

'Well, I'll see; I'll dress my old woman later on, since she worries you,' he said. 'But meanwhile I shall do her like that. You understand, she amuses me.'

He never reverted to the subject again, remaining silently obstinate, merely shrugging his shoulders and smiling with embarrassment whenever any allusion betrayed the general astonishment which was felt at the sight of that Venus emerging triumphantly from the froth of the Seine amidst all the omnibuses on the quays and the lightermen working at the Port of St. Nicolas.

Spring had come round again, and Claude had once more resolved to work at his large picture, when in a spirit of prudence he and Christine modified their daily life. She, at times, could not help feeling uneasy at seeing all their money so quickly spent. Since the supply had seemed inexhaustible, they had ceased counting. But, at the end of four years, they had woke up one morning quite frightened, when, on asking for accounts, they found that barely three thousand francs were left out of the twenty thousand. They immediately reverted to severe economy, stinting themselves as to bread, planning the cutting down of the most elementary expenses; and it was thus that, in the first impulse of self-sacrifice, they left the Rue de Douai. What was the use of paying two rents? There was room enough in the old drying-shed in the Rue Tourlaque—still stained with the dyes of former days —to afford accommodation for three people. Settling there was, nevertheless, a difficult affair; for -however big the place was, it provided them, after all, with but one room. It was like a gipsy's shed, where everything had to be done in common. As the landlord was unwilling, the painter himself had to divide it at one end by a partition of boards, behind which he devised a kitchen and a bedroom. They were then delighted with the place, despite the chinks through which the wind blew, and although on rainy days they had to set basins beneath the broader cracks in the roof. The whole looked mournfully bare; their few poor sticks seemed to dance alongside the naked walls. They themselves pretended to be proud at being lodged so spaciously; they told their friends that Jacques would at least have a little room to run about. Poor Jacques, in spite of his nine years, did not seem to be growing; his head alone became larger and larger. They could not send him to school for more than a week at a stretch, for he came back absolutely dazed, ill from having tried to learn, in such wise that they nearly always allowed him to live on all fours around them, crawling from one corner to another.

Christine, who for quite a long while had not shared Claude's daily work, now once more found herself beside him throughout his long hours of toil. She helped him to scrape and pumice the old canvas of the big picture, and gave him advice about attaching it more securely to the wall. But they found that another disaster had befallen them—the steps had become warped by the water constantly trickling through the roof, and, for fear of an accident, Claude had to strengthen them with an oak cross-piece, she handing him the necessary nails one by one. Then once more, and for the second time, everything was ready. She watched him again outlining the work, standing behind him the while, till she felt faint with fatigue, and finally dropping to the floor, where she remained squatting, and still looking at him.

Ah! how she would have liked to snatch him from that painting which had seized hold of him! It was for that purpose that she made herself his servant, only too happy to lower herself to a labourer's toil. Since she shared his work again, since the three of them, he, she, and the canvas, were side by side, her hope revived. If he had escaped her when she, all alone, cried her eyes out in the Rue de Douai, if he lingered till late in the Rue Tourlaque, fascinated as by a mistress, perhaps now that she was present she might regain her hold over him. Ah, painting, painting! in what jealous hatred she held it! Hers was no longer the revolt of a girl of the *bourgeoisie*, who painted neatly in water-colours, against independent, brutal, magnificent art. No, little by little she had come to understand it; drawn towards it at first by her love for the painter, and gained over afterwards by the feast of light, by the original charm of the bright tints which Claude's works displayed. And now she had accepted everything, even lilac-tinted soil and blue trees. Indeed, a kind of respect made her quiver before those works which had at first seemed so horrid to her. She recognised their power well enough, and treated them like rivals about whom one could no longer joke. But her vindictiveness grew in proportion to her admiration; she revolted at having to stand by and witness, as it were, a diminution of herself, the blow of another love beneath her own roof.

At first there was a silent struggle of every minute. She thrust herself forward, interposed whatever she could, a hand, a shoulder, between the painter and his picture. She was always there, encompassing him with her breath, reminding him that he was hers. Then her old idea revived —she also would paint; she would seek and join him in the depths of his art fever. Every day for a whole month she put on a blouse, and worked like a pupil by the side of a master, diligently copying one of his sketches, and she only gave in when she found the effort turn against her object; for, deceived, as it were, by their joint work, he finished by forgetting that she was a woman, and lived with her on a footing of mere comradeship as between man and man. Accordingly she resorted to what was her only strength.

To perfect some of the small figures of his latter pictures, Claude had many a time already taken the hint of a head, the

pose of an arm, the attitude of a body from Christine. He
threw a cloak over her shoulders, and caught her in the posture
he wanted, shouting to her not to stir.   These were little
services which she showed herself only too pleased to render
him, but she had not hitherto cared to go further, for she was
hurt by the idea of being a model now that she was his wife.
However, since Claude had broadly outlined the large,
upright female figure which was to occupy the centre of his
picture, Christine had looked at the vague silhouette in a
dreamy way, worried by an ever-pursuing thought before
which all scruples vanished. And so, when he spoke of
taking a model, she offered herself, reminding him that she
had posed for the figure in the ' Open Air ' subject, long ago.
' A model,' she added, ' would cost you seven francs a sitting.
We are not so rich, we may as well save the money.'

The question of economy decided him at once.

' I'm agreeable, and it's even very good of you to show
such courage, for you know that it is not a bit of pastime to
sit for me. Never mind, you had better confess to it, you
big silly, you are afraid of another woman coming here ; you
are jealous.'

Jealous !   Yes, indeed she was jealous, so jealous that
she suffered agony. But she snapped her fingers at other
women ; all the models in Paris might have sat to him for
what she cared. She had but one rival, that painting, that
art which robbed her of him.

Claude, who was delighted, at first made a study, a
simple academic study, in the attitude required for his
picture.   They waited until Jacques had gone to school,
and the sitting lasted for hours. During the earlier days
Christine suffered a great deal from being obliged to remain
in the same position ; then she grew used to it, not daring to
complain, lest she might vex him, and even restraining her
tears when he roughly pushed her about. And he soon
acquired the habit of doing so, treating her like a mere
model ; more exacting with her, however, than if he had
paid her, never afraid of unduly taxing her strength, since
she was his wife. He employed her for every purpose, at every
minute, for an arm, a foot, the most trifling detail that he
stood in need of. And thus in a way he lowered her to the
level of a ' living lay figure,' which he stuck in front of him
and copied as he might have copied a pitcher or a stew-pan
for a bit of still life.

This time Claude proceeded leisurely, and before roughing in the large figure he tired Christine for months by making her pose in twenty different ways. At last, one day, he began the roughing in. It was an autumnal morning, the north wind was already sharp, and it was by no means warm even in the big studio, although the stove was roaring. As little Jacques was poorly again and unable to go to school, they had decided to lock him up in the room at the back, telling him to be very good. And then the mother settled herself near the stove, motionless, in the attitude required.

During the first hour, the painter, perched upon his steps, kept glancing at her, but did not speak a word. Unutterable sadness stole over her, and she felt afraid of fainting, no longer knowing whether she was suffering from the cold or from a despair that had come from afar, and the bitterness of which she felt to be rising within her. Her fatigue became so great that she staggered and hobbled about on her numbed legs.

'What, already?' cried Claude. 'Why, you haven't been at it more than a quarter of an hour. You don't want to earn your seven francs, then?'

He was joking in a gruff voice, delighted with his work. And she had scarcely recovered the use of her limbs, beneath the dressing-gown she had wrapped round her, when he went on shouting: 'Come on, come on, no idling! It's a grand day to-day is! I must either show some genius or else kick the bucket.'

Then, in a weary way, she at last resumed the pose.

The misfortune was that before long, both by his glances and the language he used, she fully realised that she herself was as nothing to him. If ever he praised a limb, a tint, a contour, it was solely from the artistic point of view. Great enthusiasm and passion he often showed, but it was not passion for herself as in the old days. She felt confused and deeply mortified. Ah! this was the end; in her he no longer loved aught but his art, the example of nature and life! And then, with her eyes gazing into space, she would remain rigid, like a statue, keeping back the tears which made her heart swell, lacking even the wretched consolation of being able to cry. And day by day the same sorry life began afresh for her. To stand there as his model had become her profession. She could not refuse, however bitter her grief. Their once happy life was all over, there now seemed to be three people in the place ; it was as if Claude had introduced a mistress into it —that woman he was painting. The huge picture rose up between them, parted them as with a wall, beyond which he lived with the other. That duplication of herself well nigh drove Christine mad with jealousy, and yet she was conscious of the pettiness of her sufferings, and did not dare to confess them lest he should laugh at her. However, she did not deceive herself ; she fully realised that he preferred her counterfeit to herself, that her image was the worshipped one, the sole thought, the affection of his every hour. He almost killed her with long sittings in that cold draughty studio, in order to enhance the beauty of the other ; upon whom depended all his joys and sorrows according as to whether he beheld her live or languish beneath his brush. Was not this love ? And what suffering to have to lend herself so that the other might be created, so that she might be haunted by a nightmare of that rival, so that the latter might for ever rise between them, more powerful than reality ! To think of it ! So much dust, the veriest trifle, a patch of colour on a canvas, a mere semblance destroying all their happiness !—he, silent, indifferent, brutal at times, and she, tortured by his desertion, in despair at being unable to drive away that creature who ever encroached more and more upon their daily life !

And it was then that Christine, finding herself altogether beaten in her efforts to regain Claude's love, felt all the sovereignty of art weigh down upon her. That painting, which she had already accepted without restriction, she raised still higher in her estimation, placed inside an awesome tabernacle before which she remained overcome, as before those powerful divinities of wrath which one honours from the very hatred and fear that they inspire. Hers was a holy awe, a conviction that struggling was henceforth useless, that she would be crushed like a bit of straw if she persisted in her obstinacy. Each of her husband's canvases became magnified in her eyes, the smallest assumed triumphal dimensions, even the worst painted of them overwhelmed her with victory, and she no longer judged them, but grovelled, trembling, thinking them all formidable, and invariably replying to Claude's questions :

'Oh, yes ; very good ! Oh, superb ! Oh, very, very extra-ordinary that one !'

Nevertheless, she harboured no anger against him ; she

still worshipped him with tearful tenderness, as she saw him thus consume himself with efforts. After a few weeks of successful work, everything got spoilt again; he could not finish his large female figure. At times he almost killed his model with fatigue, keeping hard at work for days and days together, then leaving the picture untouched for a whole month. The figure was begun anew, relinquished, painted all over again at least a dozen times. One year, two years went by without the picture reaching completion. Though sometimes it was almost finished, it was scratched out the next morning and painted entirely over again.

Ah! what an effort of creation it was, an effort of blood and tears, filling Claude with agony in his attempt to beget flesh and instil life! Ever battling with reality, and ever beaten, it was a struggle with the Angel. He was wearing himself out with this impossible task of making a canvas hold all nature; he became exhausted at last with the pains which racked his muscles without ever being able to bring his genius to fruition. What others were satisfied with, a more or less faithful rendering, the various necessary bits of trickery, filled him with remorse, made him as indignant as if in resorting to such practices one were guilty of ignoble cowardice; and thus he began his work over and over again, spoiling what was good through his craving to do better. He would always be dissatisfied with his women—so his friends jokingly declared—until they flung their arms round his neck. What was lacking in his power that he could not endow them with life? Very little, no doubt. Sometimes he went beyond the right point, sometimes he stopped short of it. One day the words, 'an incomplete genius,' which he overheard, both flattered and frightened him. Yes, it must be that; he jumped too far or not far enough; he suffered from a want of nervous balance; he was afflicted with some hereditary derangement which, because there were a few grains the more or the less of some substance in his brain, was making him a lunatic instead of a great man. Whenever a fit of despair drove him from his studio, whenever he fled from his work, he now carried about with him that idea of fatal impotence, and he heard it beating against his skull like the obstinate tolling of a funeral bell.

His life became wretched. Never had doubt of himself pursued him in that way before. He disappeared for whole days together; he even stopped out a whole night, coming

back the next morning stupefied, without being able to say
where he had gone. It was thought that he had been tramping through the outskirts of Paris rather than find himself
face to face with his spoilt work. His sole relief was to flee
the moment that work filled him with shame and hatred, and
to remain away until he felt sufficient courage to face it once
more. And not even his wife dared to question him on his
return—indeed, she was only too happy to see him back again
after her anxious waiting. At such times he madly scoured
Paris, especially the outlying quarters, from a longing to
debase himself and hob-nob with labourers. He expressed at
each recurring crisis his old regret at not being some mason's
hodman. Did not happiness consist in having solid limbs,
and in performing the work one was built for well and
quickly? He had wrecked his life; he ought to have got
himself engaged in the building line in the old times when
he had lunched at the 'Dog of Montargis,' Gomard's tavern,
where he had known a Limousin, a big, strapping, merry
fellow, whose brawny arms he envied. Then, on coming
back to the Rue Tourlaque, with his legs faint and his head
empty, he gave his picture much the same distressful,
frightened glance as one casts at a corpse in a mortuary, until
fresh hope of resuscitating it, of endowing it with life, brought
a flush to his face once more.

One day Christine was posing, and the figure of the
woman was again well nigh finished. For the last hour,
however, Claude had been growing gloomy, losing the childish
delight that he had displayed at the beginning of the sitting.
So his wife scarcely dared to breathe, feeling by her own discomfort that everything must be going wrong once more,
and afraid that she might accelerate the catastrophe if she
moved as much as a finger. And, surely enough, he suddenly
gave a cry of anguish, and launched forth an oath in a
thunderous voice.

'Oh, curse it! curse it!'

He had flung his handful of brushes from the top of the
steps. Then, blinded with rage, with one blow of his fist he
transpierced the canvas.

Christine held out her trembling hands.

'My dear, my dear!'

But when she had flung a dressing-gown over her
shoulders, and approached the picture, she experienced keen
delight, a burst of satisfied hatred. Claude's fist had struck

'the other one' full in the bosom, and there was a gaping hole! At last, then, that other one was killed!

Motionless, horror-struck by that murder, Claude stared at the perforated bosom. Poignant grief came upon him at the sight of the wound whence the blood of his work seemed to flow. Was it possible? Was it he who had thus murdered what he loved best of all on earth? His anger changed into stupor; his fingers wandered over the canvas, drawing the ragged edges of the rent together, as if he had wished to close the bleeding gash. He was choking; he stammered, distracted with boundless grief:

'She is killed, she is killed!'

Then Christine, in her maternal love for that big child of an artist, felt moved to her very entrails. She forgave him as usual. She saw well enough that he now had but one thought—to mend the rent, to repair the evil at once; and she helped him; it was she who held the shreds together, whilst he from behind glued a strip of canvas against them. When she dressed herself, 'the other one' was there again, immortal, simply retaining near her heart a slight scar, which seemed to make her doubly dear to the painter.

As this unhinging of Claude's faculties increased, he drifted into a sort of superstition, into a devout belief in certain processes and methods. He banished oil from his colours, and spoke of it as of a personal enemy. On the other hand, he held that turpentine produced a solid unpolished surface, and he had some secrets of his own which he hid from everybody; solutions of amber, liquefied copal, and other resinous compounds that made colours dry quickly, and prevented them from cracking. But he experienced some terrible worries, as the absorbent nature of the canvas at once sucked in the little oil contained in the paint. Then the question of brushes had always worried him greatly; he insisted on having them with special handles; and objecting to sable, he used nothing but oven-dried badger hair. More important, however, than everything else was the question of palette-knives, which, like Courbet, he used for his backgrounds. He had quite a collection of them, some long and flexible, others broad and squat, and one which was triangular like a glazier's, and which had been expressly made for him. It was the real Delacroix knife. Besides, he never made use of the scraper or razor, which he considered beneath an artist's dignity. But, on the other hand, he indulged in all sorts of mysterious practices in applying his colours, concocted recipes and changed them every month, and suddenly fancied that he had hit on the right system of painting, when, after repudiating oil and its flow, he began to lay on successive touches until he arrived at the exact tone he required. One of his fads for a long while was to paint from right to left; for, without confessing as much, he felt sure that it brought him luck. But the terrible affair which unhinged him once more was an all-invading theory respecting the complementary colours. Gagnière had been the first to speak to him on the subject, being himself equally inclined to technical speculation. After which Claude, impelled by the exuberance of his passion, took to exaggerating the scientific principles whereby, from the three primitive colours, yellow, red, and blue, one derives the three secondary ones, orange, green, and violet, and, further, a whole series of complementary and similar hues, whose composites are obtained mathematically from one another. Thus science entered into painting, there was a method for logical observation already. One only had to take the predominating hue of a picture, and note the complementary or similar colours, to establish experimentally what variations would occur; for instance, red would turn yellowish if it were near blue, and a whole landscape would change in tint by the refractions and the very decomposition of light, according to the clouds passing over it. Claude then accurately came to this conclusion : That objects have no real fixed colour; that they assume various hues according to ambient circumstances; but the misfortune was that when he took to direct observation, with his brain throbbing with scientific formulas, his prejudiced vision lent too much force to delicate shades, and made him render what was theoretically correct in too vivid a manner : thus his style, once so bright, so full of the palpitation of sunlight, ended in a reversal of everything to which the eye was accustomed, giving, for instance, flesh of a violet tinge under tricoloured skies. Insanity seemed to be at the end of it all.

Poverty finished off Claude. It had gradually increased, while the family spent money without counting; and, when the last copper of the twenty thousand francs had gone, it swooped down upon them—horrible and irreparable. Christine, who wanted to look for work, was incapable of doing anything, even ordinary needlework. She bewailed her lot, twirling her fingers and inveighing against the idiotic young lady's education that she had received, since it had given her no profession, and her only resource would be to enter into domestic service, should life still go against them. Claude, on his side, had become a subject of chaff with the Parisians, and no longer sold a picture. An independent exhibition at which he and some friends had shown some pictures, had finished him off as regards amateurs—so merry had the public become at the sight of his canvases, streaked with all the colours of the rainbow. The dealers fled from him. M. Hue alone now and then made a pilgrimage to the Rue Tourlaque, and remained in ecstasy before the exaggerated bits, those which blazed in unexpected pyrotechnical fashion, in despair at being unable to cover them with gold. And though the painter wanted to make him a present of them, implored him to accept them, the old fellow displayed extraordinary delicacy of feeling. He pinched himself to amass a small sum of money from time to time, and then religiously took away the seemingly delirious picture, to hang it beside his masterpieces. Such windfalls came too seldom, and Claude was obliged to descend to 'trade art,' repugnant as it was to him. Such, indeed, was his despair at having fallen into that poison house, where he had sworn never to set foot, that he would have preferred starving to death, but for the two poor beings who were dependent on him and who suffered like himself. He became familiar with 'viæ dolorosæ' painted at reduced prices, with male and female saints at so much per gross, even with 'pounced' shop blinds—in short, all the ignoble jobs that degrade painting and make it so much idiotic delineation, lacking even the charm of *naïveté*. He even suffered the humiliation of having portraits at five-and-twenty francs a-piece refused, because he failed to produce a likeness; and he reached the lowest degree of distress—he worked according to size for the petty dealers who sell daubs on the bridges, and export them to semi-civilised countries. They bought his pictures at two and three francs a-piece, according to the regulation dimensions. This was like physical decay, it made him waste away; he rose from such tasks feeling ill, incapable of serious work, looking at his large picture in distress, and leaving it sometimes untouched for a week, as if he had felt his hands befouled and unworthy of working at it.

They scarcely had bread to eat, and the huge shanty, which Christine had shown herself so proud of, on settling in it, became uninhabitable in the winter. She, once such an active housewife, now dragged herself about the place, without courage even to sweep the floor, and thus everything lapsed into abandonment. In the disaster little Jacques was sadly weakened by unwholesome and insufficient food, for their meals often consisted of a mere crust, eaten standing. With their lives thus ill-regulated, uncared for, they were drifting to the filth of the poor who lose even all self-pride.

At the close of another year, Claude, on one of those days of defeat, when he fled from his miscarried picture, met an old acquaintance. This time he had sworn he would never go home again, and he had been tramping across Paris since noon, as if at his heels he had heard the wan spectre of the big, nude figure of his picture—ravaged by constant retouching, and always left incomplete—pursuing him with a passionate craving for birth. The mist was melting into a yellowish drizzle, befouling the muddy streets. It was about five o'clock, and he was crossing the Rue Royale like one walking in his sleep, at the risk of being run over, his clothes in rags and mud-bespattered up to his neck, when a brougham suddenly drew up.

'Claude, eh? Claude!—is that how you pass your friends?'

It was Irma Bécot who spoke, Irma in a charming grey silk dress, covered with Chantilly lace. She had hastily let down the window, and she sat smiling, beaming in the framework of the carriage door.

'Where are you going?'

He, staring at her open-mouthed, replied that he was going nowhere. At which she merrily expressed surprise in a loud voice, looking at him with her saucy eyes.

'Get in, then; it's such a long while since we met,' said she. 'Get in, or you'll be knocked down.'

And, in fact, the other drivers were getting impatient, and urging their horses on, amidst a terrible din, so he did as he was bidden, feeling quite dazed; and she drove him away, dripping, with the unmistakable signs of his poverty upon him, in the brougham lined with blue satin, where he sat partly on the lace of her skirt, while the cabdrivers jeered at the elopement before falling into line again.

When Claude came back to the Rue Tourlaque he was in a dazed condition, and for a couple of days remained musing whether after all he might not have taken the wrong course in life. He seemed so strange that Christine questioned him, whereupon he at first stuttered and stammered, and finally confessed everything. There was a scene; she wept for a long while, then pardoned him once more, full of infinite indulgence for him. And, indeed, amidst all her bitter grief there sprang up a hope that he might yet return to her, for if he could deceive her thus he could not care as much as she had imagined for that hateful painted creature who stared down from the big canvas.

The days went by, and towards the middle of the winter Claude's courage revived once more. One day, while putting some old frames in order, he came upon a roll of canvas which had fallen behind the other pictures. On opening the roll he found on it the nude figure, the reclining woman of his old painting, 'In the Open Air,' which he had cut out when the picture had come back to him from the Salon of the Rejected. And, as he gazed at it, he uttered a cry of admiration:

'By the gods, how beautiful it is!'

He at once secured it to the wall with four nails, and remained for hours in contemplation before it. His hands shook, the blood rushed to his face. Was it possible that he had painted such a masterly thing? He had possessed genius in those days then. So his skull, his eyes, his fingers had been changed. He became so feverishly excited and felt such a need of unburthening himself to somebody, that at last he called his wife.

'Just come and have a look. Isn't her attitude good, eh? How delicately her muscles are articulated! Just look at that bit there, full of sunlight. And at the shoulder here. Ah, heavens! it's full of life; I can feel it throb as I touch it.'

Christine, standing by, kept looking and answering in monosyllables. This resurrection of herself, after so many years, had at first flattered and surprised her. But on seeing him become so excited, she gradually felt uncomfortable and irritated, without knowing why.

'Tell me,' he continued, 'don't you think her beautiful enough for one to go on one's knees to her?'

'Yes, yes. But she has become rather blackish——'

Claude protested vehemently. Become blackish, what an idea! That woman would never grow black; she possessed immortal youth! Veritable passion had seized hold

of him; he spoke of the figure as of a living being; he
had sudden longings to look at her that made him leave
everything else, as if he were hurrying to an appointment.

Then, one morning, he was taken with a fit of work.

'But, confound it all, as I did that, I can surely do it
again,' he said. 'Ah, this time, unless I'm a downright
brute, we'll see about it.'

And Christine had to give him a sitting there and then.
For eight hours a day, indeed, during a whole month he kept
her before him, without compassion for her increasing
exhaustion or for the fatigue he felt himself. He obstinately
insisted upon producing a masterpiece; he was determined
that the upright figure of his big picture should equal that
reclining one which he saw on the wall, beaming with life.
He constantly referred to it, compared it with the one he was
painting, distracted by the fear of being unable to equal it.
He cast one glance at it, another at Christine, and a third at
his canvas, and burst into oaths whenever he felt dissatisfied.
He ended by abusing his wife.

She was no longer young. Age had spoilt her figure,
and that it was which spoilt his work. She listened, and
staggered in her very grief. Those sittings, from which she
had already suffered so much, were becoming unbearable
torture now. What was this new freak of crushing her with
her own girlhood, of fanning her jealousy by filling her with
regret for vanished beauty? She was becoming her own rival,
she could no longer look at that old picture of herself without
being stung at the heart by hateful envy. Ah, how heavily
had that picture, that study she had sat for long ago, weighed
upon her existence! The whole of her misfortunes sprang
from it. It had changed the current of her existence. And
it had come to life again, it rose from the dead, endowed with
greater vitality than herself, to finish killing her, for there
was no longer aught but one woman for Claude—she who
was shown reclining on the old canvas, and who now arose
and became the upright figure of his new picture.

Then Christine felt herself growing older and older at
each successive sitting. And she experienced the infinite
despair which comes upon passionate women when love, like
beauty, abandons them. Was it because of this that Claude
no longer cared for her, that he sought refuge in an unnatural
passion for his work? She soon lost all clear perception of
things; she fell into a state of utter neglect, going about in a

dressing jacket and dirty petticoats, devoid of all coquettish feeling, discouraged by the idea that it was useless for her to continue struggling, since she had become old.

There were occasionally abominable scenes between her and Claude, who this time, however, obstinately stuck to his work and finished his picture, swearing that, come what might, he would send it to the Salon. He lived on his steps, cleaning up his backgrounds until dark. At last, thoroughly exhausted, he declared that he would touch the canvas no more; and Sandoz, on coming to see him one day, at four o'clock, did not find him at home. Christine declared that he had just gone out to take a breath of air on the height of Montmartre.

The breach between Claude and his old friends had gradually widened. With time the latters' visits had become brief and far between, for they felt uncomfortable when they found themselves face to face with that disturbing style of painting; and they were more and more upset by the un-hinging of a mind which had been the admiration of their youth. Now all had fled; none excepting Sandoz ever came. Gagnière had even left Paris, to settle down in one of the two houses he owned at Melun, where he lived frugally upon the proceeds of the other one, after suddenly marrying, to every one's surprise, an old maid, his music mistress, who played Wagner to him of an evening. As for Mahoudeau, he alleged work as an excuse for not coming, and indeed he was beginning to earn some money, thanks to a bronze manu-facturer, who employed him to touch up his models. Matters were different with Jory, whom no one saw, since Mathilde despotically kept him sequestrated. She had conquered him, and he had fallen into a kind of domesticity comparable to that of a faithful dog, yielding up the keys of his cashbox, and only carrying enough money about him to buy a cigar at a time. It was even said that Mathilde, like the devotee she had once been, had thrown him into the arms of the Church, in order to consolidate her conquest, and that she was con-stantly talking to him about death, of which he was horribly afraid. Fagerolles alone affected a lively, cordial feeling towards his old friend Claude whenever he happened to meet him. He then always promised to go and see him, but never did so. He was so busy since his great success, in such request, advertised, celebrated, on the road to every imagin-able honour and form of fortune! And Claude regretted

nobody save Dubuche, to whom he still felt attached, from a
feeling of affection for the old reminiscences of boyhood,
notwithstanding the disagreements which difference of disposition had provoked later on. But Dubuche, it appeared,
was not very happy either. No doubt he was gorged with
millions, but he led a wretched life, constantly at logger-
heads with his father-in-law (who complained of having been
deceived with regard to his capabilities as an architect), and
obliged to pass his life amidst the medicine bottles of his
ailing wife and his two children, who, having been prema-
turely born, had to be reared virtually in cotton wool.

Of all the old friends, therefore, there only remained
Sandoz, who still found his way to the Rue Tourlaque. He
came thither for little Jacques, his godson, and for the
sorrowing woman also, that Christine whose passionate
features amidst all this distress moved him deeply, like a
vision of one of the ardently amorous creatures whom he
would have liked to embody in his books. But, above all,
his feeling of artistic brotherliness had increased since he
had seen Claude losing ground, foundering amidst the heroic
folly of art. At first he had remained utterly astonished at it,
for he had believed in his friend more than in himself.
Since their college days, he had always placed himself second,
while setting Claude very high on fame's ladder—on the
same rung, indeed, as the masters who revolutionise a period.
Then he had been grievously affected by that bankruptcy of
genius; he had become full of bitter, heartfelt pity at the
sight of the horrible torture of impotency. Did one ever
know who was the madman in art? Every failure touched
him to the quick, and the more a picture or a book verged
upon aberration, sank to the grotesque and lamentable, the
more did Sandoz quiver with compassion, the more did he
long to lull to sleep, in the soothing extravagance of their
dreams, those who were thus blasted by their own work.

On the day when Sandoz called, and failed to find Claude
at home, he did not go away; but, seeing Christine's eyelids
red with crying, he said :

' If you think that he'll be in soon, I'll wait for him.'

' Oh ! he surely won't be long.'

' In that case I'll wait, unless I am in your way.'

Never had her demeanour, the crushed look of a neglected
woman, her listless movements, her slow speech, her indifference for everything but the passion that was consuming her,

moved him so deeply. For the last week, perhaps, she had
not put a chair in its place, or dusted a piece of furniture ;
she left the place to go to wreck and ruin, scarcely having
the strength to drag herself about. And it was enough to
break one's heart to behold that misery ending in filth
beneath the glaring light from the big window ; to gaze on
that ill-pargetted shanty, so bare and disorderly, where one
shivered with melancholy although it was a bright February
afternoon.

Christine had slowly sat down beside an iron bedstead,
which Sandoz had not noticed when he came in.

'Hallo,' he said, ' is Jacques ill ? '

She was covering up the child, who constantly flung off
the bedclothes.

'Yes, he hasn't been up these three days. We brought
his bed in here so that he might be with us. He was never
very strong. But he is getting worse and worse, it's dis-
tracting.'

She had a fixed stare in her eyes and spoke in a
monotonous tone, and Sandoz felt frightened when he drew
up to the bedside. The child's pale head seemed to have
grown bigger still, so heavy that he could no longer support
it. He lay perfectly still, and one might have thought he
was dead, but for the heavy breathing coming from between
his discoloured lips.

'My poor little Jacques, it's I, your godfather. Won't you
say how d'ye do ? '

The child made a fruitless, painful effort to lift his head ;
his eyelids parted, showing his white eyeballs, then closed
again.

'Have you sent for a doctor ? '

Christine shrugged her shoulders.

'Oh ! doctors, what do they know ? ' she answered. ' We
sent for one ; he said that there was nothing to be done.
Let us hope that it will pass over again. He is close upon
twelve years old now, and maybe he is growing too fast.'

Sandoz, quite chilled, said nothing for fear of increasing
her anxiety, since she did not seem to realise the gravity of
the disease. He walked about in silence and stopped in front
of the picture.

'Ho, ho ! it's getting on ; it's on the right road this
time.'

'It's finished.'

' What ! finished ? '

And when she told him that the canvas was to be sent to the Salon that next week, he looked embarrassed, and sat down on the couch, like a man who wishes to judge the work leisurely. The background, the quays, the Seine, whence arose the triumphal point of the Cité, still remained in a sketchy state—masterly, however, but as if the painter had been afraid of spoiling the Paris of his dream by giving it greater finish. There was also an excellent group on the left, the lightermen unloading the sacks of plaster being carefully and powerfully treated. But the boat full of women in the centre transpierced the picture, as it were, with a blaze of flesh-tints which were quite out of place; and the brilliancy and hallucinatory proportions of the large nude figure which Claude had painted in a fever seemed strangely, disconcertingly false amidst the reality of all the rest.

Sandoz, silent, felt despair steal over him as he sat in front of that magnificent failure. But he saw Christine's eyes fixed upon him, and had sufficient strength of mind to say :

' Astounding !—the woman, astounding ! '

At that moment Claude came in, and on seeing his old chum he uttered a joyous exclamation and shook his hand vigorously. Then he approached Christine, and kissed little Jacques, who had once more thrown off the bedclothes.

' How is he ? '

' Just the same.'

' To be sure, to be sure; he is growing too fast. A few days' rest will set him all right. I told you not to be uneasy.'

And Claude thereupon sat down beside Sandoz on the couch. They both took their ease, leaning back, with their eyes surveying the picture; while Christine, seated by the bed, looked at nothing, and seemingly thought of nothing, in the everlasting desolation of her heart. Night was slowly coming on, the vivid light from the window paled already, losing its sheen amidst the slowly-falling crepuscular dimness.

' So it's settled; your wife told me that you were going to send it in.'

' Yes.'

' You are right; you had better have done with it once

for all. Oh, there are some magnificent bits in it. The quay in perspective to the left, the man who shoulders that sack below. But——'

He hesitated, then finally took the bull by the horns.

'But, it's odd that you have persisted in leaving those women nude. It isn't logical, I assure you; and, besides, you promised me you would dress them—don't you remember? You have set your heart upon them very much then?'

'Yes.'

Claude answered curtly, with the obstinacy of one mastered by a fixed idea and unwilling to give any explanations. Then he crossed his arms behind his head, and began talking of other things, without, however, taking his eyes off his picture, over which the twilight began to cast a slight shadow.

'Do you know where I have just come from?' he asked. 'I have been to Courajod's. You know, the great landscape painter, whose "Pond of Gagny" is at the Luxembourg. You remember, I thought he was dead, and we were told that he lived hereabouts, on the other side of the hill, in the Rue de l'Abreuvoir. Well, old boy, he worried me, did Courajod. While taking a breath of air now and then up there, I discovered his shanty, and I could no longer pass in front of it without wanting to go inside. Just think, a master, a man who invented our modern landscape school, and who lives there, unknown, done for, like a mole in its hole! You can have no idea of the street or the caboose: a village street, full of fowls, and bordered by grassy banks; and a caboose like a child's toy, with tiny windows, a tiny door, a tiny garden. Oh! the garden—a mere patch of soil, sloping down abruptly, with a bed where four pear trees stand, and the rest taken up by a fowl-house, made out of green boards, old plaster, and wire network, held together with bits of string.'

His words came slowly; he blinked while he spoke as if the thought of his picture had returned to him and was gradually taking possession of him, to such a degree as to hamper him in his speech about other matters.

'Well, as luck would have it, I found Courajod on his doorstep to-day. An old man of more than eighty, wrinkled and shrunk to the size of a boy. I should like you to see him, with his clogs, his peasant's jersey and his coloured handkerchief wound over his head as if he were an old market-woman. I pluckily went up to him, saying, "Monsieur Courajod, I know you very well ; you have a picture in the Luxembourg Gallery which is a masterpiece. Allow a painter to shake hands with you as he would with his master." And then you should have seen him take fright, draw back and stutter, as if I were going to strike him. A regular flight! However, I followed him, and gradually he recovered his composure, and showed me his hens, his ducks, his rabbits and dogs—an extraordinary collection of birds and beasts ; there was even a raven among them. He lives in the midst of them all ; he speaks to no one but his animals. As for the view, it's simply magnificent ; you see the whole of the St. Denis plain for miles upon miles ; rivers and towns, smoking factory-chimneys, and puffing railway-engines ; in short, the place is a real hermitage on a hill, with its back turned to Paris and its eyes fixed on the boundless country. As a matter of course, I came back to his picture. "Oh, Monsieur Courajod," said I, "what talent you showed! If you only knew how much we all admire you. You are one of our illustrious men ; you'll remain the ancestor of us all." But his lips began to tremble again ; he looked at me with an air of terror-stricken stupidity ; I am sure he would not have waved me back with a more imploring gesture if I had unearthed under his very eyes the corpse of some forgotten comrade of his youth. He kept chewing disconnected words between his toothless gums ; it was the mumbling of an old man who had sunk into second childhood, and whom it's impossible to understand. "Don't know—so long ago—too old—don't care a rap." To make a long story short, he showed me the door ; I heard him hurriedly turn the key in lock, barricading himself and his birds and animals against the admiration of the outside world. Ah, my good fellow, the idea of it ! That great man ending his life like a retired grocer ; that voluntary relapse into "nothingness" even before death. Ah, the glory, the glory for which we others are ready to die ! '

Claude's voice, which had sunk lower and lower, died away at last in a melancholy sigh. Darkness was still coming on ; after gradually collecting in the corners, it rose like a slow, inexorable tide, first submerging the legs of the chairs and the table, all the confusion of things that littered the tiled floor. The lower part of the picture was already growing dim, and Claude, with his eyes still desperately fixed on it, seemed to be watching the ascent of the darkness as if he had at last judged his work in the expiring light. And no sound was heard save the stertorous breathing of the sick child, near whom there still loomed the dark silhouette of the motionless mother.

Then Sandoz spoke in his turn, his hands also crossed behind his head, and his back resting against one of the cushions of the couch.

'Does one ever know? Would it not be better, perhaps, to live and die unknown? What a sell it would be if artistic glory existed no more than the Paradise which is talked about in catechisms and which even children nowadays make fun of! We, who no longer believe in the Divinity, still believe in our own immortality. What a farce it all is!'

Then, affected to melancholy himself by the mournfulness of the twilight, and stirred by all the human suffering he beheld around him, he began to speak of his own torments.

'Look here, old man, I, whom you envy, perhaps—yes, I, who am beginning to get on in the world, as middle-class people say—I, who publish books and earn a little money— well, I am being killed by it all. I have often already told you this, but you don't believe me, because, as you only turn out work with a deal of trouble and cannot bring yourself to public notice, happiness in your eyes could naturally consist in producing a great deal, in being seen, and praised or slated. Well, get admitted to the next Salon, get into the thick of the battle, paint other pictures, and then tell me whether that suffices, and whether you are happy at last. Listen; work has taken up the whole of my existence. Little by little, it has robbed me of my mother, of my wife, of everything I love. It is like a germ thrown into the cranium, which feeds on the brain, finds its way into the trunk and limbs, and gnaws up the whole of the body. The moment I jump out of bed of a morning, work clutches hold of me, rivets me to my desk without leaving me time to get a breath of fresh air; then it pursues me at luncheon—I audibly chew my sentences with my bread. Next it accompanies me when I go out, comes back with me and dines off the same plate as myself; lies down with me on my pillow, so utterly pitiless that I am never able to set the book in hand on one side; indeed, its growth continues even in the depth of my sleep. And nothing outside of it exists for me. True, I go upstairs to embrace my mother, but in so absent-minded a way, that ten minutes after leaving her I ask myself whether I have really been to wish her good-morning. My poor wife has no husband; I am not with her even when our hands touch. Sometimes I have an acute feeling that I am making their lives very sad, and I feel very remorseful, for happiness is solely composed of kindness, frankness and gaiety in one's home; but how can I escape from the claws of the monster? I at once relapse into the somnambulism of my working hours, into the indifference and moroseness of my fixed idea. If the pages I have written during the morning have been worked off all right, so much the better; if one of them has remained in distress, so much the worse. The household will laugh or cry according to the whim of that all-devouring monster—Work. No, no! I have nothing that I can call my own. In my days of poverty I dreamt of rest in the country, of travel in distant lands; and now that I might make those dreams reality, the work that has been begun keeps me shut up. There is no chance of a walk in the morning's sun, no chance of running round to a friend's house, or of a mad bout of idleness! My strength of will has gone with the rest; all this has become a habit; I have locked the door of the world behind me, and thrown the key out of the window. There is no longer anything in my den but work and myself—and work will devour me, and then there will be nothing left, nothing at all!'

He paused, and silence reigned once more in the deepening gloom. Then he began again with an effort:

'And if one were only satisfied, if one only got some enjoyment out of such a nigger's life! Ah! I should like to know how those fellows manage who smoke cigarettes and complacently stroke their beards while they are at work. Yes, it appears to me that there are some who find production an easy pleasure, to be set aside or taken up without the least excitement. They are delighted, they admire themselves, they cannot write a couple of lines but they find those lines of a rare, distinguished, matchless quality. Well, as for myself, I bring forth in anguish, and my offspring seems a horror to me. How can a man be sufficiently wanting in self-doubt as to believe in himself? It absolutely amazes me to see men, who furiously deny talent to everybody else, lose all critical acumen, all common-sense, when it becomes a question of their own bastard creations. Why, a book is always very ugly. To like it one mustn't have had a hand in the cooking of it. I say nothing of the jugsful of insults that are showered upon one. Instead of annoying, they rather encourage me. I see men who are upset by attacks, who feel a humiliating craving to win sympathy. It is a simple question of temperament; some women would die if they failed to please. But, to my thinking, insult is a very good medicine to take; unpopularity is a very manly school to be brought up in. Nothing keeps one in such good health and strength as the hooting of a crowd of imbeciles. It suffices that a man can say that he has given his life's blood to his work; that he expects neither immediate justice nor serious attention; that he works without hope of any kind, and simply because the love of work beats beneath his skin like his heart, irrespective of any will of his own. If he can do all this, he may die in the effort with the consoling illusion that he will be appreciated one day or other. Ah! if the others only knew how jauntily I bear the weight of their anger. Only there is my own choler, which overwhelms me; I fret that I cannot live for a moment happy. What hours of misery I spend, great heavens! from the very day I begin a novel. During the first chapters there isn't so much trouble. I have plenty of room before me in which to display genius. But afterwards I become distracted, and am never satisfied with the daily task; I condemn the book before it is finished, judging it inferior to its elders; and I torture myself about certain pages, about certain sentences, certain words, so that at last the very commas assume an ugly look, from which I suffer. And when it is finished—ah! when it is finished, what a relief! Not the enjoyment of the gentleman who exalts himself in the worship of his offspring, but the curse of the labourer who throws down the burden that has been breaking his back. Then, later on, with another book, it all begins afresh; it will always begin afresh, and I shall die under it, furious with myself, exasperated at not having had more talent, enraged at not leaving a "work" more complete, of greater dimensions—books upon books, a pile of mountain height! And at my death I shall feel horrible doubts about the task I may have accomplished, asking myself whether I ought not to have gone to the left when I went to the right, and my last word, my last gasp, will be to recommence the whole over again——'

He was thoroughly moved; the words stuck in his throat; he was obliged to draw breath for a moment before delivering

himself of this passionate cry in which all his impenitent
lyricism took wing :

'Ah, life ! a second span of life, who shall give it to me,
that work may rob me of it again—that I may die of it once
more ?'

It had now become quite dark; the mother's rigid silhouette was no longer visible; the hoarse breathing of the
child sounded amidst the obscurity like a terrible and distant
signal of distress, uprising from the streets. In the whole
studio, which had become lugubriously black, the big canvas
only showed a glimpse of pallidity, a last vestige of the
waning daylight. The nude figure, similar to an agonising
vision, seemed to be floating about, without definite shape,
the legs having already vanished, one arm being already
submerged, and the only part at all distinct being the trunk,
which shone like a silvery moon.

After a protracted pause, Sandoz inquired :

'Shall I go with you when you take your picture ?'

Getting no answer from Claude, he fancied he could hear
him crying. Was it with the same infinite sadness, the
despair by which he himself had been stirred just now ? He
waited for a moment, then repeated his question, and at last
the painter, after choking down a sob, stammered :

'Thanks, the picture will remain here ; I sha'n't send it.'

'What ? Why, you had made up your mind ?'

'Yes, yes, I had made up my mind ; but I had not seen
it as I saw it just now in the waning daylight. I have failed
with it, failed with it again—it struck my eyes like a blow, it
went to my very heart.'

His tears now flowed slow and scalding in the gloom that
hid him from sight. He had been restraining himself, and
now the silent anguish which had consumed him burst forth
despite all his efforts.

'My poor friend,' said Sandoz, quite upset; 'it is hard to
tell you so, but all the same you are right, perhaps, in delaying matters to finish certain parts rather more. Still I am
angry with myself, for I shall imagine that it was I who
discouraged you by my everlasting stupid discontent with
things.'

Claude simply answered :

'You! what an idea! I was not even listening to you.
No; I was looking, and I saw everything go helter-skelter
in that confounded canvas. The light was dying away, and

all at once, in the greyish dusk, the scales suddenly dropped from my eyes. The background alone is pretty; the nude woman is altogether too loud; what's more, she's out of the perpendicular, and her legs are badly drawn. When I noticed that, ah! it was enough to kill me there and then; I felt life departing from me. Then the gloom kept rising and rising, bringing a whirling sensation, a foundering of everything, the earth rolling into chaos, the end of the world. And soon I only saw the trunk waning like a sickly moon. And look, look! there now remains nothing of her, not a glimpse; she is dead, quite black!'

In fact, the picture had at last entirely disappeared. But the painter had risen and could be heard swearing in the dense obscurity.

'D——n it all, it doesn't matter, I'll set to work at it again——'

Then Christine, who had also risen from her chair, against which he stumbled, interrupted him, saying:

'Take care, I'll light the lamp.'

She lighted it and came back looking very pale, casting a glance of hatred and fear at the picture. It was not to go then? The abomination was to begin once more!

'I'll set to work at it again,' repeated Claude, 'and it shall kill me, it shall kill my wife, my child, the whole lot; but, by heaven, it shall be a masterpiece!'

Christine sat down again; they approached Jacques, who had thrown the clothes off once more with his feverish little hands. He was still breathing heavily, lying quite inert, his head buried in the pillow like a weight, with which the bed seemed to creak. When Sandoz was on the point of going, he expressed his uneasiness. The mother appeared stupefied; while the father was already returning to his picture, the masterpiece which awaited creation, and the thought of which filled him with such passionate illusions that he gave less heed to the painful reality of the sufferings of his child, the true living flesh of his flesh.

On the following morning, Claude had just finished dressing, when he heard Christine calling in a frightened voice. She also had just woke with a start from the heavy sleep which had benumbed her while she sat watching the sick child.

'Claude! Claude! Oh, look! He is dead.'

The painter rushed forward, with heavy eyes, stumbling,

and apparently failing to understand, for he repeated with an air of profound amazement, ' What do you mean by saying he is dead ? '

For a moment they remained staring wildly at the bed. The poor little fellow, with his disproportionate head—the head of the progeny of genius, exaggerated as to verge upon cretinism—did not appear to have stirred since the previous night ; but no breath came from his mouth, which had widened and become discoloured, and his glassy eyes were open. His father laid his hands upon him and found him icy cold.

' It is true, he is dead.'

And their stupor was such that for yet another moment they remained with their eyes dry, simply thunderstruck, as it were, by the abruptness of that death which they considered incredible.

Then, her knees bending under her, Christine dropped down in front of the bed, bursting into violent sobs which shook her from head to foot, and wringing her hands, whilst her forehead remained pressed against the mattress. In that first moment of horror her despair was aggravated above all by poignant remorse—the remorse of not having sufficiently cared for the poor child. Former days started up before her in a rapid vision, each bringing with it regretfulness for unkind words, deferred caresses, rough treatment even. And now it was all over ; she would never be able to compensate the lad for the affection she had withheld from him. He whom she thought so disobedient had obeyed but too well at last. She had so often told him when at play to be still, and not to disturb his father at his work, that he was quiet at last, and for ever. The idea suffocated her ; each sob drew from her a dull moan.

Claude had begun walking up and down the studio, unable to remain still. With his features convulsed, he shed a few big tears, which he brushed away with the back of his hand. And whenever he passed in front of the little corpse he could not help glancing at it. The glassy eyes, wide open, seemed to exercise a spell over him. At first he resisted, but a confused idea assumed shape within him, and would not be shaken off. He yielded to it at last, took a small canvas, and began to paint a study of the dead child. For the first few minutes his tears dimmed his sight, wrapping everything in a mist ; but he kept wiping them away, and persevered with his work, even though his brush shook. Then the passion for art dried his tears and steadied his hand, and in a little while it was no longer his icy son that lay there, but merely a model, a subject, the strange interest of which stirred him. That huge head, that waxy flesh, those eyes which looked like holes staring into space—all excited and thrilled him. He stepped back, seemed to take pleasure in his work, and vaguely smiled at it.

When Christine rose from her knees, she found him thus occupied. Then, bursting into tears again, she merely said :

'Ah ! you can paint him now, he'll never stir again.'

For five hours Claude kept at it, and on the second day, when Sandoz came back with him from the cemetery, after the funeral, he shuddered with pity and admiration at the sight of the small canvas. It was one of the fine bits of former days, a masterpiece of limpidity and power, to which was added a note of boundless melancholy, the end of every-thing—all life ebbing away with the death of that child.

But Sandoz, who had burst out into exclamations full of praise, was quite taken aback on hearing Claude say to him :

'You are sure you like it ? In that case, as the other machine isn't ready, I'll send this to the Salon.'

X

ONE morning, as Claude, who had taken 'The Dead Child' to the Palais de l'Industrie the previous day, was roaming round about the Parc Monceau, he suddenly came upon Fagerolles.

'What ! ' said the latter, cordially, 'is it you, old fellow ? What's becoming of you ? What are you doing ? We see so little of each other now.'

Then, Claude having mentioned what he had sent to the Salon—that little canvas which his mind was full of—Fagerolles added :

'Ah ! you've sent something ; then I'll get it "hung" for you. You know that I'm a candidate for the hanging committee this year.'

Indeed, amid the tumult and everlasting discontent of the artists, after attempts at reform, repeated a score of times and then abandoned, the authorities had just invested the exhi-bitors with the privilege of electing the members of the

hanging committee; and this had quite upset the world of
painters and sculptors, a perfect electoral fever had set in,
with all sorts of ambitious cabals and intrigues—all the low
jobbery, indeed, by which politics are dishonoured.

'I'm going to take you with me,' continued Fagerolles;
'you must come and see how I'm settled in my little house,
in which you haven't yet set foot, in spite of all your
promises. It's there, hard by, at the corner of the Avenue de
Villiers.'

Claude, whose arm he had gaily taken, was obliged to
follow him. He was seized with a fit of cowardice; the idea
that his old chum might get his picture 'hung' for him
filled him with mingled shame and desire. On reaching the
avenue, he stopped in front of the house to look at its frontage,
a bit of coquettish, *precioso* architectural tracery—the exact
copy of a Renaissance house at Bourges, with lattice windows,
a staircase tower, and a roof decked with leaden ornaments.
It looked like the abode of a harlot; and Claude was struck
with surprise when, on turning round, he recognised Irma
Bécot's regal mansion just over the way. Huge, substantial,
almost severe of aspect, it had all the importance of a palace
compared to its neighbour, the dwelling of the artist, who
was obliged to limit himself to a fanciful nick-nack.

'Ah! that Irma, eh?' said Fagerolles with just a shade
of respect in his tone. 'She has got a cathedral and no
mistake! But come in.'

The interior of Fagerolles' house was strangely and mag-
nificently luxurious. Old tapestry, old weapons, a heap of
old furniture, Chinese and Japanese curios were displayed
even in the very hall. On the left there was a dining-room,
panelled with lacquer work and having its ceiling draped with
a design of a red dragon. Then there was a staircase of
carved wood above which banners drooped, whilst tropical
plants rose up like plumes. Overhead, the studio was a
marvel, though rather small and without a picture visible.
The walls, indeed, were entirely covered with Oriental
hangings, while at one end rose up a huge chimney-piece
with chimerical monsters supporting the tablet, and at the
other extremity appeared a vast couch under a tent—the
latter quite a monument, with lances upholding the sumptu-
ous drapery, above a collection of carpets, furs and cushions
heaped together almost on a level with the flooring.

Claude looked at it all, and there came to his lips a

question which he held back—Was all this paid for?
Fagerolles, who had been decorated with the Legion of
Honour the previous year, now asked, it was said, ten
thousand francs for painting a mere portrait. Naudet, who,
after launching him, duly turned his success to profit in a
methodical fashion, never let one of his pictures go for less
than twenty, thirty, forty thousand francs. Orders would
have fallen on the painter's shoulders as thick as hail, if he
had not affected the disdain, the weariness of the man
whose slightest sketches are fought for. And yet all this
display of luxury smacked of indebtedness, there was only so
much paid on account to the upholsterers; all the money—
the money won by lucky strokes as on 'Change—slipped
through the artist's fingers, and was spent without trace of it
remaining. Moreover, Fagerolles, still in the full flush of
his sudden good fortune, did not calculate or worry, being
confident that he would always sell his works at higher and
higher prices, and feeling glorious at the high position he was
acquiring in contemporary art.

Eventually, Claude espied a little canvas on an ebony
easel, draped with red plush. Excepting a rosewood tube
case and box of crayons, forgotten on an article of furniture,
nothing reminding one of the artistic profession could be seen
lying about.

'Very finely treated,' said Claude, wishing to be amiable,
as he stood in front of the little canvas. 'And is your picture
for the Salon sent?'

'Ah! yes, thank heavens! What a number of people I
had here! A perfect procession which kept me on my legs
from morning till evening during a week. I didn't want to
exhibit it, as it lowers one to do so, and Naudet also opposed it.
But what would you have done? I was so begged and prayed;
all the young fellows want to set me on the committee, so that I
may defend them. Oh! my picture is simple enough—I call
it "A Picnic." There are a couple of gentlemen and three
ladies under some trees—guests at some château, who have
brought a collation with them and are eating it in a glade.
You'll see, it's rather original.'

He spoke in a hesitating manner, and when his eyes met
those of Claude, who was looking at him fixedly, he lost
countenance altogether, and joked about the little canvas
on the easel.

'That's a daub Naudet asked me for. Oh! I'm not

ignorant of what I lack—a little of what you have too much of, old man. You know that I'm still your friend ; why, I defended you only yesterday with some painters.'

He tapped Claude on the shoulders, for he had divined his old master's secret contempt, and wished to win him back by his old-time caresses—all the wheedling practices of a hussy. Very sincerely and with a sort of anxious deference he again promised Claude that he would do everything in his power to further the hanging of his picture, ' The Dead Child.'

However, some people arrived ; more than fifteen persons came in and went off in less than an hour—fathers bringing young pupils, exhibitors anxious to say a good word on their own behalf, friends who wanted to barter influence, even women who placed their talents under the protection of their charms. And one should have seen the painter play his part as a candidate, shaking hands most lavishly, saying to one visitor : ' Your picture this year is so pretty, it pleases me so much ! ' then feigning astonishment with another: 'What! you haven't had a medal yet ? ' and repeating to all of them : ' Ah ! If I belonged to the committee, I'd make them walk straight.' He sent every one away delighted, closed the door behind each visitor with an air of extreme amiability, through which, however, there pierced the secret sneer of an ex-lounger on the pavement.

'You see, eh ? ' he said to Claude, at a moment when they happened to be left alone. ' What a lot of time I lose with those idiots ! '

Then he approached the large window, and abruptly opened one of the casements ; and on one of the balconies of the house over the way a woman clad in a lace dressing-gown could be distinguished waving her handkerchief. Fagerolles on his side waved his hand three times in succession. Then both windows were closed again.

Claude had recognised Irma ; and amid the silence which fell Fagerolles quietly explained matters :

'It's convenient, you see, one can correspond. We have a complete system of telegraphy. She wants to speak to me, so I must go——'

Since he and Irma had resided in the avenue, they met, it was said, on their old footing. It was even asserted that he, so 'cute,' so well-acquainted with Parisian humbug, let himself be fleeced by her, bled at every moment of some good round sum, which she sent her maid to ask for—now to pay a tradesman, now to satisfy a whim, often for nothing at all, or rather for the sole pleasure of emptying his pockets ; and this partly explained his embarrassed circumstances, his indebtedness, which ever increased despite the continuous rise in the quotations of his canvases.

Claude had put on his hat again. Fagerolles was shuffling about impatiently, looking nervously at the house over the way.

' I don't send you off, but you see she's waiting for me,' he said. ' Well, it's understood, your affair's settled—that is, unless I'm not elected. Come to the Palais de l'Industrie on the evening the voting-papers are counted. Oh ! there will be a regular crush, quite a rumpus ! Still, you will always learn if you can rely on me.'

At first, Claude inwardly swore that he would not trouble about it. Fagerolles' protection weighed heavily upon him ; and yet, in his heart of hearts, he really had but one fear, that the shifty fellow would not keep his promise, but would ultimately be taken with a fit of cowardice at the idea of protecting a defeated man. However, on the day of the vote Claude could not keep still, but went and roamed about the Champs Elysées under the pretence of taking a long walk. He might as well go there as elsewhere, for while waiting for the Salon he had altogether ceased work. He himself could not vote, as to do so it was necessary to have been 'hung' on at least one occasion. However, he repeatedly passed before the Palais de l'Industrie[1], the foot pavement in front of which interested him with its bustling aspect, its procession of artist electors, whom men in dirty blouses caught hold of, shouting to them the titles of their lists of candidates—lists some thirty in number emanating from every possible coterie, and representing every possible opinion. There was the list of the studios of the School of Arts, the liberal list, the list of the uncompromising radical painters, the conciliatory list, the young painters' list, even the ladies' list, and so forth. The scene suggested all the turmoil at the door of an electoral polling booth on the morrow of a riot.

At four o'clock in the afternoon, when the voting was over, Claude could not resist a fit of curiosity to go and have a look. The staircase was now free, and whoever chose could

---

[1] This palace, for many years the home of the ' Salon,' was built for the first Paris International Exhibition, that of 1855, and demolished in connection with that of 1900.—ED.

enter. Upstairs, he came upon the huge gallery, overlooking
the Champs Elysées, which was set aside for the hanging
committee. A table, forty feet long, filled the centre of this
gallery, and entire trees were burning in the monumental
fireplace at one end of it. Some four or five hundred electors,
who had remained to see the votes counted, stood there,
mingled with friends and inquisitive strangers, talking,
laughing, and setting quite a storm loose under the lofty
ceiling. Around the table, parties of people who had volun-
teered to count the votes were already settled and at work;
there were some fifteen of these parties in all, each com-
prising a chairman and two scrutineers. Three or four more
remained to be organised, and nobody else offered assistance;
in fact, every one turned away in fear of the crushing labour
which would rivet the more zealous people to the spot far
into the night.

It precisely happened that Fagerolles, who had been in
the thick of it since the morning, was gesticulating and
shouting, trying to make himself heard above the hubbub.

'Come, gentlemen, we need one more man here! Come,
some willing person, over here!'

And at that moment, perceiving Claude, he darted forward
and forcibly dragged him off.

'Ah! as for you, you will just oblige me by sitting down
there and helping us! It's for the good cause, dash it all!'

Claude abruptly found himself chairman of one of the
counting committees, and began to perform his functions
with all the gravity of a timid man, secretly experiencing a
good deal of emotion, as if the hanging of his canvas would
depend upon the conscientiousness he showed in his work.
He called out the names inscribed upon the voting-papers,
which were passed to him in little packets, while the scrutineers, on sheets of paper prepared for the purpose, noted
each successive vote that each candidate obtained. And all
this went on amidst a most frightful uproar, twenty and
thirty names being called out at the same time by different
voices, above the continuous rumbling of the crowd. As
Claude could never do anything without throwing passion
into it, he waxed excited, became despondent whenever a
voting-paper did not bear Fagerolles' name, and grew happy
as soon as he had to shout out that name once more. Moreover, he often tasted that delight, for his friend had made
himself popular, showing himself everywhere, frequenting the

cafés where influential groups of artists assembled, even ven-
turing to expound his opinions there, and binding himself
to young artists, without neglecting to bow very low to the
members of the Institute. Thus there was a general current
of sympathy in his favour. Fagerolles was, so to say, everybody's spoilt child.

Night came on at about six o'clock that rainy March day.
The assistants brought lamps; and some mistrustful artists,
who, gloomy and silent, were watching the counting askance,
drew nearer. Others began to play jokes, imitated the cries
of animals, or attempted a *tyrolienne*. But it was only at
eight o'clock, when a collation of cold meat and wine was
served, that the gaiety reached its climax. The bottles were
hastily emptied, the men stuffed themselves with whatever
they were lucky enough to get hold of, and there was a free-
and-easy kind of Kermesse in that huge hall which the logs
in the fireplace lit up with a forge-like glow. Then they all
smoked, and the smoke set a kind of mist around the yellow
light from the lamps, whilst on the floor trailed all the spoilt
voting-papers thrown away during the polling; indeed, quite
a layer of dirty paper, together with corks, breadcrumbs, and
a few broken plates. The heels of those seated at the table
disappeared amidst this litter. Reserve was cast aside; a
little sculptor with a pale face climbed upon a chair to
harangue the assembly, and a painter, with stiff moustaches
under a hook nose, bestrode a chair and galloped, bowing,
round the table, in mimicry of the Emperor.

Little by little, however, a good many grew tired and
went off. At eleven o'clock there were not more than a
couple of hundred persons present. Past midnight, however,
some more people arrived, loungers in dress-coats and white
ties, who had come from some theatre or *soirée* and wished
to learn the result of the voting before all Paris knew it.
Reporters also appeared; and they could be seen darting one
by one out of the room as soon as a partial result was communicated to them.

Claude, hoarse by now, still went on calling names. The
smoke and the heat became intolerable, a smell like that of
a cow-house rose from the muddy litter on the floor. One
o'clock, two o'clock in the morning struck, and he was still
unfolding voting-papers, the conscientiousness which he displayed delaying him to such a point that the other parties
had long since finished their work, while his was still a maze

of figures. At last all the additions were centralised and the definite result proclaimed. Fagerolles was elected, coming fifteenth among forty, or five places ahead of Bongrand, who had been a candidate on the same list, but whose name must have been frequently struck out. And daylight was breaking when Claude reached home in the Rue Tourlaque, feeling both worn out and delighted.

Then, for a couple of weeks he lived in a state of anxiety. A dozen times he had the idea of going to Fagerolles' for information, but a feeling of shame restrained him. Besides, as the committee proceeded in alphabetical order, nothing perhaps was yet decided. However, one evening, on the Boulevard de Clichy, he felt his heart thump as he saw two broad shoulders, with whose lolloping motion he was well acquainted, coming towards him.

They were the shoulders of Bongrand, who seemed embarrassed. He was the first to speak, and said :

'You know matters aren't progressing very well over yonder with those brutes. But everything isn't lost. Fagerolles and I are on the watch. Still, you must rely on Fagerolles ; as for me, my dear fellow, I am awfully afraid of compromising your chances.'

To tell the truth, there was constant hostility between Bongrand and the President of the hanging committee, Mazel, a famous master of the School of Arts, and the last rampart of the elegant, buttery, conventional style of art. Although they called each other 'dear colleague' and made a great show of shaking hands, their hostility had burst forth the very first day ; one of them could never ask for the admission of a picture without the other one voting for its rejection. Fagerolles, who had been elected secretary, had, on the contrary, made himself Mazel's amuser, his vice, and Mazel forgave his old pupil's defection, so skilfully did the renegade flatter him. Moreover, the young master, a regular turncoat, as his comrades said, showed even more severity than the members of the Institute towards audacious beginners. He only became lenient and sociable when he wanted to get a picture accepted, on those occasions showing himself extremely fertile in devices, intriguing and carrying the vote with all the supple deftness of a conjurer.

The committee work was really a hard task, and even Bongrand's strong legs grew tired of it. It was cut out every day by the assistants. An endless row of large pictures rested on the ground against the handrails, all along the first-floor galleries, right round the Palace; and every afternoon, at one o'clock precisely, the forty committee-men, headed by their president, who was equipped with a bell, started off on a promenade, until all the letters in the alphabet, serving as exhibitors' initials, had been exhausted. They gave their decisions standing, and the work was got through as fast as possible, the worst canvases being rejected without going to the vote. At times, however, discussions delayed the party, there came a ten minutes' quarrel, and some picture which caused a dispute was reserved for the evening revision. Two men, holding a cord some thirty feet long, kept it stretched at a distance of four paces from the line of pictures, so as to restrain the committee-men, who kept on pushing each other in the heat of their dispute, and whose stomachs, despite everything, were ever pressing against the cord. Behind the committee marched seventy museum-keepers in white blouses, executing evolutions under the orders of a brigadier. At each decision communicated to them by the secretaries, they sorted the pictures, the accepted paintings being separated from the rejected ones, which were carried off like corpses after a battle. And the round lasted during two long hours, without a moment's respite, and without there being a single chair to sit upon. The committee-men had to remain on their legs, tramping on in a tired way amid icy draughts, which compelled even the least chilly among them to bury their noses in the depths of their fur-lined overcoats.

Then the three o'clock snack proved very welcome: there was half an hour's rest at a buffet, where claret, chocolate, and sandwiches could be obtained. It was there that the market of mutual concessions was held, that the bartering of influence and votes was carried on. In order that nobody might be forgotten amid the hailstorm of applications which fell upon the committee-men, most of them carried little note-books, which they consulted; and they promised to vote for certain exhibitors whom a colleague protected on condition that this colleague voted for the ones in whom they were interested. Others, however, taking no part in these intrigues, either from austerity or indifference, finished the interval in smoking a cigarette and gazing vacantly about them.

Then the work began again, but more agreeably, in a

gallery where there were chairs, and even tables with pens and paper and ink. All the pictures whose height did not reach four feet ten inches were judged there—'passed on the easel,' as the expression goes—being ranged, ten or twelve together, on a kind of trestle covered with green baize. A good many committee-men then grew absent-minded, several wrote their letters, and the president had to get angry to obtain presentable majorities. Sometimes a gust of passion swept by; they all jostled each other; the votes, usually given by raising the hand, took place amid such feverish excitement that hats and walking-sticks were waved in the air above the tumultuous surging of heads.

And it was there, 'on the easel,' that 'The Dead Child' at last made its appearance. During the previous week Fagerolles, whose pocket-book was full of memoranda, had resorted to all kinds of complicated bartering in order to obtain votes in Claude's favour; but it was a difficult business, it did not tally with his other engagements, and he only met with refusals as soon as he mentioned his friend's name. He complained, moreover, that he could get no help from Bongrand, who did not carry a pocket-book, and who was so clumsy, too, that he spoilt the best causes by his outbursts of unseasonable frankness. A score of times already would Fagerolles have forsaken Claude, had it not been for his obstinate desire to try his power over his colleagues by asking for the admittance of a work by Lantier, which was a reputed impossibility. However, people should see if he wasn't yet strong enough to force the committee into compliance with his wishes. Moreover, perhaps from the depths of his conscience there came a cry for justice, an unconfessed feeling of respect for the man whose ideas he had stolen.

As it happened, Mazel was in a frightfully bad humour that day. At the outset of the sitting the brigadier had come to him, saying: 'There was a mistake yesterday, Monsieur Mazel. A *hors-concours*[1] picture was rejected. You know, No. 2520, a nude woman under a tree.'

In fact, on the day before, this painting had been consigned to the grave amid unanimous contempt, nobody

[1] A painting by one of those artists who, from the fact that they had obtained medals at previous Salons, had the right to go on exhibiting as long as they lived, the committee being debarred from rejecting their work, however bad it might be.—ED.

having noticed that it was the work of an old classical painter highly respected by the Institute; and the brigadier's fright, and the amusing circumstance of a picture having thus been condemned by mistake, enlivened the younger members of the committee and made them sneer in a provoking manner.

Mazel, who detested such mishaps, which he rightly felt were disastrous for the authority of the School of Arts, made an angry gesture, and drily said:

'Well, fish it out again, and put it among the admitted pictures. It isn't so surprising, there was an intolerable noise yesterday. How can one judge anything like that at a gallop, when one can't even obtain silence?'

He rang his bell furiously, and added:

'Come, gentlemen, everything is ready—a little good will, if you please.'

Unluckily, a fresh misfortune occurred as soon as the first paintings were set on the trestle. One canvas among others attracted Mazel's attention, so bad did he consider it, so sharp in tone as to make one's very teeth grate. As his sight was failing him, he leant forward to look at the signature, muttering the while: 'Who's the pig——'

But he quickly drew himself up, quite shocked at having read the name of one of his friends, an artist who, like himself, was a rampart of healthy principles. Hoping that he had not been overheard, he thereupon called out:

'Superb! No. 1, eh, gentlemen?'

No. 1 was granted—the formula of admission which entitled the picture to be hung on the line. Only, some of the committee-men laughed and nudged each other, at which Mazel felt very hurt, and became very fierce.

Moreover, they all made such blunders at times. A great many of them eased their feelings at the first glance, and then recalled their words as soon as they had deciphered the signature. This ended by making them cautious, and so with furtive glances they made sure of the artist's name before expressing any opinion. Besides, whenever a colleague's work, some fellow committee-man's suspicious-looking canvas, was brought forward, they took the precaution to warn each other by making signs behind the painter's back, as if to say, 'Take care, no mistake, mind; it's his picture.'

Fagerolles, despite his colleagues' fidgety nerves, carried the day on a first occasion. It was a question of admitting a frightful portrait painted by one of his pupils, whose family, a very wealthy one, received him on a footing of intimacy. To achieve this he had taken Mazel on one side in order to try to move him with a sentimental story about an unfortunate father with three daughters, who were starving. But the president let himself be entreated for a long while, saying that a man shouldn't waste his time painting when he was dying for lack of food, and that he ought to have a little more consideration for his three daughters! However, in the result, Mazel raised his hand, alone, with Fagerolles. Some of the others then angrily protested, and even two members of the Institute seemed disgusted, whereupon Fagerolles whispered to them in a low key:

'It's for Mazel! He begged me to vote. The painter's a relative of his, I think; at all events, he greatly wants the picture to be accepted.'

At this the two academicians promptly raised their hands, and a large majority declared itself in favour of the portrait.

But all at once laughter, witticisms, and indignant cries rang out: 'The Dead Child' had just been placed on the trestle. Were they to have the Morgue sent to them now? said some. And while the old men drew back in alarm, the younger ones scoffed at the child's big head, which was plainly that of a monkey who had died from trying to swallow a gourd.

Fagerolles at once understood that the game was lost. At first he tried to spirit the vote away by a joke, in accordance with his skilful tactics:

'Come, gentlemen, an old combatant——'

But furious exclamations cut him short. Oh, no! not that one. They knew him, that old combatant! A madman who had been persevering in his obstinacy for fifteen years past—a proud, stuck-up fellow who posed for being a genius, and who had talked about demolishing the Salon, without even sending a picture that it was possible to accept. All their hatred of independent originality, of the competition of the 'shop over the way,' which frightened them, of that invincible power which triumphs even when it is seemingly defeated, resounded in their voices. No, no; away with it!

Then Fagerolles himself made the mistake of getting irritated, yielding to the anger he felt at finding what little real influence he possessed.

'You are unjust; at least, be impartial,' he said.

Thereupon the tumult reached a climax. He was surrounded and jostled, arms waved about him in threatening fashion, and angry words were shot out at him like bullets.

'You dishonour the committee, monsieur!'

'If you defend that thing, it's simply to get your name in the newspapers!'

'You aren't competent to speak on the subject!'

Then Fagerolles, beside himself, losing even the pliancy of his bantering disposition, retorted:

'I'm as competent as you are.'

'Shut up!' resumed a comrade, a very irascible little painter with a fair complexion. 'You surely don't want to make us swallow such a turnip as that?'

Yes, yes, a turnip! They all repeated the word in tones of conviction—that word which they usually cast at the very worst smudges, at the pale, cold, glairy painting of daubers.

'All right,' at last said Fagerolles, clenching his teeth. 'I demand the vote.'

Since the discussion had become envenomed, Mazel had been ringing his bell, extremely flushed at finding his authority ignored.

'Gentlemen—come, gentlemen; it's extraordinary that one can't settle matters without shouting—I beg of you, gentlemen——'

At last he obtained a little silence. In reality, he was not a bad-hearted man. Why should not they admit that little picture, although he himself thought it execrable? They admitted so many others!

'Come, gentlemen, the vote is asked for.'

He himself was, perhaps, about to raise his hand, when Bongrand, who had hitherto remained silent, with the blood rising to his cheeks in the anger he was trying to restrain, abruptly went off like a pop-gun, most unseasonably giving vent to the protestations of his rebellious conscience.

'But, curse it all! there are not four among us capable of turning out such a piece of work!'

Some grunts sped around; but the sledge-hammer blow had come upon them with such force that nobody answered.

'Gentlemen, the vote is asked for,' curtly repeated Mazel, who had turned pale.

His tone sufficed to explain everything: it expressed all his latent hatred of Bongrand, the fierce rivalry that lay hidden under their seemingly good-natured handshakes.

Things rarely came to such a pass as this. They almost always arranged matters. But in the depths of their ravaged pride there were wounds which always bled; they secretly waged duels which tortured them with agony, despite the smile upon their lips.

Bongrand and Fagerolles alone raised their hands, and 'The Dead Child,' being rejected, could only perhaps be rescued at the general revision.

This general revision was the terrible part of the task. Although, after twenty days' continuous toil, the committee allowed itself forty-eight hours' rest, so as to enable the keepers to prepare the final work, it could not help shuddering on the afternoon when it came upon the assemblage of three thousand rejected paintings, from among which it had to rescue as many canvases as were necessary for the then regulation total of two thousand five hundred admitted works to be complete. Ah! those three thousand pictures, placed one after the other alongside the walls of all the galleries, including the outer one, deposited also even on the floors, and lying there like stagnant pools, between which the attendants devised little paths—they were like an inundation, a deluge, which rose up, streamed over the whole Palais de l'Industrie, and submerged it beneath the murky flow of all the mediocrity and madness to be found in the river of Art. And but a single afternoon sitting was held, from one till seven o'clock—six hours of wild galloping through a maze! At first they held out against fatigue and strove to keep their vision clear; but the forced march soon made their legs give way, their eyesight was irritated by all the dancing colours, and yet it was still necessary to march on, to look and judge, even until they broke down with fatigue. By four o'clock the march was like a rout—the scattering of a defeated army. Some committee-men, out of breath, dragged themselves along very far in the rear; others, isolated, lost amid the frames, followed the narrow paths, renouncing all prospect of emerging from them, turning round and round without any hope of ever getting to the end! How could they be just and impartial, good heavens? What could they select from amid that heap of horrors? Without clearly distinguishing a landscape from a portrait, they made up the number they required in pot-luck fashion. Two hundred, two hundred and forty—another eight, they still wanted eight more. That one? No, that other. As you like! Seven, eight, it was over! At last

they had got to the end, and they hobbled away, saved—
free!

In one gallery a fresh scene drew them once more round
'The Dead Child,' lying on the floor among other waifs. But
this time they jested. A joker pretended to stumble and set
his foot in the middle of the canvas, while others trotted
along the surrounding little paths, as if trying to find out
which was the picture's top and which its bottom, and declaring that it looked much better topsy-turvy.

Fagerolles himself also began to joke.

'Come, a little courage, gentlemen; go the round, examine
it, you'll be repaid for your trouble. Really now, gentlemen,
be kind, rescue it; pray do that good action!'

They all grew merry in listening to him, but with cruel
laughter they refused more harshly than ever. No, no,
never!

'Will you take it for your "charity"?' cried a comrade.

This was a custom; the committee-men had a right to a
'charity'; each of them could select a canvas among the
lot, no matter how execrable it might be, and it was thereupon admitted without examination. As a rule, the bounty
of this admission was bestowed upon poor artists. The
forty paintings thus rescued at the eleventh hour, were those
of the beggars at the door—those whom one allowed to glide
with empty stomachs to the far end of the table.

'For my "charity,"' repeated Fagerolles, feeling very much
embarrassed; 'the fact is, I meant to take another painting
for my "charity." Yes, some flowers by a lady——'

He was interrupted by loud jeers. Was she pretty? In
front of the women's paintings the gentlemen were particularly prone to sneer, never displaying the least gallantry.
And Fagerolles remained perplexed, for the 'lady' in question
was a person whom Irma took an interest in. He trembled
at the idea of the terrible scene which would ensue should
he fail to keep his promise. An expedient occurred to him.

'Well, and you, Bongrand? You might very well take
this funny little dead child for *your* charity.'

Bongrand, wounded to the heart, indignant at all the
bartering, waved his long arms:

'What! *I?* *I* insult a real painter in that fashion? Let
him be prouder, dash it, and never send anything to the
Salon!'

Then, as the others still went on sneering, Fagerolles,

desirous that victory should remain to him, made up his
mind, with a proud air, like a man who is conscious of his
strength and does not fear being compromised.

'All right, I'll take it for my "charity,"' he said.

The others shouted bravo, and gave him a bantering
ovation, with a series of profound bows and numerous hand-
shakes. All honour to the brave fellow who had the courage
of his opinions! And an attendant carried away in his arms
the poor derided, jolted, soiled canvas; and thus it was that
a picture by the painter of 'In the Open Air' was at last
accepted by the hanging committee of the Salon.

On the very next morning a note from Fagerolles apprised
Claude, in a couple of lines, that he had succeeded in getting
'The Dead Child' admitted, but that it had not been managed
without trouble. Claude, despite the gladness of the tidings,
felt a pang at his heart; the note was so brief, and was
written in such a protecting, pitying style, that all the
humiliating features of the business were apparent to him.
For a moment he felt sorry over this victory, so much so
that he would have liked to take his work back and hide it.
Then his delicacy of feeling, his artistic pride again gave
way, so much did protracted waiting for success make
his wretched heart bleed. Ah! to be seen, to make his
way despite everything! He had reached the point when
conscience capitulates; he once more began to long for
the opening of the Salon with all the feverish impatience of
a beginner, again living in a state of illusion which showed
him a crowd, a press of moving heads acclaiming his canvas.

By degrees Paris had made it the fashion to patronise
'varnishing day'—that day formerly set aside for painters
only to come and finish the toilets of their pictures. Now,
however, it was like a feast of early fruit, one of those
solemnities which set the city agog and attract a tremendous
crowd. For a week past the newspaper press, the streets,
and the public had belonged to the artists. They held Paris
in their grasp; the only matters talked of were themselves,
their exhibits, their sayings or doings—in fact, everything
connected with them. It was one of those infatuations
which at last draw bands of country folk, common soldiers,
and even nursemaids to the galleries on days of gratuitous
admission, in such wise that fifty thousand visitors are
recorded on some fine Sundays, an entire army, all the rear
battalions of the ignorant lower orders, following society,

and marching, with dilated eyes, through that vast picture shop.

That famous 'varnishing day' at first frightened Claude, who was intimidated by the thought of all the fine people whom the newspapers spoke about, and he resolved to wait for the more democratic day of the real inauguration. He even refused to accompany Sandoz. But he was consumed by such a fever, that after all he started off abruptly at eight o'clock in the morning, barely taking time to eat a bit of bread and cheese beforehand. Christine, who lacked the courage to go with him, kissed him again and again, feeling anxious and moved.

'Mind, my dear, don't worry, whatever happens,' said she.

Claude felt somewhat oppressed as he entered the Gallery of Honour. His heart was beating fast from the swiftness with which he had climbed the grand staircase. There was a limpid May sky out of doors, and through the linen awnings, stretched under the glazed roof, there filtered a bright white light, while the open doorways, communicating with the garden gallery, admitted moist gusts of quivering freshness. For a moment Claude drew breath in that atmosphere which was already tainted with a vague smell of varnish and the odour of the musk with which the women present perfumed themselves. At a glance he took stock of the pictures on the walls: a huge massacre scene in front of him, streaming with carmine; a colossal, pallid, religious picture on his left; a Government order, the commonplace delineation of some official festivity, on the right; and then a variety of portraits, landscapes, and indoor scenes, all glaring sharply amid the fresh gilding of their frames. However, the fear which he retained of the folks usually present at this solemnity led him to direct his glances upon the gradually increasing crowd. On a circular settee in the centre of the gallery, from which sprang a sheaf of tropical foliage, there sat three ladies, three monstrously fat creatures, attired in an abominable fashion, who had settled there to indulge in a whole day's backbiting. Behind him he heard somebody crushing harsh syllables in a hoarse voice. It was an Englishman in a check-pattern jacket, explaining the massacre scene to a yellow woman buried in the depths of a travelling ulster. There were some vacant spaces; groups of people formed, scattered, and formed again further on; all heads were raised; the men carried walking-sticks and had overcoats on their arms, the women strolled about slowly, showing distant profiles as they stopped before the pictures; and Claude's artistic eye was caught by the flowers in their hats and bonnets, which seemed very loud in tint amid the dark waves of the men's silk hats. He perceived three priests, two common soldiers who had found their way there no one knew whence, some endless processions of gentlemen decorated with the ribbon of the Legion of Honour, and troops of girls and their mothers, who constantly impeded the circulation. However, a good many of these people knew each other; there were smiles and bows from afar, at times a rapid handshake in passing. And conversation was carried on in a discreet tone of voice, above which rose the continuous tramping of feet.

Then Claude began to look for his own picture. He tried to find his way by means of the initial letters inscribed above the entrances of the galleries, but made a mistake, and went through those on the left hand. There was a succession of open entrances, a perspective of old tapestry door-hangings, with glimpses of the distant pictures. He went as far as the great western gallery, and came back by the parallel suite of smaller galleries without finding that allotted to the letter L. And when he reached the Gallery of Honour again, the crowd had greatly increased. In fact, it was now scarcely possible for one to move about there. Being unable to advance, he looked around, and recognised a number of painters, that nation of painters which was at home there that day, and was therefore doing the honours of its abode. Claude particularly remarked an old friend of the Boutin Studio—a young fellow consumed with the desire to advertise himself, who had been working for a medal, and who was now pouncing upon all the visitors possessed of any influence and forcibly taking them to see his pictures. Then there was a celebrated and wealthy painter who received his visitors in front of his work with a smile of triumph on his lips, showing himself compromisingly gallant with the ladies, who formed quite a court around him. And there were all the others: the rivals who execrated one another, although they shouted words of praise in full voices; the savage fellows who covertly watched their comrades' success from the corner of a doorway; the timid ones whom one could not for an empire induce to pass through the gallery where their pictures were hung; the jokers who hid the bitter mortification of their defeat under an amusing witticism ; the sincere ones who were absorbed in contemplation, trying to understand the various works, and already in fancy distributing the medals. And the painters' families were also there. One charming young woman was accompanied by a coquettishly bedecked child ; a sour-looking, skinny matron of middle-class birth was flanked by two ugly urchins in black ; a fat mother had foundered on a bench amid quite a tribe of dirty brats ; and a lady of mature charms, still very good-looking, stood beside her grown-up daughter, quietly watching a hussy pass—this hussy being the father's mistress. And then there were also the models—women who pulled one another by the sleeve, who showed one another their own forms in the various pictorial nudities, talking very loudly the while and dressed without taste, spoiling their superb figures by such wretched gowns that they seemed to be hump-backed beside the well-dressed dolls—those Parisiennes who owed their figures entirely to their dressmakers.

When Claude got free of the crowd, he enfiladed the line of doorways on the right hand. His letter was on that side ; but he searched the galleries marked with an L without finding anything. Perhaps his canvas had gone astray and served to fill up a vacancy elsewhere. So when he had reached the large eastern gallery, he set off along a number of other little ones, a secluded suite visited by very few people, where the pictures seemed to frown with boredom. And there again he found nothing. Bewildered, distracted, he roamed about, went on to the garden gallery, searching among the superabundant exhibits which overflowed there, pallid and shivering in the crude light ; and eventually, after other distant excursions, he tumbled into the Gallery of Honour for the third time.

There was now quite a crush there. All those who in any way create a stir in Paris were assembled together—the celebrities, the wealthy, the adored, talent, money and grace, the masters of romance, of the drama and of journalism, clubmen, racing men and speculators, women of every category, hussies, actresses and society belles. And Claude, angered by his vain search, grew amazed at the vulgarity of the faces thus massed together, at the incongruity of the toilets—but a few of which were elegant, while so many were common looking—at the lack of majesty which that vaunted 'society' displayed, to such a point, indeed, that the fear which had made him tremble was changed into contempt. Were these the people, then, who were going to jeer at his picture, provided it were found again? Two little reporters with fair complexions were completing a list of persons whose names they intended to mention. A critic pretended to take some notes on the margin of his catalogue; another was holding forth in professor's style in the centre of a party of beginners; a third, all by himself, with his hands behind his back, seemed rooted to one spot, crushing each work beneath his august impassibility. And what especially struck Claude was the jostling flock-like behaviour of the people, their banded curiosity in which there was nothing youthful or passionate, the bitterness of their voices, the weariness to be read on their faces, their general appearance of suffering. Envy was already at work; there was the gentleman who makes himself witty with the ladies; the one who, without a word, looks, gives a terrible shrug of the shoulders, and then goes off; and there were the two who remain for a quarter of an hour leaning over the handrail, with their noses close to a little canvas, whispering very low and exchanging the knowing glances of conspirators.

But Fagerolles had just appeared, and amid the continuous ebb and flow of the groups there seemed to be no one left but him. With his hand outstretched, he seemed to show himself everywhere at the same time, lavishly exerting himself to play the double part of a young 'master' and an influential member of the hanging committee. Overwhelmed with praise, thanks, and complaints, he had an answer ready for everybody without losing aught of his affability. Since early morning he had been resisting the assault of the petty painters of his set who found their pictures badly hung. It was the usual scamper of the first moment, everybody looking for everybody else, rushing to see one another and bursting into recriminations—noisy, interminable fury. Either the picture was too high up, or the light did not fall upon it properly, or the paintings near it destroyed its effect; in fact, some talked of unhooking their works and carrying them off. One tall thin fellow was especially tenacious, going from gallery to gallery in pursuit of Fagerolles, who vainly explained that he was innocent in the matter and could do nothing. Numerical order was followed, the pictures for each wall were deposited on the floor below and then hung up without anybody being favoured. He carried his obligingness so far

as to promise his intervention when the galleries were
rearranged after the medals had been awarded; but even then
he did not manage to calm the tall thin fellow, who still
continued pursuing him.

Claude for a moment elbowed his way through the crowd
to go and ask Fagerolles where his picture had been hung.
But on seeing his friend so surrounded, pride restrained
him. Was there not something absurd and painful about this
constant need of another's help? Besides, he suddenly reflected that he must have skipped a whole suite of galleries
on the right-hand side; and, indeed, there were fresh leagues
of painting there. He ended by reaching a gallery where a
stifling crowd was massed in front of a large picture which
filled the central panel of honour. At first he could not see
it, there was such a surging sea of shoulders, such a thick wall
of heads, such a rampart of hats. People rushed forward with
gaping admiration. At length, however, by dint of rising on
tiptoe, he perceived the marvel, and recognised the subject,
by what had been told him.

It was Fagerolles' picture. And in that 'Picnic' he found
his own forgotten work, 'In the Open Air,' the same light
key of colour, the same artistic formula, but softened, trick-
ishly rendered, spoilt by skin-deep elegance, everything being
'arranged' with infinite skill to satisfy the low ideal of the
public. Fagerolles had not made the mistake of stripping his
three women; but, clad in the audacious toilets of women of
society, they showed no little of their persons. As for the
two gallant gentlemen in summer jackets beside them, they
realised the ideal of everything most *distingué;* while afar
off a footman was pulling a hamper off the box of a landau
drawn up behind the trees. The whole of it, the figures, the
drapery, the bits of still life of the repast, stood out gaily in
full sunlight against the darkened foliage of the background;
and the supreme skill of the painter lay in his pretended
audacity, in a mendacious semblance of forcible treatment
which just sufficed to send the multitude into ecstasies. It
was like a storm in a cream-jug!

Claude, being unable to approach, listened to the remarks
around him. At last there was a man who depicted real
truth! He did not press his points like those fools of the
new school; he knew how to convey everything without
showing anything. Ah! the art of knowing where to draw
the line, the art of letting things be guessed, the respect due

to the public, the approval of good society! And withal such delicacy, such charm and art! He did not unseasonably deliver himself of passionate things of exuberant design; no, when he had taken three notes from nature, he gave those three notes, nothing more. A newspaper man who arrived went into raptures over the 'Picnic,' and coined the expression 'a very Parisian style of painting.' It was repeated, and people no longer passed without declaring that the picture was 'very Parisian' indeed.

All those bent shoulders, all those admiring remarks rising from a sea of spines, ended by exasperating Claude; and seized with a longing to see the faces of the folk who created success, he manœuvred in such a way as to lean his back against the handrail hard by. From that point, he had the public in front of him in the grey light filtering through the linen awning which kept the centre of the gallery in shade; whilst the brighter light, gliding from the edges of the blinds, illumined the paintings on the walls with a white flow, in which the gilding of the frames acquired a warm sunshiny tint. Claude at once recognised the people who had formerly derided him—if these were not the same, they were at least their relatives—serious, however, and enraptured, their appearance greatly improved by their respectful attention. The evil look, the weariness, which he had at first remarked on their faces, as envious bile drew their skin together and dyed it yellow, disappeared here while they enjoyed the treat of an amiable lie. Two fat ladies, open-mouthed, were yawning with satisfaction. Some old gentlemen opened their eyes wide with a knowing air. A husband explained the subject to his young wife, who jogged her chin with a pretty motion of the neck. There was every kind of marvelling, beatifical, astonished, profound, gay, austere, amidst unconscious smiles and languid postures of the head. The men threw back their black silk hats, the flowers in the women's bonnets glided to the napes of their necks. And all the faces, after remaining motionless for a moment, were then drawn aside and replaced by others exactly like them.

Then Claude, stupefied by that triumph, virtually forgot everything else. The gallery was becoming too small, fresh bands of people constantly accumulated inside it. There were no more vacant spaces, as there had been early in the morning; no more cool whiffs rose from the garden amid the ambient smell of varnish; the atmosphere was now becoming hot and bitter with the perfumes scattered by the women's dresses. Before long the predominant odour suggested that of a wet dog. It must have been raining outside; one of those sudden spring showers had no doubt fallen, for the last arrivals brought moisture with them—their clothes hung about them heavily and seemed to steam as soon as they encountered the heat of the gallery. And, indeed, patches of darkness had for a moment been passing above the awning of the roof. Claude, who raised his eyes, guessed that large clouds were galloping onward lashed by the north wind, that driving rain was beating upon the glass panes. Moire-like shadows darted along the walls, all the paintings became dim, the spectators themselves were blended in obscurity until the cloud was carried away, whereupon the painter saw the heads again emerge from the twilight, ever agape with idiotic rapture.

But there was another cup of bitterness in reserve for Claude. On the left-hand panel, facing Fagerolles', he perceived Bongrand's picture. And in front of that painting there was no crush whatever; the visitors walked by with an air of indifference. Yet it was Bongrand's supreme effort, the thrust he had been trying to give for years, a last work conceived in his obstinate craving to prove the virility of his decline. The hatred he harboured against the ' Village Wedding,' that first masterpiece which had weighed upon all his toilsome after-life, had impelled him to select a contrasting but corresponding subject : the ' Village Funeral '—the funeral of a young girl, with relatives and friends straggling among fields of rye and oats. Bongrand had wrestled with himself, saying that people should see if he were done for, if the experience of his sixty years were not worth all the lucky dash of his youth ; and now experience was defeated, the picture was destined to be a mournful failure, like the silent fall of an old man, which does not even stay passers-by in their onward course. There were still some masterly bits, the choirboy holding the cross, the group of daughters of the Virgin carrying the bier, whose white dresses and ruddy flesh furnished a pretty contrast with the black Sunday toggery of the rustic mourners, among all the green stuff; only the priest in his alb, the girl carrying the Virgin's banner, the family following the body, were drily handled ; the whole picture, in fact, was displeasing in its very science and the obstinate stiffness of its treatment. One found in it a fatal, unconscious return to the troubled romanticism which had been the starting-point of the painter's career. And the worst of the business was that there was justification for the indifference with which the public treated that art of another period, that cooked and somewhat dull style of painting, which no longer stopped one on one's way, since great blazes of light had come into vogue.

It precisely happened that Bongrand entered the gallery with the hesitating step of a timid beginner, and Claude felt a pang at his heart as he saw him give a glance at his neglected picture and then another at Fagerolles', which was bringing on a riot. At that moment the old painter must have been acutely conscious of his fall. If he had so far been devoured by the fear of slow decline, it was because he still doubted; and now he obtained sudden certainty; he was surviving his reputation, his talent was dead, he would never more give birth to living, palpitating works. He became very pale, and was about to turn and flee, when Chambouvard, the sculptor, entering the gallery by the other door, followed by his customary train of disciples, called to him without caring a fig for the people present :

'Ah! you humbug, I catch you at it—admiring yourself!'

He, Chambouvard, exhibited that year an execrable 'Reaping Woman,' one of those stupidly spoilt figures which seemed like hoaxes on his part, so unworthy they were of his powerful hands; but he was none the less radiant, feeling certain that he had turned out yet another masterpiece, and promenading his god-like infallibility through the crowd which he did not hear laughing at him.

Bongrand did not answer, but looked at him with eyes scorched by fever.

'And my machine downstairs?' continued the sculptor. 'Have you seen it? The little fellows of nowadays may try it on, but we are the only masters—we, old France!'

And thereupon he went off, followed by his court and bowing to the astonished public.

'The brute!' muttered Bongrand, suffocating with grief, as indignant as at the outburst of some low-bred fellow beside a deathbed.

He perceived Claude, and approached him. Was it not cowardly to flee from this gallery? And he determined to show his courage, his lofty soul, into which envy had never entered.

'Our friend Fagerolles has a success and no mistake,' he said. 'I should be a hypocrite if I went into ecstasies over his picture, which I scarcely like ; but he himself is really a very nice fellow indeed. Besides, you know how he exerted himself on your behalf.'

Claude was trying to find a word of admiration for the 'Village Funeral.'

'The little cemetery in the background is so pretty ! ' he said at last. 'Is it possible that the public——'

But Bongrand interrupted him in a rough voice :

'No compliments of condolence, my friend, eh ? I see clear enough.'

At this moment somebody nodded to them in a familiar way, and Claude recognised Naudet—a Naudet who had grown and expanded, gilded by the success of his colossal strokes of business. Ambition was turning his head ; he talked about sinking all the other picture dealers ; he had built himself a palace, in which he posed as the king of the market, centralising masterpieces, and there opening large art shops of the modern style. One heard a jingle of millions on the very threshold of his hall ; he held exhibitions there, even ran up other galleries elsewhere ; and each time that May came round, he awaited the visits of the American amateurs whom he charged fifty thousand francs for a picture which he himself had purchased for ten thousand. Moreover, he lived in princely style, with a wife and children, a mistress, a country estate in Picardy, and extensive shooting grounds. His first large profits had come from the rise in value of works left by illustrious artists, now defunct, whose talent had been denied while they lived, such as Courbet, Millet, and Rousseau ; and this had ended by making him disdain any picture signed by a still struggling artist. However, ominous rumours were already in circulation. As the number of well-known pictures was limited, and the number of amateurs could barely be increased, a time seemed to be coming when business would prove very difficult. There was talk of a syndicate, of an understanding with certain bankers to keep up the present high prices ; the expedient of simulated sales was resorted to at the Hôtel Drouot—pictures being bought in at a big figure by the dealer himself—and bankruptcy seemed to be at the end of all that Stock Exchange jobbery, a perfect tumble head-over-heels after all the excessive, mendacious *agiotage*.

'Good-day, dear master,' said Naudet, who had drawn near. 'So you have come, like everybody else, to see my Fagerolles, eh?'

He no longer treated Bongrand in the wheedling, respectful manner of yore. And he spoke of Fagerolles as of a painter belonging to him, of a workman to whom he paid wages, and whom he often scolded. It was he who had settled the young artist in the Avenue de Villiers, compelling him to have a little mansion of his own, furnishing it as he would have furnished a place for a hussy, running him into debt with supplies of carpets and nick-nacks, so that he might afterwards hold him at his mercy; and now he began to accuse him of lacking orderliness and seriousness, of compromising himself like a feather-brain. Take that picture, for instance, a serious painter would never have sent it to the Salon; it made a stir, no doubt, and people even talked of its obtaining the medal of honour; but nothing could have a worse effect on high prices. When a man wanted to get hold of the Yankees, he ought to know how to remain at home, like an idol in the depths of his tabernacle.

'You may believe me or not, my dear fellow,' he said to Bongrand, 'but I would have given twenty thousand francs out of my pocket to prevent those stupid newspapers from making all this row about my Fagerolles this year.'

Bongrand, who, despite his sufferings, was listening bravely, smiled.

'In point of fact,' he said, 'they are perhaps carrying indiscretion too far. I read an article yesterday in which I learnt that Fagerolles ate two boiled eggs every morning.'

He laughed over the coarse puffery which, after a first article on the 'young master's' picture, as yet seen by nobody, had for a week past kept all Paris occupied about him. The whole fraternity of reporters had been campaigning, stripping Fagerolles to the skin, telling their readers all about his father, the artistic zinc manufacturer, his education, the house in which he resided, how he lived, even revealing the colour of his socks, and mentioning a habit he had of pinching his nose. And he was the passion of the hour, the 'young master' according to the tastes of the day, one who had been lucky enough to miss the Prix de Rome, and break off with the School of Arts, whose principles, however, he retained. After all, the success of that style of painting which aims merely at approximating reality, not at rendering it in all its truth, was the fortune of a season which the wind brings and blows away again, a mere whim on the part of the great lunatic city; the stir it caused was like that occasioned by some accident, which upsets the crowd in the morning and is forgotten by night amidst general indifference.

However, Naudet noticed the 'Village Funeral.'

'Hullo! that's your picture, eh?' he said. 'So you wanted to give a companion to the "Wedding"? Well, I should have tried to dissuade you! Ah! the "Wedding"! the "Wedding"!'

Bongrand still listened to him without ceasing to smile. Barely a twinge of pain passed over his trembling lips. He forgot his masterpieces, the certainty of leaving an immortal name, he was only cognisant of the vogue which that youngster, unworthy of cleaning his palette, had so suddenly and easily acquired, that vogue which seemed to be pushing him, Bongrand, into oblivion—he who had struggled for ten years before he had succeeded in making himself known. Ah! when the new generations bury a man, if they only knew what tears of blood they make him shed in death!

However, as he had remained silent, he was seized with the fear that he might have let his suffering be divined. Was he falling to the baseness of envy? Anger with himself made him raise his head—a man should die erect. And instead of giving the violent answer which was rising to his lips, he said in a familiar way:

'You are right, Naudet, I should have done better if I had gone to bed on the day when the idea of that picture occurred to me.'

'Ah! there he is; excuse me!' cried the dealer, making off.

It was Fagerolles showing himself at the entrance of the gallery. He discreetly stood there without entering, carrying his good fortune with the ease of a man who knows what he is about. Besides, he was looking for somebody; he made a sign to a young man, and gave him an answer, a favourable one, no doubt, for the other brimmed over with gratitude. Then two other persons sprang forward to congratulate him; a woman detained him, showing him, with a martyr's gesture, a bit of still life hung in a dark corner. And finally he disappeared, after casting but one glance at the people in raptures before his picture.

Claude, who had looked and listened, was overwhelmed with sadness. The crush was still increasing, he now had nought before him but faces gaping and sweating in the heat, which had become intolerable. Above the nearer shoulders rose others, and so on and so on as far as the door, whence those who could see nothing pointed out the painting to each other with the tips of their umbrellas, from which dripped the water left by the showers outside. And Bongrand remained there out of pride, erect in defeat, firmly planted on his legs, those of an old combatant, and gazing with limpid eyes upon ungrateful Paris. He wished to finish like a brave man, whose kindness of heart is boundless. Claude, who spoke to him without receiving any answer, saw very well that there was nothing behind that calm, gay face; the mind was absent, it had flown away in mourning, bleeding with frightful torture; and thereupon, full of alarm and respect, he did not insist, but went off. And Bongrand, with his vacant eyes, did not even notice his departure.

A new idea had just impelled Claude onward through the crowd. He was lost in wonderment at not having been able to discover his picture. But nothing could be more simple. Was there not some gallery where people grinned, some corner full of noise and banter, some gathering of jesting spectators, insulting a picture? That picture would assuredly be his. He could still hear the laughter of the bygone Salon of the Rejected. And now at the door of each gallery he listened to ascertain if it were there that he was being hissed.

However, as he found himself once more in the eastern gallery, that hall where great art agonises, that depository where vast, cold, and gloomy historical and religious compositions are accumulated, he started, and remained motionless with his eyes turned upward. He had passed through that gallery twice already, and yet that was certainly his picture up yonder, so high up that he hesitated about recognising it. It looked, indeed, so little, poised like a swallow at the corner of a frame—the monumental frame of an immense painting five-and-thirty feet long, representing the Deluge, a swarming of yellow figures turning topsy-turvy in water of the hue of wine lees. On the left, moreover, there was a pitiable ashen portrait of a general; on the right a colossal nymph in a moonlit landscape, the bloodless corpse of a murdered woman rotting away on some grass; and everywhere around there were mournful violet-shaded things, mixed up with a comic scene of some bibulous monks, and an 'Opening of the

Chamber of Deputies,' with a whole page of writing on a gilded cartouch, bearing the heads of the better-known deputies, drawn in outline, together with their names. And high up, high up, amid those livid neighbours, the little canvas, over-coarse in treatment, glared ferociously with the painful grimace of a monster.

Ah! 'The Dead Child.' At that distance the wretched little creature was but a confused lump of flesh, the lifeless carcase of some shapeless animal. Was that swollen, whitened head a skull or a stomach? And those poor hands twisted among the bedclothes, like the bent claws of a bird killed by cold! And the bed itself, that pallidity of the sheets, below the pallidity of the limbs, all that white looking so sad, those tints fading away as if typical of the supreme end! Afterwards, however, one distinguished the light eyes staring fixedly, one recognised a child's head, and it all seemed to suggest some disease of the brain, profoundly and frightfully pitiful.

Claude approached, and then drew back to see the better. The light was so bad that refractions darted from all points across the canvas. How they *had* hung his little Jacques! no doubt out of disdain, or perhaps from shame, so as to get rid of the child's lugubrious ugliness. But Claude evoked the little fellow such as he had once been, and beheld him again over yonder in the country, so fresh and pinky, as he rolled about in the grass; then in the Rue de Douai, growing pale and stupid by degrees, and then in the Rue Tourlaque, no longer able to carry his head, and dying one night, all alone, while his mother was asleep; and he beheld her also, that mother, the sad woman who had stopped at home, to weep there, no doubt, as she was now in the habit of doing for entire days. No matter, she had done right in not coming; 'twas too mournful—their little Jacques, already cold in his bed, cast on one side like a pariah, and so brutalised by the dancing light that his face seemed to be laughing, distorted by an abominable grin.

But Claude suffered still more from the loneliness of his work. Astonishment and disappointment made him look for the crowd, the rush which he had anticipated. Why was he not hooted? Ah! the insults of yore, the mocking, the indignation that had rent his heart, but made him live! No, nothing more, not even a passing expectoration: this was death. The visitors filed rapidly through the long gallery, seized with boredom. There were merely some people in front of the 'Opening of the Chamber,' where they collected to read the inscriptions, and show each other the deputies' heads. At last, hearing some laughter behind him, he turned round ; but nobody was jeering, some visitors were simply making merry over the tipsy monks, the comic success of the Salon, which some gentlemen explained to some ladies, declaring that it was brilliantly witty. And all these people passed beneath little Jacques, and not a head was raised, not a soul even knew that he was up there.

However, the painter had a gleam of hope. On the central settee, two personages, one of them fat and the other thin, and both of them decorated with the Legion of Honour, sat talking, reclining against the velvet, and looking at the pictures in front of them. Claude drew near them and listened.

'And I followed them,' said the fat fellow. 'They went along the Rue St. Honoré, the Rue St. Roch, the Rue de la Chaussée d'Antin, the Rue la Fayette——'

'And you spoke to them ? ' asked the thin man, who appeared to be deeply interested.

'No, I was afraid of getting in a rage.'

Claude went off and returned on three occasions, his heart beating fast each time that some visitor stopped short and glanced slowly from the line to the ceiling. He felt an unhealthy longing to hear one word, but one. Why exhibit ? How fathom public opinion ? Anything rather than such torturing silence ! And he almost suffocated when he saw a young married couple approach, the husband a good-looking fellow with little fair moustaches, the wife, charming, with the delicate slim figure of a shepherdess in Dresden china. She had perceived the picture, and asked what the subject was, stupefied that she could make nothing out of it ; and when her husband, turning over the leaves of the catalogue, had found the title, 'The Dead Child,' she dragged him away, shuddering, and raising this cry of affright :

'Oh, the horror ! The police oughtn't to allow such horrors ! '

Then Claude remained there, erect, unconscious and haunted, his eyes raised on high, amid the continuous flow of the crowd which passed on, quite indifferent, without one glance for that unique sacred thing, visible to him alone.

And it was there that Sandoz came upon him, amid the jostling.

The novelist, who had been strolling about alone—his wife having remained at home beside his ailing mother—had just stopped short, heart-rent, below the little canvas, which he had espied by chance. Ah! how disgusted he felt with life! He abruptly lived the days of his youth over again. He recalled the college of Plassans, his freaks with Claude on the banks of the Viorne, their long excursions under the burning sun, and all the flaming of their early ambition; and, later on, when they had lived side by side, he remembered their efforts, their certainty of coming glory, that fine irresistible, immoderate appetite that had made them talk of swallowing Paris at one bite! How many times, at that period, had he seen in Claude a great man, whose unbridled genius would leave the talent of all others far behind in the rear! First had come the studio of the Impasse des Bourdonnais; later, the studio of the Quai de Bourbon, with dreams of vast compositions, projects big enough to make the Louvre burst; and, meanwhile, the struggle was incessant; the painter laboured ten hours a day, devoting his whole being to his work. And then what? After twenty years of that passionate life he ended thus—he finished with that poor, sinister little thing, which nobody noticed, which looked so distressfully sad in its leper-like solitude! So much hope and torture, a lifetime spent in the toil of creating, to come to that, to that, good God!

Sandoz recognised Claude standing by, and fraternal emotion made his voice quake as he said to him:

'What! so you came? Why did you refuse to call for me, then?'

The painter did not even apologise. He seemed very tired, overcome with somniferous stupor.

'Well, don't stay here,' added Sandoz. 'It's past twelve o'clock, and you must lunch with me. Some people were to wait for me at Ledoyen's; but I shall give them the go-by. Let's go down to the buffet; we shall pick up our spirits there, eh, old fellow?'

And then Sandoz led him away, holding his arm, pressing it, warming it, and trying to draw him from his mournful silence.

'Come, dash it all! you mustn't give way like that. Although they have hung your picture badly, it is all the same superb, a real bit of genuine painting. Oh! I know that you dreamt of something else ! But you are not dead yet, it will be for later on. And, just look, you ought to be proud, for it's you who really triumph at the Salon this year. Fage-rolles isn't the only one who pillages you ; they all imitate you now ; you have revolutionised them since your " Open Air," which they laughed so much about. Look, look! there's an " open air " effect, and there's another, and here and there—they all do it.'

He waved his hand towards the pictures as he and Claude passed along the galleries. In point of fact, the dash of clear light, introduced by degrees into contemporary painting, had fully burst forth at last. The dingy Salons of yore, with their pitchy canvases, had made way for a Salon full of sunshine, gay as spring itself. It was the dawn, the aurora which had first gleamed at the Salon of the Rejected, and which was now rising and rejuvenating art with a fine, diffuse light, full of infinite shades. On all sides you found Claude's famous ' bluey tinge,' even in the portraits and the *genre* scenes, which had acquired the dimensions and the serious character of his-torical paintings. The old academical subjects had disap-peared with the cooked juices of tradition, as if the con-demned doctrine had carried its people of shadows away with it ; rare were the works of pure imagination, the cadaverous nudities of mythology and catholicism, the legendary subjects painted without faith, the anecdotic bits destitute of life—in fact, all the *bric-à-brac* of the School of Arts used up by generations of tricksters and fools ; and the influence of the new principle was evident even among those artists who lingered over the antique recipes, even among the former masters who had now grown old. The flash of sunlight had penetrated to their studios. From afar, at every step you took, you saw a painting transpierce the wall and form, as it were, a window open upon Nature. Soon the walls themselves would fall, and Nature would walk in ; for the breach was a broad one, and the assault had driven routine away in that gay battle waged by audacity and youth.

' Ah! your lot is a fine one, all the same, old fellow !' continued Sandoz. ' The art of to-morrow will be yours; you have made them all.'

Claude thereupon opened his mouth, and, with an air of gloomy brutality, said in a low voice :

' What do I care if I *have* made them all, when I haven't

made myself? See here, it's too big an affair for me, and that's what stifles me.'

He made a gesture to finish expressing his thought, his consciousness of his inability to prove the genius of the formula he had brought with him, the torture he felt at being merely a precursor, the one who sows the idea without reaping the glory, his grief at seeing himself pillaged, devoured by men who turned out hasty work, by a whole flight of fellows who scattered their efforts and lowered the new form of art, before he or another had found strength enough to produce the masterpiece which would make the end of the century a date in art.

But Sandoz protested, the future lay open. Then, to divert Claude, he stopped him while crossing the Gallery of Honour, and said :

'Just look at that lady in blue before that portrait! What a slap Nature does give to painting! You remember when we used to look at the dresses and the animation of the galleries in former times? Not a painting then withstood the shock. And yet now there are some which don't suffer overmuch. I even noticed over there a landscape, the general yellowish tinge of which completely eclipsed all the women who approached it.'

Claude was quivering with unutterable suffering.

'Pray, let's go,' he said. 'Take me away—I can't stand it any longer.'

They had all the trouble in the world to find a free table in the refreshment room. People were pressed together in that big, shady retreat, girt round with brown serge drapery under the girders of the lofty iron flooring of the upstairs galleries. In the background, and but partially visible in the darkness, stood three dressers displaying dishes of preserved fruit symmetrically ranged on shelves ; while, nearer at hand, at counters placed on the right and left, two ladies, a dark one and a fair one, watched the crowd with a military air ; and from the dim depths of this seeming cavern rose a sea of little marble tables, a tide of chairs, serried, entangled, surging, swelling, overflowing and spreading into the garden, under the broad, pallid light which fell from the glass roof.

At last Sandoz saw some people rise. He darted forward and conquered the vacant table by sheer struggling with the mob.

'Ah! dash it! we are here at all events. What will you have to eat?'

Claude made a gesture of indifference. The lunch was execrable; there was some trout softened by over-boiling, some undercut of beef dried up in the oven, some asparagus smelling of moist linen, and, in addition, one had to fight to get served; for the hustled waiters, losing their heads, remained in distress in the narrow passages which the chairs were constantly blocking. Behind the hangings on the left, one could hear a racket of saucepans and crockery; the kitchen being installed there on the sand, like one of those Kermesse cook-shops set up by the roadside in the open air.

Sandoz and Claude had to eat, seated obliquely and half strangled between two parties of people whose elbows almost ended by getting into their plates; and each time that a waiter passed he gave their chairs a shake with his hips. However, the inconvenience, like the abominable cookery, made one gay. People jested about the dishes, different tables fraternised together, common misfortune brought about a kind of pleasure party. Strangers ended by sympathising; friends kept up conversations, although they were seated three rows distant from one another, and were obliged to turn their heads and gesticulate over their neighbours' shoulders. The women particularly became animated, at first rather anxious as to the crush, and then ungloving their hands, catching up their skirts, and laughing at the first thimbleful of neat wine they drank.

However, Sandoz, who had renounced finishing his meat, raised his voice amid the terrible hubbub caused by the chatter and the serving:

'A bit of cheese, eh? And let's try to get some coffee.'

Claude, whose eyes looked dreamy, did not hear. He was gazing into the garden. From his seat he could see the central clump of verdure, some lofty palms which stood in relief against the grey hangings with which the garden was decorated all round. A circle of statues was set out there; and you could see the back of a faun; the profile of a young girl with full cheeks; the face of a bronze Gaul, a colossal bit of romanticism which irritated one by its stupid assumption of patriotism; the trunk of a woman hanging by the wrists, some Andromeda of the Place Pigalle; and others, and others still following the bends of the pathways; rows of shoulders and hips, heads, breasts, legs, and arms, all mingling and growing indistinct in the distance. On the left stretched a line of busts—such delightful ones—furnishing a most comical

and uncommon suite of noses. There was the huge pointed
nose of a priest, the tip-tilted nose of a soubrette, the handsome classical nose of a fifteenth-century Italian woman, the
mere fancy nose of a sailor—in fact, every kind of nose, both
the magistrate's and the manufacturer's, and the nose of the
gentleman decorated with the Legion of Honour—all of them
motionless and ranged in endless succession!

However, Claude saw nothing of them; to him they were
but grey spots in the hazy, greenish light. His stupor still
lasted, and he was only conscious of one thing, the luxurious-
ness of the women's dresses, of which he had formed a wrong
estimate amid the pushing in the galleries, and which were
here freely displayed, as if the wearers had been promenading
over the gravel in the conservatory of some château. All the
elegance of Paris passed by, the women who had come to
show themselves, in dresses thoughtfully combined and destined to be described in the morrow's newspapers. People
stared a great deal at an actress, who walked about with a
queen-like tread, on the arm of a gentleman who assumed
the complacent airs of a prince consort. The women of
society looked like so many hussies, and they all of them
took stock of one another with that slow glance which
estimates the value of silk and the length of lace, and which
ferrets everywhere, from the tips of boots to the feathers
upon bonnets. This was neutral ground, so to say; some
ladies who were seated had drawn their chairs together, after
the fashion in the garden of the Tuileries, and occupied themselves exclusively with criticising those of their own sex who
passed by. Two female friends quickened their pace, laughing. Another woman, all alone, walked up and down, mute,
with a black look in her eyes. Some others, who had lost
one another, met again, and began ejaculating about the
adventure. And, meantime, the dark moving mass of men
came to a standstill, then set off again till it stopped short
before a bit of marble, or eddied back to a bit of bronze.
And among the mere *bourgeois*, who were few in number,
though all of them looked out of their element there, moved
men with celebrated names—all the *illustrations* of Paris. A
name of resounding glory re-echoed as a fat, ill-clad gentleman passed by; the winged name of a poet followed as a pale
man with a flat, common face approached. A living wave
was rising from this crowd in the even, colourless light, when
suddenly a flash of sunshine, from behind the clouds of a

final shower, set the glass panes on high aflame, making the stained window on the western side resplendent, and raining down in golden particles through the still atmosphere; and then everything became warm—the snowy statues amid the shiny green stuff, the soft lawns parted by the yellow sand of the pathways, the rich dresses with their glossy satin and bright beads, even the very voices, whose hilarious murmur seemed to crackle like a bright fire of vine shoots. Some gardeners, completing the arrangements of the flower-beds, turned on the taps of the stand-pipes and promenaded about with their pots, the showers squirting from which came forth again in tepid steam from the drenched grass. And meanwhile a plucky sparrow, who had descended from the iron girders, despite the number of people, dipped his beak in the sand in front of the buffet, eating some crumbs which a young woman threw him by way of amusement. Of all the tumult, however, Claude only heard the ocean-like din afar, the rumbling of the people rolling onwards in the galleries. And a recollection came to him, he remembered that noise which had burst forth like a hurricane in front of his picture at the Salon of the Rejected. But nowadays people no longer laughed at him; upstairs the giant roar of Paris was acclaiming Fagerolles.

It so happened that Sandoz, who had turned round, said to Claude : ' Hallo ! there's Fagerolles ! '

And, indeed, Fagerolles and Jory had just laid hands on a table near by without noticing their friends, and the journalist, continuing in his gruff voice a conversation which had previously begun, remarked :

' Yes, I saw his " Dead Child " ! Ah ! the poor devil ! what an ending ! '

But Fagerolles nudged Jory, and the latter, having caught sight of his two old comrades, immediately added :

' Ah ! that dear old Claude ! How goes it, eh ? You know that I haven't yet seen your picture. But I'm told that it's superb.'

' Superb ! ' declared Fagerolles, who then began to express his surprise. ' So you lunched here. What an idea ! Everything is so awfully bad. We two have just come from Ledoyen's. Oh ! such a crowd and such hustling, such mirth ! Bring your table nearer and let us chat a bit.'

They joined the two tables together. But flatterers and petitioners were already after the triumphant young master.

Three friends rose up and noisily saluted him from afar. A
lady became smilingly contemplative when her husband had
whispered his name in her ear. And the tall, thin fellow, the
artist whose picture had been badly hung, and who had pursued
him since the morning, as enraged as ever, left a table where
he was seated at the further end of the buffet, and again
hurried forward to complain, imperatively demanding 'the
line' at once.

'Oh! go to the deuce!' at last cried Fagerolles, his pa-
tience and amiability exhausted. And he added, when the
other had gone off, mumbling some indistinct threats: 'It's
true; a fellow does all he can to be obliging, but those chaps
would drive one mad! All of them on the "line"! leagues
of "line" then! Ah! what a business it is to be a committee-man! One wears out one's legs, and one only reaps
hatred as reward.'

Claude, who was looking at him with his oppressed air,
seemed to wake up for a moment, and murmured:

'I wrote to you; I wanted to go and see you to thank you.
Bongrand told me about all the trouble you had. So thanks
again.'

But Fagerolles hastily broke in:

'Tut, tut! I certainly owed that much to our old
friendship. It's I who am delighted to have given you any
pleasure.'

He showed the embarrassment which always came upon
him in presence of the acknowledged master of his youth, that
kind of humility which filled him perforce when he was with
the man whose mute disdain, even at this moment, sufficed to
spoil all his triumph.

'Your picture is very good,' slowly added Claude, who
wished to be kind-hearted and generous.

This simple praise made Fagerolles' heart swell with
exaggerated, irresistible emotion, springing he knew not
whence; and this rascal, who believed in nothing, who
was usually so proficient in humbug, answered in a shaky
voice:

'Ah! my dear fellow, ah! it's very kind of *you* to tell me
that!'

Sandoz had at last obtained two cups of coffee, and as the
waiter had forgotten to bring any sugar, he had to content
himself with some pieces which a party had left on an
adjoining table. A few tables, indeed, had now become

vacant, but the general freedom had increased, and one
woman's laughter rang out so loudly that every head turned
round. The men were smoking, and a bluish cloud slowly
rose above the straggling tablecloths, stained by wine and
littered with dirty plates and dishes. When Fagerolles, on
his side, succeeded in obtaining two glasses of chartreuse for
himself and Jory, he began to talk to Sandoz, whom he
treated with a certain amount of deference, divining that
the novelist might become a power. And Jory thereupon
appropriated Claude, who had again become mournful and
silent.

'You know, my dear fellow,' said the journalist, 'I didn't
send you any announcement of my marriage. On account of
our position we managed it on the quiet without inviting any
guests. All the same, I should have liked to let you know.
You will excuse me, won't you?'

He showed himself expansive, gave particulars, full of the
happiness of life, and egotistically delighted to feel fat and
victorious in front of that poor vanquished fellow. He
succeeded with everything, he said. He had given up leader-
writing, feeling the necessity of settling down seriously, and
he had risen to the editorship of a prominent art review, on
which, so it was asserted, he made thirty thousand francs a
year, without mentioning certain profits realised by shady
trafficking in the sale of art collections. The middle-class
rapacity which he had inherited from his mother, the
hereditary passion for profit which had secretly impelled him
to embark in petty speculations as soon as he had gained a few
coppers, now openly displayed itself, and ended by making
him a terrible customer, who bled all the artists and amateurs
who came under his clutches.

It was amidst this good luck of his that Mathilde, now all-
powerful, had brought him to the point of begging her, with
tears in his eyes, to become his wife, a request which she had
proudly refused during six long months.

'When folks are destined to live together,' he continued,
'the best course is to set everything square. You experienced
it yourself, my dear fellow; you know something about it, eh?
And if I told you that she wouldn't consent at first—yes, it's
a fact—for fear of being misjudged and of doing me harm.
Oh! she has such grandeur, such delicacy of mind! No,
nobody can have an idea of that woman's qualities. Devoted,
taking all possible care of one, economical, and acute, too,

and such a good adviser ! Ah ! it was a lucky chance that I met her ! I no longer do anything without consulting her ; I let her do as she likes ; she manages everything, upon my word.'

The truth was that Mathilde had finished by reducing him to the frightened obedience of a little boy. The once dissolute she-ghoul had become a dictatorial spouse, eager for respect, and consumed with ambition and love of money. She showed, too, every form of sourish virtue. It was said that they had been seen taking the Holy Communion together at Notre Dame de Lorette. They kissed one another before other people, and called each other by endearing nicknames. Only, of an evening, he had to relate how he had spent his time during the day, and if the employment of a single hour remained suspicious, if he did not bring home all the money he had received, down to the odd coppers, she led him the most abominable life imaginable.

This, of course, Jory left unmentioned. By way of conclusion he exclaimed : 'And so we waited for my father's death, and then I married her.'

Claude, whose mind had so far been wandering, and who had merely nodded without listening, was struck by that last sentence.

'What ! you married her—married Mathilde ? '

That exclamation summed up all the astonishment that the affair caused him, all the recollections that occurred to him of Mahoudeau's shop. That Jory, why, he could still hear him talking about Mathilde in an abominable manner ; and yet he had married her ! It was really stupid for a fellow to speak badly of a woman, for he never knew if he might not end by marrying her some day or other !

However, Jory was perfectly serene, his memory was dead, he never allowed himself an allusion to the past, never showed the slightest embarrassment when his comrades' eyes were turned on him. Besides, Mathilde seemed to be a new-comer. He introduced her to them as if they knew nothing whatever about her.

Sandoz, who had lent an ear to the conversation, greatly interested by this fine business, called out as soon as Jory and Claude became silent :

'Let's be off, eh ? My legs are getting numbed.'

But at that moment Irma Bécot appeared, and stopped in front of the buffet. With her hair freshly gilded, she had put on her best looks—all the tricky sheen of a tawny hussy, who seemed to have just stepped out of some old Renaissance frame; and she wore a train of light blue brocaded silk, with a satin skirt covered with Alençon lace, of such richness that quite an escort of gentlemen followed her in admiration. On perceiving Claude among the others, she hesitated for a moment, seized, as it were, with cowardly shame in front of that ill-clad, ugly, derided devil. Then, becoming valiant, as it were, it was his hand that she shook the first amid all those well-dressed men, who opened their eyes in amazement. She laughed with an affectionate air, and spoke to him in a friendly, bantering way.

Fagerolles, however, was already paying for the two chartreuses he had ordered, and at last he went off with Irma, whom Jory also decided to follow. Claude watched them walk away together, she between the two men, moving on in regal fashion, greatly admired, and repeatedly bowed to by people in the crowd.

'One can see very well that Mathilde isn't here,' quietly remarked Sandoz. 'Ah! my friend, what clouts Jory would receive on getting home!'

The novelist now asked for the bill. All the tables were becoming vacant; there only remained a litter of bones and crusts. A couple of waiters were wiping the marble slabs with sponges, whilst a third raked up the soiled sand. Behind the brown serge hangings the staff of the establishment was lunching—one could hear a grinding of jaws and husky laughter, a rumpus akin to that of a camp of gipsies devouring the contents of their saucepans.

Claude and Sandoz went round the garden, where they discovered a statue by Mahoudeau, very badly placed in a corner near the eastern vestibule. It was the bathing girl at last, standing erect, but of diminutive proportions, being scarcely as tall as a girl ten years old, but charmingly delicate—with slim hips and a tiny bosom, displaying all the exquisite hesitancy of a sprouting bud. The figure seemed to exhale a perfume, that grace which nothing can give, but which flowers where it lists, stubborn, invincible, perennial grace, springing still and ever from Mahoudeau's thick fingers, which were so ignorant of their special aptitude that they had long treated this very grace with derision.

Sandoz could not help smiling.

'And to think that this fellow has done everything he

could to warp his talent. If his figure were better placed, it would meet with great success.'

'Yes, great success,' repeated Claude. 'It is very pretty.'

Precisely at that moment they perceived Mahoudeau, already in the vestibule, and going towards the staircase. They called him, ran after him, and then all three remained talking together for a few minutes. The ground-floor gallery stretched away, empty, with its sanded pavement, and the pale light streaming through its large round windows. One might have fancied oneself under a railway bridge. Strong pillars supported the metallic framework, and an icy chillness blew from above, moistening the sand in which one's feet sank. In the distance, behind a torn curtain, one could see rows of statues, the rejected sculptural exhibits, the casts which poor sculptors did not even remove, gathered together in a livid kind of Morgue, in a state of lamentable abandonment. But what surprised one, on raising one's head, was the continuous din, the mighty tramp of the public over the flooring of the upper galleries. One was deafened by it; it rolled on without a pause, as if interminable trains, going at full speed, were ever and ever shaking the iron girders.

When Mahoudeau had been complimented, he told Claude that he had searched for his picture in vain. In the depths of what hole could they have put it? Then, in a fit of affectionate remembrance for the past, he asked anxiously after Gagnière and Dubuche. Where were the Salons of yore which they had all reached in a band, the mad excursions through the galleries as in an enemy's country, the violent disdain they had felt on going away, the discussions which had made their tongues swell and emptied their brains? Nobody now saw Dubuche. Two or three times a month Gagnière came from Melun, in a state of bewilderment, to attend some concert; and he now took such little interest in painting that he had not even looked in at the Salon, although he exhibited his usual landscape, the same view of the banks of the Seine which he had been sending for the last fifteen years—a picture of a pretty greyish tint, so conscientious and quiet that the public had never remarked it.

'I was going upstairs,' resumed Mahoudeau. 'Will you come with me?'

Claude, pale with suffering, raised his eyes every second. Ah! that terrible rumbling, that devouring gallop of the

monster overhead, the shock of which he felt in his very
limbs !

He held out his hand without speaking.

'What! are you going to leave us ?' exclaimed Sandoz.
Take just another turn with us, and we'll go away together.'

Then, on seeing Claude so weary, a feeling of pity made
his heart contract. He divined that the poor fellow's
courage was exhausted, that he was desirous of solitude,
seized with a desire to fly off alone and hide his wound.

'Then, good-bye, old man ; I'll call and see you to-
morrow.'

Staggering, and as if pursued by the tempest upstairs,
Claude disappeared behind the clumps of shrubbery in the
garden. But two hours later Sandoz, who after losing
Mahoudeau had just found him again with Jory and
Fagerolles, perceived the unhappy painter again standing in
front of his picture, at the same spot where he had met him
the first time. At the moment of going off the wretched
fellow had come up there again, harassed and attracted
despite himself.

There was now the usual five o'clock crush. The crowd,
weary of winding round the galleries, became distracted, and
pushed and shoved without ever finding its way out. Since
the coolness of the morning, the heat of all the human
bodies, the odour of all the breath exhaled there had made
the atmosphere heavy, and the dust of the floors, flying about,
rose up in a fine mist. People still took each other to see
certain pictures, the subjects of which alone struck and
attracted the crowd. Some went off, came back, and walked
about unceasingly. The women were particularly obstinate
in not retiring ; they seemed determined to remain there till
the attendants should push them out when six o'clock began
to strike. Some fat ladies had foundered. Others, who had
failed to find even the tiniest place to sit down, leaned heavily
on their parasols, sinking, but still obstinate. Every eye was
turned anxiously and supplicatingly towards the settees
laden with people. And all that those thousands of sight-
seers were now conscious of, was that last fatigue of theirs,
which made their legs totter, drew their features together,
and tortured them with headache—that headache peculiar to
fine-art shows, which is caused by the constant straining of
one's neck and the blinding dance of colours.

Alone on the little settee where at noon already they had been talking about their private affairs, the two decorated gentlemen were still chatting quietly, with their minds a hundred leagues away from the place. Perhaps they had returned thither, perhaps they had not even stirred from the spot.

'And so,' said the fat one, 'you went in, pretending not to understand?'

'Quite so,' replied the thin one. 'I looked at them and took off my hat. It was clear, eh?'

'Astonishing! You really astonish me, my dear friend.'

Claude, however, only heard the low beating of his heart, and only beheld the 'Dead Child' up there in the air, near the ceiling. He did not take his eyes off it, a prey to a fascination which held him there, quite independent of his will. The crowd turned round him, people's feet trod on his own, he was pushed and carried away; and, like some inert object, he abandoned himself, waved about, and ultimately found himself again on the same spot as before without having once lowered his head, quite ignorant of what was occurring below, all his life being concentrated up yonder beside his work, his little Jacques, swollen in death. Two big tears which stood motionless between his eyelids prevented him from seeing clearly. And it seemed to him as if he would never have time to see enough.

Then Sandoz, in his deep compassion, pretended he did not perceive his old friend; it was as if he wished to leave him there, beside the tomb of his wrecked life. Their comrades once more went past in a band. Fagerolles and Jory darted on ahead, and, Mahoudeau having asked Sandoz where Claude's picture was hung, the novelist told a lie, drew him aside and took him off. All of them went away.

In the evening Christine only managed to draw curt words from Claude; everything was going on all right, said he; the public showed no ill-humour; the picture had a good effect, though it was hung perhaps rather high up. However, despite this semblance of cold tranquillity, he seemed so strange that she became frightened.

After dinner, as she returned from carrying the dirty plates into the kitchen, she no longer found him near the table. He had opened a window which overlooked some waste ground, and he stood there, leaning out to such a degree that she could scarcely see him. At this she sprang forward, terrified, and pulled him violently by his jacket.

' Claude ! Claude ! what are you doing ? '

He turned round, with his face as white as a sheet and his eyes haggard.

' I'm looking,' he said.

But she closed the window with trembling hands, and after that significant incident such anguish clung to her that she no longer slept at night-time.

XI

CLAUDE set to work again on the very next day, and months elapsed, indeed the whole summer went by, in heavy quietude. He had found a job, some little paintings of flowers for England, the proceeds of which sufficed for their daily bread. All his available time was again devoted to his large canvas, and he no longer went into the same fits of anger over it, but seemed to resign himself to that eternal task, evincing obstinate, hopeless industry. However, his eyes retained their crazy expression—one could see the death of light, as it were, in them, when they gazed upon the failure of his existence.

About this period Sandoz also experienced great grief. His mother died, his whole life was upset—that life of three together, so homely in its character, and shared merely by a few friends. He began to hate the pavilion of the Rue Nollet, and, moreover, success suddenly declared itself with respect to his books, which hitherto had sold but moderately well. So, prompted by the advent of comparative wealth, he rented in the Rue de Londres a spacious flat, the arrangements of which occupied him and his wife for several months. Sandoz's grief had drawn him closer to Claude again, both being disgusted with everything. After the terrible blow of the Salon, the novelist had felt very anxious about his old chum, divining that something had irreparably snapped within him, that there was some wound by which life ebbed away unseen. Then, however, finding Claude so cold and quiet, he ended by growing somewhat reassured.

Sandoz often walked up to the Rue Tourlaque, and whenever he found only Christine at home, he questioned her, realising that she also lived in apprehension of a calamity of which she never spoke. Her face bore a look of worry, and now and again she started nervously, like a mother who watches over her child and trembles at the slightest sound, with the fear that death may be entering the chamber.

One July morning Sandoz asked her: 'Well, are you pleased? Claude's quiet, he works a deal.'

She gave the large picture her usual glance, a side glance full of terror and hatred.

' Yes, yes, he works,' she said. ' He wants to finish everything else before taking up the woman again.' And without confessing the fear that harassed her, she added in a lower tone : ' But his eyes—have you noticed his eyes ? They always have the same wild expression. I know very well that he lies, despite his pretence of taking things so easily. Pray, come and see him, and take him out with you, so as to change the current of his thoughts. He only has you left; help me, do help me !'

After that Sandoz diligently devised motives for various walks, arriving at Claude's early in the morning, and carrying him away from his work perforce. It was almost always necessary to drag him from his steps, on which he habitually sat, even when he was not painting. A feeling of weariness stopped him, a kind of torpor benumbed him for long minutes, during which he did not give a single stroke with the brush. In those moments of mute contemplation, his gaze reverted with pious fervour to the woman's figure which he no longer touched : it was like a hesitating desire combined with sacred awe, a passion which he refused to satisfy, as he felt certain that it would cost him his life. When he set to work again at the other figures and the background of the picture, he well knew that the woman's figure was still there, and his glance wavered whenever he espied it; he felt that he would only remain master of himself as long as he did not touch it again.

One evening, Christine, who now visited at Sandoz's and never missed a single Thursday there, in the hope of seeing her big sick child of an artist brighten up in the society of his friends, took the novelist aside and begged him to drop in at their place on the morrow. And on the next day Sandoz, who, as it happened, wanted to take some notes for a novel, on the other side of Montmartre, went in search of Claude, carried him off and kept him idling about until night-time.

On this occasion they went as far as the gate of Clignancourt, where a perpetual fair was held, with merry-go-rounds, shooting-galleries, and taverns, and on reaching the spot they were stupefied to find themselves face to face with Chaîne, who was enthroned in a large and stylish booth. It was a kind of chapel, highly ornamented. There were four circular revolving stands set in a row and loaded with articles in china and glass, all sorts of ornaments and nick-nacks, whose gilding and polish shone amid an harmonica-like tinkling whenever the hand of a gamester set the stand in motion. It then spun round, grating against a feather, which, on the rotatory movement ceasing, indicated what article, if any, had been won. The big prize was a live rabbit, adorned with pink favours, which waltzed and revolved unceasingly, intoxicated with fright. And all this display was set in red hangings, scalloped at the top; and between the curtains one saw three pictures hanging at the rear of the booth, as in the sanctuary of some tabernacle. They were Chaîne's three masterpieces, which now followed him from fair to fair, from one end of Paris to the other. The ' Woman taken in Adultery ' in the centre, the copy of the Mantegna on the left, and Mahoudeau's stove on the right. Of an evening, when the petroleum lamps flamed and the revolving stands glowed and radiated like planets, nothing seemed finer than those pictures hanging amid the blood-tinged purple of the hangings, and a gaping crowd often flocked to view them.

The sight was such that it wrung an exclamation from Claude : ' Ah, good heavens ! But those paintings look very well—they were surely intended for this."

The Mantegna, so naïvely harsh in treatment, looked like some faded coloured print nailed there for the delectation of simple-minded folk ; whilst the minutely painted stove, all awry, hanging beside the gingerbread Christ absolving the adulterous woman, assumed an unexpectedly gay aspect.

However, Chaîne, who had just perceived the two friends, held out his hand to them, as if he had left them merely the day before. He was calm, neither proud nor ashamed of his booth, and he had not aged, having still a leathery aspect; though, on the other hand, his nose had completely vanished between his cheeks, whilst his mouth, clammy with prolonged silence, was buried in his moustache and beard.

' Hallo ! so we meet again ! ' said Sandoz, gaily. ' Do you know, your paintings have a lot of effect ? '

' The old humbug ! ' added Claude. ' Why, he has his little Salon all to himself. That's very cute indeed.'

Chaîne's face became radiant, and he dropped the remark : ' Of course ! '

Then, as his artistic pride was roused, he, from whom people barely wrung anything but growls, gave utterance to a whole sentence :

'Ah! it's quite certain that if I had had any money, like you fellows, I should have made my way, just as you have done, in spite of everything.'

That was his conviction. He had never doubted of his talent, he had simply forsaken the profession because it did not feed him. When he visited the Louvre, at sight of the masterpieces hanging there he felt convinced that time alone was necessary to turn out similar work.

'Ah, me!' said Claude, who had become gloomy again. 'Don't regret what you've done; you alone have succeeded. Business is brisk, eh ? '

But Chaîne muttered bitter words. No, no, there was nothing doing, not even in his line. People wouldn't play for prizes; all the money found its way to the wine-shops. In spite of buying paltry odds and ends, and striking the table with the palm of one's hand, so that the feather might not indicate one of the big prizes, a fellow barely had water to drink nowadays. Then, as some people had drawn near, he stopped short in his explanation to call out : 'Walk up, walk up, at every turn you win!' in a gruff voice which the two others had never known him to possess, and which fairly stupefied them.

A workman who was carrying a sickly little girl with large covetous eyes, let her play two turns. The revolving stands grated and the nick-nacks danced round in dazzling fashion, while the live rabbit, with his ears lowered, revolved and revolved so rapidly that the outline of his body vanished and he became nothing but a whitish circle. There was a moment of great emotion, for the little girl had narrowly missed winning him.

Then, after shaking hands with Chaîne, who was still trembling with the fright this had given him, the two friends walked away.

'He's happy,' said Claude, after they had gone some fifty paces in silence.

'He!' cried Sandoz ; 'why, he believes he has missed becoming a member of the Institute, and it's killing him.'

Shortly after this meeting, and towards the middle of August, Sandoz devised a real excursion which would take up a whole day. He had met Dubuche—Dubuche, careworn and mournful, who had shown himself plaintive and affectionate, raking up the past and inviting his two old chums to lunch at La Richaudière, where he should be alone with his two children for another fortnight. Why shouldn't they go and surprise him there, since he seemed so desirous of renewing the old intimacy? But in vain did Sandoz repeat that he had promised Dubuche on oath to bring Claude with him; the painter obstinately refused to go, as if he were frightened at the idea of again beholding Bennecourt, the Seine, the islands, all the stretch of country where his happy years lay dead and buried. It was necessary for Christine to interfere, and he finished by giving way, although full of repugnance to the trip. It precisely happened that on the day prior to the appointment he had worked at his painting until very late, being taken with the old fever again. And so the next morning—it was Sunday—being devoured with a longing to paint, he went off most reluctantly, tearing himself away from his picture with a pang. What was the use of returning to Bennecourt? All that was dead, it no longer existed. Paris alone remained, and even in Paris there was but one view, the point of the Cité, that vision which haunted him always and everywhere, that one corner where he ever left his heart.

Sandoz, finding him nervous in the railway carriage, and seeing that his eyes remained fixed on the window as if he had been leaving the city—which had gradually grown smaller and seemed shrouded in mist—for years, did all he could to divert his mind, telling him, for instance, what he knew about Dubuche's real position. At the outset, old Margaillan, glorifying in his bemedalled son-in-law, had trotted him about and introduced him everywhere as his partner and successor. There was a fellow who would conduct business briskly, who would build houses more cheaply and in finer style than ever, for hadn't he grown pale over books? But Dubuche's first idea proved disastrous; on some land belonging to his father-in-law in Burgundy he established a brickyard in so unfavourable a situation, and after so defective a plan, that the venture resulted in the sheer loss of two hundred thousand francs. Then he turned his attention to erecting houses, insisting upon bringing personal ideas into execution, a certain general scheme of his which would revolutionise the building art. These ideas were the old theories he held from the revolutionary chums of his

youth, everything that he had promised he would realise
when he was free; but he had not properly reduced the
theories to method, and he applied them unseasonably, with
the awkwardness of a pupil lacking the sacred fire; he
experimented with terra-cotta and pottery ornamentation,
large bay windows, and especially with the employment of
iron—iron girders, iron staircases, and iron roofings; and as
the employment of these materials increased the outlay, he
again ended with a catastrophe, which was all the greater as
he was a pitiful manager, and had lost his head since he had
become rich, rendered the more obtuse, it seemed, by money,
quite spoilt and at sea, unable even to revert to his old habits
of industry. This time Margaillan grew angry; he for thirty
years had been buying ground, building and selling again,
estimating at a glance the cost and return of house property;
so many yards of building at so much the foot having to yield
so many suites of rooms at so much rent. He wouldn't
have anything more to do with a fellow who blundered about
lime, bricks, millstones, and in fact everything, who employed
oak when deal would have suited, and who could not bring
himself to cut up a storey—like a consecrated wafer—into as
many little squares as was necessary. No, no, none of that!
He rebelled against art, after having been ambitious to introduce a little of it into his routine, in order to satisfy a long-
standing worry about his own ignorance. And after that
matters had gone from bad to worse, terrible quarrels had
arisen between the son-in-law and the father-in-law, the
former disdainful, intrenching himself behind his science, and
the latter shouting that the commonest labourer knew more
than an architect did. The millions were in danger, and one
fine day Margaillan turned Dubuche out of his offices, forbid-
ding him ever to set foot in them again, since he did not even
know how to direct a building-yard where only four men
worked. It was a disaster, a lamentable failure, the School
of Arts collapsing, derided by a mason!

At this point of Sandoz's story, Claude, who had begun
to listen to his friend, inquired:

'Then what is Dubuche doing now?'

'I don't know—nothing probably,' answered Sandoz. 'He
told me that he was anxious about his children's health, and
was taking care of them.'

That pale woman, Madame Margaillan, as slender as the
blade of a knife, had died of tubercular consumption, which

was plainly the hereditary disease, the source of the family's degeneracy, for her daughter, Régine, had been coughing ever since her marriage. She was now drinking the waters at Mont-Dore, whither she had not dared to take her children, as they had been very poorly the year before, after a season spent in that part, where the air was too keen for them. This explained the scattering of the family: the mother over yonder with her maid; the grandfather in Paris, where he had resumed his great building enterprises, battling amid his four hundred workmen, and crushing the idle and the incapable beneath his contempt; and the father in exile at La Richaudière, set to watch over his son and daughter, shut up there, after the very first struggle, as if it had broken him down for life. In a moment of effusion Dubuche had even let Sandoz understand that as his wife was so extremely delicate he now lived with her merely on friendly terms.

'A nice marriage,' said Sandoz, simply, by way of conclusion.

It was ten o'clock when the two friends rang at the iron gate of La Richaudière. The estate, with which they were not acquainted, amazed them. There was a superb park, a garden laid out in the French style, with balustrades and steps spreading away in regal fashion; three huge conservatories and a colossal cascade—quite a piece of folly, with its rocks brought from afar, and the quantity of cement and the number of conduits that had been employed in arranging it. Indeed, the owner had sunk a fortune in it, out of sheer vanity. But what struck the friends still more was the melancholy, deserted aspect of the domain; the gravel of the avenues carefully raked, with never a trace of footsteps; the distant expanses quite deserted, save that now and then a solitary gardener passed by; and the house looking lifeless, with all its windows closed, excepting two, which were barely set ajar.

However, a valet who had decided to show himself began to question them, and when he learnt that they wished to see 'monsieur,' he became insolent, and replied that 'monsieur' was behind the house in the gymnasium, and then went indoors again.

Sandoz and Claude followed a path which led them towards a lawn, and what they saw there made them pause. Dubuche, who stood in front of a trapeze, was raising his arms to support his son, Gaston, a poor sickly boy who, at ten years of age, still had the slight, soft limbs of early childhood; while

the girl, Alice, sat in a perambulator awaiting her turn. She
was so imperfectly developed that, although she was six years
old, she could not yet walk. The father, absorbed in his task,
continued exercising the slim limbs of his little boy, swinging
him backwards and forwards, and vainly trying to make him
raise himself up by his wrists. Then, as this slight effort
sufficed to bring on perspiration, he removed the little fellow
from the trapeze and rolled him in a rug. And all this was
done amid complete silence, alone under the far expanse of
sky, his face wearing a look of distressful pity as he knelt
there in that splendid park. However, as he rose up he
perceived the two friends.

'What! it's you? On a Sunday, and without warning
me!'

He had made a gesture of annoyance, and at once explained that the maid, the only woman to whom he could
trust the children, went to Paris on Sundays, and that it was
consequently impossible for him to leave Gaston and Alice
for a minute.

'I'll wager that you came to lunch?' he added.

As Claude gave Sandoz an imploring glance, the novelist
made haste to answer:

'No, no. As it happens, we only have time enough to
shake hands with you. Claude had to come down here on a
business matter. He lived at Bennecourt, as you know. And
as I accompanied him, we took it into our heads to walk as
far as here. But there are people waiting for us, so don't
disturb yourself in the least.'

Thereupon, Dubuche, who felt relieved, made a show of
detaining them. They certainly had an hour to spare, dash
it all! And they all three began to talk. Claude looked at
Dubuche, astonished to find him so aged; his flabby face had
become wrinkled—it was of a yellowish hue, and streaked
with red, as if bile had splashed his skin; whilst his hair and
his moustaches were already growing grey. In addition, his
figure appeared to have become more compact; a bitter
weariness made each of his gestures seem an effort. Were
defeats in money matters as hard to bear, then, as defeats in
art? Everything about this vanquished man—his voice, his
glance—proclaimed the shameful dependency in which he
had to live: the bankruptcy of his future which was cast in
his teeth, with the accusation of having allowed a talent he
did not possess to be set down as an asset in the marriage

contract. Then there was the family money which he
nowadays stole, the money spent on what he ate, the clothes
he wore, and the pocket-money he needed—in fact, the
perpetual alms which were bestowed upon him, just as they
might have been bestowed upon some vulgar swindler, whom
one unluckily could not get rid of.

'Wait a bit,' resumed Dubuche; 'I have to stop here five
minutes longer with one of my poor duckies, and afterwards
we'll go indoors.'

Gently, and with infinite motherly precautions, he removed little Alice from the perambulator and lifted her to
the trapeze. Then, stammering coaxing words and smiling, he encouraged her, and left her hanging for a couple of
minutes, so as to develop her muscles; but he remained with
open arms, watching each movement with the fear of seeing
her smashed to pieces, should her weak little wax-like hands
relax their hold. She did not say anything, but obeyed him
in spite of the terror that this exercise caused her; and she
was so pitifully light in weight that she did not even fully
stretch the ropes, being like one of those poor scraggy little
birds which fall from a young tree without as much as
bending it.

At this moment, Dubuche, having given Gaston a glance,
became distracted on remarking that the rug had slipped and
that the child's legs were uncovered.

'Good heavens! good heavens! Why, he'll catch cold
on this grass! And I, who can't move! Gaston, my little
dear! It's the same thing every day; you wait till I'm
occupied with your sister. Sandoz, pray cover him over!
Ah, thanks! Pull the rug up more; don't be afraid!'

So this was the outcome of his splendid marriage—those
two poor, weak little beings, whom the least breath from the
sky threatened to kill like flies. Of the fortune he had married, all that remained to him was the constant grief of
beholding those woeful children stricken by the final degeneracy of scrofula and phthisis. However, this big, egotistical
fellow showed himself an admirable father. The only energy
that remained to him consisted in a determination to make
his children live, and he struggled on hour after hour, saving
them every morning, and dreading to lose them every night.
They alone existed now amid his finished existence, amid
the bitterness of his father-in-law's insulting reproaches, the
coldness of his sorry, ailing wife. And he kept to his task in

desperation; he finished bringing those children into the world, as it were, by dint of unremitting tenderness.

'There, my darling, that's enough, isn't it?' he said. 'You'll soon see how big and pretty you'll become.'

He then placed Alice in the perambulator again, took Gaston, who was still wrapped up, on one of his arms; and when his friends wished to help him, he declined their offer, pushing the little girl's vehicle along with his right hand, which had remained free.

'Thanks,' he said, 'I'm accustomed to it. Ah! the poor darlings are not heavy; and besides, with servants one can never be sure of anything.'

On entering the house, Sandoz and Claude again saw the valet who had been so insolent; and they noticed that Dubuche trembled before him. The kitchen and the hall shared the contempt of the father-in-law, who paid for everything, and treated 'madame's' husband like a beggar whose presence was merely tolerated out of charity. Each time that a shirt was got ready for him, each time that he asked for some more bread, the servants' impolite gestures made him feel that he was receiving alms.

'Well, good-bye, we must leave you,' said Sandoz, who suffered at the sight of it all.

'No, no, wait a bit. The children are going to breakfast, and afterwards I'll accompany you with them. They must go for their outing.'

Each day was regulated hour by hour. Of a morning came the baths and the gymnastics; then the breakfast, which was quite an affair, as the children needed special food, which was duly discussed and weighed. And matters were carried to such a point that even their wine and water was slightly warmed, for fear that too chilly a drop might give them a cold. On this occasion they each partook of the yolk of an egg diluted in some broth, and a mutton cutlet, which the father cut up into tiny morsels. Then, prior to the siesta, came the promenade.

Sandoz and Claude found themselves once more out-of-doors, walking down the broad avenues with Dubuche, who again propelled Alice's perambulator, whilst Gaston walked beside him. They talked about the estate as they went towards the gate. The master glanced over the park with timid, nervous eyes, as if he did not feel at home. Besides, he did not know anything; he did not occupy himself about

anything. He appeared even to have forgotten the profession
which he was said to be ignorant of, and seemed to have gone
astray, to be bowed down by sheer inaction.

'And your parents, how are they?' asked Sandoz.

A spark was once more kindled in Dubuche's dim eyes.

'Oh! my parents are happy,' he said; 'I bought them a
little house, where they live on the annuity which I had
specified in my marriage contract. Well, you see, mamma
had advanced enough money for my education, and I had to
return it to her, as I had promised, eh? Yes, I can at least
say that my parents have nothing to reproach me with.'

Having reached the gate, they tarried there for a few
minutes. At last, still looking crushed, Dubuche shook hands
with his old comrades; and retaining Claude's hand in his, he
concluded, as if making a simple statement of fact quite devoid
of anger:

'Good-bye; try to get out of worry! As for me, I've spoilt
my life.'

And they watched him walk back towards the house, pushing the perambulator, and supporting Gaston, who was already
stumbling with fatigue—he, Dubuche, himself having his
back bent and the heavy tread of an old man.

One o'clock was striking, and they both hurried down
towards Bennecourt, saddened and ravenous. But mournfulness awaited them there as well; a murderous blast had
swept over the place, both Faucheurs, husband and wife, and
old Porrette, were all dead; and the inn, having fallen into
the hands of that goose Mélie, was becoming repugnant with
its filth and coarseness. An abominable repast was served
them, an omelette with hairs in it, and cutlets smelling of
grease, in the centre of the common room, to which an open
window admitted the pestilential odour of a dung heap, while
the place was so full of flies that they positively blackened
the tables. The heat of the burning afternoon came in with
the stench, and Claude and Sandoz did not even feel the
courage to order any coffee; they fled.

'And you who used to extol old Mother Faucheur's
omelettes!' said Sandoz. 'The place is done for. We are
going for a turn, eh?'

Claude was inclined to refuse. Ever since the morning
he had had but one idea—that of walking on as fast as possible,
as if each step would shorten the disagreeable task and bring
him back to Paris. His heart, his head, his whole being had

remained there. He looked neither to right nor to left, he glided along without distinguishing aught of the fields or trees, having but one fixed idea in his brain, a prey to such hallucinations that at certain moments he fancied the point of the Cité rose up and called to him from amid the vast expanse of stubble. However, Sandoz's proposal aroused memories in his mind ; and, softening somewhat, he replied :

'Yes, that's it, we'll have a look.'

But as they advanced along the river bank, he became indignant and grieved. He could scarcely recognise the place. A bridge had been built to connect Bennecourt with Bonnières : a bridge, good heavens ! in the place of the old ferry-boat, grating against its chain—the old black boat which, cutting athwart the current, had been so full of interest to the artistic eye. Moreover, a dam established down-stream at Port-Villez had raised the level of the river, most of the islands of yore were now submerged, and the little armlets of the stream had become broader. There were no more pretty nooks, no more rippling alleys amid which one could lose oneself ; it was a disaster that inclined one to strangle all the river engineers !

'Why, that clump of pollards still emerging from the water on the left,' cried Claude, 'was the Barreux Island, where we used to chat together, lying on the grass ! You remember, don't you ? Ah ! the scoundrels ! '

Sandoz, who could never see a tree felled without shaking his fist at the wood-cutter, turned pale with anger, and felt exasperated that the authorities had thus dared to mutilate nature.

Then, as Claude approached his old home, he became silent, and his teeth clenched. The house had been sold to some middle-class folk, and now there was an iron gate, against which he pressed his face. The rose-bushes were all dead, the apricot trees were dead also ; the garden, which looked very trim, with its little pathways and its square-cut beds of flowers and vegetables, bordered with box, was reflected in a large ball of plated glass set upon a stand in the very centre of it ; and the house, newly whitewashed and painted at the corners and round the doors and windows, in a manner to imitate freestone, suggested some clownish parvenu awkwardly arrayed in his Sunday toggery. The sight fairly enraged the painter. No, no, nothing of himself, nothing of Christine, nothing of the great love of their youth remained there ! He wished to look still further ; he turned round behind the house, and sought for the wood of oak trees where they had left the living quiver of their embraces ; but the wood was dead, dead like all the rest, felled, sold, and burnt ! Then he made a gesture of anathema, in which he cast all his grief to that stretch of country which was now so changed that he could not find in it one single token of his past life. And so a few years sufficed to efface the spot where one had laboured, loved, and suffered ! What was the use of man's vain agitation if the wind behind him swept and carried away all the traces of his footsteps ? He had rightly realised that he ought not to return thither, for the past is simply the cemetery of our illusions, where our feet for ever stumble against tombstones !

'Let us go ! ' he cried ; 'let us go at once ! It's stupid to torture one's heart like this ! '

When they were on the new bridge, Sandoz tried to calm him by showing him the view which had not formerly existed, the widened bed of the Seine, full to the brim, as it were, and the water flowing onward, proudly and slowly. But this water failed to interest Claude, until he reflected that it was the same water which, as it passed through Paris, had bathed the old quay walls of the Cité ; and then he felt touched, he leant over the parapet of the bridge for a moment, and thought that he could distinguish glorious reflections in it—the towers of Notre-Dame, and the needle-like spire of the Sainte Chapelle, carried along by the current towards the sea.

The two friends missed the three o'clock train, and it was real torture to have to spend two long hours more in that region, where everything weighed so heavily on their shoulders. Fortunately, they had forewarned Christine and Madame Sandoz that they might return by a night train if they were detained. So they resolved upon a bachelor dinner at a restaurant on the Place du Hâvre, hoping to set themselves all right again by a good chat at dessert as in former times. Eight o'clock was about to strike when they sat down to table.

Claude, on leaving the terminus, with his feet once more on the Paris pavement, had lost his nervous agitation, like a man who at last finds himself once more at home. And with the cold, absent-minded air which he now usually displayed, he listened to Sandoz trying to enliven him. The novelist treated his friend like a mistress whose head he wished to turn; they partook of delicate, highly spiced dishes and heady wines. But mirth was rebellious, and Sandoz himself ended by becoming gloomy. All his hopes of immortality were shaken by his excursion to that ungrateful country village, that Bennecourt, so loved and so forgetful, where he and Claude had not found a single stone retaining any recollection of them. If things which are eternal forget so soon, can one place any reliance for one hour on the memory of man?

'Do you know, old fellow,' said the novelist, 'it's that which sometimes sends me into a cold sweat. Have you ever reflected that posterity may not be the faultless dispenser of justice that we dream of? One consoles oneself for being insulted and denied, by relying on the equity of the centuries to come; just as the faithful endure all the abominations of this earth in the firm belief of another life, in which each will be rewarded according to his deserts. But suppose Paradise exists no more for the artist than it does for the Catholic, suppose that future generations prolong the misunderstanding and prefer amiable little trifles to vigorous works! Ah! what a sell it would be, eh? To have led a convict's life— to have screwed oneself down to one's work—all for a mere delusion! Please notice that it's quite possible, after all. There are some consecrated reputations which I wouldn't give a rap for. Classical education has deformed everything, and has imposed upon us as geniuses men of correct, facile talent, who follow the beaten track. To them one may prefer men of free tendencies, whose work is at times unequal; but these are only known to a few people of real culture, so that it looks as if immortality might really go merely to the middle-class "average" talent, to the men whose names are forced into our brains at school, when we are not strong enough to defend ourselves. But no, no, one mustn't say those things; they make me shudder! Should I have the courage to go on with my task, should I be able to remain erect amid all the jeering around me if I hadn't the consoling illusion that I shall some day be appreciated?'

Claude had listened with his dolorous expression, and he now made a gesture of indifference tinged with bitterness.

'Bah! what does it matter? Well, there's nothing hereafter. We are even madder than the fools who kill themselves for a woman. When the earth splits to pieces in space like a dry walnut, our works won't add one atom to its dust.'

'That's quite true,' summed up Sandoz, who was very pale. 'What's the use of trying to fill up the void of space? And to think that we know it, and that our pride still battles all the same!'

They left the restaurant, roamed about the streets, and foundered again in the depths of a café, where they philosophised. They had come by degrees to raking up the memories of their childhood, and this ended by filling their hearts with sadness. One o'clock in the morning struck when they decided to go home.

However, Sandoz talked of seeing Claude as far as the Rue Tourlaque. That August night was a superb one, the air was warm, the sky studded with stars. And as they went the round by way of the Quartier de l'Europe, they passed before the old Café Baudequin on the Boulevard des Batignolles. It had changed hands three times. It was no longer arranged inside in the same manner as formerly; there were now a couple of billiard tables on the right hand; and several strata of customers had followed each other thither, one covering the other, so that the old frequenters had disappeared like buried nations. However, curiosity, the emotion they had derived from all the past things they had been raking up together, induced them to cross the boulevard and to glance into the café through the open doorway. They wanted to see their table of yore, on the left hand, right at the back of the room.

'Oh, look!' said Sandoz, stupefied.

'Gagnière!' muttered Claude.

It was indeed Gagnière, seated all alone at that table at the end of the empty café. He must have come from Melun for one of the Sunday concerts to which he treated himself; and then, in the evening, while astray in Paris, an old habit of his legs had led him to the Café Baudequin. Not one of the comrades ever set foot there now, and he, who had beheld another age, obstinately remained there alone. He had not yet touched his glass of beer; he was looking at it, so absorbed in thought that he did not even stir when the waiters began piling the chairs on the tables, in order that everything might be ready for the morrow's sweeping.

The two friends hurried off, upset by the sight of that dim

figure, seized as it were with a childish fear of ghosts. They parted in the Rue Tourlaque.

'Ah! that poor devil Dubuche!' said Sandoz as he pressed Claude's hand, 'he spoilt our day for us.'

As soon as November had come round, and when all the old friends were back in Paris again, Sandoz thought of gathering them together at one of those Thursday dinners which had remained a habit with him. They were always his greatest delight. The sale of his books was increasing, and he was growing rich; the flat in the Rue de Londres was becoming quite luxurious compared with the little house at Batignolles; but he himself remained immutable. On this occasion, he was anxious, in his good nature, to procure real enjoyment for Claude by organising one of the dear evenings of their youth. So he saw to the invitations; Claude and Christine naturally must come; next Jory and his wife, the latter of whom it had been necessary to receive since her marriage; then Dubuche, who always came alone, with Fagerolles, Mahoudeau, and finally Gagnière. There would be ten of them—all the men comrades of the old band, without a single outsider, in order that the good understanding and jollity might be complete.

Henriette, who was more mistrustful than her husband, hesitated when this list of guests was decided upon.

'Oh! Fagerolles? You believe in having Fagerolles with the others? They hardly like him—nor Claude either; I fancied I noticed a coolness——'

But he interrupted her, bent on not admitting it.

'What! a coolness? It's really funny, but women can't understand that fellows chaff each other. All that doesn't prevent them from having their hearts in the right place.'

Henriette took especial care in preparing the menu for that Thursday dinner. She now had quite a little staff to overlook, a cook, a man-servant, and so on; and if she no longer prepared any of the dishes herself, she still saw that very delicate fare was provided, out of affection for her husband, whose sole vice was gluttony. She went to market with the cook, and called in person on the tradespeople. She and her husband had a taste for gastronomical curiosities from the four corners of the world. On this occasion they decided to have some ox-tail soup, grilled mullet, undercut of beef with mushrooms, *raviolis* in the Italian fashion, hazel-hens from Russia, and a salad of truffles, without counting caviare and *kilkis* as side-dishes, a *glace pralinée*, and a little emerald-coloured Hungarian cheese, with fruit and pastry. As wine, some old Bordeaux claret in decanters, chambertin with the roast, and sparkling moselle at dessert, in lieu of champagne, which was voted common-place.

At seven o'clock Sandoz and Henriette were waiting for their guests, he simply wearing a jacket, and she looking very elegant in a plain dress of black satin. People dined at their house in frock-coats, without any fuss. The drawing-room, the arrangements of which they were now completing, was becoming crowded with old furniture, old tapestry, nick-nacks of all countries and all times—a rising and now overflowing stream of things which had taken source at Batignolles with an old pot of Rouen ware, which Henriette had given her husband on one of his fête days. They ran about to the curiosity shops together; a joyful passion for buying possessed them. Sandoz satisfied the longings of his youth, the romanticist ambitions which the first books he had read had given birth to. Thus this writer, so fiercely modern, lived amid the worm-eaten middle ages which he had dreamt of when he was a lad of fifteen. As an excuse, he laughingly declared that handsome modern furniture cost too much, whilst with old things, even common ones, you immediately obtained something with effect and colour. There was nothing of the collector about him, he was entirely concerned as to decoration and broad effects; and to tell the truth, the drawing-room, lighted by two lamps of old Delft ware, had quite a soft warm tint with the dull gold of the dalmaticas used for upholstering the seats, the yellowish incrustations of the Italian cabinets and Dutch show-cases, the faded hues of the Oriental door-hangings, the hundred little notes of the ivory, crockery and enamel work, pale with age, which showed against the dull red hangings of the room.

Claude and Christine were the first to arrive. The latter had put on her only silk dress—an old, worn-out garment which she preserved with especial care for such occasions. Henriette at once took hold of both her hands and drew her to a sofa. She was very fond of her, and questioned her, seeing her so strange, touchingly pale, and with anxious eyes. What was the matter? Did she feel poorly? No, no, she answered that she was very gay and very pleased to come; but while she spoke, she kept on glancing at Claude, as if to study him, and then looked away. He seemed excited, evincing a feverishness in his words and gestures which he had not shown for a month past. At intervals, however, his agitation subsided, and he remained silent, with his eyes wide open, gazing vacantly into space at something which he fancied was calling him.

'Ah! old man,' he said to Sandoz, 'I finished reading your book last night. It's deucedly clever; you have shut up their mouths this time!'

They both talked standing in front of the chimney-piece, where some logs were blazing. Sandoz had indeed just published a new novel, and although his critics did not disarm, there was at last that stir of success which establishes a man's reputation despite the persistent attacks of his adversaries. Besides, he had no illusions; he knew very well that the battle, even if it were won, would begin again at each fresh book he wrote. The great work of his life was advancing, that series of novels which he launched forth in volumes one after another in stubborn, regular fashion, marching towards the goal he had selected without letting anything, obstacles, insults, or fatigue, conquer him.

'It's true,' he gaily replied, 'they are weakening this time. There's even one who has been foolish enough to admit that I'm an honest man! See how everything degenerates! But they'll make up for it, never fear! I know some of them whose nuts are too much unlike my own to let them accept my literary formula, my boldness of language, and my physiological characters acting under the influence of circumstances; and I refer to brother writers who possess self-respect; I leave the fools and the scoundrels on one side. For a man to be able to work on pluckily, it is best for him to expect neither good faith nor justice. To be in the right he must begin by dying.'

At this Claude's eyes abruptly turned towards a corner of the drawing-room, as if to pierce the wall and go far away yonder, whither something had summoned him. Then they became hazy and returned from their journey, whilst he exclaimed:

'Oh! you speak for yourself! I should do wrong to kick the bucket. No matter, your book sent me into a deuced fever. I wanted to paint to-day, but I couldn't. Ah! it's lucky that I can't get jealous of you, else you would make me too unhappy.'

However, the door had opened, and Mathilde came in, followed by Jory. She was richly attired in a tunic of nasturtium-

hued velvet and a skirt of straw-coloured satin, with diamonds in her ears and a large bouquet of roses on her
bosom. What astonished Claude the most was that he did
not recognise her, for she had become plump, round, and fair
skinned, instead of thin and sunburnt as he had known her.
Her disturbing ugliness had departed in a swelling of the
face; her mouth, once noted for its black voids, now displayed
teeth which looked over-white whenever she condescended
to smile, with a disdainful curling of the upper lip. You
could guess that she had become immoderately respectable;
her five and forty summers gave her weight beside her
husband, who was younger than herself and seemed to be her
nephew. The only thing of yore that clung to her was a
violent perfume; she drenched herself with the strongest
essences, as if she had been anxious to wash from her skin
the smell of all the aromatic simples with which she had
been impregnated by her herbalist business; however, the
sharpness of rhubarb, the bitterness of elder-seed, and the
warmth of peppermint clung to her; and as soon as she
crossed the drawing-room, it was filled with an undefinable
smell like that of a chemist's shop, relieved by an acute odour
of musk.

Henriette, who had risen, made her sit down beside
Christine, saying:

'You know each other, don't you? You have already met
here.'

Mathilde gave but a cold glance at the modest attire of
that woman who had lived for a long time with a man, so it
was said, before being married to him. She herself was
exceedingly rigid respecting such matters since the tolerance
prevailing in literary and artistic circles had admitted her to a
few drawing-rooms. Henriette hated her, however, and after
the customary exchange of courtesies, not to be dispensed
with, resumed her conversation with Christine.

Jory had shaken hands with Claude and Sandoz, and,
standing near them, in front of the fireplace, he apologised
for an article slashing the novelist's new book which had
appeared that very morning in his review.

'As you know very well, my dear fellow, one is never the
master in one's own house. I ought to see to everything,
but I have so little time! I hadn't even read that article,
I relied on what had been told me about it. So you will
understand how enraged I was when I read it this afternoon.
I am dreadfully grieved, dreadfully grieved——'

'Oh, let it be! It's the natural order of things,' replied Sandoz, quietly. 'Now that my enemies are beginning to praise me, it's only proper that my friends should attack me.'

The door again opened, and Gagnière glided in softly, like a will-o'-the-wisp. He had come straight from Melun, and was quite alone, for he never showed his wife to anybody. When he thus came to dinner he brought the country dust with him on his boots, and carried it back with him the same night on taking the last train. On the other hand, he did not alter; or, rather, age seemed to rejuvenate him; his complexion became fairer as he grew old.

'Hallo! Why, Gagnière's here!' exclaimed Sandoz.

Then, just as Gagnière was making up his mind to bow to the ladies, Mahoudeau entered. He had already grown grey, with a sunken, fierce-looking face and childish, blinking eyes. He still wore trousers which were a good deal too short for him, and a frock-coat which creased in the back, in spite of the money which he now earned; for the bronze manufacturer for whom he worked had brought out some charming statuettes of his, which one began to see on middle-class mantel-shelves and consoles.

Sandoz and Claude had turned round, inquisitive to witness the meeting between Mahoudeau and Mathilde. However, matters passed off very quietly. The sculptor bowed to her respectfully, while Jory, the husband, with his air of serene unconsciousness, thought fit to introduce her to him, for the twentieth time, perhaps.

'Eh! It's my wife, old fellow. Shake hands together.'

Thereupon, both very grave, like people of society who are forced somewhat over-promptly into familiarity, Mathilde and Mahoudeau shook hands. Only, as soon as the latter had got rid of the job and had found Gagnière in a corner of the drawing-room, they both began sneering and recalling, in terrible language, all the abominations of yore.

Dubuche was expected that evening, for he had formally promised to come.

'Yes,' explained Henriette, 'there will only be nine of us. Fagerolles wrote this morning to apologise; he is forced to go to some official dinner, but he hopes to escape, and will join us at about eleven o'clock.'

At that moment, however, a servant came in with a telegram. It was from Dubuche, who wired: 'Impossible to stir. Alice has an alarming cough.'

'Well, we shall only be eight, then,' resumed Henriette, with the somewhat peevish resignation of a hostess disappointed by her guests.

And the servant having opened the dining-room door and announced that dinner was ready, she added:

'We are all here. Claude, offer me your arm.'

Sandoz took Mathilde's, Jory charged himself with Christine, while Mahoudeau and Gagnière brought up the rear, still joking coarsely about what they called the beautiful herbalist's padding.

The dining-room which they now entered was very spacious, and the light was gaily bright after the subdued illumination of the drawing-room. The walls, covered with specimens of old earthenware, displayed a gay medley of colours, reminding one of cheap coloured prints. Two sideboards, one laden with glass and the other with silver plate, sparkled like jewellers' show-cases. And in the centre of the room, under the big hanging lamp girt round with tapers, the table glistened like a *catafalque* with the whiteness of its cloth, laid in perfect style, with decorated plates, cut-glass decanters white with water or ruddy with wine, and symmetrical side-dishes, all set out around the centre-piece, a silver basket full of purple roses.

They sat down, Henriette between Claude and Mahoudeau, Sandoz with Mathilde and Christine beside him, Jory and Gagnière at either end; and the servant had barely finished serving the soup, when Madame Jory made a most unfortunate remark. Wishing to show herself amiable, and not having heard her husband's apologies, she said to the master of the house:

'Well, were you pleased with the article in this morning's number? Edouard personally revised the proofs with the greatest care!'

On hearing this, Jory became very much confused and stammered:

'No, no! you are mistaken! It was a very bad article indeed, and you know very well that it was "passed" the other evening while I was away.'

By the silent embarrassment which ensued she guessed her blunder. But she made matters still worse, for, giving her husband a sharp glance, she retorted in a very loud voice, so as to crush him, as it were, and disengage her own responsibility:

'Another of your lies! I repeat what you told me. I won't allow you to make me ridiculous, do you hear?'

This threw a chill over the beginning of the dinner. Henriette recommended the *kilkis*, but Christine alone found them very nice. When the grilled mullet appeared, Sandoz, who was amused by Jory's embarrassment, gaily reminded him of a lunch they had had together at Marseilles in the old days. Ah! Marseilles, the only city where people know how to eat!

Claude, who for a little while had been absorbed in thought, now seemed to awaken from a dream, and without any transition he asked:

'Is it decided? Have they selected the artists for the new decorations of the Hôtel de Ville?'

'No,' said Mahoudeau, 'they are going to do so. I sha'n't get anything, for I don't know anybody. Fagerolles himself is very anxious. If he isn't here to-night, it's because matters are not going smoothly. Ah! he has had his bite at the cherry; all that painting for millions is cracking to bits!'

There was a laugh, expressive of spite finally satisfied, and even Gagnière at the other end of the table joined in the sneering. Then they eased their feelings in malicious words, and rejoiced over the sudden fall of prices which had thrown the world of 'young masters' into consternation. It was inevitable, the predicted time was coming, the exaggerated rise was about to finish in a catastrophe. Since the amateurs had been panic-stricken, seized with consternation like that of speculators when a 'slump' sweeps over a Stock Exchange, prices were giving way day by day, and nothing more was sold. It was a sight to see the famous Naudet amid the rout; he had held out at first, he had invented 'the dodge of the Yankee'—the unique picture hidden deep in some gallery, in solitude like an idol—the picture of which he would not name the price, being contemptuously certain that he could never find a man rich enough to purchase it, but which he finally sold for two or three hundred thousand francs to some pig-dealer of Chicago, who felt glorious at carrying off the most expensive canvas of the year. But those fine strokes of business were not to be renewed at present, and Naudet, whose expenditure had increased with his gains, drawn on and swallowed up in the mad craze which was his own work, could now hear his regal mansion crumbling beneath him, and was reduced to defend it against the assault of creditors.

'Won't you take some more mushrooms, Mahoudeau?' obligingly interrupted Henriette.

The servant was now handing round the undercut. They ate, and emptied the decanters; but their bitterness was so great that the best things were offered without being tasted, which distressed the master and mistress of the house.

'Mushrooms, eh?' the sculptor ended by repeating. 'No, thanks.' And he added: 'The funny part of it all is, that Naudet is suing Fagerolles. Oh, quite so! he's going to distrain on him. Ah! it makes me laugh! We shall see a pretty scouring in the Avenue de Villiers among all those petty painters with mansions of their own. House property will go for nothing next spring! Well, Naudet, who had compelled Fagerolles to build a house, and who furnished it for him as he would have furnished a place for a hussy, wanted to get hold of his nick-nacks and hangings again. But Fagerolles had borrowed money on them, so it seems. You can imagine the state of affairs; the dealer accuses the artist of having spoilt his game by exhibiting with the vanity of a giddy fool; while the painter replies that he doesn't mean to be robbed any longer; and they'll end by devouring each other—at least, I hope so.'

Gagnière raised his voice, the gentle but inexorable voice of a dreamer just awakened.

'Fagerolles is done for. Besides, he never had any success.'

The others protested. Well, what about the hundred thousand francs' worth of pictures he had sold a year, and his medals and his cross of the Legion of Honour? But Gagnière, still obstinate, smiled with a mysterious air, as if facts could not prevail against his inner conviction. He wagged his head and, full of disdain, replied:

'Let me be! He never knew anything about chiaroscuro.'

Jory was about to defend the talent of Fagerolles, whom he considered to be his own creation, when Henriette solicited a little attention for the *raviolis*. There was a short slackening of the quarrel amid the crystalline clinking of the glasses and the light clatter of the forks. The table, laid with such fine symmetry, was already in confusion, and seemed to sparkle still more amid the ardent fire of the quarrel. And Sandoz, growing anxious, felt astonished.

What was the matter with them all that they attacked Fagerolles so harshly ? Hadn't they all begun together, and were they not all to reach the goal in the same victory ? For the first time, a feeling of uneasiness disturbed his dream of eternity, that delight in his Thursdays, which he had pictured following one upon another, all alike, all of them happy ones, into the far distance of the future. But the feeling was as yet only skin deep, and he laughingly exclaimed :

'Husband your strength, Claude, here are the hazel-hens. Eh ! Claude, where are you ? '

Since silence had prevailed, Claude had relapsed into his dream, gazing about him vacantly, and taking a second help of *raviolis* without knowing what he was about; Christine, who said nothing, but sat there looking sad and charming, did not take her eyes off him. He started when Sandoz spoke, and chose a leg from amid the bits of hazel-hen now being served, the strong fumes of which filled the room with a resinous smell.

'Do you smell that ? ' exclaimed Sandoz, amused; ' one would think one were swallowing all the forests of Russia.'

But Claude returned to the matter which worried him.

'Then you say that Fagerolles will be entrusted with the paintings for the Municipal Council's assembly room ? '

And this remark sufficed ; Mahoudeau and Gagnière, set on the track, at once started off again. Ah ! a nice wishy-washy smearing it would be if that assembly room were allotted to him ; and he was doing plenty of dirty things to get it. He, who had formerly pretended to spit on orders for work, like a great artist surrounded by amateurs, was basely cringing to the officials, now that his pictures no longer sold. Could anything more despicable be imagined than a painter soliciting a functionary, bowing and scraping, showing all kinds of cowardice and making all kinds of concessions ? It was shameful that art should be dependent upon a Minister's idiotic good pleasure ! Fagerolles, at that official dinner he had gone to, was no doubt conscientiously licking the boots of some chief clerk, some idiot who was only fit to be made a guy of.

'Well,' said Jory, ' he effects his purpose, and he's quite right. *You* won't pay his debts.'

'Debts ? Have I any debts, I who have always starved ? ' answered Mahoudeau in a roughly arrogant tone. ' Ought a fellow to build himself a palace and spend money on creatures like that Irma Bécot, who's ruining Fagerolles?'

At this Jory grew angry, while the others jested, and Irma's name went flying over the table. But Mathilde, who had so far remained reserved and silent by way of making a show of good breeding, became intensely indignant. 'Oh! gentlemen, oh! gentlemen,' she exclaimed, 'to talk before *us* about that creature. No, not that creature, I implore you!'

After that Henriette and Sandoz, who were in consternation, witnessed the rout of their menu. The truffle salad, the ice, the dessert, everything was swallowed without being at all appreciated amidst the rising anger of the quarrel; and the chambertin and sparkling moselle were imbibed as if they had merely been water. In vain did Henriette smile, while Sandoz good-naturedly tried to calm them by making allowances for human weakness. Not one of them retreated from his position; a single word made them spring upon each other. There was none of the vague boredom, the somniferous satiety which at times had saddened their old gatherings; at present there was real ferocity in the struggle, a longing to destroy one another. The tapers of the hanging lamp flared up, the painted flowers of the earthenware on the walls bloomed, the table seemed to have caught fire amid the upsetting of its symmetrical arrangements and the violence of the talk, that demolishing onslaught of chatter which had filled them with fever for a couple of hours past.

And amid the racket, when Henriette made up her mind to rise so as to silence them, Claude at length remarked:

'Ah! if I only had the Hôtel de Ville work, and if I could! It used to be my dream to cover all the walls of Paris!'

They returned to the drawing-room, where the little chandelier and the bracket-candelabra had just been lighted. It seemed almost cold there in comparison with the kind of hothouse which had just been left; and for a moment the coffee calmed the guests. Nobody beyond Fagerolles was expected. The house was not an open one by any means, the Sandozes did not recruit literary dependents or muzzle the press by dint of invitations. The wife detested society, and the husband said with a laugh that he needed ten years to take a liking to anybody, and then he must like him always. But was not that real happiness, seldom realised? A few sound friendships and a nook full of family affection. No music was

ever played there, and nobody had ever read a page of his
composition aloud.

On that particular Thursday the evening seemed a long
one, on account of the persistent irritation of the men. The
ladies had begun to chat before the smouldering fire; and
when the servant, after clearing the table, reopened the door
of the dining-room, they were left alone, the men repairing to
the adjoining apartment to smoke and sip some beer.

Sandoz and Claude, who were not smokers, soon returned,
however, and sat down, side by side, on a sofa near the doorway. The former, who was glad to see his old friend excited
and talkative, recalled the memories of Plassans apropos of a
bit of news he had learnt the previous day. Pouillaud, the
old jester of their dormitory, who had become so grave a
lawyer, was now in trouble over some adventure with a
woman. Ah! that brute of a Pouillaud! But Claude did
not answer, for, having heard his name mentioned in the
dining-room, he listened attentively, trying to understand.

Jory, Mahoudeau, and Gagnière, unsatiated and eager for
another bite, had started on the massacre again. Their
voices, at first mere whispers, gradually grew louder, till at
last they began to shout.

'Oh! the man, I abandon the man to you,' said Jory, who
was speaking of Fagerolles. 'He isn't worth much. And he
out-generalled you, it's true. Ah! how he did get the better of
you fellows, by breaking off from you and carving success for
himself on your backs! You were certainly not at all cute.'

Mahoudeau, waxing furious, replied:

'Of course! It sufficed for us to be with Claude, to be
turned away everywhere.'

'It was Claude who did for us!' so Gagnière squarely
asserted.

And thus they went on, relinquishing Fagerolles, whom
they reproached for toadying the newspapers, for allying himself with their enemies and wheedling sexagenarian baronesses,
to fall upon Claude, who now became the great culprit. Well,
after all, the other was only a hussy, one of the many found
in the artistic fraternity, fellows who accost the public at
street corners, leave their comrades in the lurch, and victimise
them so as to get the *bourgeois* into their studios. But Claude,
that abortive great artist, that impotent fellow who couldn't
set a figure on its legs in spite of all his pride, hadn't he
utterly compromised them, hadn't he let them in altogether?

Ah! yes, success might have been won by breaking off. If they had been able to begin over again, they wouldn't have been idiots enough to cling obstinately to impossible principles! And they accused Claude of having paralysed them, of having traded on them—yes, traded on them, but in so clumsy and dull-witted a manner that he himself had not derived any berefit by it.

'Why, as for me,' resumed Mahoudeau, 'didn't he make me quite idiotic at one moment? When I think of it, I sound myself, and remain wondering why I ever joined his band. Am I at all like him? Was there ever any one thing in common between us, eh? Ah! it's exasperating to find the truth out so late in the day!'

'And as for myself,' said Gagnière, 'he robbed me of my originality. Do you think it has amused me, each time I have exhibited a painting during the last fifteen years, to hear people saying behind me, "That's a Claude!" Oh! I've had enough of it, I prefer not to paint any more. All the same, if I had seen clearly in former times, I shouldn't have associated with him.'

It was a stampede, the snapping of the last ties, in their stupefaction at suddenly finding that they were strangers and enemies, after a long youth of fraternity together. Life had disbanded them on the road, and the great dissimilarity of their characters stood revealed; all that remained in them was the bitterness left by the old enthusiastic dream, that erstwhile hope of battle and victory to be won side by side, which now increased their spite.

'The fact is,' sneered Jory, 'that Fagerolles did not let himself be pillaged like a simpleton.'

But Mahoudeau, feeling vexed, became angry. 'You do wrong to laugh,' he said, 'for you are a nice backslider yourself. Yes, you always told us that you would give us a lift up when you had a paper of your own.'

'Ah! allow me, allow me——'

Gagnière, however, united with Mahoudeau: 'That's quite true!' he said. 'You can't say any more that what you write about us is cut out, for you are the master now. And yet, never a word! You didn't even name us in your articles on the last Salon.'

Then Jory, embarrassed and stammering, in his turn flew into a rage.

'Ah! well, it's the fault of that cursed Claude! I don't

care to lose my subscribers simply to please you fellows. It's impossible to do anything for you! There! do you understand? You, Mahoudeau, may wear yourself out in producing pretty little things; you, Gagnière, may even never do anything more; but you each have a label on the back, and you'll need ten years' efforts before you'll be able to get it off. In fact, there have been some labels that would never come off! The public is amused by it, you know; there were only you fellows to believe in the genius of that big ridiculous lunatic, who will be locked up in a madhouse one of these fine mornings!'

Then the dispute became terrible, they all three spoke at once, coming at last to abominable reproaches, with such outbursts, and such furious motion of the jaw, that they seemed to be biting one another.

Sandoz, seated on the sofa, and disturbed in the gay memories he was recalling, was at last obliged to lend ear to the tumult which reached him through the open doorway.

'You hear them?' whispered Claude, with a dolorous smile; 'they are giving it me nicely! No, no, stay here, I won't let you stop them; I deserve it, since I have failed to succeed.'

And Sandoz, turning pale, remained there, listening to that bitter quarrelling, the outcome of the struggle for life, that grappling of conflicting personalities, which bore all his chimera of everlasting friendship away.

Henriette, fortunately, became anxious on hearing the violent shouting. She rose and went to shame the smokers for thus forsaking the ladies to go and quarrel together. They then returned to the drawing-room, perspiring, breathing hard, and still shaken by their anger. And as Henriette, with her eyes on the clock, remarked that they certainly would not see Fagerolles that evening, they began to sneer again, exchanging glances. Ah! he had a fine scent, and no mistake; he wouldn't be caught associating with old friends, who had become troublesome, and whom he hated.

In fact, Fagerolles did not come. The evening finished laboriously. They once more went back to the dining-room, where the tea was served on a Russian tablecloth embroidered with a stag-hunt in red thread; and under the tapers a plain cake was displayed, with plates full of sweetstuff and pastry, and a barbarous collection of liqueurs and spirits, whisky, hollands, Chio raki, and kümmel. The servant also brought

some punch, and bestirred himself round the table, while the
mistress of the house filled the teapot from the samovar
boiling in front of her. But all the comfort, all the feast for
the eyes and the fine perfume of the tea did not move their
hearts. The conversation again turned on the success that
some men achieved and the ill-luck that befell others. For
instance, was it not shameful that art should be dishonoured
by all those medals, all those crosses, all those rewards,
which were so badly distributed to boot? Were artists
always to remain like little boys at school? All the universal
platitude came from the docility and cowardice which were
shown, as in the presence of ushers, so as to obtain good marks.

They had repaired to the drawing-room once more, and
Sandoz, who was greatly distressed, had begun to wish that
they would take themselves off, when he noticed Mathilde and
Gagnière seated side by side on a sofa and talking languish-
ingly of music, while the others remained exhausted, lacking
saliva and power of speech. Gagnière philosophised and
poetised in a state of ecstasy, while Mathilde rolled up her
eyes and went into raptures as if titillated by some invisible
wing. They had caught sight of each other on the previous
Sunday at the concert at the Cirque, and they apprised each
other of their enjoyment in alternate, far-soaring sentences.

'Ah! that Meyerbeer, monsieur, the overture of "Struen-
see," that funereal strain, and then that peasant dance, so full
of dash and colour ; and then the mournful burden which
returns, the *duo* of the violoncellos. Ah! monsieur, the
violoncellos, the violoncellos ! '

'And Berlioz, madame, the festival air in "Romeo." Oh!
the *solo* of the clarionets, the beloved women, with the harp
accompaniment ! Something enrapturing, something white
as snow which ascends ! The festival bursts upon you, like
a picture by Paul Veronese, with the tumultuous magnificence of the "Marriage of Cana " ; and then the love-song
begins again, oh, how softly ! oh ! always higher ! higher
still——'

'Did you notice, monsieur, in Beethoven's Symphony in A,
that knell which ever and ever comes back and beats upon
your heart ? Yes, I see very well, you feel as I do, music
is a communion—Beethoven, ah, me ! how sad and sweet it
is to be two to understand him and give way——'

'And Schumann, madame, and Wagner, madame—Schumann's "Reverie," nothing but the stringed instruments, a warm

shower falling on acacia leaves, a sunray which dries them, barely a tear in space. Wagner! ah, Wagner! the overture of the "Flying Dutchman," are you not fond of it?—tell me you are fond of it! As for myself, it overcomes me. There is nothing left, nothing left, one expires——'

Their voices died away; they did not even look at each other, but sat there elbow to elbow, with their faces turned upward, quite overcome.

Sandoz, who was surprised, asked himself where Mathilde could have picked up that jargon. In some article of Jory's, perhaps. Besides, he had remarked that women talk music very well, even without knowing a note of it. And he, whom the bitterness of the others had only grieved, became exasperated at sight of Mathilde's languishing attitude. No, no, that was quite enough; the men tore each other to bits; still that might pass, after all; but what an end to the evening it was, that feminine fraud, cooing and titillating herself with thoughts of Beethoven's and Schumann's music!

Fortunately, Gagnière suddenly rose. He knew what o'clock it was even in the depths of his ecstasy, and he had only just time left him to catch his last train. So, after exchanging nerveless and silent handshakes with the others, he went off to sleep at Melun.

'What a failure he is!' muttered Mahoudeau. 'Music has killed painting; he'll never do anything!'

He himself had to leave, and the door had scarcely closed behind his back when Jory declared:

'Have you seen his last paperweight? He'll end by sculpturing sleeve-links. There's a fellow who has missed his mark! To think that he prided himself on being vigorous!'

But Mathilde was already afoot, taking leave of Christine with a curt little inclination of the head, affecting social familiarity with Henriette, and carrying off her husband, who helped her on with her cloak in the ante-room, humble and terrified at the severe glance she gave him, for she had an account to settle.

Then, the door having closed behind them, Sandoz, beside himself, cried out: 'That's the end! The journalist was bound to call the others abortions—yes, the journalist who, after patching up articles, has fallen to trading upon public credulity! Ah! luckily there's Mathilde the Avengeress!'

Of the guests Christine and Claude alone were left. The

latter, since the drawing-room had been growing empty, had remained ensconced in the depths of an arm-chair, no longer speaking, but overcome by that species of magnetic slumber which stiffened him, and fixed his eyes on something far away beyond the walls. He protruded his face, a convulsive kind of attention seemed to carry it forward; he certainly beheld something invisible, and heard a summons in the silence.

Christine having risen in her turn, and apologised for being the last to leave, Henriette took hold of her hands, repeated how fond she was of her, begged her to come and see her frequently, and to dispose of her in all things as she would with a sister. But Claude's sorrowful wife, looking so sadly charming in her black dress, shook her head with a pale smile.

'Come,' said Sandoz in her ear, after giving a glance at Claude, 'you mustn't distress yourself like that. He has talked a great deal, he has been gayer this evening. He's all right.'

But in a terrified voice she answered:

'No, no; look at his eyes—I shall tremble as long as he has his eyes like that. You have done all you could, thanks. What you haven't done no one will do. Ah! how I suffer at being unable to hope, at being unable to do anything!'

Then in a loud tone she asked:

'Are you coming, Claude?'

She had to repeat her question twice, for at first he did not hear her; he ended by starting, however, and rose to his feet, saying, as if he had answered the summons from the horizon afar off:

'Yes, I'm coming, I'm coming.'

When Sandoz and his wife at last found themselves alone in the drawing-room, where the atmosphere now was stifling —heated by the lights and heavy, as it were, with melancholy silence after all the outbursts of the quarrelling—they looked at one another and let their arms fall, quite heart-rent by the unfortunate issue of their dinner party. Henriette tried to laugh it off, however, murmuring:

'I warned you, I quite understood——'

But he interrupted her with a despairing gesture. What! was that, then, the end of his long illusion, that dream of eternity which had made him set happiness in a few friendships, formed in childhood, and shared until extreme old age?

Ah! what a wretched band, what a final rending, what a terrible balance-sheet to weep over after that bankruptcy of the human heart! And he grew astonished on thinking of the friends who had fallen off by the roadside, of the great affections lost on the way, of the others unceasingly changing around himself, in whom he found no change. His poor Thursdays filled him with pity, so many memories were in mourning, it was the slow death of all that one loves! Would his wife and himself have to resign themselves to live as in a desert, to cloister themselves in utter hatred of the world? Ought they rather to throw their doors wide open to a throng of strangers and indifferent folk? By degrees a certainty dawned in the depths of his grief: everything ended and nothing began again in life. He seemed to yield to evidence, and, heaving a big sigh, exclaimed:

'You were right. We won't invite them to dinner again —they would devour one another.'

As soon as Claude and Christine reached the Place de la Trinité on their way home, the painter let go of his wife's arm; and, stammering that he had to go somewhere, he begged her to return to the Rue Tourlaque without him. She had felt him shuddering, and she remained quite scared with surprise and fear. Somewhere to go at that hour—past midnight! Where had he to go, and what for? He had turned round and was making off, when she overtook him, and, pretending that she was frightened, begged that he would not leave her to climb up to Montmartre alone at that time of night. This consideration alone brought him back. He took her arm again; they ascended the Rue Blanche and the Rue Lepic, and at last found themselves in the Rue Tourlaque. And on reaching their door, he rang the bell, and then again left her.

'Here you are,' he said; 'I'm going.'

He was already hastening away, taking long strides, and gesticulating like a madman. Without even closing the door which had been opened, she darted off, bent on following him. In the Rue Lepic she drew near; but for fear of exciting him still more she contented herself with keeping him in sight, walking some thirty yards in the rear, without his knowing that she was behind him. On reaching the end of the Rue Lepic he went down the Rue Blanche again, and then proceeded by way of the Rue de la Chaussée-d'Antin and the Rue du Dix Décembre as far as the Rue de Richelieu.

When she saw him turn into the last-named thoroughfare, a mortal chill came over her : he was going towards the Seine ; it was the realisation of the frightful fear which kept her of a night awake, full of anguish ! And what could she do, good Lord ? Go with him, hang upon his neck over yonder ? She was now only able to stagger along, and as each step brought them nearer to the river, she felt life ebbing from her limbs. Yes, he was going straight there ; he crossed the Place du Théâtre Français, then the Carrousel, and finally reached the Pont des Saints-Pères. After taking a few steps along the bridge, he approached the railing overlooking the water ; and at the thought that he was about to jump over, a loud cry was stifled in her contracted throat.

But no ; he remained motionless. Was it then only the Cité over yonder that haunted him, that heart of Paris which pursued him everywhere, which he conjured up with his fixed eyes, even through walls, and which, when he was leagues away, cried out the constant summons heard by him alone ? She did not yet dare to hope it ; she had stopped short, in the rear, watching him with giddy anxiety, ever fancying that she saw him take the terrible leap, but resisting her longing to draw nearer, for fear lest she might precipitate the catastrophe by showing herself. Oh, God ! to think that she was there with her devouring passion, her bleeding motherly heart—that she was there beholding everything, without daring to risk one movement to hold him back !

He stood erect, looking very tall, quite motionless, and gazing into the night.

It was a winter's night, with a misty sky of sooty blackness, and was rendered extremely cold by a sharp wind blowing from the west. Paris, lighted up, had gone to sleep, showing no signs of life save such as attached to the gas-jets, those specks which scintillated and grew smaller and smaller in the distance till they seemed but so much starry dust. The quays stretched away showing double rows of those luminous beads whose reverberation glimmered on the nearer front-ages. On the left were the houses of the Quai du Louvre, on the right the two wings of the Institute, confused masses of monuments and buildings, which became lost to view in the darkening gloom, studded with sparks. Then between those cordons of burners, extending as far as the eye could reach, the bridges stretched bars of lights, ever slighter and slighter, each formed of a train of spangles, grouped together

and seemingly hanging in mid-air. And in the Seine there
shone the nocturnal splendour of the animated water of cities ;
each gas-jet there cast a reflection of its flame, like the nucleus
of a comet, extending into a tail. The nearer ones, mingling
together, set the current on fire with broad, regular, symmetrical fans of light, glowing like live embers, while the
more distant ones, seen under the bridges, were but little
motionless sparks of fire. But the large burning tails
appeared to be animated, they waggled as they spread out,
all black and gold, with a constant twirling of scales, in which
one divined the flow of the water. The whole Seine was
lighted up by them, as if some fête were being given in its
depths—some mysterious, fairy-like entertainment, at which
couples were waltzing beneath the river's red-flashing window-
panes. High above those fires, above the starry quays, the
sky, in which not a planet was visible, showed a ruddy mass
of vapour, that warm, phosphorescent exhalation which every
night, above the sleep of the city, seems to set the crater of a
volcano.

The wind blew hard, and Christine, shivering, her eyes full
of tears, felt the bridge move under her, as if it were bearing
her away amid a smash up of the whole scene. Had not
Claude moved ? Was he not climbing over the rail ? No ;
everything became motionless again, and she saw him still
on the same spot, obstinately stiff, with his eyes turned
towards the point of the Cité, which he could not see.

It had summoned him, and he had come, and yet he
could not see it in the depths of the darkness. He could
only distinguish the bridges, with their light framework
standing out blackly against the sparkling water. But farther
off everything became confused, the island had disappeared, he
could not even have told its exact situation if some belated
cabs had not passed from time to time over the Pont-Neuf,
with their lamps showing like those shooting sparks which
dart at times through embers. A red lantern, on a level with
the dam of the Mint, cast a streamlet of blood, as it were,
into the water. Something huge and lugubrious, some drifting form, no doubt a lighter which had become unmoored,
slowly descended the stream amid the reflections. Espied for
a moment, it was immediately afterwards lost in the darkness.
Where had the triumphal island sunk ? In the depths of
that flow of water ? Claude still gazed, gradually fascinated
by the great rushing of the river in the night. He leant over

its broad bed, chilly like an abyss, in which the mysterious flames were dancing. And the loud, sad wail of the current attracted him, and he listened to its call, despairing, unto death.

By a shooting pain at her heart, Christine this time realised that the terrible thought had just occurred to him. She held out her quivering hands which the wind was lashing. But Claude remained there, struggling against the sweetness of death; indeed he did not move for another hour, he lingered there unconscious of the lapse of time, with his eyes still turned in the direction of the Cité, as if by a miracle of power they were about to create light, and conjure up the island so that he might behold it.

When Claude at last left the bridge, with stumbling steps, Christine had to pass in front and run in order to be home in the Rue Tourlaque before him.

XII

IT was nearly three o'clock when they went to bed that night, with the bitter cold November wind blowing through their little room and the big studio. Christine, breathless from her run, had quickly slipped between the sheets so that he might not know that she had followed him; and Claude, quite overcome, had taken his clothes off, one garment after another, without saying a word. For long months they had been as strangers; until then, however, she had never felt such a barrier between them, such tomb-like coldness.

She struggled for nearly a quarter of an hour against the sleepiness coming over her. She was very tired, and a kind of torpor numbed her; still she would not give way, feeling anxious at leaving him awake. She thus waited every night until he dozed off, so that she herself might afterwards sleep in peace. But he had not extinguished the candle, he lay there with his eyes open, fixed upon its flame. What could he be thinking of? Had he remained in fancy over yonder in the black night, amid the moist atmosphere of the quays, in front of Paris studded with stars like a frosty sky? And what inner conflict, what matter that had to be decided, contracted his face like that? Then, resistance being impossible, she succumbed and glided into the slumber following upon great weariness.

An hour later, the consciousness of something missing, the anguish of uneasiness awoke her with a sudden start. She at once felt the bed beside her, it was already cold: he was no longer there, she had already divined it while asleep. And she was growing alarmed, still but half awake, her head heavy and her ears buzzing, when through the doorway, left ajar, she perceived a ray of light coming from the studio. She then felt reassured, she thought that in a fit of sleeplessness he had gone to fetch some book or other; but at last, as he did not return, she ended by softly rising so as to take a peep. What she beheld quite unsettled her, and kept her standing on the tiled floor, with her feet bare, in such surprise that she did not at first dare to show herself.

Claude, who was in his shirt-sleeves, despite the coldness of the temperature, having merely put on his trousers and slippers in his haste, was standing on the steps in front of his large picture. His palette was lying at his feet, and with one hand he held the candle, while with the other he painted. His eyes were dilated like those of a somnambulist, his gestures were precise and stiff; he stooped every minute to take some colour on his brush, and then rose up, casting a large fantastic shadow on the wall. And there was not a sound; frightful silence reigned in the big dim room.

Christine guessed the truth and shuddered. The besetting worry, made more acute by that hour spent on the Pont des Saints-Pères, had prevented him from sleeping and had brought him once more before his canvas, consumed with a longing to look at it again, in spite of the lateness of the hour. He had, no doubt, only climbed the steps to fill his eyes the nearer. Then, tortured by the sight of some faulty shade, upset by some defect, to such a point that he could not wait for daylight, he had caught up a brush, at first merely wishing to give a simple touch, and then had been carried on from correction to correction, until at last, with the candle in his hand, he painted there like a man in a state of hallucination, amid the pale light which darted hither and thither as he gesticulated. His powerless creative rage had seized hold of him again, he was wearing himself out, oblivious of the hour, oblivious of the world; he wished to infuse life into his work at once.

Ah, what a pitiful sight! And with what tear-drenched eyes did Christine gaze at him! At first she thought of leaving him to that mad work, as a maniac is left to the

pleasures of his craziness. He would never finish that
picture, that was quite certain now. The more desperately
he worked at it, the more incoherent did it become; the
colouring had grown heavy and pasty, the drawing was losing
shape and showing signs of effort. Even the background
and the group of labourers, once so substantial and satis-
factory, were getting spoiled; yet he clung to them, he had
obstinately determined to finish everything else before re-
painting the central figure, the nude woman, which remained
the dread and the desire of his hours of toil, and which
would finish him off whenever he might again try to invest
it with life. For months he had not touched it, and this
had tranquillised Christine and made her tolerant and com-
passionate, amid her jealous spite; for as long as he did
not return to that feared and desired mistress, she thought
that he betrayed her less.

Her feet were freezing on the tiles, and she was turning
to get into bed again when a shock brought her back to the
door. She had not understood at first, but now at last she
saw. With broad curved strokes of his brush, full of colour,
Claude was at once wildly and caressingly modelling flesh.
He had a fixed grin on his lips, and did not feel the burning
candle-grease falling on his fingers, while with silent, passionate see-sawing, his right arm alone moved against the wall,
casting black confusion upon it. He was working at the
nude woman.

Then Christine opened the door and walked into the
studio. An invincible revolt, the anger of a wife buffeted at
home, impelled her forward. Yes, he was with that other,
he was painting her like a visionary, whom wild craving fôr
truth had brought to the madness of the unreal; and those
limbs were being gilded like the columns of a tabernacle, that
trunk was becoming a star, shimmering with yellow and red,
splendid and unnatural. Such strange nudity—like unto a
monstrance gleaming with precious stones and intended for
religious adoration—brought her anger to a climax. She had
suffered too much, she would not tolerate it.

And yet at first she simply showed herself despairing and
supplicating. It was but the mother remonstrating with her
big mad boy of an artist that spoke.

'What are you doing there, Claude? Is it reasonable,
Claude, to have such ideas? Come to bed, I beg of you,
don't stay on those steps where you will catch your death of
cold!'

He did not answer; he stooped again to take some more paint on his brush, and made the figure flash with two bright strokes of vermilion.

'Listen to me, Claude, in pity come to me—you know that I love you—you see how anxious you have made me. Come, oh! come, if you don't want me to die of cold and waiting for you.'

With his face haggard, he did not look at her; but while he bedecked a part of the figure with carmine, he grumbled in a husky voice:

'Just leave me alone, will you? I'm working.'

Christine remained silent for a moment. She was drawing herself erect, her eyes began to gleam with fire, rebellion inflated her gentle, charming form. Then she burst forth, with the growl of a slave driven to extremities.

'Well, no, I won't leave you alone! I've had enough of it. I'll tell you what's stifling me, what has been killing me ever since I have known you. Ah! that painting, yes, your painting, she's the murderess who has poisoned my life! I had a presentiment of it on the first day; your painting frightened me as if it were a monster. I found it abominable, execrable; but then, one's cowardly, I loved you too much not to like it also; I ended by growing accustomed to it! But later on, how I suffered!—how it tortured me! For ten years I don't recollect having spent a day without shedding tears. No, leave me! I am easing my mind, I must speak out, since I have found strength enough to do so. For ten years I have been abandoned and crushed every day. Ah! to be nothing more to you, to feel myself cast more and more on one side, to fall to the rank of a servant; and to see that other one, that thief, place herself between you and me and clutch hold of you and triumph and insult me! For dare, yes, dare to say that she hasn't taken possession of you, limb by limb, glided into your brain, your heart, your flesh, everywhere! She holds you like a vice, she feeds on you; in fact, she's your wife, not I. She's the only one you care for! Ah! the cursed wretch, the hussy!'

Claude was now listening to her, in his astonishment at that dolorous outburst; and being but half roused from his exasperated creative dream, he did not as yet very well understand why she was talking to him like that. And at sight of his stupor, the shuddering of a man surprised in a debauch, she flew into a still greater passion; she mounted

the steps, tore the candlestick from his hand, and in her turn
flashed the light in front of the picture.

'Just look!' she cried, 'just tell me how you have
improved matters? It's hideous, it's lamentable and
grotesque; you'll end by seeing so yourself. Come, isn't it
ugly, isn't it idiotic? You see very well that you are conquered, so why should you persist any longer? There is no
sense in it, that's what upsets me. If you can't be a great
painter, life, at least, remains to us. Ah! life, life!'

She had placed the candle on the platform of the steps,
and as he had gone down, staggering, she sprang off to join
him, and they both found themselves below, he crouching
on the last step, and she pressing his inert, dangling hands
with all her strength.

'Come, there's life! Drive your nightmare away, and let
us live, live together. Isn't it too stupid, to be we two
together, to be growing old already, and to torture ourselves,
and fail in every attempt to find happiness? Oh! the grave
will take us soon enough, never fear. Let's try to live, and
love one another. Remember Bennecourt! Listen to my
dream. I should like to be able to take you away to-morrow.
We would go far from this cursed Paris, we would find a quiet
spot somewhere, and you would see how pleasant I would
make your life; how nice it would be to forget everything
together! Of a morning there are strolls in the sunlight, the
breakfast which smells nice, the idle afternoon, the evening
spent side by side under the lamp! And no more worrying
about chimeras, nothing but the delight of living! Doesn't it
suffice that I love you, that I adore you, that I am willing to
be your servant, your slave, to exist solely for your pleasures?
Do you hear, I love you, I love you? there is nothing else,
and that is enough—I love you!'

He had freed his hands, and making a gesture of refusal,
he said, in a gloomy voice:

No, it is not enough! I *won't* go away with you, I *won't*
be happy, I *will* paint!'

'And I shall die of it, eh? And you will die of it, and we
shall end by leaving all our blood and all our tears in it!
There's nothing beyond Art, that is the fierce almighty
god who strikes us with his thunder, and whom you honour!
he may crush us, since he is the master, and you will still
bless his name!'

'Yes, I belong to that god, he may do what he pleases with

me. I should die if I no longer painted, and I prefer to paint and die of it. Besides, my will is nothing in the matter. Nothing exists beyond art; let the world burst!'

She drew herself up in a fresh spurt of anger. Her voice became harsh and passionate again.

'But I—I am alive, and the women you love are lifeless! Oh! don't say no! I know very well that all those painted women of yours are the only ones you care about! Before I was yours I had already perceived it. Then, for a short time you appeared to love me. It was at that period you told me all that nonsense about your fondness for your creations. You held such shadows in pity when you were with me; but it didn't last. You returned to them, oh! like a maniac returns to his mania. I, though living, no longer existed for you; it was they, the visions, who again became the only realities of your life. What I then endured you never knew, for you are wonderfully ignorant of women. I have lived by your side without your ever understanding me. Yes, I was jealous of those painted creatures. When I posed to you, only one idea lent me the courage that I needed. I wanted to fight them, I hoped to win you back; but you granted me nothing, not even a kiss on my shoulder! Oh, God! how ashamed I sometimes felt! What grief I had to force back at finding myself thus disdained and thus betrayed!'

She continued boldly, she spoke out freely—she, so strangely compounded of passion and modesty. And she was not mistaken in her jealousy when she accused his art of being responsible for his neglect of herself. At the bottom of it all, there was the theory which he had repeated a hundred times in her presence: genius should be chaste, an artist's only spouse should be his work.

'You repulse me,' she concluded violently; 'you draw back from me as if I displeased you! And you love what? A nothing, a mere semblance, a little dust, some colour spread upon a canvas! But, once more, look at her, look at your woman up yonder! See what a monster you have made of her in your madness! Are there any women like that? Have any women golden limbs, and flowers on their bodies? Wake up, open your eyes, return to life again!'

Claude, obeying the imperious gesture with which she pointed to the picture, had now risen and was looking. The candle, which had remained upon the platform of the steps, illumined the nude woman like a taper in front of an altar,

whilst the whole room around remained plunged in darkness.
He was at length awakening from his dream, and the woman
thus seen from below, at a distance of a few paces, filled him
with stupefaction. Who had just painted that idol of some
unknown religion? Who had wrought her of metals, marbles,
and gems? Was it he who had unconsciously created that
symbol of insatiable passion, that unhuman presentment of
flesh, which had become transformed into gold and diamonds
under his fingers, in his vain effort to make it live? He
gasped and felt afraid of his work, trembling at the thought
of that sudden plunge into the infinite, and understanding at
last that it had become impossible for him even to depict
Reality, despite his long effort to conquer and remould it,
making it yet more real with his human hands.

'You see! you see!' Christine repeated, victoriously.

And he, in a very low voice, stammered:

'Oh! what have I done? Is it impossible to create, then?
Haven't our hands the power to create beings?'

She felt that he was giving way, and she caught him in
her arms:

'But why all this folly?—why think of anyone but me—I
who love you? You took me for your model, but what was
the use, say? Are those paintings of yours worth me? They
are frightful, they are as stiff, as cold as corpses. But I am
alive, and I love you!'

She seemed to be at that moment the very incarnation of
passionate love. He turned and looked at her, and little
by little he returned her embrace; she was softening him and
conquering him.

'Listen!' she continued. 'I know that you had a frightful
thought; yes, I never dared to speak to you about it, because
one must never bring on misfortune; but I no longer sleep
of a night, you frighten me. This evening I followed you
to that bridge which I hate, and I trembled, oh! I thought
that it was all over—that I had lost you. Oh, God! what
would become of me? I need you—you surely do not wish
to kill me! Let us live and love one another—yes, love one
another!'

Then, in the emotion caused him by her infinite passion
and grief, he yielded. He pressed her to him, sobbing and
stammering:

'It is true I had that frightful thought—I should have
done it, and I only resisted on thinking of that unfinished

picture. But can I still live if work will have nothing more to do with me? How can I live after that, after what's there, what I spoilt just now?'

'I will love you, and you will live.'

'Ah! you will never love me enough—I know myself. Something which does not exist would be necessary—something which would make me forget everything. You were already unable to change me. You cannot accomplish a miracle!'

Then, as she protested and kissed him passionately, he went on: 'Well, yes, save me! Yes, save me, if you don't want me to kill myself! Lull me, annihilate me, so that I may become your thing, slave enough, small enough to dwell under your feet, in your slippers. Ah! to live only on your perfume, to obey you like a dog, to eat and sleep—if I could, if I only *could!*'

She raised a cry of victory: 'At last you are mine! There is only I left, the other is quite dead!'

And she dragged him from the execrated painting, she carried him off triumphantly. The candle, now nearly consumed, flared up for a minute behind them on the steps, before the big painting, and then went out. It was victory, yes, but could it last?

Daylight was about to break, and Christine lay asleep beside Claude. She was breathing softly, and a smile played upon her lips. He had closed his eyes; and yet, despite himself, he opened them afresh and gazed into the darkness. Sleep fled from him, and confused ideas again ascended to his brain. As the dawn appeared, yellowishly dirty, like a splash of liquid mud on the window-panes, he started, fancying that he heard a loud voice calling to him from the far end of the studio. Then, irresistibly, despite a few brief hours' forgetfulness, all his old thoughts returned, overflowing and torturing him, hollowing his cheeks and contracting his jaws in the disgust he felt for mankind. Two wrinkles imparted intense bitterness to the expression of his face, which looked like the wasted countenance of an old man. And suddenly the loud voice from the far end of the studio imperiously summoned him a second time. Then he quite made up his mind: it was all over, he suffered too much, he could no longer live, since everything was a lie, since there was nothing left upon earth. Love! what was it? Nought but a passing illusion. This thought at last mastered him, possessed him entirely; and soon the craving for nothingness as his only refuge came on him stronger than ever. At first he let Christine's head slip down from his shoulder on which it rested. And then, as a third summons rang out in his mind, he rose and went to the studio, saying:

'Yes, yes, I'm coming.'

The sky did not clear, it still remained dirty and mournful—it was one of those lugubrious winter dawns; and an hour later Christine herself awoke with a great chilly shiver. She did not understand at first. How did it happen that she was alone? Then she remembered: she had fallen asleep with her cheek against his. How was it then that he had left her? Where could he be? Suddenly, amid her torpor, she sprang out of bed and ran into the studio. Good God! had he returned to the other then? Had the other seized hold of him again, when she herself fancied that she had conquered him for ever?

She saw nothing at the first glance she took; in the cold and murky morning twilight the studio seemed to her to be deserted. But whilst she was tranquillising herself at seeing nobody there, she raised her eyes to the canvas, and a terrible cry leapt from her gaping mouth:

'Claude! oh, Claude!'

Claude had hanged himself from the steps in front of his spoilt work. He had simply taken one of the cords which held the frame to the wall, and had mounted the platform, so as to fasten the rope to an oaken crosspiece, which he himself had one day nailed to the uprights to consolidate them. Then from up above he had leapt into space. He was hanging there in his shirt, with his feet bare, looking horrible, with his black tongue protruding, and his bloodshot eyes starting from their orbits; he seemed to have grown frightfully tall in his motionless stiffness, and his face was turned towards the picture, close to the nude woman, as if he had wished to infuse his soul into her with his last gasp, and as if he were still looking at her with his expressionless eyes.

Christine, however, remained erect, quite overwhelmed with the grief, fright, and anger which dilated her body. Only a continuous howl came from her throat. She opened her arms, stretched them towards the picture, and clenched both hands.

'Oh, Claude! oh, Claude!' she gasped at last, 'she has

taken you back—the hussy has killed you, killed you, killed
you ! '

Then her legs gave way. She span round and fell all of
a heap upon the tiled flooring. Her excessive suffering had
taken all the blood from her heart, and, fainting away, she
lay there, as if she were dead, like a white rag, miserable,
done for, crushed beneath the fierce sovereignty of Art.
Above her the nude woman rose radiant in her symbolic idol's
brightness ; painting triumphed, alone immortal and erect,
even when mad.

At nine o'clock on the Monday morning, when Sandoz,
after the formalities and delay occasioned by the suicide,
arrived in the Rue Tourlaque for the funeral, he found only
a score of people on the footway. Despite his great grief, he
had been running about for three days, compelled to attend
to everything. At first, as Christine had been picked up
half dead, he had been obliged to have her carried to the
Hôpital de Lariboisière ; then he had gone from the municipal
offices, to the undertaker's and the church, paying everywhere,
and full of indifference so far as that went, since the priests
were willing to pray over that corpse with a black circle round
its neck. Among the people who were waiting he as yet
only perceived some neighbours, together with a few inquisitive folk ; while other people peered out of the house
windows and whispered together, excited by the tragedy.
Claude's friends would, no doubt, soon come. He, Sandoz,
had not been able to write to any members of the family, as
he did not know their addresses. However, he retreated into
the background on the arrival of two relatives, whom three
lines in the newspapers had roused from the forgetfulness in
which Claude himself, no doubt, had left them. There was
an old female cousin,[1] with the equivocal air of a dealer in
second-hand goods, and a male cousin, of the second degree,
a wealthy man, decorated with the Legion of Honour, and
owning one of the large Paris drapery shops. He showed
himself good-naturedly condescending in his elegance, and
desirous of displaying an enlightened taste for art. The
female cousin at once went upstairs, turned round the studio,
sniffed at all the bare wretchedness, and then walked down

---

[1] Madame Sidonie, who figures in M. Zola's novel, ' La Curée.' The
male cousin, mentioned immediately afterwards, is Octave Mouret, the
leading character of ' Pot-Bouille ' and ' Au Bonheur des Dames.'—ED.

again, with a hard mouth, as if she were irritated at having taken the trouble to come. The second cousin, on the contrary, drew himself up and walked first behind the hearse, filling the part of chief mourner with proud and pleasant fitness.

As the procession was starting off, Bongrand came up, and, after shaking hands with Sandoz, remained beside him. He was gloomy, and, glancing at the fifteen or twenty strangers who followed, he murmured :

'Ah ! poor chap ! What ! are there only we two ?'

Dubuche was at Cannes with his children. Jory and Fagerolles kept away, the former hating the deceased and the latter being too busy. Mahoudeau alone caught the party up at the rise of the Rue Lepic, and he explained that Gagnière must have missed the train.

The hearse slowly ascended the steep thoroughfare which winds round the flanks of the height of Montmartre; and now and then cross streets, sloping downward, sudden gaps amid the houses, showed one the immensity of Paris as deep and as broad as a sea. When the party arrived in front of the Church of St. Pierre, and the coffin was carried up the steps, it overtopped the great city for a moment. There was a grey wintry sky overhead, large masses of clouds swept along, carried away by an icy wind, and in the mist Paris seemed to expand, to become endless, filling the horizon with threatening billows. The poor fellow who had wished to conquer it, and had broken his neck in his fruitless efforts, now passed in front of it, nailed under an oaken board, returning to the earth like one of the city's muddy waves.

On leaving the church the female cousin disappeared, Mahoudeau likewise; while the second cousin took his position behind the hearse. Seven other unknown persons decided to follow, and they started for the new cemetery of St. Ouen, to which the populace has given the disquieting and lugubrious name of Cayenne. There were ten mourners in all.

'Well, we two shall be the only old friends,' repeated Bongrand as he walked on beside Sandoz.

The procession, preceded by the mourning coach in which the priest and the choirboy were seated, now descended the other side of the height, along winding streets as precipitous as mountain paths. The horses of the hearse slipped over the slimy pavement; one could hear the wheels jolting

noisily. Right behind, the ten mourners took short and
careful steps, trying to avoid the puddles, and being so
occupied with the difficulty of the descent that they refrained
from speaking. But at the bottom of the Rue du Ruisseau,
when they reached the Porte de Clignancourt and the vast
open spaces, where the boulevard running round the city,
the circular railway, the talus and moat of the fortifications
are displayed to view, there came sighs of relief, a few words
were exchanged, and the party began to straggle.

Sandoz and Bongrand by degrees found themselves behind
all the others, as if they had wished to isolate themselves from
those folk whom they had never previously seen. Just as the
hearse was passing the city gate, the painter leant towards
the novelist.

'And the little woman, what is going to be done with
her?'

'Ah! how dreadful it is!' replied Sandoz. 'I went to
see her yesterday at the hospital. She has brain fever. The
house doctor maintains that they will save her, but that she
will come out of it ten years older and without any strength.
Do you know that she had come to such a point that she no
longer knew how to spell. Such a crushing fall, a young lady
abased to the level of a drudge! Yes, if we don't take care
of her like a cripple, she will end by becoming a scullery-maid
somewhere.'

'And not a copper, of course?'

'Not a copper. I thought I should find the studies
Claude made from nature for his large picture, those superb
studies which he afterwards turned to such poor account.
But I ferreted everywhere; he gave everything away; people
robbed him. No, nothing to sell, not a canvas that could be
turned to profit, nothing but that huge picture, which I
demolished and burnt with my own hands, and right gladly,
I assure you, even as one avenges oneself.'

They became silent for a moment. The broad road
leading to St. Ouen stretched out quite straight as far as
the eye could reach; and over the plain went the procession,
pitifully small, lost, as it were, on that highway, along which
there flowed a river of mud. A line of palings bordered it
on either side, waste land extended both to right and left,
while afar off one only saw some factory chimneys and a few
lofty white houses, standing alone, obliquely to the road.
They passed through the Clignancourt fête, with booths,

circuses, and roundabouts on either side, all shivering in the abandonment of winter, empty dancing cribs, mouldy swings, and a kind of stage homestead, ' The Picardy Farm,' looking dismally sad between its broken fences.

'Ah! his old canvases,' resumed Bongrand, ' the things he had at the Quai de Bourbon, do you remember them? There were some extraordinary bits among them. The landscapes he brought back from the south and the academy studies he painted at Boutin's—a girl's legs and a woman's trunk, for instance. Oh, that trunk! Old Malgras must have it. A magisterial study it was, which not one of our "young masters" could paint. Yes, yes, the fellow was no fool— simply a great painter.'

' When I think,' said Sandoz, ' that those little humbugs of the School and the press accused him of idleness and ignorance, repeating one after the other that he had always refused to learn his art. Idle! good heavens! why, I have seen him faint with fatigue after sittings ten hours long; he gave his whole life to his work, and killed himself in his passion for toil! And they call him ignorant—how idiotic! They will never understand that the individual gift which a man brings in his nature is superior to all acquired know- ledge. Delacroix also was ignorant of his profession in their eyes, simply because he could not confine himself to hard and fast rules! Ah! the ninnies, the slavish pupils who are incapable of painting anything incorrectly!'

He took a few steps in silence, and then he added:

'A heroic worker, too—a passionate observer whose brain was crammed with science—the temperament of a great artist endowed with admirable gifts. And to think that he leaves nothing, nothing!'

'Absolutely nothing, not a canvas,' declared Bongrand. 'I know nothing of his but rough drafts, sketches, notes carelessly jotted down, as it were, all that artistic parapher- nalia which can't be submitted to the public. Yes, indeed, it is really a dead man, dead completely, who is about to be lowered into the grave.'

However, the painter and the novelist now had to hasten their steps, for they had got far behind the others while talking; and the hearse, after rolling past taverns and shops full of tombstones and crosses, was turning to the right into the short avenue leading to the cemetery. They overtook it, and passed through the gateway with the little procession. The

priest in his surplice and the choirboy carrying the holy
water receiver, who had both alighted from the mourning
coach, walked on ahead.

It was a large flat cemetery, still in its youth, laid out
by rule and line in the suburban waste land, and divided into
squares by broad symmetrical paths. A few raised tombs
bordered the principal avenues, but most of the graves, already
very numerous, were on a level with the soil. They were
hastily arranged temporary sepulchres, for five-year grants
were the only ones to be obtained, and families hesitated
to go to any serious expense. Thus, the stones sinking
into the ground for lack of foundations, the scrubby ever-
greens which had not yet had time to grow, all the provisional
slop kind of mourning that one saw there, imparted to that
vast field of repose a look of poverty and cold, clean, dismal
bareness like that of a barracks or a hospital. There was not
a corner to be found recalling the graveyard nooks sung of in
the ballads of the romantic period, not one leafy turn quivering with mystery, not a single large tomb speaking of pride
and eternity. You were in the new style of Paris cemetery,
where everything is set out straight and duly numbered—
the cemetery of democratic times, where the dead seem to
slumber at the bottom of an office drawer, after filing past
one by one, as people do at a fête under the eyes of the police,
so as to avoid obstruction.

'Dash it!' muttered Bongrand, 'it isn't lively here.'

'Why not?' asked Sandoz. 'It's commodious; there is
plenty of air. And even although there is no sun, see what a
pretty colour it all has.'

In fact, under the grey sky of that November morning, in
the penetrating quiver of the wind, the low tombs, laden with
garlands and crowns of beads, assumed soft tints of charming
delicacy. There were some quite white, and others all black,
according to the colour of the beads. But the contrast lost
much of its force amid the pale green foliage of the dwarfish
trees. Poor families exhausted their affection for the dear
departed in decking those five-year grants; there were piles
of crowns and blooming flowers—freshly brought there on
the recent Day of the Dead. Only the cut flowers had as yet
faded, between their paper collars. Some crowns of yellow
immortelles shone out like freshly chiselled gold. But the
beads predominated to such a degree that at the first glance
there seemed to be nothing else; they gushed forth every-

where, hiding the inscriptions and covering the stones and railings. There were beads forming hearts, beads in festoons and medallions, beads framing either ornamental designs or objects under glass, such as velvet pansies, wax hands entwined, satin bows, or, at times, even photographs of women —yellow, faded, cheap photographs, showing poor, ugly, touching faces that smiled awkwardly.

As the hearse proceeded along the Avenue du Rond Point, Sandoz, whose last remark—since it was of an artistic nature —had brought him back to Claude, resumed the conversation, saying:

'This is a cemetery which he would have understood, he who was so mad on modern things. No doubt he suffered physically, wasted away by the over-severe lesion that is so often akin to genius, "three grains too little, or three grains too much, of some substance in the brain," as he himself said when he reproached his parents for his constitution. However, his disorder was not merely a personal affair, he was the victim of our period. Yes, our generation has been soaked in romanticism, and we have remained impregnated with it. It is in vain that we wash ourselves and take baths of reality, the stain is obstinate, and all the scrubbing in the world won't take it away.'

Bongrand smiled. 'Oh! as for romanticism,' said he, 'I'm up to my ears in it. It has fed my art, and, indeed, I'm impenitent. If it be true that my final impotence is due to that, well, after all, what does it matter? I can't deny the religion of my artistic life. However, your remark is quite correct; you other fellows, you are rebellious sons. Claude, for instance, with his big nude woman amid the quays, that extravagant symbol——'

'Ah, that woman!' interrupted Sandoz, 'it was she|who throttled him! If you knew how he worshipped her! I was never able to cast her out of him. And how can one possibly have clear perception, a solid, properly-balanced brain when such phantasmagoria sprouts forth from your skull? Though coming after yours, our generation is too imaginative to leave healthy work behind it. Another generation, perhaps two, will be required before people will be able to paint and write logically, with the high, pure simplicity of truth. Truth, nature alone, is the right basis, the necessary guide, outside of which madness begins; and the toiler needn't be afraid of flattening his work, his temperament is there, which will

always carry him sufficiently away. Does any one dream of
denying personality, the involuntary thumb-stroke which
deforms whatever we touch and constitutes our poor creative-
ness?'

However, he turned his head, and involuntarily added :

'Hallo! what's burning? Are they lighting bonfires here?'

The procession had turned on reaching the Rond Point,
where the ossuary was situated—the common vault gradually
filled with all the remnants removed from the graves, and the
stone slab of which, in the centre of a circular lawn, disappeared under a heap of wreaths, deposited there by the pious
relatives of those who no longer had an individual resting-
place. And, as the hearse rolled slowly to the left in transversal Avenue No. 2, there had come a sound of crackling, and
thick smoke had risen above the little plane trees bordering
the path. Some distance ahead, as the party approached,
they could see a large pile of earthy things beginning to burn,
and they ended by understanding. The fire was lighted at
the edge of a large square patch of ground, which had been dug
up in broad parallel furrows, so as to remove the coffins before
allotting the soil to other corpses ; just as the peasant turns
the stubble over before sowing afresh. The long empty
furrows seemed to yawn, the mounds of rich soil seemed to be
purifying under the broad grey sky ; and the fire thus burning
in that corner was formed of the rotten wood of the coffins
that had been removed—slit, broken boards, eaten into by
the earth, often reduced to a ruddy humus, and gathered
together in an enormous pile. They broke up with faint de-
tonations, and being damp with human mud, they refused
to flame, and merely smoked with growing intensity. Large
columns of the smoke rose into the pale sky, and were beaten
down by the November wind, and torn into ruddy shreds, which
flew across the low tombs of quite one half of the cemetery.

Sandoz and Bongrand had looked at the scene without
saying a word. Then, having passed the fire, the former
resumed :

'No, he did not prove to be the man of the formula he
laid down. I mean that his genius was not clear enough to
enable him to set that formula erect and impose it upon the
world by a definite masterpiece. And now see how other
fellows scatter their efforts around him, after him ! They go
no farther than roughing off, they give us mere hasty impressions, and not one of them seems to have strength enough to

become the master who is awaited. Isn't it irritating, this
new notion of light, this passion for truth carried as far
as scientific analysis, this evolution begun with so much
originality, and now loitering on the way, as it were, falling
into the hands of tricksters, and never coming to a head,
simply because the necessary man isn't born? But pooh!
the man will be born; nothing is ever lost, light must be.'

'Who knows? not always,' said Bongrand. 'Life mis-
carries, like everything else. I listen to you, you know, but
I'm a despairer. I am dying of sadness, and I feel that
everything else is dying. Ah! yes, there is something unhealthy in the atmosphere of the times—this end of a century
is all demolition, a litter of broken monuments, and soil
that has been turned over and over a hundred times, the
whole exhaling a stench of death! Can anybody remain in
good health amid all that? One's nerves become unhinged,
the great neurosis is there, art grows unsettled, there is
general bustling, perfect anarchy, all the madness of self-love
at bay. Never have people quarrelled more and seen less
clearly than since it is pretended that one knows everything.'

Sandoz, who had grown pale, watched the large ruddy
coils of smoke rolling in the wind.

'It was fated,' he mused in an undertone. 'Our excessive
activity and pride of knowledge were bound to cast us back
into doubt. This century, which has already thrown so much
light over the world, was bound to finish amid the threat
of a fresh flow of darkness—yes, our discomfort comes from
that! Too much has been promised, too much has been hoped
for; people have looked forward to the conquest and explanation of everything, and now they growl impatiently. What!
don't things go quicker than that? What! hasn't science
managed to bring us absolute certainty, perfect happiness, in
a hundred years? Then what is the use of going on, since
one will never know everything, and one's bread will always
be as bitter? It is as if the century had become bankrupt,
as if it had failed; pessimism twists people's bowels, mysticism fogs their brains; for we have vainly swept phantoms
away with the light of analysis, the supernatural has resumed
hostilities, the spirit of the legends rebels and wants to
conquer us, while we are halting with fatigue and anguish.
Ah! I certainly don't affirm anything; I myself am tortured.
Only it seems to me that this last convulsion of the old

religious terrors was to be foreseen. We are not the end, we are but a transition, a beginning of something else. It calms me and does me good to believe that we are marching towards reason, and the substantiality of science.'

His voice had become husky with emotion, and he added :

'That is, unless madness plunges us, topsy-turvy, into night again, and we all go off throttled by the ideal, like our old friend who sleeps there between his four boards.'

The hearse was leaving transversal Avenue No. 2 to turn, on the right, into lateral Avenue No. 3, and the painter, without speaking, called the novelist's attention to a square plot of graves, beside which the procession was now passing.

There was here a children's cemetery, nothing but children's tombs, stretching far away in orderly fashion, separated at regular intervals by narrow paths, and looking like some infantile city of death. There were tiny little white crosses, tiny little white railings, disappearing almost beneath an efflorescence of white and blue wreaths, on a level with the soil; and that peaceful field of repose, so soft in colour, with the bluish tint of milk about it, seemed to have been made flowery by all the childhood lying in the earth. The crosses recorded various ages, two years, sixteen months, five months. One poor little cross, destitute of any railing, was out of line, having been set up slantingly across a path, and it simply bore the words : 'Eugénie, three days.' Scarcely to exist as yet, and withal to sleep there already, alone, on one side, like the children who on festive occasions dine at a little side table !

However, the hearse had at last stopped, in the middle of the avenue ; and when Sandoz saw the grave ready at the corner of the next division, in front of the cemetery of the little ones, he murmured tenderly :

'Ah! my poor old Claude, with your big child's heart, you will be in your place beside them.'

The under-bearers removed the coffin from the hearse. The priest, who looked surly, stood waiting in the wind; some sextons were there with their shovels. Three neighbours had fallen off on the road, the ten had dwindled into seven. The second cousin, who had been holding his hat in his hand since leaving the church, despite the frightful weather, now drew nearer. All the others uncovered, and the prayers were about to begin, when a loud piercing whistle made everybody look up.

Beyond this corner of the cemetery as yet untenanted, at the end of lateral Avenue No. 3, a train was passing along the high embankment of the circular railway which overlooked the graveyard. The grassy slope rose up, and a number of geometrical lines, as it were, stood out blackly against the grey sky; there were telegraph-posts, connected by thin wires, a superintendent's box, and a red signal plate, the only bright throbbing speck visible. When the train rolled past, with its thunder-crash, one plainly distinguished, as on the transparency of a shadow play, the silhouettes of the carriages, even the heads of the passengers showing in the light gaps left by the windows. And the line became clear again, showing like a simple ink stroke across the horizon; while far away other whistles called and wailed unceasingly, shrill with anger, hoarse with suffering, or husky with distress. Then a guard's horn resounded lugubriously.

'*Revertitur in terram suam unde erat*,' recited the priest, who had opened a book and was making haste.

But he was not heard, for a large engine had come up puffing, and was manœuvring backwards and forwards near the funeral party. It had a loud thick voice, a guttural whistle, which was intensely mournful. It came and went, panting; and seen in profile it looked like a heavy monster. Suddenly, moreover, it let off steam, with all the furious blowing of a tempest.

'*Requiescat in pace*,' said the priest.

'Amen,' replied the choirboy.

But the words were again lost amid the lashing, deafening detonation, which was prolonged with the continuous violence of a fusillade.

Bongrand, quite exasperated, turned towards the engine. It became silent, fortunately, and every one felt relieved. Tears had risen to the eyes of Sandoz, who had already been stirred by the words which had involuntarily passed his lips, while he walked behind his old comrade, talking as if they had been having one of their familiar chats of yore; and now it seemed to him as if his youth were about to be consigned to the earth. It was part of himself, the best part, his illusions and his enthusiasm, which the sextons were taking away to lower into the depths. At that terrible moment an accident occurred which increased his grief. It had rained so hard during the preceding days, and the ground was so soft, that a sudden subsidence of soil took place. One of the sextons had to jump into the grave and empty it with his shovel with a slow rhythmical movement. There was no end to the matter, the funeral seemed likely to last for ever amid the impatience of the priest and the interest of the four neighbours who had followed on to the end, though nobody could say why. And up above, on the embankment, the engine had begun manœuvring again, retreating and howling at each turn of its wheels, its fire-box open the while, and lighting up the gloomy scene with a rain of sparks.

At last the pit was emptied, the coffin lowered, and the aspergillus passed round. It was all over. The second cousin, standing erect, did the honours with his correct, pleasant air, shaking hands with all these people whom he had never previously seen, in memory of the relative whose name he had not remembered the day before.

'That linen-draper is a very decent fellow,' said Bongrand, who was swallowing his tears.

'Quite so,' replied Sandoz, sobbing.

All the others were going off, the surplices of the priest and the choirboy disappeared between the green trees, while the straggling neighbours loitered reading the inscriptions on the surrounding tombs.

Then Sandoz, making up his mind to leave the grave, which was now half filled, resumed:

'We alone shall have known him. There is nothing left of him, not even a name!'

'He is very happy,' said Bongrand; 'he has no picture on hand, in the earth where he sleeps. It is as well to go off as to toil as we do merely to turn out infirm children, who always lack something, their legs or their head, and who don't live.'

'Yes, one must really be wanting in pride to resign oneself to turning out merely approximate work and resorting to trickery with life. I, who bestow every care on my books—I despise myself, for I feel that, despite all my efforts, they are incomplete and untruthful.'

With pale faces, they slowly went away, side by side, past the children's white tombs, the novelist then in all the strength of his toil and fame, the painter declining but covered with glory.

'There, at least, lies one who was logical and brave,' continued Sandoz; 'he confessed his powerlessness and killed himself.'

'That's true,' said Bongrand; 'if we didn't care so much for our skins we should all do as he has done, eh?'

'Well, yes; since we cannot create anything, since we are but feeble copyists, we might as well put an end to ourselves at once.'

Again they found themselves before the burning pile of old rotten coffins, now fully alight, sweating and crackling; but there were still no flames to be seen, the smoke alone had increased—a thick acrid smoke, which the wind carried along in whirling coils, so that it now covered the whole cemetery as with a cloud of mourning.

'Dash it! Eleven o'clock!' said Bongrand, after pulling out his watch. 'I must get home again.'

Sandoz gave an exclamation of surprise:

'What, already eleven?'

Over the low-lying graves, over the vast bead-flowered field of death, so formal of aspect and so cold, he cast a long look of despair, his eyes still bedimmed by his tears. And then he added:

'Let's go to work.'

THE END

THE WORLD IN YOUR POCKET
some Pocket Classics from Alan Sutton
Good reading in a handy pocket size, attractively produced
and priced, featuring the works of major writers generally
not available elsewhere in paperback.

POCKET CLASSICS
W.N.P. BARBELLION – The Journal of a Disappointed Man
ARNOLD BENNETT – Elsie and the Child and other stories
Whom God Hath Joined – Helen with the High Hand
JOSEPH CONRAD – Within the Tides
DANIEL DEFOE – Captain Singleton
MRS GASKELL – The Manchester Marriage
My Lady Ludlow
THOMAS HARDY – Life's Little Ironies
JACK LONDON – The Star Rover
CAPTAIN MARRYAT – Peter Simple
THOMAS LOVE PEACOCK – Gryll Grange
HESTHER LYNCH PIOZZI – Anecdotes of Samuel Johnson
R. S. SURTEES – Ask Mamma
Mr Facey Romford's Hounds – Mr Sponge's Sporting Tour
WILLIAM THACKERAY
Samuel Titmarsh and the Great Hoggarty Diamond
ANTHONY TROLLOPE – The Bertrams
Lady Anna – An Old Man's Love – The Three Clerks
FANNY TROLLOPE – Domestic Manners
of the Americans

CONTINENTAL CLASSICS
HONORÉ DE BALZAC – A Passion in the Desert
RÉTIF DE LA BRETONNE – My Father's Life
ANTON CHEKHOV – The Black Monk and Other Stories
ALEXANDRE DUMAS – The Lady of the Camellias
IVAN TURGENEV – Smoke
EMILE ZOLA – The Fortune of the Rougons

TRAVEL CLASSICS
FREDERICK BURNABY – On Horseback Through
Asia Minor
HENRY SEEBOHM – The Birds of Siberia:
To the Petchora Valley – The Birds of Siberia: The Yenesei
ANTHONY TROLLOPE – The West Indies and the
Spanish Main
FANNY TROLLOPE – Paris and the Parisians

Available from all good bookshops. Complete catalogue from:
Alan Sutton Publishing, 30 Brunswick Road, Gloucester GL1 1JJ

ARNOLD BENNETT

HELEN WITH THE HIGH HAND

It is difficult to say who is the more delightful in this charming domestic comedy: James Ollerenshaw or high handed Helen who arrives to disturb his miserly, measured existence.

When Helen Rathbone met her estranged step-uncle James on a park bench in one of the Five Towns, no citizen of this provincial manufacturing region could have guessed what a turn events would take, least of all the two protagonists. Helen was quite convinced she could change James Ollerenshaw for the better, whilst he was equally determined that she should not. From that moment their lives were inextricably bound together and would affect many more inside and outside their circle.

WILKIE COLLINS

THE BITER BIT
& OTHER STORIES

Here are tales of detection, mystery and suspense, from the author of *The Moonstone* and *The Woman in White*.

The title story is an investigation into an unusual robbery, revealing Wilkie Collins' little known comic talents. Others selected for inclusion are *A Terribly Strange Bed*, set in a Parisian gambling den, where a young Englishman encounters the 'fiendish murder machine' after breaking the bank; *Mad Monkton*, a fine thriller; *Gabriel's Marriage*, set at the time of the French Revolution and an intriguing mystery, *The Lady of Glenwith Grange*.

DANIEL DEFOE

CAPTAIN SINGLETON

Defoe had that power to create the illusion of truth which is the very life force of fiction and nowhere is ·this more evident than in his portrait of the piratical Captain Singleton.

Taken by a gypsy child-stealer, Singleton soon finds himself cast ashore on the island of Madagascar. How he crosses Africa with a party of marooned sailors from Mozambique to the Gold Coast is a book in itself. His years of piracy are still to come. The story moves to the West Indies where he falls in with William the Quaker, an unusual pirate with whom Singleton becomes a lifelong friend, sharing adventures from the Spanish Main to the Indian Ocean before, filled with remorse, he decides to end it all . . .

ARTHUR CONAN DOYLE

THE LOST WORLD

The Lost World is the story of an expedition by four men to a remote plateau in South America, a region out of time, cut off from the outside world by unscalable, vertical cliffs. In an area the size of an English county, pterodactyls, iguanodons, ape men and dinosaurs still exist.

Into this nightmare world come Professor Challenger, Summerbee, Lord John Roxton and the reporter Malone. After many adventures they return at last to London with proof of their incredible discovery.

Conan Doyle tried in vain to kill off his more famous creation, Sherlock Holmes, but in the character of Challenger, he was content.